Enter the enchanted islands of Naipon, and meet the acclaimed hero of Jessica Amanda Sa son's first novel:

TOMOE GOZ

"TOMOE GOZEN is the f ntasy series, but one unlike any counter . . . This first novel is o ooks I've read in years, writte style . . . I would suspect this is ontender."

—Don D'Ammassa
Fiction Chronicle

". . . an unusual, rather stern fantasy . . . Admirers of the filmmaker Kurosawa will see some similarities between movies like *Yojimbo* and TOMOE GOZEN's blend of lyricism and violence."

—Carol McGuirk
New York Daily News

"Sandwiched between bloodbaths and grotesqueries are finely etched passages of introspection, with flourishes as delicate as hummingbirds . . . Superbly illustrated by Wendy Adrian Shultz."

—Don Strachan
Los Angeles Times

"This striking first novel in a proposed trilogy will fascinate a wide variety of readers. The sf reader will enjoy the parallel universe idea employed by the author, who uses an island nation that 'bears a striking resemblance to old Japan' as the setting for the heroic tale of a female samurai who will delight feminists and martial arts enthusiasts with her unflinching courage, strength of will, and perseverance in the face of wondrous and horrific challenges . . ."

—*Library Journal*

"TOMOE GOZEN, by Jessica Amanda Salmonson, places the historical woman warrior Tomoe Gozen in a series of adventures in the mythical world of Naipon, which has just enough in common with our own Japan to delight samurai film lovers."

—Valerie Eads
Ms. Magazine

"Salmonson is able to skillfully blend the magical and the 'real world' into one . . . All in all, for a good read, I recommend TOMOE GOZEN."

—Nina Boal
Fighting Women's News

"For those who enjoy magic and adventure, it is all here . . . I recommend this book."

—Karen Frank
Seattle Gay News

THE GOLDEN NAGINATA

JESSICA AMANDA
SALMONSON

A Division of Charter Communications Inc.
A GROSSET & DUNLAP COMPANY
51 Madison Avenue
New York, New York 10010

An ACE Book

Ace printing: February 1982
Published Simultaneously in Canada

2 4 6 8 0 9 7 5 3 1
Manufactured in the United States of America

THE GOLDEN NAGINATA

DEDICATION:

to Junko Fuji, Michiyo Yasuda, Yoho Matsuyama,
Junko Miyazono, Keiko
Nakamura, Meiko Kaji
"and many other stars"

also
to Susan and Terri

LIST OF ILLUSTRATIONS
by Wendy Adrian Shultz

PART ONE

The Vengeance Swords of Okio

Azo Hono-o awaited Tomoe Gozen where two rivers forged themselves into one, north of Daki village in the province of Heida. Azo wore a pair of baggy trousers or split skirt called *hakama*, printed brown on black, over a short kimono of blue slik. Her family seal—a gingko leaf—was printed on the back of the kimono and in the front at each shoulder. Through her sash or *obi* she bore two swords: long and short. Around her head was tied a towel, symbol of her readiness to meet with Tomoe.

She watched the two rivers blend, as she and her sword would blend to become a mighty machine by which another samurai might fall. One of the rivers was smaller than the other. It was overwhelmed by the turbulence of the larger one. The froth and noise of the clashing rivers vanished into serene greatness further on, beyond the destruction of the smaller.

There had been too many occasions when Azo heard it said that among the women warriors of Naipon, only Tomoe Gozen could defeat Azo Hono-o. Azo disagreed; no samurai, be he man or be she woman, was match for Azo's blade. She believed this devoutly. She would demonstrate the truth of her belief. It was a matter of pride.

Tomoe was more famous, it was true; she had slain the Shogun's champion Ugo Mohri and won reestablishment of the Shigeno clan. The clan's only heir was a woman named Toshima-no-Shigeno. It was rare that a clan survived the lack of male heirs. The fact that a woman samurai championed a woman Lord was naturally a fascinating incident. To Azo, none of this meant that Tomoe was special. It grated that Tomoe should become so famous because of unusual circumstances. Defeating her would bring Azo deserved recognition, and bring honor to her family and her sword instructor.

The violence of the two rivers provided a monotonous roar which soothed Azo's anger over having to wait. Tomoe Gozen had not arrived within the time allocated! It would do Azo no good to succumb to rage. When the duel commenced, she must apply herself with calm precision and not be daunted by the cheap maneuver of disrespectful tardiness.

More time passed. Despite her resolve, Azo began to seethe. It was inconceivable that an honorable warrior should accept a challenge and then keep the challenger waiting so long! A good fighter would never stoop to it. Therefore, Tomoe Gozen was not a good fighter. Deciding this, Azo let herself experience the rage after all. She let it sweep over her, and what matter if it weakened her, when her nemesis was famous without warrant!

Enmity peaked. It washed away like silt to a distant delta. If anger was meant to weaken Azo, Tomoe had waited too long to reap the advantage. After a while, the only thing the waiting woman felt was contempt.

Shining Amaterasu passed Her zenith and began the long descent toward twilight. Azo paced along the upper banks of the rivers. She began to suspect Tomoe would not come at all. This was even more inconceivable than tardiness, that Tomoe was a coward.

Azo reeled about, thumb pushing her sword a little ways loose of the scabbard.

There was a thrashing among the bushes along the smaller of the two rivers. Azo caught a glimpse of a varnished straw hat. Tomoe Gozen burst from cover and scrambled up a steep bank. She wore a long kimono, tied up between her legs to allow for running and wading. She was soiled and wet, scratched and sweaty. Her sword was drawn.

Azo drew her sword, though puzzled by the dirty specter who earlier that day had been a regal warrior, wholesome and beautifully dangerous. As Tomoe topped the hillside, she stopped, fell to her knees, and said, "Please accept my apology. Trouble kept me from your commission."

Along the river from the direction of Daki village there came the sound of splashing feet and shouting samurai.

"You were detained?" asked Azo, trying to see who was coming in a loud hurry.

Tomoe bowed to Azo, humbled and ashamed to be so late. "My father decided my marriage! I was not informed until shortly after your challenge that I was to meet the man today. I refused, saying that my duty was to the Lady of Shigeno Valley, to whom I am a vassal. My father knew of my commitment and previously honored it . . . but . . . intrigues! Even the Shogun's concubines become rambunctious knowing that one woman killed his Champion and another woman is overlord in a distant valley. My master, Toshima-no-Shigeno, is politically powerful and cannot be compelled to marry. But I am vulnerable through my father. The Shogun's agents hinted that a dutiful daughter should be married. He bowed to the pressure and said I must accept betrothal and not be so famous as a bachelor. When I refused, my father grew wroth. He said no woman can place her career first, that all women bow in youth to the father, in prime to the husband, and in old age to the son. I disagreed further, saying a samurai's duty is first to a master and to family second. It made him furious that I spoke so boldly. He turned his retainers on me; I killed many of them. Then I realized I was late in coming to you. I came as fast as I could run, but have been followed. My father's men have orders to bring me back to meet with my fiancé, or, if that is not possible, to kill me for my disobedience."

"A harsh father!" said Azo.

"A difficult daughter," Tomoe confessed. "He and I both are at an impasse. He too must act according to a master; family ties are indeed secondary."

Azo Hono-o barely had time to consider Tomoe's situation when six men burst out of the brush. They stopped at the foot of the hill and spotted Tomoe at the top. Tomoe leapt to her feet and sprinted alongside Azo to a stand of trees.

"Before we can have our match," said Azo, "it seems we must first kill them. I will wear your hat. It will confuse them."

Tomoe exchanged her varnished hat for Azo's towel. The six men saw the two women separate in opposite directions. Three of them followed after Azo and three after Tomoe. Azo led her three through a ravine, turned quickly to slay the foremost pursuer with a surprise sweep of her sword. The trick could only work once. She jumped up from the ravine and took a stand by a tree, so the two men could not get her between them. They immediately saw their mistake. "Not Tomoe!" one of them said. The other said, "Good. We needn't hesitate to avenge our friend murdered in the ravine."

They charged together. Azo caught both their swords on her one. When they fell back for another run, she did not wait against the tree as would be expected. She became the aggressor, following them several paces. A quick downward slice cut through shoulder bones, continued through ribs, and found a man's heart. She did not see him fall, already having turned to her third and final opponent.

"Who kills me!" cried the final man, backing away and shaking.

Azo pursued him to the edge of the ravine. "Azo Hono-o," she replied. Her sword cut through his forehead, and he fell into the ravine without another sound.

It was quickly done. She did not hear the sound of fighting elsewhere, and presumed the other battle was finished as quickly.

"Tomoe Gozen!" she called. There was no answer. Azo Hono-o rushed toward a figure half hidden by brush. It was Tomoe, sitting on her knees cleaning blood from her sword. Three corpses lay around her. She looked up and said to Azo,

"You make a lot of noise killing. I finished these three at one stroke."

"Stand up and duel," said Azo. "It is our turn."

Tomoe stood, sheathed her sword, and left the three corpses. She returned to the bank overlooking the two rivers, then sat down upon her knees once again.

"What are you doing?" demanded Azo. "We will fight now!"

"I won't," said Tomoe.

Azo looked stricken. She took the varnished hat from off her head and tossed it away. She said, "It was agreed!"

"I don't care."

"It was agreed!" Azo repeated, more confused than angry. There was nothing in tradition to allow for behavior such as Tomoe's.

"Chop off my head, then. I won't stop you."

Azo looked at the unreasonable woman intensely, feeling unhappy about the direction of events. She walked around Tomoe slowly, striking threatening postures. "I want to test your blade!" she exclaimed.

"Take it. Test it."

"I want to test you!"

"I refuse. Kill me if you want to. I won't resist."

"Tell me why!" Azo pleaded, her tone dwindling from fierce to exasperated.

"All of my life," said Tomoe, "I have been faithful to the Way of the Warrior, to *bushido*. Suddenly I am told to break faith with my master by marrying. If my master were not a woman, no one would insult her by commanding one of her samurai to be unfaithful. If I were not a woman, they would not be so surprised that I balk and fight when given orders contrary to my master's will."

Azo Hono-o sat down on her knees facing Tomoe. They looked each other eye to eye. "Surely you will be allowed to serve the Lady of Shigeno Valley your requisite amount of time," said Azo. "Meeting your betrothed is not the same as an immediate marriage."

"That is true," said Tomoe. "It is not reasonable that I refuse to marry." She sighed heavily. "But I have tasted adventure, Azo! I have seen too many good fighting women given to the defense of households, never riding off to battle, never fighting for more than a husband's holdings or their own dubious virtue. I have never wanted to be like them."

"I am still too young to have your worry," said Azo, for in Naipon marriage was not encouraged until mid-twenties for women, early thirties for men, as it was not a good idea to begin a family at too young an age in a tangibly finite island nation. Azo added, "But when my father eventually arranges my marriage, I will be glad to serve Naipon by serving my husband."

"How can you say so?" asked Tomoe, leaning toward Azo. "You are famous too! You would trade it for a husband?"

"Women must provide heirs. We are still allowed to fight."

"*Hai!* Like my mother fought—and died bearing my younger brother."

"Death is always near a samurai," said Azo. "Man or woman."

"Death by these!" exclaimed Tomoe, pulling her sword out a ways and shoving it back. "Not by this!" She struck her own belly.

These were not acceptable notions and Azo Hono-o shook them off. If women thought as Tomoe Gozen, soon they would not be allowed the choice of a warrior's life before marrying. Not many women chose the life of Azo or Tomoe, it was true; it was not precisely encouraged. Yet the choice was there; it existed because women would yet obey their parents' plans of marriage when the time was ripe.

"Perhaps you will like your husband," Azo suggested uneasily.

"I don't care to like him," Tomoe said stubbornly. "My father says he is a powerful warlord: Kiso Yoshinake of Kiso Province. You may have heard of him."

"Yoshinake! He is called the Rising Sun General and is known to be fierce in battle. I hope my father plans so well for me!"

Tomoe made a disparaging sound. Azo said,

"It is said that the Shogun would not be half as secure if not for Yoshinake. You are lucky if you wed a general favored by the Shogun."

"The Shogun favors Yoshinake, but not me. He despises the example I set for other women. Why, then, would he have his most valued warlord marry me? He wants me contained by someone strong!"

"That is impressive!" said Azo. "I wish I could make a

claim like yours. The Shogun does not even know that I exist. Consider yourself fortunate! Bushido is different for women, Tomoe. We must have strong sons."

"So! Sons you say! What is wrong with a daughter? I was a fine daughter! What has it brought me?"

"It has brought you the promise of an excellent marriage with an important warlord," Azo argued. "It is no worse a mess than Kiso Yoshinake's. Perhaps he counts himself even more unlucky than you, if he waits to meet you now, and hears you killed your father's retainers rather than go ahead with a mere meeting."

Tomoe was insulted. "He is luckier than me!"

"How so? Because you could defend his household better than another wife?"

Tomoe's face reddened. She said angrily, "Because I can fight at his side across Naipon!"

"You see? You *do* want to marry him."

"I did not mean that," she said, and looked away from Azo. She scrunched down into herself, pouting.

"If you honor my challenge as you are supposed to do," said Azo, "you will not have to worry about marriage, because I will kill you."

"No. I will kill you."

Now Azo Hono-o was amused. "You hate your betrothed though you have never seen him, and you say you can defeat me though you have never tried."

"I heard your sloppy killing."

"Still. I always win."

"I won't fight." Tomoe was adamant.

"Then," said Azo, rising to her feet and drawing her sword, "I will claim your ear as my trophy." She slashed without hesitation in the direction of Tomoe's head.

Her steel met steel instead of ear. Tomoe's sword had slid from its scabbard with lightning speed. It blocked Azo's blow then returned to the scabbard. Tomoe had not moved from her sitting position. Azo Hono-o's eyes were momentarily round. She said, "That was very good! I have never seen it done before. Once more, please?" She made another sweeping approach with her sword. Again Tomoe performed an amazingly swift draw, not even rising to one knee as was usually necessary. She struck Azo's sword aside without difficulty. Azo said, "Now it is certain we must fight! I must know who is better."

"Azo: I defeated the Shogun's champion. I have survived a dozen terrible wars. I wield steel forged and tempered by Okio, the Imperial Smith, and blessed by the Mikado himself. With it I have slain men and demons. By contrast, you have acquired most of your skills in a *dojo*; and while your school is of the highest repute, it is never the same as practical experience. If you wish to kill me, do so in five years, when I am older and you are stronger than today."

"An insult!" said Azo. "I have distinguished myself in two battles. I've killed more men than I remember!" She raised her sword above her head. "I will show you my strength!" She whirled around and sliced toward a squat, thick tree. When her sword was sheathed, the tree began to fall. The trunk was thrice the width of a hand, but had been shorn through effortlessly. The tree fell directly in front of Tomoe. If she was impressed, it did not show.

Tomoe took two long breaths, then said, "We have chosen the wrong place," relenting a little. "If you wish so strongly to be killed by me, it must be announced publicly."

Azo was delighted. "Excellent! How will it be arranged?"

"It may take a while," said Tomoe. "First I must escape my father's wrath. I can kill his retainers and break no law; but if he comes for me himself, I would be guilty of patricide."

"I can help!" Azo promised. "We will trade clothing. Your family seal will cause me to be followed. I will keep my face shadowed under your hat. By the time the error is realized, you can be far away!"

Tomoe nodded. "A good plan." Azo began to untie the straps of her hakama. Tomoe doffed kimono.

"You have gained momentary respite," said Azo boastfully, trying on Tomoe's clothing. "Next time we meet, we will fight."

"As you say," agreed Tomoe. "My advice: Practice for that day. Be worthy of the contest." She finished dressing in

Azo's hakama and short kimono. "Until then," she said, "farewell."

Tomoe rested comfortably on her knees and watched the street from the inn's upper story window. Beside her an oil lamp glowed within a columnar paper lantern. In front of her on a small black tray was an untouched meal: rice, pickles and braised eggplant, each in different bowls. Her longsword rested on a rack against a wall. Her shortsword was in her *obi*. She had long since traded Azo's kimono for a plain one without family seal. She still wore Azo's cotton hakama, somewhat worn from a month's hard travel, yet fastidiously clean and pleated.

She had sent a message to Toshima-no-Shigeno three weeks earlier, explaining her plight and saying she would await Toshima's instruction at Chogi Inn on a certain date. As Tomoe watched the street, a bare-legged messenger appeared from an alley near the edge of town. He wore a bandana around his head and chin. Over one shoulder he carried a long stick with a letter pinned to one end. Tomoe slid the rice paper window closed. She reached for the bowl of rice and pair of pointed chopsticks and began eating while she waited.

Several pairs of feet clambered up the steps at once. Tomoe heard the coarse laughter of men and the giggling of geishas. The party entered one of the other rooms. By her keen sense of hearing, Tomoe knew that one of those pairs of feet had not passed by her door.

The door slid aside abruptly. It was not the messenger standing there, but a burly, cruel looking man with a spear. He grinned wickedly as he charged into the room.

Tomoe's longsword was on a rack beyond reach. She raised her right hand to the side of her head, the points of both chopsticks held outward from the knuckles. With a single flick of her hand and wrist, the burly man dropped his spear and began shouting. He grabbed at the chopsticks in his eyes. As he stumbled to his knees, Tomoe's shortsword silenced him with a quick slash to the throat.

The bowl of rice was still in her left hand. She calmly set it on the tray. Outside the open door stood the messenger with his carrying stick and the letter. His bare knees were shaking. Tomoe asked,

"Did you know you were followed?" The messenger shook his head, plopped down on both knees, and crawled forward with the letter for Tomoe. She unfolded it section by section. It was a long piece of paper, but only a small part of it was used. Tomoe read quietly. Toshima's message was a simple one, agreeing to give the samurai leave of her duties in Shigeno Valley for however long it took to resolve her troubles.

"I have no letter for you to take back," said Tomoe, dismissing the messenger. "Please have someone come and clean my room as you leave." The man looked at the untidy corpse, then at Tomoe. He bowed several times before he stood and backed out of the room. As he turned in the hall to scurry away, Tomoe noticed that his feet were not very calloused for a runner. When she was alone, Tomoe pivoted on her knees and faced the lantern. She held the letter above the warmth of the burning wick. A second message had been written with invisible clear fruit juice. The heat darkened the writing so that Tomoe could read it.

"You will have realized as quickly as I that the messenger is a spy," the missive began. *"Yet your father's search has been halfhearted and I think he has forgiven you. The spies serve someone else. I may know who.*

"Since the Mikado returned from exile, the Shogun has been uneasy. The great swordsmiths of Kyoto, our Imperial City, have been commanded to relocate in the Military Capital of Kamakura. Only one smith dared refuse: Okio, the Mikado's private smith. The Shogun meanwhile favors Okio's mortal enemy, the giant Uchida Ieoshi of a jealous family of swordsmiths. Uchida was raised to be a warrior so that force might be instigated against competitive smiths. The Shogun will almost certainly overlook any vengeful move against Okio's small clan at this time."

This was sore news, but Tomoe wasn't sure in what way the swordsmith's plight affected her own. Toshima's missive continued, *"Those of us loyal to the Mikado are striving to protect Okio. His family has been moved secretly to Isso. Tell no one! But so long as Okio himself remains in Kyoto, he is endangered by his own stubborn resolve. It's believed that Uchida Ieoshi already has possession of Okio's ledgers, which were stolen by ninja spies. From the ledgers Uchida gleaned the names of many warriors who carry swords fashioned by the Imperial Smith. One by one, Okio's fine swords are being located and broken by crafty ninja. Of course this plot necessitates the killing of whatever samurai bear Okio's weaponry, for none give up their swords willingly.*''

It was clear now what Tomoe's danger was. She glanced quickly to her sword in the rack—made by Okio and blessed by the Mikado. The letter went on to say, ''*Take care of yourself, Tomoe! It will be harder for me rebuilding my late father's holdings without the assistance of your strong arm and manner. But I give you leave with one requirement: If Okio is slain, avenge him. Do so in honor of his craft, and with the mightiness his craft has contributed to your skill.*'' The letter was signed, ''*Lady Toshima-no-Shigeno,*'' the overlord of Shigeno Valley.

Reopening the window, Tomoe saw far down the street. The messenger disappeared into the same alley he had appeared from earlier.

A girl came to the door of the room and gasped at the sight of the would-be assassin killed by Tomoe.

''You let rabble use your inn!'' Tomoe complained, rising swiftly to her feet. Her shadow enveloped the wide-eyed girl. Tomoe reached into her kimono sleeve and brought out some coins to pay for her food and lodging. She snapped at the maid, ''I will not return!''

The samurai brushed by the frightened maid; but then she stopped and faced the girl again, apologizing, ''Forgive me being peevish. Your inn is a fine one, but I must go.''

Tomoe Gozen hurried into the street, vaguely annoyed that the day's killings might not be done.

The man who had brought the letter to Tomoe moved sideways through a narrow passage between two buildings. Twice he looked back, imagining a pursuer. He came out behind a kimono refurbishing shop, where women workers bleached and redyed clothing. The smell was ferocious. The man grinned amiably and bowed many times as he skirted this industry. The workers paid him little attention. There was a ladder leading to a roof apartment. He ascended this quickly. From the top, he looked left and right at the rest of the tenement neighborhood, a shiver of paranoia at his back. Then he ducked through the opened, undersized door.

Inside the small apartment it was dark and hot. The stink of the kimono repair shop was dizzying. From a shadow, the dry voice of an old, old man asked,

"Where is the *ronin?*"

The fraudulent messenger looked afraid. He peered toward that darkest shadow of the unlit chamber. The shadow looked hardly big enough to hide a man. Although he saw no one, he replied,

"Your money was wasted on that masterless samurai. Tomoe Gozen killed him with ease."

"What help were you?" asked the dry, accusing voice. "Didn't you try to kill her?"

"I did!" the man said. "I tried hard, but she evaded me!"

"You lie, Shinichi."

"I don't lie!" he insisted. His eyes danced back and forth, looking for a good story. "I stabbed at her with my carrying-stick, but she stepped aside. She drew her sword too quickly, so I jumped out the window. That's the only reason I survived. I will try again come darkness. You won't be disappointed!"

"How will you kill her?" asked the voice in the shadow.

Shinichi jabbed his stick in front of himself as he said, "Like this! Through her eyes while she is sleeping!"

"What will you do when she is dead, Shinichi?" the voice asked sardonically.

"Take her sword and break it!" Shinichi said. "Smash it on a stone!" He made motions with his stick to illustrate.

"That will please our 'master,' Uchida Ieoshi." The voice did not call Uchida "master" with much conviction or respect. "Every sword of Okio is to be destroyed. Tomoe's will be hardest to take. You'll be rewarded if you succeed,

Shinichi. If you fail . . ."

"I won't fail! She will soon be on the road again. I will follow close behind. I'll kill her wherever she camps the night."

Throughout this exchange, Tomoe Gozen had been listening outside the small door at the top of the ladder. The furtive Shinichi was no expert and had been easily tracked. Now, Tomoe stepped into the room's interior and said,

"Kill me now, Shinichi."

Shinichi jumped like a rabbit. Tomoe's sword swept toward the pitiful hireling, but he moved backward and parried with his pole. He was better with it than Tomoe had expected. She moved forward aggressively and Shinichi deflected another murderous slash while leaping back. He could not withdraw further in the little room. He tried to block Tomoe's third blow; but a pole could only deflect at angles, not block a direct strike. The sword of Okio sliced through the pole, losing almost none of the cut's force. Shinichi grimaced and spit through his teeth, cut mortally at the temple.

Without waiting to see Shinichi collapse, Tomoe leapt toward the shadowed corner. Her sword met nothing. There was a fluttering of robes. The dark figure had jumped into the rafters. A dart was tossed toward Tomoe's face, but it rang against her sword. She thrust the curve of her blade far above her head, causing the unseen fellow to move again. This time the fluttering sounded more like wings than robes.

"Tengu!" cried Tomoe, recognizing that sound at last. A tengu was a small, winged demon with a long nose. He perched in another part of the rafters where dim light struck. His wings made him look hunchbacked. A sword was sheathed near his groin. His dry, hoary voice clicked and cackled with delight. "You know my race!" he said. "Then you will know we are good swordfighters!"

He spread his wings and lighted on the floor, longsword drawn. The tengu looked like an old man, thin and bony; but he moved with the wiry grace of a youth. There was not much space for Tomoe to maneuver against the long-nosed demon's quick style. He was smaller and could maneuver better. But Tomoe had fought demons many times; and the tengu may have been surprised that his tricks did not work. He would have to rely on skill alone, so Tomoe doubted he could win.

The tengu must have thought likewise, that he could not win. He spread his wings and returned to the rafters, abandoning the fight; then he dove like a hawk toward the small door. Tomoe moved quickly. Her sword cut the demon's tail feathers and clipped his right wing. He was unable to break his descent.

He plunged from the roof apartment into the yard of the kimono repair company. He landed in a vat of blue dye. The women working there fled into the building, screaming shrilly about the monster. Tomoe looked down at the comical sight of the tengu splashing and cussing in the vat. He climbed from his messy post and tried to fly away, but Tomoe had trimmed too many feathers.

"Vengeance!" cried the tengu, hobbling away through the narrow alleys. "I will be avenged!" When he found a shadowed place away from the sun, he turned and shook his knobby fist at Tomoe on the roof outside the vacated apartment. The tengu said, "Mine will be remembered as the Vengeance of the Blue Tengu! I will be remembered when Tomoe Gozen is forgotten!"

His promise made, the blue tengu slunk away through paths too small for Tomoe to follow.

In a clearing away from the road, Tomoe made a firepit. She had previously pulled some edible roots. These she tied to the end of a stick and propped the stick over the coals of her fire. Her mood was somewhat gloomy, as it had been for the month since she visited her father in Heida and her troubles began. Now she was pursued by enemies of swordmaker Okio, aside from her falling out with her father. It was one trouble after another! Although her pursuers wanted only her sword, the sword was her soul and she would die before giving it up. It was an annoying situation all around. The nuisance of being on the road, rather than in Shigeno Valley aiding Toshima while her castle was being constructed against tremendous odds, was the main source of Tomoe's irritability. "I will strive to be more patient," Tomoe said to herself; for a proper samurai tries each day to be a little better than before. "I will strive to be serene."

Yellow fire lit her features: round face and small, flat nose; high eyebrows and intelligent eyes. Tough as she was, the woman was yet beautiful.

Around her camp, the forest was lost in darkness. The branches of aromatic pine provided loose shelter overhead. Tomoe looked up and saw stars through the limbs. *Ama-no-kawa* the "heavenly river" was a sharp, bright waterway between Naipon and the High Plain of the Gods, *Taka-ma-no-hara*. It was almost the time of year for the Star Festival, when the sky should be especially appreciated. The beautiful sight of the heavenly river helped settle Tomoe's turbulent feelings. She thought that her own route was like *Ama-no-kawa*, with many wonders along the banks.

Against that backdrop of stars, she caught sight of a fluttering shadow. It disappeared near the top of the pine. It might have been an owl, but Tomoe was wary. She watched carefully until she saw another. It, too, landed in the pine beneath which Tomoe camped. She could not see or hear these birds. As she watched with narrow eyes, a falling star streaked the night's sky and vanished: an omen which was sometimes lucky and sometimes not. A third dark shadow moved against *Ama-no-kawa,* like a minor deity swimming down from heaven.

The campfire was dwindling. Tomoe's meal was cooked. She pretended not to notice the three birds watching from the tree as she removed the roots from the cooking-stick. Rather than eating, she stoked the fire with the stick. There was a restless sound above her head, like crows nudging each other on their roost. Tomoe lifted the stick above her head, fire on its end, and three baby tengu squawked and fluttered.

"Why do children come to gawk at Tomoe Gozen?" Tomoe asked.

The three tengu chittered excitedly. At young ages, tengu did not have the long noses which took years to develop. They looked like starving but pretty children crouching on the limbs of the pine, huddling close together and ruffling their wings. One of them, the lankest, answered,

"Old Uncle is furious with you. He says we are to follow you about and haunt you until he grows his flight feathers back and can come to take revenge."

The other two were giggling frantically. One of them, with a bloated belly but elsewhere as scrawny as the others, piped, "Old Uncle has turned blue!" The two tittered some more. The first one to speak, who was more serious than his brothers, added, "We won't let you sleep! We'll play tricks on you! We'll be awful pests!"

Tomoe lowered the flaming stick, because the tengu children did not like light. Fire was something adult tengu used in casting spells; it was never used carelessly as it was by humans. Tomoe said, "I presume you are sent as part of your training, so that you can become properly mischievous tengus when grown. But such dainty, unlearned goblins as yourselves will surely get yourselves murdered if you tease very many samurai. It might not be wise to bother me."

The main speaker for the three was indignant, but the others shushed their tittering and were scared by the warning. "We are too clever for that!" boasted the leader. "Tengu trained the skulking *ninja* many generations ago. That's how clever we are!"

Before the boast was completed, Tomoe moved with unpredicted swiftness. She jumped straight up, drawing her sword and slashing the pine's limb. She landed on her feet away from where the limb fell. The surprised tengu children tried to fly away. They beat their wings in panicky awkwardness and smashed into one another. Tomoe's sword was sheathed. She gathered up the tengu by their legs and held them in a bunch, upside down like roosters fetched for slaughter. The three squawked and wept and pleaded and flapped their wings uselessly. Finally, Tomoe let them go.

The tengus flew to a higher limb this time, quivering. Tomoe calmly broke the severed pine branch and placed it on the fire, lighting the area better. The talkative, lankiest tengu gathered his wits the fastest. He asked,

"Why did you let us go when you had us so quickly?"

"I took an oath with myself to be more patient," said

Tomoe. "Earlier today I killed a masterless samurai so down on his luck that he accepted a foolish commission to attack me. Afterward I killed a stupid peasant who thought a little skill in stick-fighting qualified him as an assassin. I'm not tickled with the notion of killing baby goblins simply because their uncle is an idiot."

The samurai picked up the long pieces of cooked roots and broke them into handy lengths. "Come down to my camp and eat with me," she invited, holding the roots up for the tengus to see. They chattered among themselves for a few moments, then decided to trust her since she could have killed them already had she wished. The roots were tasty but tough; their young teeth gnawed and gnawed on the pieces. After a while, they were all comfortable with each other, and Tomoe plied them carefully, "Tell me, my young friends: Why does your uncle serve Uchida Ieoshi?"

Their eyes grew large at the mention of the name. "The giant!" said the round-bellied tengu, who was eating two pieces of root at once. The littlest one, who had not yet spoken, covered his eyes with his palms and patted his forehead with his fingers. Their lank leader replied, "Old Uncle owes a favor to Uchida's swordsmithing clan. A long time ago they gave our tribe of tengus some good iron from another island of the archipelago. No one really likes Uchida."

"Do you know what Uchida wants your Old Uncle to do in order to redeem the old favor?"

They didn't.

"Your Old Uncle is supposed to see that my longsword is broken. That means his mission is to kill Tomoe Gozen."

"Kill you?" said the littlest one who hadn't talked before. A piece of root was hanging out of his mouth. The samurai nodded.

"I gather that your uncle raised you," said Tomoe, "or he wouldn't risk your lives so blithely. When you fly home to your mountain, tell him that I would hate to make his nephews orphans. Tell him that a blue tengu shines in the dark and cannot hide so well."

The children quailed at the thought of sassing Old Uncle.

"He would beat us up!" the leader said.

"Not until he regains his flight feathers," said Tomoe. "You can drop rocks on his head or anything you like. He can't get you."

Their eyes lit up. Tomoe continued,

"I think it will be a safer first lesson in mischief."

The tengus tittered and clapped their bony little hands in front of their faces. Their wings shook excitedly; they could hardly wait to begin teasing Old Uncle. But they couldn't leave Tomoe's camp without permission, because it would be impolite after accepting the meal. Tomoe laughed with them and said, "You may go home now if you want," and the Tengu children were off into the night, trailing happy noises across *Ama-no-kawa* and toward a nearby mountain.

Tomoe tried not to feel too well-pleased with her actions, since egoism and self-satisfaction detracted from any deed. Still, she knew that a less considerate individual would have killed the demon brats without hesitation, believing supernatural creatures to be obscene. Allowing them to go safely on their way soothed Tomoe's weeks-old edginess. It demonstrated that she had successfully bettered herself despite recent misfortunes. Because of this she was able to sleep through the night with her dreams more restful than usual.

The permanently borrowed hakama trousers were neatly folded and placed inside the large, plain straw hat at her side. She slumbered sitting up against the big pine, her legs and arms drawn inside her kimono for warmth, her sword laying across her lap. Before dawn, she opened her eyes. In spite of the peaceful night, it was a sense of danger that awoke her so early.

She sat forward abruptly, lifting the sword and scabbard off her knees. Dew chilled the recent sleeper. Amaterasu had not yet risen; it was difficult to see in the dark. For light and warmth, Tomoe took an unburnt end of firewood and stirred the ashes of the firepit, uncovering a few coals exactly where she'd buried them. Hours earlier she had placed some brown leaves in her kimono so that they'd stay dry against her body; now she brought them forth and piled them on the exposed coals. When she blew on the coals, the leaves flared. However, before she could get anything more substantial burning, a momentary wind, cold as death, issued from the surrounding pines and put the fire out.

A sad, lonesome voice whispered eerily in the woods: "To-mo-eh. To-mo-eh." It was a *gaki* or "hungry ghost," she was certain. Ghosts hungered sometimes for revenge, sometimes for love lost during life, or for money left behind in dying . . . occasionally, they hungered for the blood of living folk. Whatever the cause of their hunger, it made them haunt the world, morose and dissatisfied.

"Who are you?" Tomoe asked cautiously, betraying no fear. There was no reply, but her sword rattled in its scabbard for no cause. This was an unprecedented power for a gaki, affecting a samurai's weapons! It caused Tomoe to ask more vehemently, "*Who are you?*"

The gaki drifted out of the forest, a dim phosphorescent fog with no particular shape. It began to coalesce into the shape of a man whose legs were void of feet and joined as one. He drifted a little ways above the ground. His pale whiteness gained a bit of color as the materialization progressed, though he retained the translucence throughout. The gaki looked terribly sad.

"We have never met," said the ghost. "But I think you will know me anyway." Again, Tomoe's sword vibrated in its case. It seemed to do so in resonance with the gaki's deep intonations. For the first time, Tomoe noticed the gaki's small black hat. It was the cap of a Naiponese metallurgist.

"You're Okio!" Tomoe exclaimed, realizing the swordsmith must have been killed. She held the sword before her, not as a weapon but as a charm. "I am not your slayer! Why do you haunt me?"

The hungry ghost drifted toward her, his expression earnest, but seeming to mean no harm. He said, "By trickery my bodyguards were drugged. Fifty samurai attacked my house this very night, stabbing all the guards in their beds or slumbering at their posts. Against so many, I was helpless."

"Fifty to kill one!" said Tomoe. "They had no honor!"

The ghost of Okio continued, "They probably thought that

Wendy Alorian Shultz

I would be as good at fighting with swords as making them. But I have never liked to see swords dented. I was unpracticed in fencing. Not one of the fifty was injured; I'm ashamed to confess it. At this very moment they are on their way to Isso to complete their commission. They intend to kill my wife and children! Those clever men placed an amulet against ghosts in my body's mouth, thinking it would keep me from pursuing them in death. Yet a part of me lives in the swords I have forged. A part of me is carried in your own scabbard; and that part cannot be arrested by amulets. If my enemies have their way, even these remnants of myself, of my contribution to Naipon, will be wrecked. For all that, I worry more about my family than posterity. You must go to Isso, Tomoe Gozen! You must rush to my family's defense!" The ghost wrung his hands in despair, hovering nearer and saying, "Save them, Tomoe! Save them!"

"I will try," said Tomoe, bowing a little from her standing position, still holding her sword in front of her vertically lest the ghost press too near.

After her promise, the ghost withdrew a short ways and looked somewhat relieved. He said, "Of the fifty men, I can give you ten names. I will etch them on your memory so that you cannot forget." So saying, he began to recite the names of a fifth of his assassins: "Matsu Emura, Ryoichi Nomoto, Shintaro Shimokashi, Fusakuni Sumikawa . . ." As the ghost gave her the names, their heads moved before her as if carried on poles. Their features, with their names, burned into her brain. She would know them anywhere! The deep, sad voice of Okio continued: "Kajutoshi Saitoh, Hitoshi Nakazaki and his brother Tatsuo Nakazaki, Kenji Hachimura, Fudo Kuji, and Kozo Ono."

The last of the ten men's heads passed before her vision. The specter which had once been the Imperial Swordsmith grew faint, weakened by the spell he had weaved. A cold, cold wind swept through the pines as it had done when Okio first came. He became mist once more. Amaterasu's shining face peered up from below the world, banishing him and all hungry ghosts into the Land of Gloom for another day.

Tomoe raised her sword horizontally and held it from each

end. She bowed to the sword in her outstretched hands while facing the place where the ghost had been. She gave her oath.

"*Bushi no-ichi gon*," she said, the word of a samurai binding unto death. "The task will be done!"

It was more than two days by relay-palanquin to Isso. The men who bore the transport on their shoulders shouted, "Pardon us! Emergency!" to clear the road, running from palanquin-station to palanquin-station, keeping Tomoe fast upon the route day and night. At the last station there were no palanquins to be had, because *Tana-bata* or Star Festival had created extra business. Tomoe hurried the last few miles afoot, arriving amidst gentle merriment. She didn't think the fifty assassins coming from Kyoto could have closed the distance in better time. It would be hard to find out, however, since any number of men could arrive unnoticed during a celebration.

As Tana-bata was observed mainly by young women and girls, it was one of the least rowdy festivals of the year. Yet it did provide a few excuses for men to enjoy themselves, or to take advantage of sentimental girls. Tana-bata was the seventh lunar month's holiday, in praise of the High Plain of Heaven and in particular two constellations: the Herdsman, and the Weaver Maid, who met at this time of year on two sides of Heaven's River to gaze across at one another with sad love.

Tomoe walked the quietly busy street, listening to an unseen *koto* harp, traditionally played for lovers. There were puppet shows and other entertainment, each attended by a crowd. In the bamboo trees were hung rectangles of paper bearing poems about and prayers for happy marriage and love affairs. Young women had hung these compositions with strips of cloth or pieces of yarn especially to honor Weaver Maid who symbolized endless longing love.

The people wore gay colors for the occasion and went about moon-eyed and smiling. Surrounded by all this refined celebrating, Tomoe in her dark hakama and kimono was like a shadow. Her mission was an affront to the day, but it could not be helped.

Lovely, fragile-seeming women hurried to and fro, colored ribbons trailing from their wooden clogs or *geta*. Their steps were short and graceful. They sometimes bowed with admiration to the fighting woman who took long strides. Others ignored her as they passed by.

A magistrate walked slowly, looking extraordinarily pleased. He was followed by a covey of admiring girls. They were too young to interest him much; but boldness among girls was allowed during Star Festival, and the magistrate was obviously flattered to be the constant brunt of this occasion. He wore a flat metal hat and carried a *jitte* through his obi, between his swords. The jitte was a pronged instrument designed to catch an uncouth fencer's blow and, with a skilled twist, break the blade. It was also the mantle of the man's position. Tomoe approached this small group looking far too fierce for a woman during Tana-bata. The young girls backed away. The magistrate withdrew his jitte and looked officious with this badge. He asked,

"There is trouble, *bushi*?" He called her "knight." She composed her expression so that she looked more pleasant, not having intended to alarm him.

"I've need of an address," she said amiably. "The family of the Imperial Swordsmith's wife is said to live in Isso."

"Ah!" He looked relieved and pointed toward a certain street with his jitte. He described the house she would see. Thanking him, she bowed, and hurried on her way, arousing no more of his suspicions.

The house was modest but the garden was rich. As Tomoe walked along the garden path, she was disturbed by the quietude. There were no poems hanging in the bamboos of this garden. There were no offerings to Herdsman and Weaver Maid sitting on a table. There was no incense and no music. Tomoe sensed that she was about to discover a disaster. The fifty assassins had raced faster after all.

An old woman and an old man lay together in one of the rooms, pierced by the same sword-thrust while they made love. They must have been Okio's in-laws. Their *futon* cover was soaked with blood. Their faces were close to one another. By their expressions, it seemed they died at a moment of final ecstacy.

In the next room were the children and Okio's wife, scattered about in pools of blood, their faces frozen with terror. Tomoe dropped to her knees amidst this gore and silently reproached herself. She withdrew the longsword and sheath from her obi and set it on the floor in front of her and spoke to it:

"I will not fail you, Okio! I will find the ten men you named for me. Before I kill them, perhaps I can force some of the names of the other forty from their lips." She bowed to the sword until her forehead touched the *tatami* mat. She felt the floor vibrating with a footstep. She instantly grabbed the sword's handle and came to her feet, leaving the sheath on the tatami.

A young samurai stood in the hallway by the door. His forehead was neatly shaven; his *motodori* or queue of hair was pressed flat along the top and center of the shaved area. His face was pretty, but his expression was disconcerted.

"I'm too late!" he said, looking at the bodies on the floor.

Tomoe held her naked blade in the least threatening way, but was ready for any trick. "Who are you?" she asked.

He replied, "Prince Shuzo Tahara!"

Tomoe was startled. This was the son of a well known lord.

Behind Tomoe, a paper door slid aside and a monk revealed himself where he'd been hiding. Prince Tahara drew his sword. He and Tomoe stood side by side. The monk carried a staff with jangling rings on the top end, and a sword through his cloth belt. His head was entirely shaven.

"Bonze!" said Tomoe, addressing him by a common title. "Have you come to pray for these murdered people?"

"My praying is done," he said. His voice was kind. He was almost as young as Prince Shuzo Tahara but not nearly so handsome. "I intended to defend these people, but arrived moments too late. Now that their souls have been attended, I will seek revenge for their stolen lives."

Prince Tahara sheathed his sword while Tomoe retrieved her scabbard from the floor. At that moment, a broad-shouldered samurai pushed his considerable weight right through a paper door, screaming hideously and waving a sword. Woman, prince and bonze readied their weapons, but the big samurai stopped short and ceased raving. He looked amazed to see these three.

"Have I failed?" he asked, sheathing his sword and scratching his head in a befuddled way. Tomoe said,

"I am Tomoe Gozen of Heida. This is Prince Shuzo Tahara, whose family you may know. This Bonze is . . ."

"Shindo," said the monk. "A novice on leave from a mountain sanctuary."

The big samurai still looked confused. He said, "I'm Hidemi Hirota, vassal to Hirotaka-no-Hondo. My arm is strong but my mind is weak. You must tell me why we have all met here!"

The bonze stepped forward and said, "It would seem to be the plan of Okio's ghost. There is one way to be sure. Follow me into the garden." They left the house with the monk and went to a place where there was no shade. The monk said, "The light is good enough here." He proceeded to knock the pin from his sword's handle to reveal the tang. Tomoe followed this example, sitting on her knees beside the monk and removing the sword's handle. The other two copied the maneuver. Directly, they compared all four tangs and saw that each bore the signature of Okio. To be sure there was no trick, they held the flat side of the blades toward the sunlight so that they could investigate the pattern of the temper. A clever forger could imitate a signature, but none could duplicate Okio's secret method of tempering. The temper patterns of the four swords were identical.

As the four avengers peered along the edges of each others' swords, a fifth sword's blade thrust toward the sun, its tang revealed in a soiled hand.

The fifth man was an unbathed *ronin*. His forehead was unshaven. His queue of hair stuck up at a sad angle. His jaws were bristly. It was difficult to believe that so unfortunate a character owned one of Naipon's finest swords; but the sword, and his presence, were proof enough. The four introduced themselves.

The ronin hadn't the courtesy to sit with them, but stood

looking from bonze to vassal to prince and gazing overlong at the woman warrior. He scratched his whiskers and paraded back and forth. At length he said, "A ghost insisted that I come. I would be glad enough to avenge the maker of my sword, which was won from a famous warlord who likes to gamble when he's drunk. But I'm not sure I would mix with wholesome children like these!" He passed his disapproving eyes over them again. "A monk who teaches Buddha's love with a sword! A vassal who looks as intelligent as an ogre! A prince who is hardly more than a boy! A woman with swords instead of poems at Star Festival! If I join fools as these, surely it will be me who next needs an avenger."

Prince, bonze and woman were unruffled. The vassal bit back a reply. The bonze smiled with excessive politeness and asked,

"Does the lucky gambler have no name?"

A samurai with no name was no samurai at all. It was not a very subtle insult; but coming from a monk, it might be excused as ignorance of samurai manners. The ronin squinted at the daring bonze, then answered,

"Call me Ich'yama."

"Number one mountain!" said the bonze, laughing. "If that is the only name you have, it will do."

Tomoe intervened more seriously, "I presume Okio has given us each ten names. The total is fifty. Because there is a festival and many willing girls, we can assume the fifty assassins will remain in Isso for a while. They will leave at festival's end, the day after tomorrow."

The five avengers had put their swords back together and sheathed them. Hidemi Hirota leaned toward Tomoe and said, "We must kill them before they leave!"

Ich'yama snorted derisively. "Brilliant deduction, Hidemi-sama." The ronin used the suffix denoting godhood or superiority. It was too unsubtle a jab. Hidemi stood from his knees to face the ronin. They were of equal height but Hidemi was wider.

"Please," said Prince Tahara. "We must all like each other for a day or two. I suggest we divide into two pairs and investigate the saké houses and the low district. Bonze Shindo can remain here to attend the corpses. The bodies will need to be disposed of secretly, lest the magistrate discover the murders and our plot before our task is completed. We will rejoin Shindo in this garden before dusk tonight and report what we have found."

Ich'yama's scruffy face was bent over a group of flowers, sniffing. When he looked up, he sneezed. He said, "Tomoe Gozen and I will go together."

"Will that do?" young Prince Tahara asked Tomoe. She did not answer. "Then Hidemi Hirota and I will go together. None of us must be conspicuous!"

The two pairs left the misleading peace of the gardens, going slowly as to be unnoticed. The monk Shindo stood alone among the trees and blossoms. He did not move.

"It's Tana-bata," Ich'yama said to Tomoe. "Are you always this unaffected?" The ronin looked left and right at the happy couples and hopeful singles. He stopped occasionally to read the poems which hung on bamboo bushes and trees.

"There is serious business to attend," said Tomoe.

"Death is forever near the sides of samurai. This does not mean we cannot stop long enough to appreciate beauty. We should be even more appreciative of beauty than others, for it could always be the last we see."

"If a samurai has no time for baths," said Tomoe, "he has no time for beauty."

Ich'yama was struck soundly. "My scent offends you?" he asked good-naturedly. "Come with me to a public bath and we'll rectify the problem."

Tomoe repeated herself firmly: "There is serious business to attend."

A beautiful maiden in silk kimono played koto, the instrument setting in front of her on the floor of the porch. Beside her was a table filled with offerings for Weaver Maid and Herdsman. Ich'yama stopped to listen. He looked sentimental. Tomoe stopped beside him, but was annoyed by the interruption. Ich'yama said softly, so as not to bother the koto player, "On Star Festival, Tomoe, many lovers meet for the first time!"

Tomoe's eyes narrowed. She did not reply. She and

Ich'yama strolled on. The ronin still yammered,

"Some of this poetry is nice!" He dawdled again, looking at a strip of paper in a tree and quoting, " 'Star Maiden weeps but is not unhappy. Parted by the River, still Herdsman is faithful.' " He shrugged and commented on the piece, "Well, the poet's hand is young."

Tomoe's growing irritation became harder to contain. She said, "You have the mind of a young girl! Tend to the Way, ronin, and perhaps your lot will be better in the future."

Ich'yama winced. "Everytime you speak, it stings!" he complained. "What is wrong with the mind of a young girl? Have you never had a mind like that? Do you believe in the kind of love called 'Tana-bata Enlightenment'? It means 'love at first sight.' "

"I know what it means."

" I'm glad!" said Ich'yama. "You look down on me because I'm without a master. What if my fortune were better? Would you still sneer?"

"Mine is the Way of the Warrior, ronin! If you cannot attend to business today, then I will search Isso alone!"

Ich'yama was distracted and did not hear Tomoe's criticism. "Look!" he said. "A puppet show!" There were puppeteers "hiding" under black veils, holding puppets in front of themselves and performing a whimsical play in the middle of the street. Children and adults had gathered around. It was the story of the conquering Empress Jingo who, in the play, had recently returned from the Mainland a widow. Thirty-seven princes came to her in turn, asking for her favor, and each time she said:

"My soul is serene
It dwells in another heaven
Here, cranes perch on branches of plum
No man may come."

Historically speaking, Jingo never did remarry, but ruled Naipon for many years by herself. Ich'yama looked from the beautifully crafted puppet depicting the ancient amazon, and then he looked at Tomoe. The look on his face did not evade her. She turned and walked away, not caring if he followed, but he did. The uncouth behavior of ronin always appalled Tomoe. She reproached him severely,

"Go bathe, ronin! I will not walk with you until you do."

Ich'yama stopped in the middle of the street and let her go on by herself. For a moment he looked sad, but then he beamed and shouted,

"Happy Tana-bata, Tomoe!" He looked at everyone in the street and called to all, "Happy Tana-bata!" Then he went running through the crowd toward a public bath.

On her own, Tomoe investigated one of the grimmer districts of Isso. Gamblers and wanderers staggered from saké den to den. Cutthroats conspired in corners. Geishas were obscene in bright of day. Thieves patrolled the alleys. Crippled children begged—some, perhaps, crippled by their parents for precisely this occupation.

She lingered in low places, tasting stale noodles and soured sauces as an excuse to sit and overhear abominable dialogues. She heard nothing regarding the fifty men.

The ten faces shown to her by the ghost of Okio were always fresh in her mind; but she saw no one to fit these descriptions. Sometimes faces were shadowed with straw hats large as the one she wore herself. It made spying out identities difficult.

As the day progressed, she began to wonder if Ich'yama would ever catch up to her. She rather hoped he wouldn't. With his large mouth and doubtful intentions, he was too great a nuisance.

A tinkling of bells caught her attention. As custom dictated, the fortuneteller wore tiny bells around the rim of her hat, heralding her presence and profession everywhere she went. It made her rather too conspicuous as a shadow. This was the third time Tomoe had heard the ringing.

Tomoe moved quickly aside and hid between two buildings. The fortuneteller passed the place without detecting the samurai. As the belled woman walked by on bare feet, she

Wendy Adrian Shultz

leaned heavily on a staff because she was lame in one leg. She wore a red kimono with a representation of Oh-kuni-nushi, God of Occultists, embroidered on the back.

After the woman passed the place where the samurai hid, Tomoe stepped out from between the buildings and became the tracker instead of the tracked. This didn't last long. The fortuneteller realized the trick. She stopped and turned around to face Tomoe Gozen.

Tomoe couldn't see the woman's face, for a veil hung from the front of her straw hat's brim. A pair of intense eyes peered over the veil. By those eyes, it was clear that the woman beneath the hat was younger than Tomoe would have guessed; the limp, then, was the fault of injury, not age. If the occultist were ugly or beautiful, Tomoe could not tell; the eyes, at least, were normally attractive.

"Why do you follow me?" asked Tomoe.

"You followed me," the other stated. Tomoe only stared. In a moment the fortuneteller confessed, "You looked wealthier than this district's usual clientele. I had hoped to read your fortune and charge you double."

"If that were true," said Tomoe, "why reveal your ploy so easily? Now I will know if you try to cheat me."

"My services are *worth* double in this case," said the woman in red. Her bells tinkled as she talked. The staff seemed to waver in her grasp and Tomoe noted that three of five fingers were bent, as though they'd once been broken. Those eyes glared steadily from under the hat's brim and through the crack above the veil. "By my occult power," she said, "I sensed you were in danger. Demons haunt you! I would tell you what this portends—for a price."

Perhaps the fortuneteller spoke truthfully. She might have sensed the *gaki* spirit attached to Tomoe's sword; or she might have discerned that Tomoe had been recently in contact with demonic tengu. All the same, Tomoe had no interest in news of her future. She said, "A samurai is always prepared for death. Our ignorance about tomorrow helps us remain ready."

The fortuneteller nodded understanding. "I will follow you no more, then. If you see me again, it is coincidence."

As the woman turned to go away, Tomoe caught a momentary outline of the face's profile. She thought she recognized that silhouette.

"I know you!" said Tomoe. "You were a nun!" The moment she said it, she knew it wasn't possible. The nun she was thinking of had been slain a long time ago. The fortuneteller turned back to face Tomoe once more.

"You think I could have been a nun?" There was laughter. "No one forgets me who has seen my face; I can be mistaken for no other." She started to draw aside the veil, then thought better of it, preserving the mystery. "No, samurai, you cannot know me." She raised a finger and pointed over Tomoe's shoulder. "Perhaps you know *her* better."

Tomoe looked behind and saw Azo Hono-o standing in the street. "Tomoe!" Azo called, hurrying forth from the crowd. "Why are you standing in the middle of the street talking to yourself?"

"I was talking to this fortuneteller."

"To who? There is no one here!"

Tomoe scanned the street, but could not detect where the fortuneteller had gone. Azo Hono-o said,

"It's been weeks! Remember our oath: When next we met, we were to test each others' skills!"

"The time is not right," said Tomoe, agitated. "No one must know I'm in Isso. A public match is not feasible."

Azo looked annoyed. "You evade the duel too often! Could it be you fear my sword?"

"Think as you wish."

"Well, I bring encouragement for you: Your father no longer hunts you. He has declared you officially dead!"

Tomoe looked surprised, then upset.

"It's true," said Azo. "He made your grandmother fold your clothing right-over-left as for a corpse. Any possessions you kept in Heida were given to a temple for distribution among the poor. As a result your grandmother will not speak to him anymore, but lives in his house. Your brother is even angrier. But as your father is the family patriarch, none can question his authority to do these things. You are no longer Tomoe of Heida. You must take another name."

"I'll keep my name!" said Tomoe. "My father has died for me as well. *He* can take another name!"

"You speak tough! But tears are in your eyes. Will you fight me, then, Tomoe Gozen? Without filial piety, what good is life anyway?"

Tomoe drew her sword and raised it above her head. Azo stepped back, smiling, pleased, hand to hilt. The beggars and other people in the street scurried away to watch from safe distances. "Too many people try my patience today!" shouted Tomoe. She untied her straw hat with one hand and let it fall from her back to the ground. "Did you search for me to give me troubling news? If you are that eager to die, we will begin!"

The sound of a larger fracas interrupted the intended duel. A laughing, howling ronin was running down the street, pursued by four large men. Tomoe's eyes narrowed at the sight. She whispered the ronin's name as though it were a curse:

"Ich'yama."

The ronin hadn't bathed at all. He'd gotten drunk and evidently gambled. No doubt he lacked the funds to pay his losses. His pursuers were tattooed men: professional underworld gamblers. They had bared their shoulders to boastfully reveal their fierce tattoos. Although Ich'yama fled their murderous rage, he did not seem worried. He laughed uproariously, heading straight toward Tomoe Gozen and Azo Hono-o.

"I've been running all over looking for you, Tomoe!" he shouted. "I wanted you to see this!"

He reeled about and drew his sword in the direction of the gamblers. The four men were surprised by the action, but prepared themselves quickly. As they raised their swords to kill the delinquent ronin, Ich'yama was already sheathing his sword. The four men were gutted. One by one they realized they'd been mortally cut, and fell to the ground.

Tomoe's evil mood lessened with the sight. She never expected to feel admiration for the dirty ronin. She picked her hat off the ground, dusted it, and said to Ich'yama, "That was excellent."

"I know!" said Ich'yama, eyes sparkling.

Azo Hono-o inspected the clean, killing wounds approvingly. She started to slip away, for what reason Tomoe wasn't certain. "Where do you go?" asked Tomoe; but Azo Hono-o withdrew into an alley and vanished.

"Who was she?" asked Ich'yama.

"A friend who wants to duel," said Tomoe. "I expect someday we will . . . but I wonder why she ran away. It's been a day of strange meetings! As I don't believe in coincidences, I suspect occult intervention."

She and Ich'yama left the corpses for others to clear away. Since samurai could lawfully slay anyone equal to or below their own station, an investigation was unlikely, especially in the case of gamblers.

"Did you learn anything?" asked Ich'yama. "No? Me either. I went to the most despicable places searching!" He jokingly feigned disgust for the necessity. "The bathhouse was overcrowded, so I didn't get a chance to bathe . . . but . . . I *did* do something!" He blushed like a lovestruck boy as he removed a rectangle of paper and a piece of yarn from his sleeve. He had written on the paper. Seeing a rather scraggly bamboo bush nearby, he hurried toward it and began to tie the paper to a branch. "I wrote it myself!" he said. "Please read it!"

Despite herself, she was curious. If anyone had ever written a poem for her before, they had not had the nerve to show it to her. Ich'yama's poem read:

Women are inconstant
as streaks of golden sunset
under clouds.

She was immediately incensed. Doubtless it was intended to convey his sadness regarding her unresponsiveness to amorous clues; probably she was supposed to be flattered to be compared to golden sunsets. But the charge of inconstancy was entirely false! It revealed the ronin's self-centered ignorance more than any comprehension of Tomoe's strengths or nature. She tore the paper from the limb and crushed it in her palm. Ich'yama was surprised. Tomoe growled at him,

"Your sentiment would be appropriate for a courtesan or girlish page. Either might reply happily to your bid for sympathy. But to level a charge of inconstancy against a *bushi* is to challenge my very honor as a samurai! I will prove my constancy with my sword. You will agree to duel?"

Ich'yama stammered, "I—I didn't mean . . . I—I only meant . . ."

"Tomoe Gozen!"

It was Prince Shuzo Tahara hurrying out of an inn. He must have been watching this drama unfold from an upper floor window. Hidemi Hirota was with him, as they too had been spying through the low districts and doing so as a team. Tahara stopped two sword-lengths away from the man and woman samurai, and shouted as though he stood a long way off,

"Tomoe! Place your priorities according to your conscience! You want to duel the ronin! What is more important!"

"Don't meddle, Shuzo!" she said. "He has been an affront to me all day. He has even accused me of inconstancy! I cannot waver now."

"Let them fight," said Hidemi.

"No! Ich'yama has ten of the faces in his brain! Tomoe has another ten! If one dies, or they kill each other, part of our task will go uncompleted!"

"Tell us the names of the men," Hidemi suggested to Tomoe and Ich'yama. He looked at the prince and added, "Then we can let her kill the ronin."

"I said no!" The young prince had the commanding posture and tone of his class, but lacked years and experience. It took more than blood to be a strong leader to samurai as willful as these. He could only plead to their sense of duty: "If you must fight, do so with *boken*. A wooden sword won't ruin our chance of seeing our task completed."

Tomoe had pushed her sword out the length of her thumb. The sword was not yet drawn. Ich'yama looked terribly burdened and upset. He said,

"I will agree to what Shuzo Tahara says, Tomoe! We will test each other with sticks!"

Prince Tahara decided the terms: "It will be at dusk, in the gardens where we already agreed to meet. The bonze can be a witness too."

Tomoe said, "It is dusk now."

"Then we'll repair to the gardens," said the prince. "Hidemi, please run ahead and find a pair of strong bokens."

Tomoe pushed her sword tight into the scabbard, saying, "Good."

Hidemi Hirota was sweaty from having raced in search of wooden swords. He rested on his knees near the monk. Shindo sat in the gardens with his pilgrim's staff at his side, his sword next to that. He did not look pleased. Tomoe was not unaffected by Shindo's stern expression. Despite the gloomy circumstances which brought the five together, Shindo had been of bright humor. Now his humor was spent. The prospect of two in their group fighting against each other rather than a common enemy had completely overwhelmed his cheerfulness. Tomoe's guilty feelings caused her to feel defensive. When she, Prince Tahara and the ronin came into the garden, she asked the bonze coldly:

"Why wrap the sticks in straw!"

He set the padded bokens on the ground in front of him and denied Tomoe the courtesy of reply. He addressed the entire situation instead: "I will not consider either of you good warriors if you cause so much as a bruise. No, do not argue! The test of skill is not whether one of you can hurt the other. If you can control your blows so well as to cause no injury, *that* is the measure of supreme understanding of your weapons' merits and limitations. Bokens are not swords, yet they are deadly weapons; therefore I have wrapped these in straw. If one of you kills the other by accident or intent, then both of you will have shown yourselves poor samurai. Your present duty is to Okio's vengeance. When that is done, you may kill each other at leisure. I won't say more. Nor will I be a witness." Finishing his lecture, Shindo took up his sword and placed it in his sash. Then, with staff in hand, he stood and went into the house, not looking back.

Hidemi Hirota took up the straw-wrapped bokens. He

said, "The bonze was ill tempered the instant I informed him of the match. I don't understand his complaint." He let Tomoe choose first between the bokens. They were identical, but she weighed them both before choosing.

Prince Tahara said to the fighters,

"It is unfortunate that Ich'yama has alienated half his fellows. It is more unfortunate that Tomoe Gozen's temper leads to this. It is almost as unfortunate that Hidemi encourages the fight and wants so badly for the ronin to be killed. Do as the bonze directed. Do not let there be a fourth unfortunate item for my list."

Hidemi gave Ich'yama the remaining boken with far less ceremony. He said to the ronin, "Tomoe is famous! My own Lord has mentioned her merit with reverence and awe. There are perhaps five fencers anywhere in Naipon who could begin to stand against her. Think of that when she holds back and does not bruise you."

Ich'yama took a stance facing Tomoe Gozen. Tomoe held her boken straight before, the hilt gripped firmly in both hands. She dug her toes into the soil of the garden. Ich'yama slid his right foot closer.

They clashed.

Fell away.

Bits of straw scattered in the air. Hidemi looked disappointed that the ronin was not touched. Prince Tahara looked surprised and began to watch more closely. Neither of the mock-fencers revealed their feelings.

They circled one another. Ich'yama gave ground, moving backward through a thicket. Unexpectedly, he moved forward, a blow aimed for the head. Tomoe went to one knee and blocked the cut, slipped out from under the boken and struck for Ich'yama's arm as she came back to both feet. A twist of the hand and he had stopped her counter cut. Again, they backed away from one another, bokens pointing outward from their centers.

Already their brows were sweaty. It was a strain for them to hide their feelings. Neither had expected a close match. Both had thought to win instantly.

The straw hung loose from the bokens, sad padding indeed. The pair engaged in another set of exchanges which proved neither one superior.

"It could go on all night!" said Hidemi Hirota. "How can a ronin be so good?"

"Shush!" the prince reprimanded. He and Hidemi followed the fighters through the large gardens, along paths or trampling through beds of flowers. There were no lanterns lit. As twilight became night, it was harder to see what was going on. Outside the garden, a koto played love melodies. Stars winked as darkness deepened.

Tomoe stepped into a narrow brook which ran through the grounds. Ich'yama rushed her with his sword held high and his trunk entirely exposed to a sideways cut. She tried for the swift strike, but slipped on algae in the rocky brook, as Ich'yama must have expected. She started to block his blow but decided to let herself fall away instead, though it meant landing on her side in the shallow waters. Ich'yama had not expected her to perform an undignified defense. As a result, he fell forward on the momentum of his own thrust and landed face down in pepper bushes. Where the pepper scratched him, it itched.

Neither warrior looked very glamorous now, one soaked and the other scratched. Prince Shuzo called out, "Draw!"

The two had regained their feet and faced one another again. Ich'yama said, "We should accept Shuzo's declaration, Tomoe! We are evenly matched!"

She said, "I could kill you any time."

Ich'yama was indignant. "How can you say so? Admit I fight as well as you!"

"I have tested out your weak spots," said Tomoe. "I know how to land a cut. If this were true steel, I could kill you right now."

"You are too boastful!" said Ich'yama. "I will not consider Prince Tahara's decision any longer!"

Tomoe's teeth shined in the darkness. It was a smile. She said, "Good," then moved forward.

She waited for his attack. Instead of blocking, she placed

her wooden sword against his neck, hard enough to surprise him but not hard enough to bruise.

"I've killed you," said Tomoe.

Ich'yama's boken was held firmly against the side of Tomoe's ribs. A real sword would have continued to her breast bone and exposed her heart.

Prince Tahara said, "Tomoe has won the match."

Ich'yama jerked around furiously and faced Shuzo. "It was a draw! We killed each other at the same instant!"

"Victory for a samurai is more than coming away alive," said Shuzo Tahara. "Tomoe was more prepared to die. That is how she won."

The ronin's face was hot with anger. He threw the scarred and dented boken on the ground and said, "I accept defeat!" As he stomped into the house to find a place to sleep, bonze Shindo came out into the yard. He had been listening out of curiosity, though by his own oath he was not allowed to watch.

"A good night for moon gazing!" said Shindo, his positive disposition regained. But nobody listened, nor looked into the sky.

The samurai was disappointed in her behavior. She'd won the bout with the ronin, but not with herself. It was unlike her to be temperamental, to insist on a fight when one was unnecessary. Now that her anger was assuaged, her guilt was heightened. When the broad-shouldered Hidemi and child-faced Prince Shuzo suggested turning in for the night, Tomoe decided on the monk's occupation instead: moon-gazing. Shindo sat on smooth moss near a large, artificially made pond in the middle of the gardens. The rising moon reflected in the pond.

"Would I interrupt your meditation," asked Tomoe, "if I sat beside you?"

Shindo showed her his homely, pleasant face, round as the moon. He smiled welcome. They sat together. Tomoe said,

"You are a novice of the *yamahoshi*? I've met mountain men before. They're usually less pleasant that you."

The bonze was unoffended. "As you are different from many women of samurai caste, so am I different from many of my sect."

Tomoe's awkward attempt to start a conversation ended there. They were silent for a long while, listening to the night birds and insects. A frog swam through the moon's reflection, carving a transitory wedge. After a while, Shindo said,

"It's odd that no one spied a single man of the fifty today. I suspect they repaired to a shrine or hot springs to purify themselves after they completed their unholy commission. If that is true, they will be cleansed by now. They'll return to Isso tomorrow and celebrate the last day of Star Festival with abandon. We must arrange the revenge-taking in darkness, so that Okio's ghost can come up from the Land of Gloom and watch us."

Tomoe did not respond. Her thoughts were elsewhere. The bonze recognized her trouble. "Don't treat yourself so harshly," he said. "The fight with the ronin is done, and great harm was avoided."

"I try to make myself a little better every day," said Tomoe. "How could I let a mere ronin ruffle my disposition?"

Bonze Shindo grinned and looked another way.

"You think it's funny?" asked Tomoe.

"I think we must each search our hearts from time to time. See over there among the reeds? There is a brown duck sleeping alone. Is it not sad?"

Tomoe saw no duck. Ducks symbolized family love and faithfulness. Brown ducks were female. Tomoe said, "Do you suggest I'm *fond* of the ronin?"

"Did I say so? No, I realize he is uncouth by your standards. But when you returned to the gardens at dusk, you looked more like someone who had lost her family than like someone desiring a fight."

"You are perceptive, bonze." Tomoe looked unhappy. "My father has declared me dead because I refused a marriage meeting. It was bad timing for a ronin's lust."

"You think it is lust?" asked the novice yamahoshi. "Don't you believe in love?"

"I believe in duty and circumstance," said Tomoe. "Wives and husbands love each other because it is their duty. The circumstance is arranged by parents and go-betweens, not by love."

"You are cynical," said the bonze. "The yamahoshi do not prescribe celibacy for their priests—only for novices." Shindo laughed at himself. "So there is a saying among my sect: 'Devils fall when yamahoshi raise their swords. Yamahoshi fall when women raise their eyes.' "

"I'm not certain I like the saying," said Tomoe.

"The ronin might like it better!" The monk laughed again. "He is obviously very strong. Perhaps he has never been defeated before."

"He did not fall because of my eyes," said Tomoe, her voice somewhat strained. "He fell to the skill of my weapon."

"Only that? I think he loves you besides!"

"It annoys me that you say so. Monks forever give advice! How can you know what a ronin feels?"

"To fight so well, he is more than a mere ronin. He takes the name 'Number One Mountain,' which is not a name at all, although it is very boastful to call himself that. I listened to the two of you fighting. By the sound of his footwork and strikes, I recognized the style. I'm certain he studied with Mountain Priests, perhaps at my own temple before I became a novice."

"So? It proves he's from a mountain province and presently travels incognito. Yet he is too dirty to be anything but a well-trained man of bad fortune and worse manners."

"Even men of bad fortune have hearts, Tomoe."

"Do you suggest I have no heart?" asked Tomoe, her face turning red. She calmed herself immediately, breathing deeply, looking away from Shindo's moon-face to the moon reflected in the pond. "My mind dwells always on the Way of the Warrior. I am forever prepared for death, not love."

"I won't mention it again," said the bonze, seeing her upset.

"I would be grateful."

The moon's path had taken it away from their vision. It

peeped through the trees around Tomoe and Shindo, but no longer reflected on the water. The nightbirds and insects were silent, and that was strange.

"Let's move over there," said Shindo, "so I can see the moon a while longer." Tomoe followed the monk to a wooden deck built over a corner of the pond. The moon's reflection was still not visible, but the moon itself shined brightly on their faces. Tomoe changed the topic of conversation:

"I wonder if you know a man named Goro Maki. He shaved his head a long time ago to become a yamahoshi."

Shindo tried to remember. "If his head were still shaven, I would know him by that name. But once a new man in the monastery has proven his strength, he begins to grow a beard and wild mane of hair. He changes his name as well. The harrier the yamahoshi, the longer he has been a fighting monk; his beard symbolizes his strength. The change of name symbolizes the beginning of a new life, without desire for fame. If I have met your friend, it may have been by his newer name."

"He is unmistakable," said Tomoe, anxious for news of the man. "He's extraordinarily severe, yet kind in his heart. He was a samurai destined to be famous, except that he was forced to resign from the world because of circumstances beyond his control."

"You were part of his troubles?" asked Shindo, encouraging her to continue. "Today's fight reminds you of a past error?"

"It was unavoidable!" said Tomoe. "Goro and I served the same master, the father of Toshima-no-Shigeno. When the warlord died, it was my sword that killed him. I wanted to commit suicide to atone, but Toshima absolved me of guilt. Goro Maki, however, remained bound by samurai rules to fight me, despite our friendship. He was also bound to obey the warlord's heir, Toshima. To prevent the fight, she commanded Goro to leave and become a monk, forsaking all samurai privileges. She then made me her chief vassal. To other people, this is old history. To me, it is sometimes as clear as this morning's events. No one has seen Goro Maki since that terrible situation. I would like to know he bears me no animosity. It's hard to lose friends."

"There are many stories like that one among the yamahoshi," said Shindo. "My own instructor might have been a famous samurai, but circumstances drove him to cloister. He will never talk of it. My own history is less extreme, yet I might have been the priest of an important shrine but for family disputes. I volunteered for something with less prestige because I was least proud, and it ended jealousies. It was frightening at first, going to the yamahoshi monastery. I'd been told they were bitter men, for it is true that the Way of the Warrior is complex and arbitrary enough to cause many warriors to choose either *harakiri* or retiremen, through no cause of their own. Since then, I've grown fond of the yamahoshi. They are as honorable as famous men! They obey no government but their own. They practice martial skills by challenging demons such as *oni* and *tengu*. They banish evil with their swords but ask no thanks or fame. Because they understand the importance of attending supernatural events, my instructor quickly said, 'Go!' when I begged leave to avenge Okio. I'll return to the mountain after this commission and not leave again until I'm a strong warrior-monk."

"I would like to see you then," said Tomoe, "with your whiskers and long hair."

"It will hide my ugly face!" said Shindo happily.

"Not so ugly," said Tomoe. She was at ease for the first time that day. "It's a face of large character."

Shindo looked pleased.

The brown duck sleeping in the reeds was disturbed. She made frightened noises and burst from cover, flapping into the sky. Shindo stood up immediately and took a stout posture.

"Evil spirit!" cried Shindo. He struck the ground with the bottom of his staff, and the three rings at the top jangled. "Back to the mountains with you!"

Tomoe stood and looked in the direction of the reeds. She

did not see anything, but realized something was amiss since it had been quiet for so long. Shindo struck the ground again. The sound of the rings was meant to frighten devils and ghosts away.

"How do you know what it is?" asked Tomoe.

"A yamahoshi knows!" he said. "Even a novice like me. Look!" He pointed with his staff. For a split second, the moon shone on the face of a hideously ugly, brilliant red oni.

"Oni devil!" said Tomoe; but the specter slunk out of sight too fast for her to be certain.

"You know them, too," said Shindo.

"I have fought them in the past," said Tomoe. "They are fierce with weapons, but cannot speak."

Shindo struck the ground again. Something besides an oni devil appeared on the pond's opposite bank. It was a woman dressed in red and wearing a large hat with veil and bells attached. The woman spoke, and her voice carried across the water in an eerie way:

"You are mistaken, bonze. If I were an oni, how could I speak to you so easily?"

The bonze struck the ground with his staff once more. The woman did not quail, reaffirming that she was not a devil disguised. She nodded her head to make the bells of her hat jingle, returning the bonze's insult. She said,

"You are a novice after all, unable to tell a sorceress from a devil. But you must be sensitive to recognize my occult aura." The woman raised her walking staff above her head as she added, "I would like to match my staff to yours. We will see whose understanding of occult matters is better."

Shindo looked serious. He said, "The yamahoshi banish evil magic! We do not fight with spells, but with martial skill!"

The woman laughed, and the laugh was devilish indeed. She set foot on the surface of the pond and did not sink. She began to walk toward Tomoe and the bonze. Her gait was broken and surreal, for one of her legs had once been broken and healed crookedly. Tomoe reached for her sword, but the bonze said, "Leave it to me!" He waded into the pond to meet the sorceress, but the waves from his legs made the woman vanish from the pond. Tomoe gasped. She said,

"How is it possible!"

"The sorceress was not really here," said Shindo, wading back to the flat dock and climbing out of the water. The hem of his robe dripped around his bare feet. "That was her soul wandering from the body. Most people's souls wander now and then, while dreaming. When the dreamer wakes, there is rarely memory of the events. The sorceress probably won't recall having visited you and me. But it worries me. When someone of occult learning has so little control over her soul, it usually means trouble for everyone."

"Then I must do something tonight!" said Tomoe. "Or she might interfere with our vengeance tomorrow."

"What can you do?"

"I saw her earlier today. She's a fortuneteller in one of the low districts. I'll find her and wake her up!" Tomoe started toward the garden gates. If Shindo wanted to dissuade her, he disuaded himself from saying so. He said,

"Be careful, Tomoe."

The nearly deserted street appeared somehow askew, as though hinged from the stars at a slight angle. A few candles were still lit inside paper lanterns hanging outside the doors of late-night establishments. A fat woman came out of a saké house, a dirty towel tucked in her obi. She looked up and down the street, her eyes narrow and expectant. Then she took down the lantern, collapsed it, and blew out the flame. Tomoe stepped out of the night and said, "The fortuneteller who wears red. Where does she live?"

The fat woman glared at Tomoe with a blank expression: no fear, no surprise, no concern. Smoke trailed up from the extinguished candle in her collapsed lantern. Slowly, as though dreaming, the woman raised a large hand and pointed with pudgy fingers. Tomoe said, "Thank you," and strode on down the street.

She stopped outside the door of an inn which the fat woman had indicated. Its light was already taken inside; the door was bolted from within. Tomoe slapped the door with the flat of her hand. After a while, a sleepy voice called, "It's all sold out!" which meant his inn was closed.

Tomoe said, "Think well of me," a formal phrase, "and slide your door aside."

She heard grumbling, but the door was unbolted. The innkeeper was a small man who hunched down even smaller. He looked out from his establishment cautiously, but he wasn't measuring Tomoe; he was looking elsewhere on the street, as though afraid a horde of monsters might take advantage and come running in behind her. Dim candlelight shone from inside, behind the little man's back.

"There are no ghosts with me," said Tomoe, hoping to discourage his apparent fears. He let her enter. She left her *zori* sandals on the ground inside the door, then climbed onto the polished, elevated wooden floor. Tomoe said, "I need to see the woman who hides her face."

The innkeeper stepped back from Tomoe, looking as though he regretted opening the door for her. He said, "What fortunes she tells bode ill! You do not want to see that one. There are better fortunetellers in Isso—famous ones."

"I don't seek my fortune told," said Tomoe. "I come to tell her hers."

The innkeeper slapped himself on the cheek and looked even more upset. "No trouble in my inn tonight, please!" he pleaded. "It's always trouble where that one's concerned. I'd evict her but for my fright."

Tomoe moved closer to the fellow. He cowered as she neared. "What kind of trouble does she cause?" the samurai asked.

"She talks to devils!" he said, whispering as to a confidante. "When you slapped the door, I was afraid it was her pet, a red colored oni who follows her around."

There was a strange look in the man's eyes. It caused Tomoe to say, "You're too dream-sotted to answer doors. You're too free with information about your tenants."

The little man was insulted, then suspicious. He said, "Perhaps you're the oni after all, disguised as a samurai."

"Perhaps I am," said Tomoe. The innkeeper squeaked like a mouse and hopped away. Tomoe raised her chin and looked up the staircase. She asked, "Which is her room?"

He told her at once, then ducked backward into a side room and bolted himself in.

Tomoe removed an "S" shaped candlestick holder from the top of a doorframe and carried the light with her up the steps. Strangely, the candle barely penetrated the darkness of the stairwell. Tomoe felt momentarily disoriented, but caught her balance before slipping down. At the top of the stairs, she lurched forward as though forcing herself through something invisible but strong. When she tried to slide the occultist's door aside, she discovered it would move only a finger's width. The door was tied shut with red yarn. She stuck the sharp, upper part of the "S" candlestick holder into the lintel and peered into the room through the door's narrow crack.

Shadows seemed to dance within; but when Tomoe blinked and cleared her vision, there was only the shape of a woman lying on a futon rolled out on the floor. Without the slightest sound, Tomoe drew her shortsword, cut the string, sheathed the weapon, and slid the door aside. She stepped into the room.

The sense of disorientation which she had experienced on the seemingly tilted street and again while coming up the staircase was far stronger in the room. Everything felt slightly awry, although a quick glance revealed nothing overtly amiss. The trouble was as subtle as a dream's reality; everything seemed proper although nothing really was.

The woman lying on the floor jerked awake and sat up abruptly. The dreaminess of the room was instantly dispelled. Tomoe, too, felt suddenly wakened. The fortuneteller, sitting cross-legged on the futon, faced the other direction. She did not turn around, but said, "Have you come to see your future after all, samurai?"

Tomoe had left the sliding door open and the candle at the top of the doorframe. The candle's light cast appalling dark shapes up the wall and out the window. Moonlight shone into the room and cast opposing shadows. The fortuneteller, therefore, had two shadows: one from the moon, faint and long; the other from the candle, sharp and hunched down. Although the double-shadow was explicable, Tomoe was unsettled by it. She said,

"Explain yourself to me or I'll behead you without reservation. I think you are a danger to an important mission."

A wind blew from the window and the candle went out in the hall. A cloud passed before the moon. Tomoe's sword was out of the sheath at once, prepared to decapitate this woman of sorcery. But something had crawled into the open window, and it bore a sword. In the darkness, Tomoe was a shadow herself, and one shadow fought another. She sensed that her opponent was far weaker; but whatever the thing was that was fighting her, it could apparently see without light. It's better vision weighted the battle more evenly.

"Stop it," said the woman who had not moved from the futon. The specter ceased fighting. "Leave at once," she said; and the specter slunk out the window. Tomoe saw its outline for the shortest moment: a horned oni devil. She remembered seeing it before, across the garden's pond earlier that evening. The sorceress sat very still and said to Tomoe, "Forgive my friend's protectiveness. Despite what you have witnessed, please think well of me and sit down."

Tomoe sat.

The sorceress reached toward her straw hat, which lay beside her walking staff near the futon mattress. As she donned the hat, she said, "Also pardon my eccentricity." The veil attached to the front of the hat hid her face before she turned toward the window and faced Tomoe. The cloud parted from the moon, lighting the room and the sorceress.

"Do you know that you are dangerous when you sleep?" asked Tomoe. "Your soul threatened a bonze halfway across the city. Also, everyone I passed in this district was affected by your slumber."

"I do recall a dream," said the woman behind the veil. "In it, I went searching for a friend, a woman I knew long ago. I found her with a yamahoshi who had a long beard and wild hair and ticks. He told me that he was adverse to magic, but I knew he was a sorcerer. I rushed forth and killed him with my walking staff! Only, when his corpse had fallen, I saw that somehow I had killed my friend by accident."

"That is an interesting dream," said Tomoe. "You went looking for a friend and found me. You wanted to kill a yamahoshi priest, but threatened a novice instead. Fortunately, the part about the killing has no counterpart in the waking world."

"Perhaps that part of the dream is in the future," said the fortuneteller.

Tomoe said, "If that is so, then it is good I've come to kill you."

"If I were killed, the oni would be upset."

"I don't fear devils. I've fought stronger ones than yours."

"I did not mean you should be afraid. You should feel sorry for the oni's sadness if I die." The sorceress took up a flat dish containing leaves from the *kaji* tree, a tree associated with magic. She indicated a teapot full of water which was within Tomoe's reach. "If you would grant a final wish before I'm killed," said the sorceress, "let me tell your fortune. Pour water onto the kaji leaves and I will hold the saucer up so that stars reflect on the water. By the placement of the leaves and the stars, I can see your life tomorrow."

"I don't believe in destiny," said Tomoe. "There is only now."

"That may be so," said the occultist. "But 'now' has no beginning and no end. Those of us with vision can see other parts of 'now.' Unless you are afraid, grant my final wish and pour from the pot."

Tomoe did so. Then the occultist held the saucer of leaves and water up to reflect starlight. Tomoe sat between the woman and the window. Stars reflected in the fortuneteller's eyes, which were all that showed of her face.

"The stars reflect red in this saucer," she began. "That is unusual. It means you will fight many kinds of devils, human and not."

"I like adventure," Tomoe jibed, then added sardonically, "And will I fight an oni?"

"The stars suggest redder devils than my oni."

"You, too, are clad in red."

The occultist refused to be ruffled by Tomoe's failure to take the reading seriously. She concentrated on the dish of reflected stars and continued, "Blood is your nemesis. Red death. There is only one white star in the saucer, and it must be yourself; although you might be a red star, too, and the white one is someone else. A red star and white star stand together. Red stars surround these two, as though to attack. Wait! What was that? A momentary streak! The falling star was blue! I don't know what it means."

Tomoe found herself unable to make more snide comments. The blue falling star was undoubtedly the tengu, of which the occultist could know nothing by ordinary means.

"The placement of the leaves is more interesting," she said, her voice suddenly oily and sweet. "I see romance. I see marriage. I see a round-faced child . . ."

Tomoe slapped the dish from the woman's hand. It was the sort of fortune sold cheaply to romantic girls at Star Festival every year. To have her attention gained only for an insult enraged Tomoe! She had died to her family and would never have a family of her own; of this, she was certain. Painful anger caused her to draw her sword and cut toward the woman's face. The veil was clipped off. The fortuneteller turned halfway around so that Tomoe could not see her . . . but Tomoe saw the face clearly in the moon's silver light.

The fortuneteller was beautiful.

"You *are* the nun!" said Tomoe. She scooted closer, all anger cast away, looking intense and concerned. "You're Tsuki Izutsu! Once you tried to convert me to Zen. I thought you'd been killed long ago!"

The woman's profile was turned down, frowning. She said, "You have unveiled my face, but not my identity. I don't remember the name Tsuki Izutsu. If you must have a name for me, call me Naruka."

Naruka was a kind of monster that lived near the bottom of the Land of Gloom and was never seen in the living world. It was not a good name for a woman, not even if she worshipped Oh-kuni-nushi, God of sorcery. Tomoe would not consider the name appropriate. Tsuki Izutsu had been only kind! Tomoe said,

"You must recall!" She scooted nearer. "We fought side by side! You were good at *bojutsu*, fighting with your staff! We battled seven oni devils of various colors! When you were injured, I thought you died; but one of the oni carried off your corpse. It was the red oni! Why did it save your life? Why does it stay close to you now?''

''I remember nothing of the sort!'' The occultist was insistent, almost hysterically so.

''They were mountain oni although we fought them in the lowland swamps. The one who saved you must have carried your broken body to the mountain priests to be healed.''

''I despise the yamahoshi!'' said Tsuki-*cum*-Naruka. She turned her face toward Tomoe. Hate filled the woman's eyes. Tomoe gasped; for, lit plainly by the moon, she saw that half the woman's face was scarred and ugly. The cheekbone was caved in. One nostril had been torn larger. The corner of her mouth was drawn down. She spoke venomously: ''You recoil from my visage? Good! Yes, I remember the yamahoshi 'saving' my life! They had me brought back from Emma's hell, sending that foul, devoted oni after my soul! I would rather have been left dead. Of Tsuki Izutsu, there is nothing left, if that was ever my name.''

The occultist snatched up her staff and began to stand. ''You think I am some friend from your past?'' she asked in exclamation. ''I am your worst possible enemy! Did you not wonder how the young warrior Azo Hono-o found you in Isso, where you had come in secret? It was my sorcery which planted the idea of coming here, though she herself thought it intuition. You believe you could defeat her easily, but I do not think you can. She is like a younger, more impetuous Tomoe. To kill her would be *jigai*; it would be killing yourself. I think you will let her win!''

Tomoe whispered, ''Why have you this grudge?''

Tsuki-cum-Naruka looked confused by the quiet question, then replied hotly, ''I need no grudge! I am the evil Naruka and desire to do mischief only!''

''Someone makes you,'' said Tomoe. ''Someone who is a greater magician than you. I would suspect the giant who was the enemy of the swordsmith Okio, but Uchida Ieoshi is no sorcerer. Therefore my enemy is unknown to me. Will you tell me?''

The occultist looked still more confused, the ugly side of her face contorting madly. She exclaimed, ''I am your enemy! Your only one! You need suspect no other!"

For the first time Tomoe spoke loudly, "That is not your voice!"

"If you fail to kill me now," said the occultist, "then I will kill you later!" Saying this, she moved toward the samurai. Tomoe started for her sword, but could not move her hand against Tsuki Izutsu, no matter how cruel the woman had become. Despite the crooked leg, the woman leapt over Tomoe's head and out the window. Tomoe whirled around and saw her one-time friend hobbling across the lower roof. Then she jumped onto the street. She ran brokenly into the night. Behind her, the red oni followed like a faithful dog.

In the morning, Tomoe awoke, momentarily wondering where she was. She had spent the night in the fortune teller's abandoned room. The innkeeper came up the stairs and looked into the room, for the door had been open all night. Tomoe said,

"The occultist has run away. I doubt that she or her oni will return."

The little man looked doubtful, then hopeful, then gleeful. He jumped in the air and whooped happily. "A reward!" he exclaimed. "Let me show my gratitude by making you a meal and pouring you saké!"

Tomoe nodded. "Don't bring it to this room. I will eat on the main floor with your other guests." The innkeeper scurried away, singing a gay folk song as he went. Tomoe closed the door for privacy. She squatted on the *shibi* to relieve herself. She found a bowl and poured water into it so she could splash her face. She cleansed her ears and teeth. She groomed her hair with a comb kept in a small kit in her sleeve. The most difficult undertaking was to remove the wrinkles from her hakama, for she had unfortunately fallen asleep before taking them off. She removed the baggy trousers and laid them flat on the floor to press the pleats with her fingers; then she put her legs back into the garment and retied the straps around her waist, making a fine bow in front.

In all these morning practices, she took her time and tried

to be relaxed. Thoughts of Tsuki Izutsu the gentle nun changing her name and occupation to something more devilish interfered with Tomoe's sense of calm.

Other tenants were already gathering on the main floor of the inn. Tomoe joined them, descending the stairwell with her sheathed shortsword through her hakama straps and obi, and her longsword and straw hat carried in one hand. There were a few flat pillows for kneeling, but not enough to go around. Tomoe chose not to use one. She knelt upon the polished floor, aloof from the motley group around her.

The fleet-footed innkeeper brought individual trays of food for everyone, and a special gold-leafed tray for Tomoe in particular. Her presence dampened the group, for her neatness caused the others to try to be as mannerly about eating. She was not the only samurai in the room, however: there was a young samurai sitting apart from everyone else, with an even younger girl in his company. The girl was too shy to be a geisha or even a geisha's attendant. Her hair was covered with a peasant's towel; Tomoe suspected the girl was hiding the fact that there was very little hair under that towel. Most likely she served a nearby temple, which was why her hair was short, but she had run away for wont of romance. It was a common story. And the fate of such girls was generally sad. The young samurai was dressed for travel and, though he might have been sincere in meeting her during Star Festival, he obviously could not legitimize any relationship. A month later, the girl would almost certainly be a geisha's attendant, learning a more harrowing trade than temple chores.

Tomoe noted these things without attempting to judge.

When the samurai raised his face in her direction, Tomoe's muscles tensed. She recognized him, though they'd never met previously. His name was Ryoichi Nomoto. His name and his face were one of the ten burnt into her memory by the ghost of the Imperial Swordsmith.

For the barest moment, the two samurai met eye to eye. The youth looked away first, disturbed.

The innkeeper hurried back into the room with a bottle of freshly warmed saké. "A present!" he said. "It is the best I have, and not too bad—the least I can offer you for seeing an end to my poor inn's troubles!"

The young samurai and his girlfriend were moving toward the end of the elevated floor to get their shoes. Tomoe had only tasted her meal which the innkeeper had made special. She pushed the tray aside and let the innkeeper pour her a tiny cup of saké, which she drank. She held the cup out to be refilled. As he poured the second cup, Tomoe whispered, "Because I appreciate your hospitality, I must leave quickly before blood is spilled on this clean floor."

The little man frowned and quaked. He looked around his shoulder and spied the young couple moving slyly toward the exit. He scooted out of Tomoe's way while she drank the second cup of saké. After she shook out the empty cup and set it aside, she nodded a brisk appreciation to the innkeeper then stood up. He rushed ahead of her so that he could place her sandals on the step.

As she went out after the departing pair, Tomoe pulled the longsword and scabbard into place in her obi, and tied her hat so that it hung on her back. The street was damp from a brief rain during the night, but already the sky was clear and the morning pleasantly warm. Most of the people of the district were not yet out, since so many had been up late with celebrations.

The young samurai looked back with eyes large. He pulled the girl after him, hurrying toward a small, enclosed shrine where it would be a sin for Tomoe to shed his blood. The youth's fondness for the girl hindered his speed; her kimono was tight-fitting and she could not move with long strides. Tomoe overtook the couple without having to hurry.

The girl, in payment for her lover's kindness in not leaving her behind, shielded the samurai with her own body. Tomoe's sword was drawn, but she was reluctant to kill the innocent protectress.

"Don't kill him!" the girl exclaimed. "It was my fault!"

"I have not come because of your illicit affair," said Tomoe. "I have come because this youth took part in the affairs of murder."

The youth's eyes grew larger still. The girl said, "It isn't true! Ryoichi is too gentle!"

"Was Ryoichi accompanied when he came to the temple from which you ran away?" Tomoe did not wait for the girl to answer, since the answer was obvious. She said, "They came to purify themselves after the crime!"

Even with Tomoe's evidence, the girl would not move aside. Tomoe's sword raised until it was poised above her head. She took a step forward, indicating that she would kill the girl if necessary. The young assassin shrank behind his shield.

"Spare Ryoichi!" she pleaded. "Take my life instead!"

Tomoe would not consider a bargain. She said to the cringing young samurai, "Don't be a coward, Ryoichi Nomoto. Push the girl out of the way and fight me with your sword. If you are old enough to be a killer, you are old enough to be killed."

The calmness of her tone unnerved the samurai further. Instead of pushing the girl out of the way, he grabbed hold of her lest she change her mind about dying first. He held her neck and started backing toward the gate of the shrine. The girl may have been surprised to be so willingly used; but she remained stern in her resolve to protect her lover. Tomoe's sword slashed downward at an angle. The arm around the girl's neck was sliced to the bone, but the girl herself was uninjured. Blood drenched the front of her kimono. Even cut so badly, the youth would not let go.

"He has many friends!" the girl warned, holding out a hand in a feeble gesture to stay Tomoe from pressing nearer. "If you do not strike Ryoichi again, I will ask his friends to overlook your error!"

Tomoe drew her shortsword and threw it, apparently, straight up in the air. Ryoichi Nomoto looked up to see where the blade was going. It came down and took him in the right eye. As he slipped to his knees on the wet ground, the girl whirled around and shouted, "Brace up, Ryoichi!" She tried to pull him to his feet and drag him the rest of the way into the shrine. Tomoe moved quickly. Her longsword finished the task, silencing Ryoichi's pitiful whimpering.

The girl collapsed upon the corpse, wailing. Tomoe took the shortsword from the dead boy's face, saying, "He was braver when killing an unarmed family with the aid of forty-nine. But if you want him avenged, find his many friends. Tell them they will know where I am waiting."

This stated, Tomoe left the sobbing girl with a lover's corpse. The samurai strode away from the low districts without once looking back.

She arrived at the garden entrance at the same moment as did Hidemi Hirota. The big man was excited as he stumbled across her path. His sword was still drawn from a recent scuffle, and was crimson-stained. "I found one of them!" he exclaimed, then, noticing his soiled sword, swung the blade to one side to get the blood off. He sheathed the weapon and explained, "I slipped out this morning to go pray at one of the temples and to bring back some dried fruit." He reached inside of his kimono and brought out a container with enough plums for four or five people. "On my way back," he continued, "I saw one of the ten men shown me by the gaki. I killed him with ease!"

"I, too, killed one of the assassins," said Tomoe. She and Hidemi went into the garden, where the bonze Shindo was sitting on a deck which extended from the anterior of the house. His hands were held in prayer, rubbing beads between his palms. His prayer was for an enemy killed. Clearly he, too, had slain that morning. Tomoe said to Hidemi, "The ghost of Okio continues the haunting. I suspect all five of us have found one each of our requisite ten! We will know for certain when we see Prince Tahara and the ronin."

"A strange coincidence," said Hidemi, scratching behind his ear and wrinkling up his brow in consternation.

"No doubt Okio's spirit worked hard through the night to arrange the situation," said Tomoe.

Prince Shuzo Tahara appeared at one of the doors of the house. He held a bloody cloth in one hand; it had been used to clean his sword. Tomoe looked up from one of the garden's stepping-stones and asked Shuzo, "Have you also found one of our enemies?"

Tahara replied, "It seems that one of the fifty decided to return to the place of the crime, with the intent of burglarizing the house. No doubt he failed to inform the others of his plan. You can find his body lying in the hall, where I left it moments ago when I recognized him."

The monk had finished his prayer and looked at his three conspirators one at a time. He added to Tahara's statement, "The one you killed did not return here alone, Shuzo. His partner lies dead among those bushes, filched items strewn around his corpse!" Shindo stood and pointed with his staff. Then he asked, "Where is Ich'yama?"

The ronin appeared across the garden at the gate. He carried two parcels. "I had errands!" he said, looking somber as he approached the other four. One of his parcels was bloody and about the size of a head. He threw it on the ground at their feet. "This is one of the fifty," he said. "I ran into him on the market street."

"What is in the other parcel?" asked the bonze.

Ich'yama hugged the parcel close, looking furtive and mean. "It is my business!" he snapped.

"If it affects us . . ."

"Don't meddle!" he said, cutting the bonze short. "If you must know, it contains a new kimono, rice paper, writing kit, and a knife. Now, I've private matters to attend!" He entered the house, leaving the others in the morning's dewy garden. They wondered about his attitude.

"Ich'yama is in bad temper," said Hidemi, sounding slightly pleased about it. The bonze said,

"He is still upset about losing the match with Tomoe." The bonze passed a knowing eye toward Tomoe, as if to say, "Or he is temperamental because of a broken heart! See how he has bought a new kimono besides a knife to shave himself. Who does he want to impress?"

Tomoe returned the look quite differently, as though saying, "You have sworn silence on this matter, bonze!" So neither of them verbalized their ruminations.

Outside the garden there were children laughing, for the final day of Tana-bata was already in full sway. Their merriment was a harsh contrast to the mood of the four within the garden walls. Prince Shuzo spoke seriously:

"We each have nine left to kill. No doubt our morning slayings will alert the others to their danger. They will begin to get their group back together to discuss their unexpected bad fortune. Then they'll spy on the garden to learn how many their foe number."

"They could easily prepare an attack before evening," said Shindo, looking pensive and holding his monk's staff straight up to one side. "We have to delay them somehow, so that the fight will happen after sunset. Okio can't leave the Land of Gloom until then."

Tomoe suggested, "We could leave a letter of challenge posted in this garden. It might say, 'After nightfall, the five avengers of Okio will gather to fight the forty-five remaining assassins.' "

"A good plan," said Shuzo Tahara. "In the meantime, we must make ourselves scarce."

Hidemi said, "But won't they be waiting for us when we come back? We cannot surprise them! They'll grant themselves critical placement throughout these grounds!"

"It can't be helped," said the bonze. "Are you afraid of the odds?"

Hidemi Hirota puffed out his chest. "Certainly not."

"Good," said the bonze. The prince said, "Let's scatter through Isso, then. Everyone maintain a low profile for a while longer. We will return at sunset for the main encounter." Tahara looked over his shoulder at the door of the house and called, "Are you listening, Ich'yama?"

Ich'yama did not come out; but his voice carried deep and strong: "As I have recently purchased a writing kit, I will post the challenge myself, after you are gone. For myself, I prefer to remain hidden in this house."

Hidemi rushed atop the deck and looked into the house, but a premonition kept him from entering. He scowled and shouted into the unlit interior: "That is too risky! You might be found too soon!"

"It is my risk," said Ich'yama. "I am answerable to none of you."

Hidemi's cheeks shook and reddened. Ich'yama wore the broad-shouldered samurai's patience thin, but Prince Tahara intervened, saying, "Let it be."

"*Baké*!" said Hidemi, which meant "fool" or "crazy." He stormed away from the house and the others followed him. At the gate he suddenly remembered his plums and, forgetting the annoyance of Ich'yama's strange behavior, divided the dried fruit among his friends. The monk, prince and woman samurai thanked him. Hidemi's spirits were restored. Then they went opposite directions from the gate.

Throughout and around Isso there were many temples and shrines, for it was a capital of holiness since antiquity. Among the gods honored with relics, gates and buildings, however, there was no place or refuge designated for Weaver Maid and Herdsman. Yet on Star Festival's second and last day, every temple was temporarily converted into places to honor the stars of Heaven's High Plain. Novice nuns and acolytes had worked feverishly through the night making thousands of little cakes which the priests and priestesses generously gave away during the Children's Parade. Many children marched in large and small groups through the various streets of Isso and around the outskirts of that big town, making mini-pilgrimages to various temples and shrines of importance to different families. These little girls and boys wore colorful kimono with exceptionally long sleeves. They carried bamboo branches hung with bright papers, switching them in time to a song their own pretty voices made. They sang before the holy spots with happy faces, and they received the little cakes to save or eat, and then they took their parade elsewhere.

Behind the long lines of children came mothers and older sisters wearing their most festive costumes plus simple straw hats of a kind which folded in the center and were like gabled roofs on their heads. These were the children's guardians on the pilgrimage, but also they were dancers, waving fans in time to the children's songs. One song went: "Weaver Maid and Herdsman met last night in the sky. The morning dew happens to be their tears of happiness." More children and adults joined these parades as the day progressed, so that the ranks swelled and the streets grew merrier still. As these folks traipsed gayly through Isso's respectable and religious quarters, they harvested the hundreds of love-poems and -prayers hanging everywhere on bamboo trees and bushes. These would later be tossed into one of the streams or rivers running through and around Isso, with the expectation that each poem or prayer would ultimately find its way to the Heavenly River itself.

Tomoe was hard put to evade a joyous spirit. She craved solitude before the battle, not celebration. She spied one happy parade of children, girls, and women; and she went quickly the other way down a street, coming eventually to the city limits. She strode through shadowy woods, the singing city seeming much less noisy with every step she took. As she went, she chewed the tough, salty meat from the dried plums' stones. Since she had already eaten something that day, the nutritious plums were overly filling and she could not finish them. Although they would keep indefinitely if she stored them in her kimono against a hungrier moment, she was moved to offer the last of the plums to a squat, pleasantly carved rock she happened upon.

The rock was naturally shaped like a kneeling monk and had had a whimsical face added to it by means of a chisel. Someone had tied a paper bib to it in recent days, but already the bib was tattered. "Have you been neglected?" Tomoe asked as she knelt before the stone. A flat rock had been placed in front of the rough-hewn statue, and on this Tomoe placed the plums. "Since I am a samurai," she said, "it is rare that I honor rustic gods; so I hope you will forgive my presumption. Unlike many of my caste, I am more faithful to the Shinto deities than to Buddhism. Because you look very old, I know you are one of the Billions of Myriads of Shinto gods; and that is why I have given you these plums. They are from me, but also from Hidemi Hirota, who bought them this morning. I won't ask any favors in return, since I am a warrior and you appear too gentle for beseeching in matters of dueling. If my offering pleases you, however, please grant the request of the next traveller to happen by."

Her odd prayer given, Tomoe bowed, stood, and continued along the sun-dappled, shady path. She came to a stream. There was a bridge further down the way, but she did not cross it; rather, she sat upon a smooth rock and rested. There was a small, unpresuming temple on the other side of the shallow, wide stream, but she saw nobody around it. On her own side of the stream there was only one other person in view: an elderly, hunchbacked fisherman sitting under a willow tree. He fished in the old, sporting fashion, not in the commercial manner with nets; he had a line tied to a twig. He didn't seem to be having much luck, although Tomoe saw now and then that there were plenty of fish to be caught. In any event, he was far enough away that Tomoe's solitude felt no hindrance. She watched the sparkling waters and meditated on matters sometimes important and usually unimportant. Occasionally she cleared her mind entirely.

She spied a crayfish in the stream, chasing after a minnow.

A cicada cried out from a sunny spot behind her. It was commonly believed that cicadas spoke with the voices of dead loved ones reborn among the withered bushes of the field. Tomoe began to listen carefully. She thought she heard the voices of friends lost in battles. She heard especially the voice of Madoka Kawayama, who had fought at her side when the warlord Shojiro Shigeno still lived. Madoka's voice was sad because he had been slain by his own best friend; his voice seemed to call his friend's name: "Ushii! Ushii!" as the cicada chirruped. Tomoe was reminded that she should visit the grave of Madoka in Shigeno Valley as soon as it was possible to return. She was reminded also of the shrine built for Shojiro Shigeno; she had helped build it with her own hands, in partial recompense for an unavoidable killing. These things reminded her inevitably of Shojiro Shigeno's heir, Toshima-no-Shigeno, who had kindly given Tomoe leave of a vassal's duties for however long it took to resolve personal matters. Tomoe brooded deeply and realized she was an inferior vassal, to be far from Toshima's side in difficult times.

The crayfish captured the minnow and tore it to pieces.

Across the river at the small temple, acolytes began to appear, and then a priest. They looked down the path together. Soon, Tomoe heard a procession of laughing, singing children. Tomoe was shaken from her moodiness and, despite herself, was won over by the beautifully clad children and other celebrators who swarmed up the path to the temple. The children sang a special song and received their cakes. Then the parade began to cross the stream on a narrow bridge. The path brought them near the place where Tomoe was sitting on a rock. The children were delighted to happen upon a samurai. They halted and began to sing a song for her, although she had no cakes to give them. She gave them smiles and nods instead, and one pretty girl ran forward and placed her bamboo branch in Tomoe's lap and ran back to the group again, looking shy.

The mothers and older sisters came forward to the very edge of the stream. The poems and prayers which they had gleaned from bushes in Isso were thrown into the water. The papers floated away, encouraged by a farewell song to go up into heaven so that Weaver and Herder could read and enjoy the verses. When at length the parade of children started on its way back toward the city, Tomoe felt curious indeed. She couldn't explain the feeling. She reached into her kimono sleeve and pulled out a wadded piece of paper. Why she had saved it she didn't know, for it was an infuriating thing: It was the poem that Ich'yama had written her, and which she had angrily torn from a bush. Despite its false charge of inconstancy, it was a pretty poem. Tomoe thought that perhaps Weaver and Herder would like it. Therefore the samurai threw the paper into the stream where it trailed after the others.

"I am being very strange today," Tomoe said aloud, after the reveling children were gone and she was with her solitude once more. The poems had all drifted away, except a few caught on twigs and eddies. The water hurried by her vision. Miniature, mountain-like waves rose and fell and rushed away, seeming like eons of Time compressed into each second. The stream's quick, simple beauty made Tomoe feel inconsequential.

The voices of the children and women faded away into the woods. The priest and acolytes went back into their temple. Once again the only other person in eye's sight was the hunchbacked fisherman up the way.

Tomoe stood from the rock she'd been sitting on, leaving the bamboo branch behind as a small offering to Oho-iwa Dai-myo-jin, the great and unchanging rock god, and for his consort Iwa-naga-hime, Lady of Rock Perpetuity. It was fitting for a samurai to honor that strong pair on a lovers' holiday!

As there was half the day to wait before returning to fight in the gardens, Tomoe walked upstream, going slowly, watching birds and plants and insects. Her nostrils were assailed by autumn's aromatic decay. It was largely an evergreen woods, yet patches of colorful, deciduous leaves broke the greenness here and there.

Because she did not want to bother the wizened fisherman or scare the fish so that his luck was even worse, she gave him wide berth. She intended to pass him without so much as a nod. But, as she was about to go by, he hooted with delight and pulled his line from the water. There was a big toad caught on the end! The line flicked in the air and the toad came loose, landing near Tomoe's feet. She jumped one direction and the toad jumped another. The fisherman came hopping, too, and chased the toad through the grass, shouting, "A fine dinner! A fine dinner for me!" Tomoe smiled at these antics, being in a very much better mood after listening to the children sing. Then she noticed something odd about the fisherman: There were feathers showing from underneath the hem of his ragged kimono. The feathers were blue.

"Old Uncle Tengu," said Tomoe, her voice even and calm. The fisherman looked her straight in the eye, his toad held firmly in one hand. The weathered peasant-face melted away and the tengu's long-nosed face showed instead. He said,

"You have seen through my disguise."

Tomoe asked, "Have you come to exact vengeance on me?" She did not sound worried about the possibility.

"I have two reasons to wish vengeance now," he replied. "I have many lumps on my head because my nephews took your advice and flew above me, dropping stones. Until my flight-feathers have grown back, I am unable to chastise them properly. Because of my shame in not being able to fly, I have disguised myself to travel around the country afoot until the sky is mine again. However, despite my grudge against you, it seems that I will be unable to have vengeance in any usual fashion. This is because you were kind to my nephews, sparing their lives, feeding them, and even giving them useful advice, albeit advice annoying to my pate. There are tengu-diviners among my tribe who made a magic-circle flying beneath the moon; they divined that Tomoe Gozen was the Patron of Demon Children. An honorable appointment for you! Now, even an old tengu like me must honor your name, although I like the idea a very small amount."

"What you say is interesting," said Tomoe. "To be appointed Patron of Demon Children merely for feeding tengu brats a few roots I pulled in the forest! It would seem that tengu tribes bestow honorific titles for low prices."

"Well you may scoff! But famous heros of history have talked to tengu-diviners for guidance. If they have divined that you are a *kami* or deity to our race, then neither you nor I can say they are wrong. It has even been suggested to me that I should be proud to have some of my feathers clipped, and consider it a boastful mantle that the rest of my feathers were dyed blue by Tomoe-sama."

"If I accept the diviners' commission as Patron of demon brats," said Tomoe, "it does not mean I won't kill full grown demons as I decide!"

"Of course not," said the tengu, his tone matter-of-fact. "Nor does it mean that demons will no longer cause you trouble. Even I, whose hands have been tied by my tribe's authority, may find ways to make your life unhappy."

"It would be interesting to have you try."

"Good." The tengu grinned wickedly and his long nose turned up. "I will try immediately."

Tomoe bowed politely. "Please do so."

"I will start by telling you a story," said the tengu: "In a town not far from here there was an important official who often went riding on his horse. His horse was trained for war and resented that he was taken out for purposes other than fighting. The horse grew angrier and angrier each time he was ridden about casually. Finally, the horse could no longer tolerate being treated like a useless, gentle pet. He threw the official onto the ground and trampled him in the legs and belly.

"The official was taken home and the doctor came to set the broken legs as best as was possible, but said, 'He will never walk again.' The doctor gave medicine to the official's mother (for the wife had long since died birthing a son) and said, 'Give him this medicine and maybe he will live, but I doubt it. His broken legs are bad enough, but the hoof in the belly will surely cause him to die.'

"Now the official's son was behind a screen and heard the doctor's words. The son and father had been on evil terms for a while, so that now the son felt remorseful. He went out to the stables where the horse was waiting. The son took the horse into the exercise yard, bridling the murderous beast as if for war. Then the son said, 'We will have a grudge match! You have fatally injured my father. Now, show me a warhorse's better virtues!' The young man drew his sword. The horse's eyes were red with hatred and delight.

"The battle went on a long while. Sometimes the son was almost trampled. Sometimes the horse's tendons were nearly cut by the sword. Eventually the horse knocked the young man over; but he rolled aside in time to not be trampled as had happened to his father. As he rolled, he cut the horse's belly. Viscera fell out. But the horse would not give up. Although its back legs stomped upon its own innards, the horse neighed with bloodlust, not agony. It reared and jumped straight into the air. The young man moved aside too slowly to keep from having his arm broken by a ferocious kick.

"And still the battle went on, in a grisly way. The official's son fought one-handed, his broken arm dangling limp. The horse's blood reddened the exercise yard from one side to the other. Guards came to help, but the son said, 'Don't meddle!' At last he cut the horse's throat and it could only fight a little while after that.

"The doctor came again and set the young man's arm and said it would probably heal fine. 'But,' the doctor said, 'your valor will not save your father. I have looked at him again, and am more certain than ever that he will die.' So, despite his victory, the young man wept."

The tengu seemed to have finished the story, so Tomoe said, "Old Uncle Tengu is a good storyteller. How will his tale help in his vengeance?"

"I have not told you the young man's name."

"That's so," said Tomoe.

"Nor the official's."

"Then do so," Tomoe suggested.

"I will, and gladly. The official's son is Imai Kanchira."

"My brother!" Tomoe looked stricken. The tengu's evil grin grew larger. Its nose twitched back and forth.

"And the official is Nakahara Kaneto, your father!"

Tomoe fell to her knees before the tengu and cried. She said through bitter tears, "Thank you for bringing me the news."

"It was my pleasure," said the tengu. "And it is good revenge, do you think? To bring a samurai to her knees before me, thanking me for delivering pain!"

"It is good revenge," Tomoe agreed. She bowed her head to the ground and begged to know, "How long before my father dies?"

"If you left immediately," said Old Uncle Tengu, "you could see him before he dies. But you cannot leave, can you? You have an errand to complete! If you leave tomorrow, it may be too late."

Tomoe did not rise from her bowing posture. She didn't care if the tengu saw her weep. Her shoulders shook.

"Now my vengeance is complete and I am fully satisfied," said the tengu. "It will be easier for me to obey the command of the tengu-diviners from this moment on. To prove I am at least partially your friend, I'll grant you a vision. I will let you see your father before he dies."

Tomoe looked up. Her cheeks were wet. She said, "You can do this? We can see each other?"

"He cannot see you. But this toad I fished from the stream is not ordinary, for I used a special bait." The tengu held up the creature he had caught on the fishing line. It looked like an ordinary toad except its eyes. When Tomoe looked closely, she realized the eyes were like two small mirrors. She gasped and backed away on hands and knees.

"O-gama!" she exclaimed.

"The toad-goblin can grant you the vision to see all the way to your home in Heida." The tengu placed the toad on the ground. It opened its mouth like a little *shibi* urinal, and white mist began to exude. The mist swept up around Tomoe. She felt a rush of panic as her arms and limbs went numb; but the mists parted a bit so that she could see the countryside of Heida far from Isso. Her soul was being whisked away to her hometown! Directly, she was viewing her father who lay on a thick futon and was covered with two lighter futons. Tomoe's grandmother sat on her knees near the foot of this bed. Tomoe's brother, his arm bound to his breast, sat at the bedside, crying.

The inability to feel her body was unsettling to Tomoe. She struggled mentally for some control, but could not succeed. It did not seem possible to get closer to her father.

Nakahara Kaneto breathed deeply. He looked older than his years, aged by family troubles and then by sickness and injury. Yet his eyes remained open and alert; he must have known he was dying.

Tomoe's brother said, "Come to the side of the bed, Grandmother. Please make peace with Father as I have done."

"My son is dead already, Kanchira," the old woman said. She was tired but stubborn. Obviously she had been taking care of her dying son; but she was still not speaking to him, because he had declared Tomoe dead. "He is dead for as long as my granddaughter is dead," she explained. "I will not speak to his ghost. I am his ancestor; he is not mine. So I need not do his ghost honor."

It was a sorrowful situation. Kanchira was torn between love for both his father and grandmother. It caused him pain that they would not make up. He said, "Father. Is it so hard to beg Grandmother's forgiveness?"

The old man lay still, looking at the rafters.

"Grandmother!" Imai Kanchira stood up, hurried to the foot of the bed and got down on his knees again. "For my sake, Grandmother! Father cannot live much longer. How can his ghost rest if you will not forgive him?"

"As well as mine shall rest," said the old woman.

The dying man tried to speak. His son hurried back to his side and asked, "Will you speak, Father?"

He said, "I regret," then gasped for breath.

Kanchira bowed closer to his father's face. "What do you regret, Father?"

"I regret . . . that I cannot see Tomoe."

The old woman tried to remain severe, but water filled her eyes. It was the first time since pronouncing Tomoe dead that Nakahara Kaneto had said his daughter's name. It was as good as an apology. The old woman bowed to the floor and began to weep the many tears she had held back for so long. She wailed, "Do not die, Kaneto my son! I'm certain Tomoe will come home soon! We will all be united in happiness a final moment before you are gone!"

It was an impossible wish, Tomoe knew; she could not leave for home in time. Unable to face the sadness in the room, Tomoe struggled to escape back to Isso. She felt her heart beat; it was the first thing she felt as her soul returned to its body. Then she felt nothing again. The mists parted and once more Tomoe saw her weeping grandmother, sad brother, and dying father. She fought to regain her body, but the magic of the toad was stronger. "I don't want to see

anymore!'' Tomoe shouted, but didn't make a sound. She found her hands in the mist; they were the only things she could see. With them she felt near her waist and discovered where her swords were kept. She drew the shortsword and threw it. The mist popped like a bubble and vanished instantaneously.

The O-gama or goblin-toad was pinned between its eyes, dead, though its legs were kicking. The tengu's hand was about to pick it up; but he jumped back from the dashing knife and exclaimed,

''Why did you kill the O-gama? It gave you a present!''

''Your vengeance has no bounds, tengu!'' Tomoe was angry. ''You made me see my family because you knew what they would say! They wait for my return; but you know, as do I, that I must serve Okio tonight!''

''You are ungrateful, samurai!'' the tengu complained. ''I do not control the circumstances of your family's life. They were things you should want to know! The O-gama could have invented a better vision, it is true; and a pretty lie is succor in time of trouble. But lies are not salvation!''

''Tengu grant cruel favors,'' said Tomoe. ''So do not lecture me.'' She stepped forward and retrieved her knife from between the O-gama's eyes. Those eyes still shined like mirrors, closing slowly. Tomoe brandished the knife threateningly and said, ''I have killed bigger demons than you! Hobble away quickly or I'll cut off more of your feathers. I'll send you home bald!'' The tengu hopped away like a spry old man. He shed his garment to reveal his blue-tinted wings which had made him look hunchbacked in the ragged kimono. He said,

''It is unfortunate that you feel like that!''

Tomoe rushed forward with her knife. A log was drifting down the river and the tengu made a long, long leap, flapping his damaged wings awkwardly. He landed on the log and balanced himself as the stream took him away from Tomoe's wrath.

''We may spend our whole lives,'' said the tengu, ''exchanging vengeances like this!'' Tomoe hurried downstream, following the log and its rider. She outpaced it and waited on the bridge, thinking to grab the tengu as it went under. But Old Uncle Tengu made another long, awkward, flapping jump which took him straight up into the trees. From there he vanished quickly, melding with the shadows and moving safely from treetop to treetop.

Tomoe's rage faded away, revealing the sorrow that was the true cause of her quick temper. When she was calmed down, she realized that the hour was late. The trip her soul made to Heida must have taken longer than she thought; she'd have to hurry to reach the gardens in time. As she sped along the path toward Isso, she halted only once. She lingered briefly by the whimsical statue where she had previously left the plums. The plums were gone; eaten by the god, pits and all, or stolen by woodland animals. Tomoe said,

"Though I am undeserving of your notice, I have a favor to ask you after all. Keep my father alive an extra day! It is important that I see him one last time, and beg forgiveness that I have been an undutiful daughter. Do this for me and I will never fail to honor rustic gods like you!"

Then she was off once more, toward Isso.

The nighted garden was still. Tomoe saw a note pinned to a tree inside the entrance. It was the letter drafted by Ich'yama. Beneath it was a second note: "The Mukade Group accepts the challenge." It was stuck to the tree by means of a six-pointed shuriken.

There was a rustling high in the tree beneath which stood Tomoe. A man clad in ninja-costume—black, tight-fitting clothing, including hood and mask—dropped to the ground behind the woman. She turned quickly, sword slipping from scabbard. The ninja's shorter sword was already drawn, yet Tomoe was too fast for him. Her sword licked outward. The ninja jumped back into the tree when he realized his surprise attack was ineffective. Tomoe's sword slid easily into its scabbard once more. She looked up but could not see where the ninja hid.

Blood trickled down the trunk of the tree and stained the two notes pinned there. The ninja fell out of the branches, landing at Tomoe's feet. Her quick sword had cut him before he regained the tree, perhaps before he knew himself mortally wounded. She reached down to pull the dead man's mask away. She recognized him as a fellow named Fusakuni Sumikawa, one of those etched onto her memory by the ghost of Okio. She had eight left to kill.

In the sky there was a thin cloud-cover. Only the brightest stars winked through. Tana-bata was definitely ended. The new festival was a private one: a festival of death.

The garden was inexplicably colder than the city streets had been. Tomoe took this as evidence of Okio's ghost being nearby, watching, delighting at the destruction of his enemies. Tomoe wondered what influence the supernatural presence might have. Okio should see the vengeance, it was true; but if he desired to be helpful as well as witness, it could go badly, since the help, well-meant or not, was still rooted in Hell.

There was another sound behind Tomoe. She reeled again, hand to hilt. In the darkness it was hard to tell who was coming. It turned out to be the bonze Shindo. He had left his monk's staff somewhere so that the jangling rings would not scare away the hungry ghost of Okio. It was more fitting, anyway, that the steel smithed by Okio be the bonze's only weapon tonight.

"They're hiding everywhere," said Shindo, looking at the corpse Tomoe made. "Hidemi Hirota is circling around the far side of the garden, searching carefully. Fortunately not all of the assassins use ninja tricks. Some of them fight like honorable samurai, though not so well as yamahoshi. I have already killed four."

Tomoe did not reveal her amusement regarding Shindo's boast about his mountain sect. Before she could comment on the talents of samurai versus martial priests, they heard a scream of agony. Tomoe and bonze Shindo hurried toward the place of the cry and saw Prince Shuzo Tahara standing over the body of a foe. "He fought well," said Shuzo, looking at the bonze and then at Tomoe. "But the swords of Okio are vampires tonight!" The three exchanged steady glances, then separated again, scouring the garden.

The stillness was eerie. No nightbird or insect sang. It was difficult to believe nearly forty foe hid among the bushes and trees and well-arranged boulders of the silent grounds. The garden was fairly large; its design was such as to give the illusion of even greater size; there were scores of lurking-places. Moonrise was not much help in lighting the scene, for the misty clouds turned the moon into the dimmest of lanterns. Yet Tomoe, like most samurai, was hard-practiced at night-battle. In schools it was common to learn to fight blindfolded. She could see better than when blindfolded at least!

Veils of mist drifted between trees, looking like specters, tricking the eyes into believing adversaries stood where there were none, and disguising where they really were. Tomoe walked between two large stones, herself a virtual wraith, moving silently; and she came face to face with another: a man stepped out from the darkness with his sword raised, prepared to slay. Tomoe drew her sword casually and took a countering stance. But she was unable to strike. Something held her arms! She backed away from the assassin and he pursued. It was curious indeed that she could not take the offensive. The approaching man was not one of those shown her by the gaki spirit; by some supernatural interference, she was unable to kill any but her allotted portion. In using gaki-magic to reveal to each of his avengers only a fraction of Mukade Group, Okio had inadvertently bound each to slaying *only* those revealed!

The stranger pressed nearer, wisely taking advantage of her evident inability to attack. His sword begain its descent; but suddenly he grimaced, lurched into a rigid posture, than began to collapse. As he fell, Tomoe saw that Hidemi Hirota stood behind her would-be killer. Hidemi had sliced the man down the spine. He indicated the fresh corpse and said, "He was mine!"

"Where is Ich'yama?" asked Tomoe, realizing the ronin had not been in evidence. Hidemi was reluctant to answer her. She said, "He must not fail to come! There are nine fellows only he can slay, due to limitations accidentally imposed on us by Okio's hellish efforts. Ich'yama's portion will escape, or kill us, if the ronin stays away."

"He is here," said Hidemi, looking at his feet. "Only . . . he will not come out of the house."

Shocked, Tomoe asked, "How is that?"

"You arrived to the garden late," said Hidemi, seeming to evade her query.

"I was detained by a tengu monster," Tomoe explained.

"You need not excuse yourself to me," said Hidemi apologetically, for he had not meant his remark to sound disparaging. "Only, you were not here to discover Ich'yama's decision."

"What decision is that?"

Hidemi Hirota removed a paper from the fold of his obi. "Ich'yama left this letter on the door of the house. I removed it when Shindo, Shuzo and I came here at sundown. After we read it, we decided not to enter the house or rely on the ronin. Our enemies have undoubtedly read it too; but they would not have understood its cryptic meaning. I did not understand it myself until bonze Shindo explained."

"Tell me!" Tomoe demanded.

Hidemi looked embarrassed. "You read it for yourself," he said. "Ich'yama waits inside for the Hour of the Ox."

The Hour of the Ox was the spirit hour, the hour of death. At that time, monks throughout and around Isso repaired to temple yards or hillsides to strike the bosses of huge bells, frightening evil spirits away from the city and comforting the sleeping people. Tomoe meant to ask Hidemi why Ich'yama would remain inside the house until then; but Hidemi had pressed the letter into her hand and scurried off too quickly to be grilled further.

Before Tomoe could completely unfold the letter, a man's head peered at her over a rock. Tomoe held the letter in her teeth and prepared to be attacked. The man was very handsome and smiled amiably, not offering to come out from behind the rock. She recognized him as Hitoshi Nakazaki and was anxious to kill him for Okio's sake. "Come out!" she challenged, speaking with the letter in her teeth. "Show me how to duel!" Hitoshi Nakazaki only smiled more engagingly, perhaps amused by the way she made challenges with teeth clenched on paper. He watched her but didn't move.

An attack came from behind. Tomoe did not turn immediately to face her unexpected attacker, but blocked the downward cut by raising her sword sideways over her head. Steel rang on steel. She slid out from under the blow as the fellow moved out of range of her returned slice. This second man was Hitoshi Nakazaki's brother Tatsuo. Hitoshi climbed over the rock so that soon both brothers were positioned to each side of Tomoe.

She guessed their plan and wondered how best to counter. They were trained as a pair and did not attack randomly, but alternated one busying her with dangerous feints while the other strove seriously to kill. Their timing was excellent. For the moment she was entirely on the defensive. She blocked to left and right quickly enough to avoid being pierced but was given no moment to instigate an attack of her own.

She blocked them again then hurried backward in an attempt to get them both in front of her. They were too fast and clever for that. Several times she beat off their tandem assaults. Soon she was able to perceive the full and limited scope of their style and skill. They were fair swordsmen, but really excellent only in a few narrowly defined and practiced maneuvers. Finally she understood the means by which she might turn their best skills around, causing them to defeat themselves upon the edge of their own certainty.

Tatsuo attacked on her left. She evaded his cut without blocking with her sword. It was an unexpected defense. To her right Hitoshi had already launched a fierce attack, but this time his timing was incorrect, for he had expected Tomoe to remain stationary and block as she had done several times. The result was that the two men carved into each others' shoulders simultaneously. They looked at one another in stark surprise.

"Brother!" said Hitoshi Nakazaki.

"Brother!" said Tatsuo Nakazaki.

Tomoe slashed twice. Two brothers died embracing, swords crossed between their breasts. *Six left*, thought Tomoe.

One of the brothers' cuts had been close enough to her face to sheer off part of the letter she'd carried in her teeth. She quickly found where the other piece had fallen and held the parts together. A vagrant dart of moonlight escaped the prison of clouds and lit the garden. In this light Tomoe was able to see that the letter was actually one of Ich'yama's infamous poems. It read:

From her crimson sheath
a white-feathered arrow flies West
Empty dreams of love!
they fill my nights with sadness.

The reference to a crimson sheath might have had a martial meaning, or intended to be lewd; yet what took Tomoe's attention was the fact that the white feathers and the westerly direction were associated with death. Ich'yama had written a suicide poem! How could the heartbroken fool consider killing himself at this time? He could at least have waited one more day! Shindo, Shuzo and Hidemi had seen the poem already; and they had done nothing about it. Was she to be equally aloof?

If Ich'yama committed seppuku for love of Tomoe Gozen, then Okio's vengeance would be left incomplete. Tomoe's part in injuring the ronin's sensitivity would cause her to share the burden of that duty unmet. She alone was qualified to convince Ich'yama he should stray from his resolve . . . long enough, at least, to complete his other mission.

As she hurried toward the mansion and onto the deck, she heard scuffles among several people but did not see who was fighting who. On the deck one of her own enemies waited.

"You are Matsu Emura," said Tomoe. He looked more princely than Okio's ghost had indicated when showing heads on pikes. Emura was middle-aged, dignified, richly dressed; and he held his sword well. Tomoe assumed, "You must be the leader of these assassins."

"I am boss of Mukade Group," he said. " 'Mukade' means 'centipede,' symbol of unity, and trouble for a foe." He pointed to the group's seal printed on his garb's shoulders: a many-legged insect curled into a circle. "Kill one of us, and the centipede has many more legs to count on; but two of the legs you removed were especially dear to me. When you killed my adopted son Ryoichi Nomoto last morning, you sealed your misfortune."

Tomoe was unimpressed by the threat; but she was impressed by the way the older swordfighter carried himself, held his weapon, inched one foot toward her. Only a life of dedicated practice gave a man such grace. No matter which way she held her longsword, Emura held his in precisely the position appropriate to counter. Because she respected the fact of Emura's skill but had previously found Ryoichi cowardly, she said, "Ryoichi was not a worthy heir for a man of your ability. He did not try to defend himself. He used a girl as shield."

Matsu Emura shook with rage. It spoiled his princely posture. "He was still a child!" Emura shouted.

"Mukade Group kills children in their beds," Tomoe calmly reminded. "The centipede is slyness under stones! You killed the children of the Imperial Swordsmith, not for honor but for the gold of the giant Uchida Ieoshi."

It was surprising how the leader of Mukade Group seethed. The fey youth Ryoichi must have meant much to him. "For Ryoichi!" cried Matsu Emura as he charged, his face inscribed with sorrow for the loss of the gentle boy who was like a son. Tomoe dropped to one knee and hardly seemed to move her sword. Emura missed his mark and flew off the end of the deck, landing in a cluster of dwarfed pines. His stomach was cut open. Tomoe looked to where the swordsman had fallen and she was sad. He was not yet dead, but the cut was too good for him ever to rise again. Tomoe said to him,

"You should have been a more difficult opponent except that you let emotion guide your sword. The hardest lesson is often the last one learned." Then she turned and slid the mansion door open. She disappeared into the lightless interior.

There was only darkness before her; but it was a traditionally built house and its corridors were in general easy to discern by the feel of her toes. She had, of course, left her sandals at the door. She slid one foot ever before as she progressed, making scarcely a sound. Her sword was drawn and wary. Mukade Group would fight harder now that their leader was killed; the desire for vengeance would go both ways. Ninja assassins might wait for her in one of the corridor's alcoves, or behind the very walls. The hand which did not carry the sword lightly touched one wall, helping her to feel the route. She listened for any sign of Ich'yama, who would be hiding while waiting for the Hour of the Ox.

Her hand on the wall felt a slight vibration. She jerked aside when she heard a sword penetrating the thinness of the wall's panel. She thrust her own sword into that panel and heard a vague grunt. There was no way of telling which of the remaining five, among the original allotment of ten, she had just pierced; even if she could get the body out from behind the wall, it was too dark for quick identification. She thought about it no more, but noted for future reference that she had only four left to kill. For Ich'yama, however, nine remained uninjured.

Rather than slink and search, Tomoe decided on a more overt approach. "Ich'yama!" she cried out. "Tell me where you are!" It was a ninja, not Ich'yama, who replied. Tomoe sensed the presence of the black-clad spy but could not see him. "Is it Kenji Hachimura?" she asked. "Kajutoshi Saitoh? Kozo Ono? Fudo Kuji?"

"Kenji is already dead," replied the deep, bodiless voice. "You pierced him where he hid behind the wall. I am Shintaro Shimokashi of Mukade Group. By my *kyoketsu-shogi* you will die."

Tomoe was unfamiliar with the weapon he named; but she suspected it was some kind of rope or chain attached to a sickle or barbed pole, for such were the tools only ninja used. It was a matter of the profoundest concentration to face in darkness a weapon the nature of which was uncertain. She heard a whirring sound and dodged to one side, but had been anticipated. A rope which felt as though it were made of oiled human hair wrapped three times around her neck, a metal weight at its end. The ninja drew her toward him, but could not hold her long enough to slash her with his weapon. Judging by the sound the weapon made when he swung it, it was shaped like a scythe mounted at a right-angle to a short pole. It would have sliced her but that her own sword cut the rope-of-hair so that she fell back from the slashing scythe. The severed rope was still wrapped tightly about her neck. She could not breathe.

The ninja threw darts through the narrow corridor, aiming for the sound of choking. Tomoe took evasive steps as she struggled to get the slick, constricting bonds from her throat. She felt the wind of the passing darts, so close to her face she could smell the poison on the tips. She had loosened the rope enough to gasp deep breaths when the ninja leaped at her invisibly. The blade of the kyoketsu-shogi made so distinct a sound that Tomoe detected its angle of descent. Rather than fall back, she rushed closer and, one-handed, grabbed the handle behind the scythe-blade. She felt the curve of steel cut her clothing but not her flesh; it stopped next to her spine. With her other hand she thrust her sword up under the ninja's rib cage. She heard his heart give a moist, startled "pop!" as she drew the sword out and pushed the scythe away from her shoulder. The ninja collapsed.

In the next moment there was a dim light showing through a door of rice-paper. A lantern had been unshaded. Tomoe carefully slid the door open.

"Come in," Ich'yama invited. The room was pleasantly lighted. Tomoe was surprised by what she saw. Ich'yama had bathed himself. His forehead and jaws were cleanly shaven. His queue of hair was neatly tied, oiled, and pressed flat over the center of his head. He wore perfume, pilfered no doubt from somewhere in the house. He also wore fresh clothing: a flowing white kimono with a yellow crane embroidered on the back; and a white obi was bound around his waist. He wore no hakama or accouterments. He sat on his knees with his left side to Tomoe, facing a polished mirror as would a woman at her toilet. On his other side he had placed a little table on which rested a sheathed knife.

By the look of him, Ich'yama might have been a man of royal lineage.

"The ronin is transformed," said Tomoe, her tone sarcastic. "Bonze Shindo thinks you cannot be the masterless samurai you have seemed; but to me, this sudden finery which you have taken for the Final Ritual does not disguise your uncouthness. Do you think seppuku is honorable when you have another deed yet to perform? Kill yourself tomorrow! Nine men await your sword outside!''

''I await the Hour of the Ox and nothing else,'' Ich'yama said grimly, not looking at the woman. ''Not only is it an appropriate time for death, but it reminds me of the ox-headed wind-god who is also the god of a man's love.'' He sighed deeply. ''You have injured my heart, Tomoe! I no longer care about pride or honor or duty. I am undone by a woman; it is a classic case! There is nothing left.''

Tomoe circled left to see Ich'yama from the front. She was amazed by the beauty of him, as she had been amazed in the gardens when they fought with bokens until both were reduced to sweaty slovenliness. She would not reveal her impressions now, however; she must be severe with him to rekindle his sense of honor. ''You are injured to find your equal in a woman?'' she asked sardonically. ''If it has so destroyed your pride, then do not die by seppuku! Leap into a cold river instead! Die like a lovesick peasant, not like a samurai!''

He looked at her then, and his look was hard; but seeing her, the look vanished quickly. His lips trembled and his eyes held sorrow. He said, ''You have defeated me in worse ways than in practice-combat, and in more ways than you yet know. You spurned my love-poem and my love. Before we even knew each others' faces, you refused our marriage meeting, going so far as to kill our go-betweens and many of your father's retainers. I was insulted but impressed. You won my heart with those ferocious deeds!''

Tomoe was shocked by the seeming-ronin's confession. She exclaimed, ''You are Kiso Yoshinake!''

He bowed slightly. ''I am sorry I had to mislead you. When Okio's ghost requested that I help him achieve satisfaction against his assassins, I could not refuse the maker of my sword. Yet Okio had while still living aligned himself against the Shogun, who I serve as field martial. It was not possible to openly avenge the Imperial Swordsmith, so I came to Isso in disguise. When I found out you bore one of Okio's swords also, I thought that if you would not love the successful Rising Sun General you might love a roguish fellow instead. But you have no love, Tomoe! It has ruined me. My final hour approaches."

Kiso Yoshinake pushed the mirror away and moved the seppuku blade and table to a place directly in front of himself. Tomoe said, "I won't let you die by seppuku! If you refuse your duty to Okio, I will kill you myself!" To prove her meaning she raised her sword above her head, standing near enough to strike. In response, Yoshinake shoved the little table and knife beyond easy reach and said, "Very well. I will die with no honor whatsoever. Behead me." He made his neck accessible.

Tomoe lowered her sword. "I've changed my mind," she said, trying not to reveal her frustration with the unreasonable man. "Is there no appealing to you? You will be remembered as a dishonorable man if you willfully fail your promised task. Think of your duty, not yourself!"

Kiso Yoshinake flashed an angry look at Tomoe and this time it did not melt away. "Do you care of honor? What is the duty of a woman of the samurai? Have you not equally dishonored yourself by evading duty? The story of Tomoe Gozen's recent faithlessness is already spreading through Naipon! The stories of her many exploits are told in the *kodan*-houses: how she came to be a favored hero; how she served Toshima-no-Shigeno, an equally notorious woman. Lady Toshima, say the stories, had been a famous author but set aside her career to be Overseer of her slain father's lands. It was her preference not to buttress her position by a carefully chosen marriage, and thus it was necessary that she be ruthless and clever. Toshima raised a fortress where her father's mansion had been. Her political genius and manipulation restored the valley to its former importance, and she was gentle enough to peasants that they happily repopulated the area. Stability was achieved by reasonable taxation of rice and rape-seed crops, of artisans' products in the new and rebuilt towns which sprouted throughout fertile Shigeno Valley; and riches were gained because of special gifts and tributes from the old Lord Shigeno's repentant enemies and the Mikado's supporters. To protect these holdings, Lady Toshima appointed thirty-six generals, many of them famous samurai, and over them the hero Tomoe Gozen was made chief."

Yoshinake adopted an impersonal narrative and did not look at Tomoe during most of the time he spoke. She was flattered that he had taken to memory so much of her story, although it was disconcerting to think he had become obsessed with her even before the first marriage-meeting was proposed. He continued to recite what he knew about her life:

"So it was that Tomoe Gozen and Lady Toshima lived amidst burgeoning comfort and prosperity. They became models for emulation for other women of Naipon. It became almost fashionable to aspire independently. Naipon's holy emperor approved of these circumstances. His ministers were quick to say that six times in Naipon's history, even the Mikado was a woman, Jingo Kogo among the most famous of these, the greatest warrior of her age. But the Shogun, who had become the truer authority in Naipon, was concerned by the immodesty of these unmarried women. Rumor held that the Shogun's fretfulness was in direct response to happenings in his own court. The wives of his many retainers and his own concubines were becoming arrogant with men. Although it was customary that women of Naipon marry later than do girls in other countries, still their aspirations must always and appropriately be directed toward their capacity to defend households and eventually bear strong sons. If considerations other than these became fashionable among women, it would mean the downfall of the nation. Yet the Shogun and his advisers were patient for a while, hoping that either Tomoe or Toshima would marry of their own choosing so that thereafter their deeds could be viewed within a more traditional perspective.

"Then one day the Shogun attended the training session of young girls. The tiniest of these was his favorite daughter. This child was proficient with knives and spears and pole and was expected one day to become *kogo*, leader of castle women. Unfortunately, on the day in question, this girl betrayed to her noble father an unfashionable desire. She dreamed of ruling a vast estate in the manner of Lady Toshima and leading a mighty army as did Tomoe Gozen. Sadly the Shogun had to order his favorite daughter put to death, by way of example to other girls. The child, remarkably, killed her executioner and escaped, but was overtaken in the forest because she was too small to travel quickly. She was hacked to pieces by the swords of eight samurai and the pieces were left for wolves. That night the Shogun ventured to the shrine of Jizo-sama, protector of children, and lit incense for his beloved child.''

Tomoe found herself backing into a shadowed corner, as though trying to not be there, although she could not help but listen. The story Yoshinake told her was one that only someone close to the doings in Kamakura could have known. She herself had heard nothing of it before now, and would rather have remained ignorant. Yoshinake went on:

''Soon after, Nakahara Kaneto, the father of Tomoe Gozen, discovered himself compelled by methods variously subtle and forceful to decide important matters. Eventually he arranged a meeting between his famous daughter and a man of equal renown, Yoshinake of Kiso Prefecture. Any samurai—man or woman—would lose face without obedience to the father. Tomoe Gozen had always obeyed her father's edicts before, but she had become spoiled by his liberal treatment of her and because of her own glad fame. From that time on, trouble was to be compounded by Tomoe Gozen's selfish revolt. She became in the minds of many no better than *sanzoku*, who are worse than masterless samurai, who think only of themselves and benefit no one in Naipon. And all this while, the Knight of Kiso Prefecture, Kiso Yoshinake, pined in his heart and was lonely.''

Although the man sitting on his knees in the light of a square lamp had told a tale which judged her cruelly, Tomoe was curiously calm. It might be simple to deal anger for anger, but the words of Yoshinake cut more true than any sword, and she could not fight him.

Duty was not always a happy thing, but it was duty nonetheless. She had loved her freedom more. Although she had for a while convinced herself that vassalage to Toshima-no-Shingeno was the cause of her rebellion (for vassalage took precedence even above family), the fact was that Tomoe had arranged to be dismissed from that position so that she could continue her flight from the prospect of an annoying marriage. As men of the samurai give up themselves to a lord and master to be fully respectable, so must women of the samurai eventually give themselves up to a husband and his household. The inequity between man and woman, lord and vassal, samurai and peasant, god and mortal . . . these were not hers to question. Her failure to abide by ancient customs had resulted in unhappiness between the members of her family. It had caused her father to declare her dead. Nor had it aided Toshima-no-Shigeno when Tomoe was disobedient to a father. It had only caused Tomoe to stray from filial piety *and* devotion to her master. Ultimately it put her at odds with the bushido, the samurai code of ethical behavior. This had injured her growth tremendously, for she had not bettered herself each day since fleeing from Heida province. Now, even the vengeance of Okio was endangered as a result of Tomoe's stubbornness.

In the hills around Isso and around the temples of the city, many bells began to devise a simultaneous resonance denoting the Hour of the Ox. Kiso Yoshinake scooted forward so that he could reach the seppuku table, since Tomoe would not execute him after all. He took the knife and set it in his lap, placed the seppuku table behind himself so that he would not fall backward, opened his white kimono to expose his belly, then unsheathed the blade. When he held the blade toward himself, Tomoe exclaimed,

"Wait!"

The bells throughout Isso released a second sonorous note. For a moment Tomoe saw her father standing near her side, looking failed and forlorn. When the tolling died away, the specter of her father was also gone. Tomoe knew that Nakahara Kaneto's soul was gone from its body in Heida; but it was not the time to mourn.

Yoshinake's knife pricked the skin of his stomach.

"I will marry you!" Tomoe shouted. At that moment, a ninja dropped through a loosened ceiling panel. Yoshinake's seppuku blade caught the spy before he had landed on the floor. The ninja's shortsword shot through the air and stuck harmlessly in a beam of the house. At the same moment of the ninja's attack, a big half-caste man of the distant, continental kingdoms of Ho charged into the room at Tomoe. She knew him to be Fudo Kuji, the eighth of the ten men she had to kill. His girth was no advantage. Tomoe evaded his onslaught and left him instantly slain. Yoshinake stood while looking at his own quick handiwork; then he looked at Tomoe's like product as he asked, "We are engaged?"

"You heard me correctly," said Tomoe. "I am weary of fighting traditions old as the reign of the Mikados. A moment ago my father's ghost stood here. The Hour of the Ox took him from the world of the living, but he lingered to see me one last time. I should have been at his side and eased his worries about me. Also I should have agreed to my betrothal long ago, for much nuisance could have been avoided if I had. To make amends to my father, and to secure vengeance for Okio by keeping you alive, I will marry you."

"What of love?" asked Yoshinake, sounding absurd even to himself, but feeling sincere. "Is there none of that?"

"Marriages are more commonly arranged by families and go-betweens than by the parties involved," said Tomoe. "Many 'lovers' have met each other no more than twice before their wedding. What then has marriage to do with love? It has to do with necessity. I will marry you from a sense of duty. I will be an untroublesome wife."

"Your words already trouble me," said the man in white.

Tomoe removed her sheath and sword from her obi and got down on her knees. She set the sword at her side then bowed with her face to the mat. When she looked up she said, "Test my faith in any way you choose. I will be dutiful." This promise was no more and no less than required of her. It eased the guilt she had felt the many weeks since running away from Heida, away from the marriage-meeting with a man who in the end would not be avoided. It by no means eased her bitterness and resentment. How could she confess that she had twice thought Yoshinake appealing: when she saw him slay four rough gamblers in the streets of Isso, and when she fought him herself in the gardens. Nor could she bring herself to say that he was beautiful to her now, for she doubted the soul of him was as handsome as his body.

Hidemi Hirota had stated that only half a dozen swordfighters in Naipon were Tomoe's match. There were others who thought her totally without peer. Until she met this ronin-who-was-a-general, she herself feared that her equal lived nowhere in the world. How could she help but admire a man who was genuinely as proficient a fencer as herself? Yet she could not find it in herself to tell him sentiments of this sort. It seemed that he had extorted the agreement of marriage from her. He did so by threatening the entire mission which had thrown them together in the first place. She refused to have kind words extorted as well, no matter how sad his expression might be. She would forgive him in time, but not immediately.

"Don't bow before me," Yoshinake said peevishly. "You are my equal; and after we are wed you will lead armies for me. My destiny is to be a great one and you will share it. In the mountainous county of my birth, wives do not guard castles because we do not build them. Wives fight beside their husbands and, as our whole lives are devoted to conquest, we live in tent-camps. It is not a bad fate for you. Yet we have begun our romance ill-omened; and as you have asked to be tested it may be that you will be tested more cruelly than you imagine. I hope this isn't so, but lives weave eerie tapestries and it is presently the Autumn season overseen by the Lady of Brocade, who understands the ironies of the cloth."

Tomoe stood from kneeling as she had been directed. Yoshinake went to one side of the room where his sword was mounted on a rack. He took the weapon and put it in his white obi. The seppuku blade he put inside his kimono. He did not tie back his sleeves but only straightened the lines of his kimono and pulled his arms inside, looking more prepared for relaxation than battle.

"As token of my feeling of our equality," said Yoshinake, "and to indicate your marriage to me does not mean subservience, it is my wish that you lead me from the house into the gardens rather than walk behind me. I have eight more men to kill. I am impatient to kill them so that bonze Shindo can say the necessary prayers as we sip the nuptial cups. Remember: No one must know I am the Knight of Kiso. In this fight, I am the ronin Ich'yama."

As commanded, Tomoe led the way from the mansion. Though she walked in front, already she felt the easy power of the Rising Sun General. He walked behind her but no one would have mistook Tomoe for the master, not with Yoshinake's cocksure gait and his arms in his sleeves. Tomoe felt like the road-clearer for some rich lord's procession. She had served lords before and had been glad to do so; so she was not certain what it was she resented. A samurai was meant to serve. Should she complain to serve a husband? At least he valued her warrior assistance. Yet inside, she was seething. She wished it were otherwise, but it was not.

They went out through a lightless corridor. At the doorway she paused and slipped her feet into her sandals. When she stepped outside, the ninth of the ten men alloted Tomoe stood as though awaiting her appearance. The duel consisted of two strokes. The man—Kajutoshi Saitoh—who had been only a face and name imprinted upon her mind, lay dead. There was something other than calm justice in Tomoe's death-dealing. It was as though she struck at things besides mere men.

The mists had cleared from the sky. Yoshinake stepped over the corpse Tomoe had made and emerged into moonlight. He strolled into a clearing of the garden, his arms still inside his sleeves, and he looked up at the Guardian of the Night, the brother of Amaterasu the Shining Goddess. He said, "It is a good night for killing." He said this but did not move.

The strange, hellish magic of the gaki had influenced the members of Mukade Group, eight of whom were drawn from hiding in order to take up positions surrounding Kiso Yoshinake. He was a magnet to them; they could not resist. Yet they did not look frightened, for eight against one seemed to be in their favor. Four of them crouched, dressed in black. They were sly ninja who might try anything. The other four stood tall, the sleeves of their kimonos tied back. They were samurai who undoubtedly considered themselves honorable men, regardless of the ruthless occupation given them by their slain master, Matsu Emura.

From four directions, shurikens shot toward Yoshinake. He seemed hardly to move and did not draw his arms from their resting place inside his sleeves; but the four metal stars missed him. The four ninja slunk in and out of the darkness, shadows against shadows, wolfish. The four samurai drew their swords but preferred not to attack until their adversary showed some readiness.

Bonze Shindo, Prince Shuzo Tahara and the vassal Hidemi Hirota gathered near Tomoe Gozen on the porch of the mansion. They had slain their alotted number. They had learned, during the long night of killing, that it would do no good to try to help the supposed ronin with the remaining eight; they were his and his alone. So they only watched the grim spectacle unfolding.

Yoshinake's arms remained inside his kimono, the sleeves swinging gracefully when he turned slowly. His attention was captured once more by the moon. His breath was white as his clothing on that unusually cold night.

Two samurai wearied of waiting for their opponent to draw steel. They charged as one, but Yoshinake evaded them with easy steps. They withdrew to take new stances. Yoshinake had moved almost carelessly in the direction of two waiting ninja. They drew their shortswords instantly. Yoshinake's right arm appeared from its sleeve holding a seppuku blade. It cut through one ninja's windpipe before he could fight; then the white-clad warrior sank the knife into the other ninja's heart. He left it there, turning to face the rest. They eased backward, then forced themselves not to retreat.

The two remaining ninja tossed darts. Yoshinake turned his left hip toward them and the darts seemed to have struck him through the obi and into the flesh. Actually he had caught the poisonous darts on the lacquered wood of his undrawn sword's scabbard. His left hand came out of its sleeve, removed the darts from where they were stuck, and flung them both at once, taking one ninja in the left eye and the other in the right eye. They shouted and ran forward, half-blind, knowing they were dying of their own poisons, brandishing their swords for the last, most desperate onslaught. Yoshinake did not move; he did not draw his sword. The two ninja fell just short of him, stopped by the poison which had rushed from their pierced eyes directly to their brains. Kiso Yoshinake said,

"I judged it beneath the dignity of Okio's tempered steel to slay mere ninja. It is more than they deserve to die by any sword whatsoever. That is why I made them die without the need of this:" He drew his sword at last, to show his four opponents. They understood him, and bowed to him in unison; and he bowed to them in turn. Then he said, "Will you watch the moon with me a while? It will be setting soon, and is beautiful to see change color as it lowers."

The four men looked to each other in surprise, then back to Yoshinake. They nodded with uncertainty, then walked with their mysterious enemy on a garden path to the edge of the pond, sitting casually in a grassy place.

Hidemi Hirota, seeing this from his vantage-point on the porch, asked irritably,

"What is that about?"

"He honors them," said Prince Tahara.

Hidemi scowled and blew air. "He honors them too much."

The five men watched the moon until it was no longer visible in the gardens. The coldness of the night pressed angrily upon them, as though to remind them of their task. They stood, swords once again in their hands, and moved to an open area. One of the four men of Mukade Group stepped closest to Yoshinake and said, "You must tell us your name."

"Ich'yama," he said. "A ronin."

The speaker for the group frowned. "You mock us? You are some lord!"

"They have a point," said the bonze to Prince Tahara. "That man is no ronin."

The prince looked at Tomoe and said, "You convinced him to come out to fight. You must know who he is."

She was about to say that she did know but could not tell. At that moment, however, a raging samurai leapt upon the porch to make a lunge for Tomoe. He screamed, "For Lord Emura!" He was Kozo Ono, last of the men Tomoe had been commissioned to kill. She dodged his attack, drew her own sword, and said, "Don't annoy us now!" killing him before he could turn to strike again. Then, in reply to the curiosity of prince, bonze and vassal, she said with unexpected bellingerence, "He is Ich'yama, who I will marry!"

They couldn't have looked more surprised had she slapped them.

In the garden clearing, the speaker for the four men said, "I think we are destined to die by your sword, so tell us your real name. Otherwise the moments we shared with Amaterasu's moon-brother mean nothing."

Kiso Yoshinake looked toward the porch, where his co-conspirators in the vengeance-taking stood in hearing distance. Indeed, he had heard them, too, talking about him and wondering. Suddenly, without warning, his sword of Okio scored the darkness and the four men around him fell as stems of rice, having no chance to fight although their swords were already prepared. Yoshinake's white garment had not even caught a spatter of blood, and he stood like a ghostly warrior in the dark, the ultimate symbol of Okio's final revenge.

The leader of the four, clinging to spilled intestines steaming in the cold atmosphere, looked up from where he knelt. He forced these final words: "I was misled! I thought you an honest man," then died.

Dawn broke on the horizon. As the first warming rays of Amaterasu threatened the garden, the preternatural chill vanished, Okio's unseen spirit with it, doubtlessly satisfied that vengeance had been done.

Although none of them had slept for a day, there was too much excitement for anyone to desire rest. "Marry us!" Yoshinake brashly demanded of the bonze; and Shindo looked sideways at Tomoe, his grin almost too large for his face. Even Hidemi Hirota was affected by this, putting aside his dislike for the supposed ronin and begging to give the man a hug. He hugged Tomoe as well. Prince Tahara had momentarily vanished. He reappeared from within the mansion, carrying a beautiful pair of saké cups from which wedding vows might be sipped. These cups he had placed upon a lacquered tray; and between the cups was a small bottle of rice wine, enough for two.

The five of them paraded about the gardens, searching for a place at once beautiful enough for a wedding and unlittered by the slain. Tomoe and Yoshinake decided on a spot atop a small knoll, and sat there upon their knees, facing one another. Of the two, the man was most beautiful, dressed as he was in long white kimono with the yellow bird embroidered on the back. The woman was more dour in dark hakama and the back of her short kimono cut by a ninja's weapon during the late encounters.

Prince Tahara set the tray between the couple. He poured saké into each cup, then moved unobtrusively away to sit with Hidemi Hirota. Hidemi had found a comfortable spot near the base of the knoll to one side. He sat there hitting on his knees excitedly, as though he were a child. Bonze Shindo had put his sword aside and regained his staff, rattling its *shaku* top to frighten away any spirits which might wish the couple ill. Then he placed the staff at his side on the ground. He had already tied a pill-box hat upon his head; and from a travel pouch he'd been keeping in the house, he took a patchwork stole and draped it around his shoulders. He looked holy and officious.

In front of him, a bit higher than he was, the bride and groom waited patiently. To them he said, "A buddhist ceremony is complex and cannot be impromptu; but we of the yamahoshi do not malign the Shinto customs which are raw and more direct. Therefore I have in mind a wedding chant which is popular in a northern province, but which I admit is most often sung for peasants."

"We are not too proud," said Yoshinake.

"I am personally more fond of Shinto," said Tomoe.

"Nothing fancy is needed," Yoshinake added. "Marry us now."

"Very well," said Shindo. He swelled himself up into a

little mountain and recited the words in an old, poetic language—slowly, at the top of his lungs, and with guttural intonation:

"Infinitely greater than
the billion myriads of deities!
Is the sipping of your vows!"

He stopped, bowed to them once, and continued shouting:

"These nuptial cups
Incite the solemn grandeur
of unbounded love!
They keep you enthusiastic
in human service! They
keep you happy, sober and divine!"

He bowed a second time. A pair of butterflies, one light and one dark, performed an aerial dance between the pair upon the knoll. The monk finished his speech more loudly than before, if that were possible, with a flourish of his sleeve and arm:

"Drink now
the sincerity of your eyes
reflected in the wine!"

The third time he bowed, he did not look up until the couple before him performed their part. Tomoe and Yoshinake took up their cups and held them steadily before their faces, so that each could see the other's eyes reflected in the sake. Tomoe's heart skipped a beat when a *kaji* leaf drifted into her cup. There were no kaji trees nearby, from which it might have fallen. It was the same plant Tsuki Izutsu, as Naruka, had used to tell fortunes.

Her heart skipped again when she saw Yoshinake's eyes reflected in the cup, red as the stars in Naruka's fortune-telling saucer. But Tomoe did not shake about these omens.

She held the cup without allowing the slightest ripple, and her eyes were steady as she drank.

She and Yoshinake sipped three times; three times more; and a final three times. Then the saké cups were empty but for a kaji leaf in one.

They set the cups down on the tray between their knees, then turned to face the small audience. Yoshinake said,

"We are happy!" and Tomoe,

"Thank you very much."

Yoshinake bowed. The bonze rose from his own bowing posture at that time, and saw how Tomoe Gozen was lowering her head, but not so low as the warrior-in-white.

"The three clappings!" said Hidemi Hirota excitedly, tears of gladness in his eyes. He, the prince, and the bonze raised their hands outward as Hidemi shouted, "Yo!" and they clapped in three sets of three, plus a single additional clap for exclamation; then all three men said with one voice: "Congratulations!"

The mood of these five was incongruously happy and playful in the corpse-strewn gardens. Even Tomoe did not seem upset now that it was done. The white and brown butterfly-couple followed the newlyweds. The morning sun was warm and the air was pleasant. Tomoe went to each of her three friends in turn, thanking them for their kind attendance; and she thanked the bonze in particular for his tremendous recitation. She told each one, "I have made a good decision," without a single qualification or noticeable qualm. Yoshinake puffed up with his own good feeling. But all this happy feeling was short-lived, for a stranger stood in the entrance of the garden.

The man was a magistrate. He wore a flat, metal hat and carried a pronged *jitte*, badge of his authority. Tomoe remembered having met him briefly when first arriving in Isso.

The entry of the magistrate brought instantaneous silence to the cheerful group. They watched his disapproving vision pass over the gardens, spying a corpse here and another there and two more somewhere else. His gaze stopped finally on the body of Lord Matsu Emura whom Tomoe had killed.

Emura lay among small evergreens off the end of the mansion's porch. Doubtlessly Emura had lived a respectable life for whatever most people saw; and even a bad lord could not be slain with impunity unless by strict procedure and honest reason. Those men without rank and especially those in ninja garb incited small concern; but the death of Emura meant the magistrate could by no means withdraw his attention from the scene.

Hidemi Hirota was the least flustered. He scurried up to the magistrate, smiling ingratiatingly, and said, "As you can see, sir, the five of us have completed an important mission, in accordance with the laws of *kataki* or vengeance-taking. You will see it was legally done."

The magistrate replied harshly, "You are someone's vassal? By whose authority is this vengeance done?"

Hidemi was uncertain how to answer. He could not say it was by his own lord's authority; and he did not know if a ghost's commission would qualify. Prince Tahara approached and intervened. He bowed from the waist and introduced himself with precise formality. Because of his lineage and rank, there could be no further question about there being someone of high enough station overseeing the revenge.

Prince Shuzo Tahara explained, "These forty-seven men laying dead in the house and in the gardens, besides three others who you may already have learned were killed yesterday, were the slayers of the Imperial Swordsmith Okio and of his entire family. It was necessary to fight them because of their crime. I trust you will think well of us for acting appropriately."

"Just so," said the magistrate. Indeed, if everything was as explained, the laws of *kataki* not only permitted, but required the deed performed. Yet the magistrate was not entirely convinced. He asked, "Where are the bodies of the family you say were murdered?"

Bonze Shindo stepped forward, smiling as had Hidemi, mostly to be disarming. "I took them secretly to a nearby temple yesterday. Their unfortunate deaths will be reported to you later today, as per my instructions."

"You are a mountain priest," said the magistrate, seeming vaguely annoyed that strangers from outside his district appeared to be the only ones present. "Who else was involved in the vengeance-taking?"

"A famous warrior!" said Hidemi Hirota, indicating Tomoe. "She is Tomoe Gozen of Heida. This other fellow with his back to us is a ronin named Ich'yama, who is recently married to Tomoe."

"I will make a full report," said the magistrate. "I am sure there will be no problem."

That would have been the end to it, except for Yoshinake, who had still not turned around. With his back turned rudely to the others, he growled a query to the magistrate:

"Who told you to come here."

The others looked at him harshly, for Yoshinake's tone could cause unnecessary trouble. But he did not face them and did not see their disapproval, not that he was likely to be concerned if he had noticed. The magistrate's reply was equally abrupt:

"My informer's identify is not your business!" He pointed his pronged jitte at the back of the rude man and said, "You dress nicely for a masterless samurai! Let me see your face so that I can judge if you are a criminal!"

Yoshinake did not turn around.

"Be polite, Ich'yama," said Hidemi. The magistrate added harshly,

"Face me and bow, or I will arrest you immediately!

Yoshinake turned slowly. As he did, the magistrate backed away, lowered his jitte, and looked surprised. He fell to his knees at once and said, "I was informed correctly!" He lowered his head and begged, "Forgive my bothersome interrogations, Lord Kiso."

"Kiso!" said the bonze, equally surprised; but certainly it made sense to him. Hidemi looked puzzled, but Prince Tahara clarified the so-called ronin's identity for the vassal: "He is Yoshinake."

In that instant, Yoshinake's sword licked out like a flame. The marvelous sword of Okio cleaved through the magistrate's metal hat and divided his face to the chin. Hidemi

Hirota took a step forward, shocked by Yoshinake's grim and unexpected deed. A moment later, Hidemi's head flew off and Yoshinake turned upon Prince Tahara.

Tahara drew his sword and exclaimed, "Why this? We are friends!"

"Husband!" cried Tomoe, appalled.

"Don't meddle!" he commanded; and she dared not disobey a husband.

Shuzo Tahara managed to deflect Yoshinake's attempt to decapitate, but was not quick enough to keep himself from being gutted by the second slash of Yoshinake's weapon. Finally, Yoshinake looked toward the bonze.

Bonze Shindo had a similar kind of training and knew what to expect from Yoshinake's sword. The bonze wove a defense, striking with the metal shaku at the head of his staff. He strove to capture the tip of the deadly sword inside one of the shaku's rings. But Shindo was only a novice priest while Yoshinake was a warrior tested in a hundred battles. After a few moments of keeping the attacker at bay, the ornate, rattling shaku was shorn off its pole. The bonze hopped back, helpless, and cried, "Permission! Permission!" He fell upon his knees in a begging posture.

"Permission for what?" Yoshinake growled.

"I will tell you in a minute!" said the monk, shaking but belligerent. He remained on hands and knees and did not look up. He tried to sound rude, but his life of good-naturedness gave him no skill at it. "Explain yourself to me," he said, "if there is any respect left in you for the sect that made you so skillful!"

The warrior-in-white held back. He said, "You think you recognize my style, but it is not true that I was a student of the yamahoshi. As a matter of fact I studied with the yamabushi, your rival sect; but that is not why I attack you. Even as a mountain-born youth, I knew that I must seek more notice than the solitary lives of monastic warriors would permit, be they yamahoshi or yamabushi. So I left my prefecture and fought to my present station. I became the Rising Sun General at the center of Naipon's intrigues. A gentler warrior could not have come so far. It is unfortunate to kill you, but cannot be helped. A year from now I will be in position to snatch more power than other samurai dare imagine. That is because I am close to the Shogun, who trusts no one before me. I have treason in mind, I will tell you; and there must be no indication of it until that time. There can be no witness to my role in the revenge performed for Okio, for it is something the Shogun would not approve, and to learn of it would shake his faith in me. I have liked you, bonze. But you must die."

Shindo looked up from his posture, then sat back on his knees and folded his arms. "I am not relieved that you say you are fond of me. It seems to be no privilege. Nor am I enthused about your high-blown intentions. Talk is the measure of insincerity! Action is what matters! If you want to kill an insignificant monk, or commit treason against the high Shogun, do not worry about consequences. Only . . . be certain the action itself is meritorious."

"I do not seek merit, Shindo, and will not be swayed by your subtle insult. Humanity is essentially benign; there is no sin, no goodness. Age, illness, mishap, death . . . we are destined to be failures in the end. Human beings and humane feelings are a fleeting impermanence. Nothing we do is important. Our swords are more eternal than ourselves. Doom is all that lasts." Saying this, Yoshinake raised his sword to strike.

"Husband!" said Tomoe, who could keep obediently silent no longer. "What good is killing Shindo? He is an honorable man and if he promises to say nothing, there is no problem. There is anyway another witness: the woman who informed the magistrate."

He looked at her. "Woman? So. It must have been that young warrior who challenged you in the street, then slipped away on seeing me. I will consider her your problem. She has forced you to fulfill her desire. Kill her when next she asks to duel!"

Tomoe stared at him in disbelief, trying to think of some way to save Shindo. "You are too wise for this," she said. "You have slain a lord's heir, and the favorite vassal of another lord. They will want to know who did this! They will not rest without an answer!"

"They cannot find out," said Yoshinake. "I will break those three swords of Okio which were carried by Shindo and the two I've already killed. Thereby the blame will fall on Uchida Ieoshi, who everyone knows was jealous of the swordsmith. Uchida is smart enough to find some way out of the trouble, perhaps blaming his uncouth hirelings; but he is not smart enough to guess who sent the blame his way."

"Can my husband be so cruel?" asked Tomoe, surprised at herself for pleading like wives are known to do, surprised at her husband for considering the ruin of three of Okio's last five swords. Her eyes were sober and her thoughts unclear.

"Do not look at me as though I were a monster!" Yoshinake snapped. "I will pursue my end with strict sincerity, whatever you may feel. Nothing I do is villainy. Humanity itself is the fiend."

Tomoe lowered her eyes and said softly, "Would that your soul could be as graceful as your body."

Bonze Shindo interrupted. "I see that you cannot be swayed by my words or Tomoe's. If you will grant me the permission, then: since you are certain my death is necessary, I would prefer to die by the hand of someone I respect, not by the hand of a fellow who can kill friends unhesitantly."

"You mean Tomoe," said Kiso Yoshinake. "It is a fair request, since you so abhor my philosophy. Your wish is granted!" Yoshinake sheathed his sword and said to his wife, "Tomoe! Kill him."

Tomoe wavered. Shindo said to her, "Please grant this favor." He bowed with forehead to ground.

"As you desire," said Tomoe, but could not disguise her sorrow. She looked from bonze to Yoshinake and to Shindo once again. She drew her sword and raised it.

"One more thing," said Shindo calmly, groping for the shaku which Yoshinake had cut from the head of the staff. "If it is no burden, it would be kind of you to return this to my fight-instructor in the yamahoshi retreat. Tell him for me that I apologize for not returning as I promised."

"I will," said Tomoe, her eyes filled with tears. The bonze set the shaku down near Tomoe's feet. Then he bent his head to make his neck accessible. Tomoe took a half-step backward and said, "Human lives are too long," meaning she would rather not have lived to see this day. Then she brought her sword down swiftly. Shindo's torso slumped forward. His head with its pill-box hat was attached by the thinnest section of skin. Kiso Yoshinake's severity softened and he said to his wife, "You are stronger than I guessed! Together, we will someday rule Naipon."

Tomoe sheathed her sword and bent to take up Shindo's shaku and placed it in her obi. "I believe you," she said to her husband. She believed him, but was not certain that she cared.

PART TWO

Into the Hollow Land

The pilgrim traveled with a largish wooden box strapped to her shoulders. She wore a flat-topped hat which hid her face. Her kimono's hem was folded upward and tucked into her obi, baring her legs, so that she could take long strides. Her sandals were woven of straw. Through her obi was a shortsword.

She entered the valley by the lesser used roads and came to a small cemetery surrounded by forest. None of the towns were nearby, so it was silent but for a few evening birds. Against the graying sky the highest towers of the valley's fortified castle were silhouetted above the trees. The pilgrim avoided looking at the castle.

At the edge of the cemetery was a house for a groundskeeper to live in. It was plain but not homely, for it was surrounded by pleasantly arranged shrubbery and thickets which made the cemetery, house and forest blend into a harmonious whole. The pilgrim put her burden down at the bottom of the steps which led to the house. She opened the top of the box, revealing the head of some stone carving. With it was a parcel which she removed and tucked under her arm. She also removed a longsword which was kept in there. Then she resealed the box and went up the mossy staircase and called out to the groundskeeper within.

A woman came to the door. It was impossible to guess her age—thirty-five or sixty. She was healthy but only the least attractive. She was dressed in white, like a Shinto priestess; but the scarf which covered her head and neck was saffron, suggesting marginal acceptance of Buddhist doctrine. In this day and age it was rare to find any pure Shintoists. The cemetery itself was a mixture of Shinto graves and Buddhist ones. Doubtlessly the two religions shared the expense of keeping a priestess here; so even if this woman were wholly Shinto in her heart, she must make some obeisance to the powerful Buddhist institutions.

A big white dog stood beside the priestess in the doorway, its tail between its legs and its ears pressed back. The pilgrim bowed from the waist and introduced herself, "I am Tomoe Gozen of Heida. I believe a messenger told you I would come."

The priestess looked surprised. The dog's ears perked up, too. "I did not expect to see the famous warrior and wife of a bakufu general in tawdry pilgrim's clothes."

Tomoe said, "You will appreciate that it is difficult for someone of my station to go anywhere without a large retinue. I thought it better to travel incognito during my vacation, or life would be as troublesome a coordinating venture as usual; and also my disguise has saved you from the imposition of thirty or forty soldiers and servants, the minimum I could otherwise have brought along."

"You are right," said the priestess. "There would be no room for them here. However, there is a growing castle-town around the recently completed Shigeno Castle, where you and a retinue could have been accommodated without problem."

"As my messenger implied," said Tomoe, "I do not want the Lady of Shigeno Castle to know of my presence. It is a bad mark on my past that I failed to be a good retainer to her, but ran off and became married instead. I don't have the strength to see her yet. I could only lose face."

"You are harsh with yourself," said the priestess, "but it will be as you desire. Please come into my house and make it your own. My name is Shan On, gardener of this place."

Tomoe entered, doffing hat and sandals, allowing the dog to sniff her hands and knees. The priestess said,

"My companion's name is Taro. He seems to like you already, which is rare."

Tomoe petted the dog vigorously and its tail went like a switch. "I like him, too," she said. "He looks familiar to me, although I cannot remember ever having seen a white dog before."

"Perhaps you knew him in a previous life," said Shan On. "He is fond of the horses of samurai which are sometimes ridden along these back roads. I think he was himself a horse before he was a dog."

The house was clean and well arranged, although very small. Tomoe looked about, quickly making herself feel comfortable. She said to the priestess, "I have brought a change of clothing." She held up her bundle. "I would not want to visit the graves of my friends dressed as I am now."

Shan On smiled. "You would boast to them a little about your good fortune, heh?" Tomoe flushed and returned the smile, admitting, "I guess you are right." She unwrapped her bundle, which contained a tightly folded pair of silk hakama and other nice garments, as well as some paper spirit-gifts and a pretty bottle of good saké. The priestess brought a shallow, wooden pail of water so that Tomoe could clean and groom herself, for she was dusty from the road. Then she dressed as befits a samurai, the priestess helping to comb out Tomoe's long hair, binding it back with a tie. When Tomoe looked the part of a general's wife, the priestess said, "I will prepare a meal for us while you visit with your friends." Tomoe thanked her and went out into the cemetery. At first she went with long, proud steps; but as she drew closer to a specific monument, her feet began to drag, her head lowered, and she looked sad or ashamed.

The largest monument in the cemetery was one which she had personally helped to raise several years earlier. It was built upon the place where a psychotic samurai named Ushii Yakushiji had been swallowed up by the earth. The other graves surrounding the monument were those of eight thousand samurai killed in the War of Shigeno Valley, of which only Tomoe and one other survived.

Buried directly beneath the monument was Ushii's victim and childhood friend Madoka Kawayama. It was considered that they were buried together, even though Ushii's body went far deeper into the ground and had never been recovered.

In front of the monument there were two narrow posts

standing upright, the names of the luckless men printed thereon. Tomoe got down on her knees between these two posts, faced the monument, set her longsword at her side, and bowed. When she raised her head, she said,

"Ushii, Madoka, forgive my not coming to see you for so long. It has been more than a year since I left Shigeno Valley and circumstances have not allowed me to return until just now." She told them of her recent adventures, including the encounter with Old Uncle Tengu, the death of her father, the plight of the Strolling Nun who was possessed by evil Naruka, the vengeance taken for the swordsmith Okio, and her marriage to Kiso Yoshinake. She unburdened herself as she rarely dared with living folk. "That was almost a year ago," said Tomoe, "and although it began ill-omened, the marriage has been good. Yoshinake and I have fought seven large battles for the Shogun, repressing rival lords, and increasing the stability of the bakufu, Kamakura's office of the military. It has been one of the happier times of my life. I have rarely been more useful to our country and to a lord. My other time of happiness was when Lord Shojiro Shigeno lived, when the two of you lived, and together with Goro Maki we four protected Lord Shigeno's estates. When tragedies separated us, I never thought to feel that closeness and importance again." Her eyes were filled with tears at these remembrances, but she stoutly wiped them away and looked severe, adding in the quietest possible voice, "I will admit to you, my friends, that all this excellent service for the Shogun leads eventually to treason. My husband has sworn many of the conquered lords to his service. He hopes they will side with him when he turns against the Shogun. Even if the other lords consider their first duty to the bakufu, or try to use the inevitable confusion to grab power for themselves, Yoshinake will be secure. We have allies in the mountain provinces, especially among the yamabushi who have been troublesome to the Shogun but are secretly Yoshinake's friends. He seeks a treaty between the yamabushi and their rivals, the yamahoshi. If these two sects of martial priests can be united in service to the Knight of Kiso, nothing can keep us from occupying Imperial Kyoto and saving the Mikado from forced seclusion. It is only through Amaterasu's god-child that the Shogun legitimizes his regency; but the Mikado resents being a figurehead and will reward whoever frees him from virtual imprisonment.

"I hope the two of you appreciate this plan and do not think ill of the conspiracy. As for my own feelings about it, I obey my husband and am glad of every victory we have. But you would be surprised, Ushii, Madoka . . . you would be surprised how little he masters me. See this crest?" She pointed to the seal printed on each shoulder of her garment. The design was of three comma-shapes arranged in a circle. "This is not Yoshinake's family seal. It is my personal seal, for he says I am his equal and not his subject. 'Tomoe' means 'comma,' so it is an appropriate symbol for me. He lets me be independent, knowing I am devoted to his cause.

"Soon that cause will blossom and bear fruit; for the agreement between the two sects of warrior monks is imminent, and every other preparation is ready for the invasion of the Imperial City. Then, with the Mikado behind us, an attack will be launched against Kamakura itself. My husband will become Shogun, and I, like Madam Hojo before me, will share the power equally."

As though just remembering, Tomoe reached suddenly for the spirit-presents she had made with her own hands. These representations of toys and practical objects she placed within a char-stained receptacle built into the monument. With a piece of flint and iron kept there, she lit the spirit-presents. The paper had been treated to smell of incense as it burned. While the small fire was burning, Tomoe produced seven little pieces of spirit-money which she had obtained before leaving on her pilgrimage. They were golden colored and oval shaped, with square holes through the center. Of them she said, "In this life we samurai are supposed to eschew wealth; but it seems to me it is often useful, and I thought you might need these in heaven." She dropped the paper coins into the receptacle where they flared. "If I misjudge your interests," she said, "please do not take offense, but give the money to someone else for me, perhaps the family of the swordsmith Okio who died in poverty."

Darkness had fallen on the graveyard, but Tomoe was unperturbed by the eeriness of the nighted place. She unstoppered the bottle of saké and poured some into each of two shallow depressions on one level of the monument. She poured a bit more directly on the poles bearing her two friends' names. Then she drank some of it herself, right from the bottle. "It's good," she said and smacked her lips, looking more carefree than before. Then she sighed heavily and said,

"I wish I had news about our best friend Goro Maki, but there has been no word of him since shortly after tragedies broke us up. I told you last year that he became a monk, retiring from the world. I hope that he is healthy, but it is hard to know what a monk does. They never seek notice."

An owl made a noise from some hiding place, but Tomoe ignored it. She spoke to her frineds about this and that, and her mood went from laughter to unhappiness to severity. After a while she got up and went to the box she had carried through two provinces on her back. She dragged it toward the monument, saying, "This is the best I have yet to offer you, Ushii, Madoka!" She took the lid off and broke away the front of the box, revealing a fat stone god sitting inside. It had a kind expression. Three names were carved on its big belly: Shindo, Shuzo and Hidemi. Of the stone god, Tomoe said, "I had this rustic deity carved to look like one I saw in Isso. I have prayed to that other one to keep my father alive an extra day, so that I might see him once more. Although the little god was unable to grant that particular request, I have sometimes gotten the feeling that my good fortune afterward was due to him. That is why I had one made for you, so that the two of you may have good luck, too, and be reunited in heaven and in the next life.

"You may want to know whose names are carved into this belly. Well, they were not such close friends as you, but they were the only ones at my wedding and I liked them. It was the sad part of my wedding day that they had to die for Yoshinake's sake and for the sake of the Great Treason he has planned. I owe them gratitude and felt that my introducing them to you would help me atone for their deaths. I am sure you will all like each other very much, and maybe end up serving the same lord in a future life, becoming happy as a result. It is the most I can hope for everyone concerned. Perhaps the children of Yoshinake and myself will be great rulers after us, and you will serve them as privileged retainers; and they will be privileged, too, if that happens."

She hefted the statue and climbed with it to the top of the monument, setting it on the flat top and making the burial place of Ushii and Madoka that much taller. Then the smell of food reminded her that the priestess had promised a meal, which might already be getting cold. So she took up her sword from where she had set it and started toward the house; but something stopped her. Her sword was as light as air, and she held it up to look at it in the darkness. "This is strange!" she said, and drew the sword out a little bit, wondering why it was weightless. The steel was phosphorescent. She sheathed it quickly, hiding the unnatural light of the blade. As she slowly turned around, she saw Ushii Yakushiji sitting where she had placed the stone god. His face was maniacal; his hair untidy; his clothing in shreds. He laughed horridly and said to Tomoe,

"Why do you pray to me in heaven when I reside in Hell!" He laughed wickedly again and stepped down from the monument. Tomoe tried to see his feet, but they were hidden under long, tattered hakama. "I am an important man in Hell!" Ushii boasted. "I am sometimes privileged to know what goes on atop the earth. In your prayer you say it should make me happy to bow down to your children in some future life. You think your children will inherit the rule of Naipon. *Baké!*" He circled her menacingly, hand on his sword's hilt. "You and the traitor Yoshinake will never rule Naipon! Forget your dream! You will be killed and come to me in Hell! There, each of your old friends will be waiting for you. They will rape you many times and cut you into pieces to feed you to the hell-flies; but you will be put back together by cruel Emma, King of the Land of Gloom, so that we can torment you again!"

Tomoe said, "Poor Ushii! Your madness followed you even into death! Your threats would frighten me, except that I

WAS

do not believe any of my friends aside from yourself reside in Hell. None of them were mad."

Ushii looked offended, but did not deny that he had lied. His face contorted into an ugly mask of hatred and he said, "Perhaps your friends are not in Hell with me, but neither am I alone! The swordsmith Okio is still here! He does not like you one bit!"

Tomoe looked upset. She said, "I avenged him and his family. They should bear no grudge for me. Okio should be in Hell no longer, for he was avenged a year ago and can feel at peace."

"Baké!" shouted Ushii. "Baké-baké! Stupid Tomoe! Monster Tomoe!"

"Stop that!" she said, and drew the weightless blade, its light bathing the monument and Ushii with silver. Ushii let go of his own sword's hilt and stepped backward, looking afraid. He said, "I will not fight you. Ghosts cannot kill living people. But you cannot kill me either, because I am already dead. Still, if you think I am wrong to call you stupid, look to the West, Tomoe, and you will see. Look to the West!" She obeyed him, and saw in the west of the cemetery that an entire family of ghosts drifted over the gravemarkers and monuments: old woman, old man, young woman, children, and a man wearing the bent cap of a swordsmith. Tomoe was horrified. "Okio!" she exclaimed.

"And his family," said Ushii. "You and Kiso Yoshinake killed his other avengers. Now Okio requires vengeance for them! The men whose names you chiseled on that rustic god's belly might forgive you; they are stupid, too. If they had lived in Hell a while, they would be more bitter. They would be less forgiving. Okio's rage is increased by the rage of his parents, his wife, his children. They have not been able to reach you yet, because it is true a Shinto deity protects you; but it is only a matter of time before the protection wears away. This is what I was sent to tell you: only two of Okio's swords are left unbroken on the face of the earth. You bear one; your husband bears the other. Through these your ruin will be achieved. Okio will find satisfaction; and I will find you here in Hell."

The woman samurai looked from the family of ghosts and then at the monstrous Ushii, wondering why he had to speak for them, why he should be any stronger than a whole family. She noticed that the ghosts of Okio's small clan never quite touched the ground, no matter how low their specters dipped and glided. Understanding this difference between them and Ushii Yakushiji, it finally made sense to Tomoe that the psychotic man had been afraid of her drawn sword despite pretending it could not hurt him.

"I see your toes!" exclaimed Tomoe. "Ghosts have no feet and cannot walk on the ground. That means you did not die when Hell swallowed you whole. How unfortunate that a living man should live the life of a demon or a spirit! I feel pity for my friend. I will release you from your misery at once!"

Laughing Ushii backed away from Tomoe's glowing sword. He said, "King Emma has granted me immortal life for as long as I reside in his country under the earth. You can cut me into pieces but I cannot die." Hearing this, Tomoe held back, afraid her sword would only make her one-time friend's existence more miserable. Ushii Yakushiji pulled his own sword from its scabbard and held it up without any grace at all. He said, "Stupid Tomoe does not want to cut me now!" He ran forward in an attempt to slice her, but a dog came growling through the night. Ushii dashed away from Taro, for a Shinto dog is enemy to any being out of Buddhist Hell. Taro worried at Ushii until the hellish man climbed back atop the stone monument. The white dog kept its paws on the gravestone, barking fiercely. When Tomoe looked up, there was nothing on top of the monument except the statue she had placed there.

Shan On came hurrying down the stairs from her house, shouting a word of exorcism: "Norito! Norito!" She threw blessed beans at the ghostly family drifting toward Tomoe. They withdrew in terror of the priestess. When the many ghosts as well as Ushii Yakushiji were gone, Tomoe's sword ceased to glow and regained its weight and balance. As the samurai sheathed her sword, she was shaking with fury and confusion. The priestess said,

"We must stay inside tonight. It is not even the Hour of the Ox and already ghosts are flying. Forgive my taking so long to hear your trouble." The priestess and the samurai bowed to one another. The white dog followed them toward the house.

Tomoe Gozen trod the road in peasant cottons. She had traveled several days afoot and now approached Yuwe, a city not far from Kyoto. She carried a cloth-wrapped parcel across her shoulders, about the length of a sword, but fatter. One hand kept the parcel from falling from its resting place; the opposite arm swung free. A pilgrim's hat hung at the parcel's further end.

The road was busy with samurai, as Yuwe was occupied by Yoshinake's eastern allies (Tomoe's relations, to be exact). A bare month before, Yoshinake together with Tomoe had quelled a certain lord's intended rebellion, giving him only enough time to commit seppuku before capture. Yoshinake had set up a headquarters in the captured castle, becoming, in the Shogun's name, a threat of chastisement should loyalists of the Imperial forces in nearby Kyoto attempt to undermine the authority in Kamakura. The threat had been enough, and no other lords had caused trouble for the past month. It was this very calm which decided Tomoe to go on a pilgrimage, but her itinerary had been cut short by the spectral visitations in Shigeno Valley Cemetery.

Although Tomoe did not hide her face under the brim of a hat, she did wear a blue bandana which held her hair out of sight and covered her chin where the knot was tied. None of the samurai passing her realized who they ignored.

One samurai approached on horseback, riding slowly. He was young and very pretty, yet clearly held some rank. Tomoe stepped off the road and bowed until he had gone by. He scarcely noticed her, expecting nothing less than quick courtesy from *heiman*. When he was past her, Tomoe bent to pick up a small stick and tossed it like a dart. It struck the young man in the middle of his back, where a small clan seal was printed. He stopped the horse immediately, then sat frozen as though shocked to immobility, considering the meaning of such an insult. He lifted one leg from its stirrup so that he could turn halfway in his saddle; but realization shone in his eyes and he said, even before he saw her,

"Tomoe?"

She had known her brother would remember his own childhood game-of-points. As a tike he had revelled in his ability to come up behind his older sister unawares, and score a point with a pebble or a twig flung at the family seal. If he missed, or if she detected him, he gave her the point. If he struck the target precisely, he would run off laughing, only to return whenever she was off guard. This was the first time she had ever returned the sport.

His name was Imai Kanchira, and since the death of their father the young man had become fixated on his brother-in-law, virtually worshiping Kiso Yoshinake. He had been made vassal to Lord Kiso, an impressive position for one so young, but not unprecedented since Imai was a family heir. An important young lord should not be seen too readily in the company of a peasant; so Tomoe scudded humbly to the side of the horse, bowing once and saying loudly, "Excuse my unnecessary presence on this highway, good samurai!" As she bowed, she slyly tucked a letter in the horse's stirrup, under Imai's foot. She looked up and said in a hoarse whisper, "My pilgrimage ends earlier than I anticipated. Expect me at the castle after nightfall. In the meanwhile, the letter is for Lord Kiso; I would entrust it to none but my own brother. Ask me nothing now. Kick me away from your horse and go on."

Imai Kanchira hesitated a moment only, then raised his foot—stirrup and letter with it—to feign a kick at Tomoe. She fell back holding the side of her face. When he rode on, she continued the other way, politely inconspicuous to others on the road.

In this manner she arrived without detection at a convent in the hills above Yuwe. The building was behind short walls and adjunct to a Buddhist temple called Yuwe-ji, which she passed without respects. She struck a wooden bell hanging at the gate to the convent. After a while she was noticed and a young novice dressed in black and yellow came to see her. The girl's head was covered, but undoubtedly shaven. Although the girl acted gracious, Tomoe sensed nothing of true regard for a peasant standing outside; for the Buddhists catered to wealthier people, save only one or two sects, and left the heiman to the Shinto ceremonialists. A Shintoist herself—though of a class rapidly converting to Buddhism—Tomoe was annoyed by the girl's patronizing friendliness rather than honest hostility. Therefore Tomoe untied her bandana, letting long hair flow back. She placed her free hand on the shortsword in her obi and fixed an authoritative eye upon the youngster.

"I recognize you!" the girl said, looking surprised. "In the recent battles, you were the woman-general outside these very gates! Why are you dressed like this? Are you *ninja*?"

"I am no spy. I have been on a pilgrimage and went about it humbly. The priestess of Shigeno Valley Cemetery bid me return to Yuwe and seek the blind nun of this convent."

The girl inside the gate looked more startled than before. She said, "She sees no one. It is the strictest rule."

"How will you stop me?"

"I would not try. But the Mothers are fighters; and the priests would come along the back trail from the temple if their help were needed."

"A child threatens a samurai?" Tomoe was almost amused. The girl, however, was terrified, but brave enought to adhere stoutly to the policies of the nun-mothers. Tomoe said,

"The blind woman was a hero when the mainland invaded Naipon sixty years ago. She was a warrior like myself." Tomoe tried to sound as polite as possible, considering what she intended to say. "You cannot deny one samurai the right to see another. The military makes the laws, not the Buddhists."

The young novice looked back over her shoulder, desiring aid; but if anyone watched and listened from the austere-looking nunnery, none came out. The girl argued, "This is her home since losing her vision. It upsets her too much to remember her life before retirement. It would be cruel to annoy her with reminders."

"Either you know too little," Tomoe complained, "or your Mothers lie to you, for that woman held inside did not retire due to blindness. She fought in three more important battles before she was forced to retire because of politics, not invalidism. A blind warrior is useful in darkness and in other ways, but powerful adversaries did not want her in their ranks. The resultant rule of seclusion was made too long ago for it to matter anymore. Others rule Naipon today; the convent will not be punished if she is allowed to speak. If you cannot let me enter on your own authority, when run and tell your Mothers that a nervous samurai in peasant clothing has threatened to kill everyone in her way to save Okumi from her prison!"

The novice's eyes bulged frightfully before she turned and ran away. Tomoe followed at leisure, dawdling to look at a stark arrangement of rocks and raked gravel around them. Before she reached the door of the convent, three nun-mothers came out. They carried staffs in case of trouble, but in fact there was none. They had listened to Tomoe and the girl arguing at the gate, and made a quick decision. They led Tomoe through the convent's interior, along bleak corridors, to the smallest of rooms in which there was no light. Incense was heavy in the atmosphere. Sutras were quietly sung by someone with a brittle voice. One of the three nuns lit a small, square lantern inside the room. It was not much light. The three nuns backed away, turned, and left without comment. Tomoe listened to be sure they did not linger close enough to hear any conversation. When she was certain they were gone, she lowered herself to her knees in the tiny, dark room and whispered,

"Okumi?"

The sutras were left off. An old, heavily built woman was sitting on her knees before a reliquary; Tomoe had not seen her at first. The old one seemed to detach from the shadows as she pivotted to face her visitor. Her eyes were shut so tightly, and for so long, that they seemed only two more wrinkles in an elderly face.

The blind nun was large of girth, almost fat, like a lucky, pleasant grandmother-goddess.

"I am Tomoe Gozen, wife of Kiso Yoshinake, Lord of Kiso, field marshal for the Kamakura military regime."

That old face leaned nearer, shaking slightly with palsy. Dim candlelight played over her features in an odd way, making her look young a moment, then older than old. Okumi asked, "Should I know you? I do not."

"You have lived in seclusion a long time," said Tomoe. "You would not know me in such a case, nor the Rising Sun General. But we are famous, yes; and you are famous, too, although no one has known where you retired."

"Okumi is famous?" The lips parted in a toothless smile.

"You are," said Tomoe. "You were the fiercest on the shores of an alien invasion; you helped repulse the foe most admirably, with a weapon charged by magic. That is what they say in the *kodan* houses; the minstrels and puppeteers say it, too. Your deeds are told throughout Naipon."

Okumi seemed to think this over very carefully. Then she said, "I did not know that. I was asked to retire by enemies of my husband, or else submit to concubinage . . . that was long ago. I have lived here since then, and prayed for the well-being of my husband's spirit."

"If anyone had known where you were," said Tomoe, "they would have set you free. The world has changed a little, Okumi. You have outlived your antagonists. Now you can walk from this place into the world anytime you desire."

"There have never been locks on my room," said Okumi. "I am held here only by my own promise, given sixty years ago. I cannot break the promise even now; 'the word of the samurai' was given. My whole world is like this anyway . . . " She indicated the shadowed perimeter of the room. "Everything is darkness. I have been treated well. I have been resigned."

Tomoe held back tears. This, she knew, was the fate of many women warriors, if they were unfortunate enough to survive a losing husband.

"You are unhappy for me?" asked Okumi, sensitive to what others felt although she could not see their faces.

"I am more selfish than that," said Tomoe. "I am thinking that someday I may be sitting in a room like yours."

"You would rather be a 'Yamato hero'?" Okumi asked, being ironic; for Yamato referred not only to Naipon's chief race, but also to a famous hero of the most ancient times, who died young. There had been many like him since.

"I would rather be a Yamato hero," Tomoe easily admitted.

Okumi laughed very gently. "Either you will have your wish," she said, "or you will change your mind. It is no trouble being old. There is time to thank the ancestors and the Buddhas. There is time for peaceful sensations and meditation."

"I rarely talk to Buddhas," said Tomoe. "The sutras are unknown to me."

"Then you will have time to thank the Billions of Myriads," the old woman said. "There are even more of them than Buddhas! But you did not come to find out what it is like to live secluded. Someone told you where I was."

"It was Shan On of Shigeno Valley Cemetery. You would not know the place, for it was recently made on the site of a terrible war."

"But I do know the place," said Okumi. "Although I do not have much news of the outside world, Shan On happens to be my daughter."

Tomoe was surprised. "I could not guess her age. I did not think she was so old as sixty."

"She is not my husband's child, but was born three years after he was killed; Shan On is not quite sixty. For a time I had a lover who was a man of the Celestial Kingdoms, a renegade who loved Naipon better. He was executed under false charges of being a spy. As a result of my affair, or because it made a good excuse, my husband's old enemies 'asked' that I retire. I complied to save my daughter. We were separated by force, and Shan On was raised by a Shinto priestess so that even the nuns could not get word to me through Buddhist routes. I knew nothing of her for many years, except that she was alive. After the Shinto priestess died, Shan On visited me here; it was a happy reunion. She took a Buddhist habit to add to her Shinto robes, this to honor my own sutras. I have word from her now and then, although I have been denied other contacts."

"The reason she has sent me," said Tomoe, "is for your

aid. I bear a sword haunted by a vengeful ghost, as does my husband.'' Tomoe unwrapped her bundle which contained her better clothing and a sword. She set the sword on the floor between herself and the large, old woman. Thick-fingered hands reached for the weapon, touched the handle, drew away. ''An evil thing!'' she exclaimed. Tomoe said, ''I feared it.'' The blind nun said,

''You must leave the sword with the priests of Yuwe-ji. I would keep it myself, but I may not live as long as it will take to appease the angry spirit. The sword will require regular services, perhaps for many years if not for generations; only then can it be made pure. The priests can do that, although you will have to make some other donation as well.''

''I will do as you advise,'' said Tomoe. ''But my husband is stubborn and may not agree to do the same with his.''

''If he fails to retire the sword,'' said Okumi, ''it will undo him in the end.''

''Shan On has told me the same thing,'' said Tomoe. ''But she informed me that it might be possible to meet with the ghost in his own country under the earth, and to beseech him to forgive my husband.''

The old woman nodded slowly, pulled her face back into the shadows. ''It would be a dangerous journey, without guarantees. The yamahoshi are responsible for guarding the gate to hell; you can enter only by their permission, and escape only by their aid. You will also need a better weapon than this sword would be, unhaunted. The weapon must be as capable of slaying creatures of the supernatural realm as of slaying mortal samurai.''

''There is such a weapon?'' urged Tomoe, who already knew the answer from the stories told in the *kodan* houses. Okumi had borne a magic weapon during the Wars with Ho. It had been a halberd-like *naginata*, a sword mounted on a pole. What became of it was part of Okumi's mystery.

''The Golden Naginata,'' said Okumi, ''rests in the crater of Kiji-san, a mountain in the north.'' Tomoe knew the mountain, one of a pair of twins: Kijiyama on the right and Kujiyama on the left (from the southern approach), the latter being the abode of the yamahoshi monks, the former being the place where the yamabushi built their monastery. "The yamabushi make prayers to Kiji-san so that the peak will not explode, for it appears always on the verge of overflow. But they are misled. The mountain is at rest, and only the naginata inside its summit causes the terrifying glow. Unless the metal is coated with the blood of the monster *kirin* who guards it, to gaze upon the nagainata's light means instant blindness!" Saying this, the old nun opened her eyes for the first time. They were shiny, black and vacant. She raised a fist and said, "But, oh!, it is a fine thing to have as one's final vision! It etches itself onto the mind and stands forever in the darkness like a beacon!" Okumi's breasts heaved excitedly, but slowly she calmed herself, lowered her quivering fist, and shut her unseeing eyes. "Until the blade is drenched in the kirin's blood, you can only use it with eyes bound shut. Samurai practice many blind styles for the sake of nightfighting and for stalking the lightless corridors of castles; but the kirin will set an unusual test of blind battle which you may not survive."

"I do not fear it."

"You will need a certain sheath. The golden naginata is so sharp that no common sheath can hold it without being cut in two. I have kept the magic sheath these years as a memento; but as Shan On thinks it important, I will part with my keepsake for you, if you will make one promise."

"I will do any favor."

"The Golden Naginata cannot be held too long in mortal hands; for one thing, the blood of the kirin filters away the blinding brightness for the space of a single month, and it is difficult to fight such a monster on a monthly basis. You will have to return the weapon to Kiji-san by then, or the mountain might not rest longer. The sheath, however, is yours to keep . . . until some other hero comes to you and needs it for Naipon's sake. That is how it has always been, and how it must always be."

"But if I become a Yamato hero," said Tomoe, "how will I keep such a promise?"

"In that case, the sheath will take care of itself; death will free you of the promise."

"Very well," said Tomoe. "If I do not become a Yamato hero, I will do as you say without fail."

The old woman stood and went through the dark of her room to a side wall, sliding a small door aside. Inside was her bedding, and hidden among the futons and blankets was the sheath. It was not an extraordinary sheath, seeming to be made of common wood, nicely carved but not lacquered, not gilded, no special attachments of any kind. Okumi said, "No doubt it looks plain to you. But to these old hands which know the feel of magic, this sheath is spectacular. It has pleased me to touch it lo these many years, so you must love it, too."

Tomoe held the plain sheath, letting her fingers trace the mystic carvings in the wood. "It has *aji*," she said, aji being a special trait of simple things, a word applied to things which should be used and are not so nice if they look unworn. The word also implied much handling, as by Okumi's loving hands throughout these sixty years.

Okumi bowed slightly to Tomoe's praise, and said, most simply, "Thank you."

Tomoe called to her brother: "Imai!" She hurried along a narrow hall in the castle. The word "castle" was barely apropos. Yuwe Castle was a fortified position surrounded by palisades; it had proven pitifully easy to win and scarcely worth having, except for its strategic location near Kyoto. Yet to Yoshinake, who began his career as a "tent general," it was almost too fancy for comfort.

Tomoe had changed into good clothing: hakama trousers and kosode blouse, her personal comma-pattern crest printed at the front of each shoulder and in the middle of her back. She said to Imai, catching up to him in the hall, "Sorry if you worried about my being late. After visiting with a nun, I was with the priests of Yuwe-ji longer than expected. Is my husband sleeping?"

Imai said, "He is in a bad mood, Tomoe, Whatever you said in your letter makes him unhappy—with me, too, for delivering it. He says you walk about the country like an unlanded peasant, or a perverse lord who enjoys sneaking among the common people in disguise. He says you are troublesome and annoying, that . . ."

"Good," said Tomoe. "If he is upset, he must believe what I have told him."

"I don't understand," her brother said, screwing up his handsome face in a look of consternation.

"Don't worry about it. He is in his quarters?"

He nodded. "Yes." Tomoe started to hurry away and, as she did, her brother flicked a secreted pebble toward the crest printed on her back. She turned swiftly and caught the stone in her hand, grinning at the fellow who threw it. He said, "You are too quick for me, Tomoe."

"You are slow in your old age," she teased, then hurried on. Momentarily she came to the rooms Yoshinake had selected for himself and his wife on the day the castle was taken. He sat against one wall with his elbow on a padded arm-table. He glowered into space, not seeming to notice who had entered. Tomoe came up to him and dropped to her knees, face tipped down a little, awaiting permission to speak. After an uncomfortable silence, Yoshinake removed the letter from his sleeve-pocket, waved it like a flag, and said with hoarse annoyance, "Why do you send such news as this in a letter? Are you afraid to speak to me in person?"

"My apologies, Lord Kiso." She bowed further, as might any cowed vassal.

"You call me that? You were less formal before you left!"

Challenged, she sat up tall, hands on knees, and admitted plainly, "Sometimes you are difficult to approach with a difficult matter, it is true."

"You should not feel like that with me! You come tonight like a vassal, not a wife; you sit there as though we are not intimate. You are my equal in everything and need not be overwhelmed by me. Haven't I given you your own crest?"

Tomoe said, "You have made me more solitary than independent. If you would command me more, perhaps it would not be true that I am less lonesome in a graveyard, and find it easier to converse with ghosts."

"I promised not to rule you!" stormed Yoshinake. "You require subjugation?"

"You are subject to the Shogun," she reminded. "Every samurai must serve."

"You serve me well!" he said. "You should think of liberty as your reward."

"I will do so," she said, still formal. Yoshinake grumbled because she would not soften. Then he said more calmly,

"Explain this letter to me. If it makes it easier, I command you to do so."

Tomoe looked toward her left, at the wall behind which three bodyguards were always sitting. She rose to her feet, went to the wall, and slid a panel aside. "Go away!" she snapped, her tone imitating that of her husband. They looked at Lord Kiso, who did not contradict Tomoe's order. They stood, bowed, and shuffled away like a short parade. Tomoe shut the panel. To Yoshinake she said, "It is as I wrote you. Because Okio's hungry ghost knows we killed three of his champions, he wishes us injury. The swords he made in life are the instruments of his vengeance, as you and I well know. The giant Uchida Ieoshi, vainly considering himself your rival in the Shogun's esteem, will no doubt consider it his victory if we both take new swords, perhaps swords made by the smiths of his own clan. It cannot be helped. My sword is already placed in retirement. You must do the same with yours."

"Absurd!" Yoshinake looked agitated to the extreme.

"Okio haunts you already," said Tomoe. "He will twist your normal stubbornness into something not sincere, but unreasonable."

Yoshinake pulled his knees up under himself, taking a more formal position and sinking down like a child pouting.

"I have talked to the priests, a priestess, and a nun," said Tomoe. "Each says the sword will be your undoing."

"I am stronger than any ghost," he said. "There is no finer sword in Naipon. I will not part with it."

Silence was like death after he said this. Tomoe watched his face, but he would not look her in the eyes. She thought she saw something of madness behind his strict expression, as though the ghost of Okio were already firmly rooted in him, making the Rising Sun General act this way. Finally,

Tomoe spoke:

"I expected this. Therefore I have already made arrangements for a journey. Since, as you say, I have my liberty, I may undertake any mission I please, and be away however long I desire."

"It cannot be just now," he said, looking at her at last. "There are no battles to be fought at the moment, it is true; but this is only the calm before the storm. While you were on your pilgrimage, the yamabushi and yamahoshi agreed to sign a treaty with each other and serve me. I mean to send you to the Karuga mountains to personally lead them on a march upon Kyoto. Our bid for ultimate power nears us, Tomoe! When the last leaves of autumn have fallen, the warlord Yoshinake will rise!"

He was excited by the news he was giving her, but Tomoe was entirely composed. She said, "I had meant to go to Karuga anyway; for upon twin mountains there, my mission lies. In the last year, you and I have been busy settling revolts; so I have been unable to keep my promise to bonze Shindo, to return the *shaku* from the head of his staff to his teacher in the yamahoshi monastery."

"You have more than that in mind, I know; but as you do not wish that I ask what it is, I will not pursue it. Only, when the last leaves fall, you must begin your march with the martial Buddhists. My plan is for Kyoto to be already won when you arrive; for with those lords sworn to my service, plus my blood clan, and your own eastern relatives, we have army enough to secure a victory and possess the Mikado's city. The Shogun will hear of it and send a strong army against me at once. They will not expect the reinforcements you will bring from the north. After the shogunate forces are defeated, we begin the fortnight's march to Kamakura, with our multitudes of allies. If we travel as the wind, we may cut four days off that harsh trek, unseating the Shogun before he has news about our exact plan."

"Before marching on Kamakura," said Tomoe, "you must win an imperial decree. Otherwise we cannot legitimize such action against the Shogun."

"The Mikado will make any decree I wish!" said Yoshinake. "He will be delighted that I free him from virtual imprisonment, and reward me with the commission I am seeking."

"If he does not?"

Yoshinake fumed at the query. He said, "Then he will be obliged to act accordingly for the sake of his own life!"

Tomoe registered no emotion, although inwardly she was sharply affected by her husband's promise to threaten even the Mikado's safety, all for personal gain. Very quietly, she asked,

"Can you see true a threat against Amaterasu's god-child?"

There was no hesitation. "I can."

"I see." She looked away from him a moment, then met his eyes until he was forced to look away from her. She said, "I will do as you say. It will be a month before the last leaves fall. I have that much time to complete my personal mission." She did not say that her mission was to save him from this madness, from possession by the hungry ghost. She stood to leave, awaiting no permission, being as she was told "at liberty." But he stopped her with an unexpected gentle voice. He said,

"It is late. Surely your mission can wait for dawn."

She hesitated in the doorway. Yoshinake's tone was plaintive. She had never heard him sound that way before. Perhaps something inside him recognized his own madness, causing him to beg for succor. Tomoe turned back to face him. With anger gone from his expression, Kiso Yoshinake was too beautiful to resist, and too much in need. She said, "Yes, it can wait that long."

In the night, Tomoe had a dream she didn't like. She dreamed it was already morning and she had started out for the Karuga mountains. She was fully armored and rode a white horse. Behind her came a retinue of seven personal retainers, also on horses, also in armor; and there were at least a dozen servants on foot, carrying flags in their hands and boxes on their backs. Two were pounding drums. For a long time, in the dream, they went along like this, quite slowly.

Up ahead, on the side of the road, a woman dressed in a red

kimono sat next to a fat, rustic god carved in stone. The god's face was pleasant. The woman wore the bell-rimmed hat of a fortuneteller. A veil hung from the hat so that it was not possible to see the woman's face. Tomoe Gozen did not realize who this was, because, in dreams, things are often like that.

Tomoe could think of no explanation for it seemed that the fortuneteller had been sitting on the right-hand side of the road a moment before, whereas she and the rustic god were now sitting on the left-hand side of the road. Besides that, the face of the rock-carved god was not as pleasant as Tomoe had first thought. As the woman samurai tried to figure these things out, she realized she was mistaken, for the fortuneteller was on the right-hand side of the road after all, although come to think of it, she was really on the left.

In the next moment, the fortuneteller was sitting on neither right nor left, but was standing in the middle of the road. The rustic god was not at all what it had seemed; instead, it was an ugly red oni devil. For some reason it wasn't as fierce as oni generally were. It crouched not as to attack, but as though cowering and afraid. When the fortuneteller limped boldly forward, leaning on a long staff, the oni devil withdrew.

It was rude for someone of low station to block a samurai's path, so Tomoe's retainers urged their horses ahead and surrounded the disrespectful woman. Nobody acted as though anything were unusual. Tomoe stopped her horse. The dozen servants stopped walking; the two stopped beating the drums. All watched.

Despite the fact that the seven retainers had penned the woman between their horses, somehow she was no longer there. She had slipped through them and was walking toward Tomoe. As she came, she took off her belled hat and threw it aside. In this way she revealed that one side of her face was horrible while the other side was unscarred and beautiful. The fortuneteller raised her fighting stick and held it above her head. When she twisted the stick in a certain way, spikes sprung out from both ends, making it a two-way spear. Tomoe still did not move, but only wondered. The fortuneteller spun around to face the seven retainers who were charging down upon her with bared swords.

The fortuneteller vanished. She instantly reappeared beside one of the retainers who had reined his horse aside. She stuck one point of her stick-cum-spear into the surprised man's throat, then lifted him off his horse with supernatural strength, throwing him at another rider. She disappeared again, before one of the other retainers could slice her. She appeared behind him, sticking him in the lower back. She lifted him into the air, holding him straight above her head while he thrashed and cried and rained blood upon her face. Then she threw him at another rider.

Now there were two men knocked from their horses but still alive. When they regained their feet, they attacked together. Her spear, sharp at both ends, took one and then the other. Once more she vanished, reappearing behind an attacker, killing him; and in like manner she killed the other two.

The servants who had been with Tomoe were gone. She had not seen them run away, but they must have done so. The horses of her retainers were also gone, but the bodies of the men still cluttered the road. In all this while, Tomoe had not moved, had not blinked her eyes. She kept staring at the monstrous woman who, alone and afoot, slew seven horsemen.

In Tomoe's obi there was no longsword, but only a short one; and beside it was a *shaku* from the head of a monk's staff. Tomoe took out the shaku and rattled its rings at the monster-woman. The monster-woman laughed. The laughter sounded as though it resounded from the depths of hell.

"You cannot frighten me with that!" said the monster-woman. Her voice was indeed a distant echo, however loud it might be; and it was not pretty, but the deep, grating voice of a powerful demon.

"I know why the shaku does not scare you," said Tomoe. "You are the *naruka* at the bottom of the Land of Gloom, who may never walk the earth. I cannot send you back to Hell because you have never left it. It is unfortunate that you have chosen my friend Tsuki Izutsu as the instrument of your terror. But I will have you soon! I am coming through the gate of Mount Kuji with the golden naginata of Mount Kiji. I will duel you in your own country, and free Tsuki from possession!"

The deep, ugly voice of Naruka challenged spitefully, "Get me if you can!" She charged forward with the two-ended spear twirling over her head. Tomoe had happened to bring along some red beans, given to her by the priestess Shan On. Tomoe did not remember getting the beans, but all the same, they were from Shan On.

She threw the beans at Naruka.

The monster screamed at the beans and pointed one end of the spear at them. All the beans stopped in mid-air, and hung there as a barrier between Naruka and Tomoe. Tomoe said,

"Tell the swordsmith Okio I will come to see him, too. Also tell my good friend Ushii Yakushiji that I have a special gift for him, better than the spirit-toys and -money, better than the good rice wine. Tell him I am bringing him his heart's desire, so that he may be happier in eternity."

The monster-woman growled like a bear, saying, "You think your enemies reside in hell? I am not your enemy! Okio is not! Ushii is not! Your enemy is . . . your enemy is . . ." Naruka began to choke, the eye on the ugly side of her face bulging. She grabbed at her throat as though something invisible were strangling her. Then, to save herself, Naruka vanished. The red oni devil scampered forward to the place where his companion had vanished, running around and around, whimpering like a forgotten puppy. At that moment, Tomoe Gozen awoke in the covers of her futon. She was sweating profusely. Kiso Yoshinake was looking at her, concern in his expression. He said,

"I did not know if I should wake you. You didn't make a sound."

Tomoe could barely speak. When her heart slowed down to normal, she said, "It is good you let me sleep. A fortuneteller visited me in my dream. She informed me that I must go upon my mission alone, for whoever travels with me will die. Additionally, the dream informed me that I had better seek a special gift for a friend of mine, although I do not know what the gift should be."

"If I can help," said Yoshinake, but he did not finish. Tomoe said,

"Make love to me again."

Yoshinake smiled. "It is the first time you said so. I was sometimes afraid I was a nuisance."

"I have been cruel to my husband," said Tomoe. Perhaps, she thought, she had never told Yoshinake that he was beautiful because of the interference of Okio's vindictive sword. Now, the sword retired, she could speak her true feelings. "You are pretty as a boy," she said. "You remind me of a girlfriend I had when I was little."

Yoshinake liked to hear this. Tomoe grinned back at him in the darkness of their bedroom. Moonlight made the translucent rice-paper windows glow, so they could see each other. She said,

"When we fought the lord of Yuwe to win this castle, we were side by side in the last onslaught, eagerness making us bold, even careless. I was aroused to see you then. I am aroused to see you now."

He pushed a gentle arm underneath her and lifted her up to him, his eyes glistening with unwept tears. "It means a lot!" he said. When she wrapped her legs around him, they began to play for a long while, and finally copulated. Tomoe held her eyes closed, and saw a field of battle, on which Yoshinake reaped.

She drew rein upon the narrow road. The horse made snuffling sounds, then stood perfectly still. The sky was darkening. Tomoe had not come to an inn as quickly as she had expected. Ahead, the road curved, and woods impinged upon the bend at either side. It was a perfect place for ambush; and as she had not left Yuwe incognito, it was possible that one or another enemy of herself and Yoshinake would arrange something unfriendly.

There was nothing visibly untoward in the shadows at the bend. Yet the stillness was perhaps *too* great; not even the evening's insects sang. Despite her suspicion, she urged the horse to continue, and pushed her sword a bit forward in its scabbard so that it would be loose and ready. It was a sword untested in her hands, so she did not yet know its reliability; still, she almost welcomed the opportunity to better acquaint herself with its mettle.

When she reached the bend, four men on horseback parted from the shadows and trees, blocking her path. They were samurai. By the quality of their dress, they were vassals of a wealthy Lord. They seemed to scrutinize her, as though to be sure of her identity.

"I am Tomoe Gozen of Heida, honored wife of Kiso Yoshinake," she said, for introductions were common before a duel. The four men did not reciprocate, which was rude. In fact their identities were carefully hidden beneath large hats, and by bits of paper sewn over the clan crests printed on the shoulders and backs of their haori.

It was unfortunate that samurai of rank should be sent as common assassins; for, no matter the reasons, excellence of encounters, or outcome, there would be no honor for anyone involved. There could only be a dog's unheralded death or, at best, a dog's reward of pats and bones.

"You will die quickly," warned Tomoe, "unless you give this up."

She was hasty in her surmise. One of the samurai whistled some code, for none of them would use voices by which they might be recognized should the prey escape. The whistle summoned more than thirty brigands from the trees. They were on foot. Several were armed with bows and arrows. This motley group's leader pushed to the fore, chewing on a twig and looking certain of himself. He wore hakama trousers and two swords like a samurai, but Tomoe suspected he was *akuto,* meaning he might be bold and skillful, but he lacked samurai lineage so that his talents could not win him a clan's commission. Such men often captained brigands.

As the akuto wore no hat, his face was visible in the closing shadows of dusk. He was scruffy, unbathed, with a scar along one side of his jaw. Since his identity was of no concern, he was not reluctant to talk:

"If you throw down your sword and ride away without it, we will let you pass unbothered."

"A samurai's sword is a samurai's soul," said Tomoe evenly.

"Samurai of station have many souls, then," the akuto retorted, sounding bitter. "You can go home and pick out another."

They looked each other eye to eye without wavering. Tomoe said, "What would you do with my sword?"

"We are brigands after all," said the akuto. "We will sell it for what it brings. We do not mind being called 'sword thieves.' "

"What about my horse?"

"We do not sell horses."

It was obviously no ordinary bit of highway robbery, or the horse would be taken too. Tomoe looked at the thirty-odd brigands, then at the four silent samurai on horseback. She asked the akuto, "Since when do brigands work for vassal samurai?"

"Since this afternoon."

It was an honest reply, but not informative. She guessed the brigands had been approached by the vassals only that afternoon because it had not been known until that morning that Tomoe Gozen had left Yuwe without escort. She doubted the whole lot of them could injure her with swords, but the arrows were perturbing.

"I will surrender my sword and leave," Tomoe said, surprising them.

The chief of the brigands said simply, "Good."

Tomoe slipped from the back of her horse. Now, at the same height as the numerous brigands, the arrows were of less concern; also, her horse or one of the other four might prove useful shields.

She stepped toward the akuto, removing her sheathed sword. She held it forth in both hands so that the brigand chief might take it. He was not very smart about it; for she had offered the sword in such a way that he had to take hold of the scabbard first. Then she withdrew the blade and, before he could drop the empty sheath and draw his own sword, she had sliced him through the forehead. He collapsed without a sound.

Arrows were unleashed at once, but she had moved away from the spot. She heard her horse give a cry of pain. The beast darted through the circle of brigands, scattering them;

then, further along the road, the poor animal fell, thrashing awhile. Tomoe had at the same time charged toward one of the four samurai, menacing the man's horse so much that it reared, rolling the rider to the ground. He was stuck by her sword before regaining a single breath. She scurried behind the slain samurai's horse so that it took arrows in its side, the brigand bowmen being that easily tricked.

The brigands ran about uselessly, confused by Tomoe's speed and maneuvers. The vassal who whistled commands could not control them.

Tomoe rushed toward the whistler, keeping her head down, but he reined his horse back. The other two vassals dismounted and came at her quickly, thinking to catch her between them. Because they would not take off their hats, she doubted they could be effective. But, the moment her barely tested sword crossed with one of the others, her weapon broke in half. If she was surprised, the vassals on each side of her were more so, for they had doubtless expected the blade to be the marvelous Sword of Okio. While her nearer opponent hesitated at the sight of the broken steel, Tomoe plunged the half-weapon into his belly, ripping up. At the same time, she kicked the man's fingers so that he released his sword even before he was dead. His sword went wildly into the air, and Tomoe caught it by the handle on its descent, in time to face the third of the four vassals.

The third vassal backed away, grabbing his horse by the reins and leaping onto its back.

The head vassal continued whistling; the sound of it was crazy. The brigands would not obey, presuming they remembered the code in their confusion. They had not been prepared for such a woman. Doubtless they had not been told who it was they were attacking; by now they would have guessed. With their akuto captain slain, there was no one to stop their retreat. The hysterical whistling ceased in an abrupt curse, and the head vassal spoke with his own voice:

"It is the wrong sword! She does not have it!"

Tomoe stood by the second samurai she had killed. It did not look as though the other two vassals intended to attack her. Clearly they had been ordered to take the Sword of Okio from her; now they were not certain whether or not it was necessary to press the situation, especially as they had so quickly lost the support of the brigands. Tomoe made their decision for them: she bent to the corpse and tore off a piece of paper which had hidden the clan crest. She revealed to her own satisfaction that the crest was that of the giant Uchida Ieoshi, and these were his vassals. The giant remained obsessed with the destruction of Okio's last remaining swords. He had never until now been so bold, or careless, as to send his personal retainers to break the blades of his swordsmithing clan's murdered rival, whose fame survived the grave. Now, if Tomoe escaped to tell the story, Ieoshi would lose face as a "sword thief," the most derogatory title any samurai could earn. He would be reviled by samurai at every level of life, and never be certain who laughed behind his back.

"Ieoshi's ninja spies must have been slow-witted," said Tomoe, "or he would have been told that I have retired my Sword of Okio. Their stupidity will cost him pride and you your lives; for now you must try to kill me to protect your master's reputation, and in that you will fail."

The two remaining vassals tore off their hats, and their eyes looked panicked. The one who had been the whistler urged his steed back and forth along the forest's margin, crying out, "Reward and amnesty for the brigand band! Reward and amnesty for brigands!"

There was rustling about in the leaves. Tomoe knew the brigands would accept the offer unless she acted fast. She leapt over the corpse and rushed forward, but Ieoshi's two vassals retreated on their horses.

The head vassal sweetened his offer: "*Wealth* and amnesty! Wealth! Amnesty!"

Tomoe tried to get close enough to cut the legs of the horses, but the vassals evaded her too well. She would tire herself out running after them, so the only thing left was to take a stand in the road. She dug her toes into the ground and stood in the young darkness, raising the sword she had taken from the second vassal slain.

Bowmen and swordfighting brigands stepped out of the woods by ones and twos, looking sheepish or afraid, but willing to risk any trouble for the promise of amnesty and enough reward to begin life anew. Tomoe growled at them in a way she had learned from watching her husband fight. Her eyes glazed in a crazed manner, seeming to shine in the night. Spittle sprayed as she shouted,

"All will die!"

It was a trick that always worked on lowbred men, raised with a fear of samurai wrath or vengeance. The brigands backed away from her crazy challenge and appearance. But the two vassals were shouting not to be tricked, mentioning the increasing size of the fortune the brigands could expect. With such encouragement, the frightened men were not cowed for long. Tomoe ducked to avoid an arrow. She moved sideways and was missed again. A number of swords were pointing in her direction, but so far no one dared rush forth to fight.

"Baké!" shouted the head vassal. "Fools! Do you stand there hoping she starves to death? Attack her! Attack her!"

They attacked together in a stupid clutter that would cause them to injure each other as much as their single foe; but it would be, ultimately, a more effective thing than trying her two or three at a time. She would cut a dozen, and a dozen more would cut their own friends by accident; but it would be hard to avoid a wound for herself if they piled themselves upon her like this.

Before they reached her, Tomoe Gozen was saved by an unexpected miracle. A blue ring of fire fell straight away from the sky, burning the two remaining horses and the vassals riding them, as well as the corpses, and every brigand without exception. There were hideous cries among the brigands, dying in the flames, while Tomoe stood in the center of this burning ring, untouched.

One of the two vassals fell from his horse, screaming. The other would not let go of his saddle. He and his steed were charred black, from the rider's head to the animal's hoofs; they were terrifyingly stout, monstrous in the light of the still-burning ring of blue flames. Everyone else writhed in pain upon the ground or had already been roasted to death; but this one vassal and his mount suddenly reined about and galloped away, hideous specters across the night. Perhaps that last samurai vassal lived long enough to report the failure to his Lord; more likely, he died along the route. To Tomoe, with more immediate concerns, the vassal no longer mattered. Although she had not been burned, the ring of fire persisted, and she was trapped in the middle.

It was tengu-fire, she could not doubt it. She had heard that tengu could weave magic out of flame, not without risk to themselves; but she had never seen such a thing with her own eyes. It was hard to understand it, but she refused to reveal sign of fear.

Above her head there was a flapping sound, and a wheezing kind of laughter. The voice of an old man called from the heavens,

"Old Uncle Tengu has grown back his flight-feathers! He has done Tomoe Gozen a favor, killing her foes. Will she try to trim him anew, or will she let us pretend to be friends?"

"You have me trapped," said Tomoe. "You cannot coerce friendship from me in this way. I will jump into the sky and cut you in half before your fire can touch me!"

The wheezing laughter proved that Old Uncle Tengu did not believe her. "You cannot jump so high as I can fly," he said. "Your bluffs won't work on a wily tengu as easily as feigned madness frightened those brigands. Still, I mean to coerce nothing from you. You may choose as you wish, without fear of fire."

With that, the blue flames vanished, leaving only the scent of cooked meat. For the moment, Tomoe Gozen was blinded by the sudden return of darkness. The wheezing laughter came nearer; Old Uncle Tengu had settled on the ground before her. She could not see him, but heard him say, "It will be a moment before your eyes adjust. I could have used this moment to drop rocks on your head, as you once had my nephews do to me. You are helpless without your sight."

To prove him wrong, Tomoe leapt at the sound of his voice, sword swinging horizontally. The tengu's laughter ceased. He flapped away barely fast enough to keep his head on his shoulders.

"You missed that time!" he said. "Please do not try again! Have I attacked you even once? Do not be too proud to accept the help of a devil tengu!"

When Tomoe's eyes had adjusted to the darkness, she tossed aside the sword she had borrowed from a dead vassal. The long-nosed devil looked relieved, but Tomoe was still not friendly. She said, "Tengu do not help samurai without reasons of their own. You and I have special enmity besides. Do not try to fool me, only, say what it is you want in return for your unrequested aid."

"You are right a little, and you are wrong a little," said Old Uncle Tengu, preening his feathers, wings and tail. He was still blue from the dye Tomoe had once landed him in, except where new feathers had grown in, and in those places he was white. He carried a sword through a narrow obi belt, and it was longer than the swords tengu usually carried, but he made no motion towards it. He said,

"I told you once before that the oracles of the tengu tribe consulted among themselves and decided you were the Patron of Demon Children. It is at their request that I have found you, although it wasn't easy to track you down, with your recent pilgrimage and everything."

Tomoe did not like such talk. A patron, or *kami*, was a tutelary deity, and to be called that made her uneasy. "It is stupid to call me *kami*," she said. "I am a mortal samurai."

"Nonetheless," said Old Uncle Tengu, "the oracles have said so, and I cannot doubt their advice, for that would be the greater blasphemy among my kind. Now I am sent here for two reasons, and one is important to your mission, while the other is important to a half-breed *bakemono*, a monster-baby."

"If I must hear you chatter," Tomoe complained, "speak faster and more plainly. The night is cold and I would rather go to an inn than stand talking to you."

"Be more patient, Tomoe Gozen. I will not keep you long. But you should not go to any inn tonight. You can reach the Twin Mountains by morning if I tell you a shorter way through the forest. You will come out at Lost Shrine, where a woman lives in misery and poverty. She will give you a place to rest before you climb the first mountain, Kiji-san, abode of the yamabushi. The woman of Lost Shrine will even provide you with a bath. You will find out about the half-bakemono child which she birthed.

"The second thing that brings me to you is this: I want to give you a certain sword, the one I am wearing. Since you have broken the one you chose at random this morning, you may require the one I have to offer . . . unless you prefer to risk the curse of stealing one from these burnt brigands and vassals. The sword I bring you is a better one in any case."

Tomoe did not seem enthused. She said, "It is an honor to be given a sword, but also an honor for you if I accept it. Why should I want such a gift from a long-nosed devil?"

"Do not be prejudiced, Tomoe Gozen!" Old Uncle Tengu was indignant. "Remember, we are pretending to be friends. If you cannot accept it as the gift of a tengu, think of it as coming from your late friend Madoka Kawayama, the young samurai buried in Shigeno Valley Cemetery in a double-grave."

Tomoe stepped forward a little bit, remembering the beautiful samurai who had died in a terrible war, at the hand of his blood-brother who became a foe. "It was Madoka's sword?" she asked. "How have you gotten it?"

"There is no need to ask how tengu get things. It will not be missed by anyone. It was not really my idea to get it for you. I bring it at the request of the priestess Shan On, groundkeeper of the cemetery you visited. I met her only this morning while I was trying to find where you had gone; and she told me that a scarred fortuneteller came to her in a dream last night. In the dream the fortuneteller said, 'Tomoe Gozen requires something special to give Ushii Yakushiji as a present.' So Shan On asked me to bring you a couple of things, one of them this sword."

It was curious that Shan On had dreamed about Tsuki/Naruka; but Tomoe had already learned, a year earlier in Isso, that the fortuneteller wandered in her sleep, her spirit unaware of its own doings. It was not a story the tengu could have made up, so Tomoe did not doubt the explanation. She said, "I believe you, because the fortuneteller visited me in a dream as well, and the necessity of some special gift for Ushii was implied by the dream. But you say there is another thing Shan On commissioned you to deliver?"

"I could not fly here with the second thing," he said, "so it awaits you at Lost Shrine. You will have to go there to get it."

Tomoe scowled. "You fool me after all," she said.

Old Uncle Tengu shrugged his shoulders and rustled his wings. He confessed, "I have tricked you a very little bit by leaving the second present there. But the trick is for the bakemono child, not for myself. You will surely take pity if you see the unhappy mother."

The severe look on Tomoe Gozen's face had mostly gone away. She said to Old Uncle Tengu, "Perhaps I should not be so stubborn. For the sake of Madoka Kawayama's sword, which is indeed a suitable gift for Ushii Yakushiji in Hell, I will offer you our pretended friendship as an honest one."

Old Uncle Tengu tried not to show any sign of happiness, but it glistened in his eyes. He took the longsword from his obi and handed it to Tomoe. "It is good of you," he said. The tengu and the samurai bowed to one another on that nighted road in the early part of autumn; and then Old Uncle Tengu told Tomoe Gozen how not to lose the forest path to Lost Shrine, and they parted.

She leaned back in the stone hot-tub, relaxing aching muscles, smiling to herself. Vapors of steam snaked through the rickety structure. "It feels good," she said, but there was no one close enough to hear. The only sounds were those of her own graceful motions in the deep tub, and the fire built in an outside wall's masonry nook, where it heated the bathhouse's simple duct system. Tomoe Gozen had slept the entire morning and into the afternoon, too weary to have bathed the instant she arrived at Lost Shrine. On waking she had felt stiff and filthy; happily, Oshina, the woman of Lost Shrine, had prepared a bath for her visitor. Tomoe was grateful.

After lengthy ablutions, she climbed from the bath, dried herself, oiled her hair with something sweet-smelling which Oshina had left for her, and clad herself handsomely in the clothing Oshina had brushed clean and folded while Tomoe had slept. Taking up her swords, and a cloth which wrapped a few possessions, she thrust these into her obi and stepped out of the tiny bathhouse.

The air was chilly off the snowcapped Karugas. The mountain range surrounded the place on three sides, with an especially notable pair of identical peaks looking larger than the others because they loomed so near. These were Kuji-san of the yamahoshi sect, and Kiji-san of the yamabushi sect, the two places Tomoe must visit. The Buddhist warriors dominated the prefecture, which might partly explain the neglect of the Shinto shrine.

A cold, cold stream ran nearby. Oshina sat on her knees on a flat, mossy bridge washing a child's clothing in the icy water. They were the size and design for a small boy. The woman was rag-clad, but the little kimonos she washed were in good repair, suggesting that the young mother took better care of her son than herself.

Tomoe had hardly looked at the grounds on arrival. It had not quite been sunrise, and she had been too weary even for decent amenities, much less for exploration. On waking, she had been so eager for a bath that again she scarcely took in her surroundings. Now she looked over the landscape, and though it had the individual elements of a pretty country place, there was in fact nothing charming about Lost Shrine. The bathhouse she came out of leaned so much that it was surprising it did not collapse. The torii gate was broken near its top. The path from the gate to the shrine's chief building was weed-grown from disuse. The shrine-building itself looked more like a weathered storage house than a holy place. From any distance, the site would be invisible, hidden by the overgrowth of flora and the shadows of the trees.

There was only one area not left wild. A cleared patch sported a healthy crop of cucumbers and autumn squash. The crop helped take the edge of eeriness off the surroundings, as did the comforting sight of a woman washing clothing in a stream. Oshina was silent in her work and, because of the stream's babbling, had not heard Tomoe come out of the bath.

"It's a good day!" Tomoe shouted. The woman on the bridge raised her head, looked at the samurai without an emotion on her face, then bowed to her work again.

Tomoe looked at the twin peaks and the Karuga range again. As viewed from Lost Shrine, the mountains were too much like the walls of a cage to be appealing. Tomoe thought the whole area was like an exceedingly finite dish-scene, and one arranged by someone with a melancholy disposition. The samurai turned full circle and mumbled to herself, "Lost Shrine could be more pleasant."

A white dog who had greeted her also before sunrise came from behind the shrine, straight to Tomoe Gozen, and licked her hand. The dog was the one named Taro, belonging to Shan On; and he was the second thing Old Uncle Tengu had been asked to deliver. Tomoe understood Shan On's reason. Since the samurai planned to enter Buddhist Hell, a Shinto dog might well be an extraordinarily beneficial companion. Tomoe said,

"Hello, Taro; do you want to fight some demons pretty soon? We will do it together. But I must go for the Golden Naginata by myself, there atop Kiji-san. See how the mountain lights the bottoms of the clouds? That is not the activity of a volcano, but the shining of the miraculous weapon I seek. I will come back here and get you before going to the second mountain, Kuji-san; and we will enter the Gate of Hell side by side and unafraid."

The dog wagged his tail as though he understood and was eager for the chance. Oshina had finished with her wash and was coming along a path with a dripping basket in her arms. Nearby, several poles had been braced across each other, on which clothing could be hung to dry. That was where Oshina went, so Tomoe walked up the path to the same spot, Taro close at her heels.

"Thank you for the fire-warmed bath. I am a new woman this afternoon."

Oshina bowed briskly and kept working, her mood not improved by the samurai's pleasantness.

"Oshina," said Tomoe. "Do you know who I am that visits you?"

"Yes," she said. "You are Tomoe Gozen. The tengu who

flew here with the white dog told me you would be coming."

"But do you know me besides that?" she asked.

"Of course. You are famous."

"I do not mean that either. I think I have seen you somewhere before, maybe a few years ago."

Oshina finished with hanging the child's clothing. Before Tomoe could grill further, the young woman had grabbed the emptied basket and hurried toward the crumbling shrine-house, in which she lived. Tomoe looked down at the dog and said,

"It seems I cannot say the proper things today, Taro. You go make her happy for a little while." Taro ran after Oshina, wagging his entire bottom like a miraculous happiness-charm. Both the woman and the dog vanished into the shrine-house's dark interior. Tomoe walked about the ruins of Lost Shrine for a while, trying to remember where she had seen Oshina before. The woman was no outstanding beauty, and her weariness leant more to a plain appearance; but even in her poverty, Oshina had a dignity and uniqueness which made her familiar to Tomoe. Tomoe said to herself, "I cannot remember," and looked puzzled.

Behind the shrine, chickens were kept under big, loosely woven reed-baskets so that they could not wander away or be taken by predators. Baby chicks came and went with more freedom, for they fit through the strands of woven reeds. They would hurry back to hide beneath their restricted mothers at the slightest sign of danger, as when Tomoe Gozen approached. There was a big rooster who lived by himself under a separate basket, although the baby chicks were evidence that the fellow was let with the hens from time to time. The rooster seemed to be a clue to the identity of Oshina, but still Tomoe could not recall.

It seemed as though Oshina had managed to make herself a reasonable home in the run-down place, with garden and fresh eggs and a dry floor to sleep on. But it was a lonely, deserted kind of place and Tomoe suspected she might well be the only human visitor Oshina had had since coming here. "It's sad," said Tomoe, still talking to herself, it being hard to strike conversations with her hostess.

There was something Tomoe had been putting off; but

soon she must face up to her duty. She had promised Old Uncle Tengu that she would look in on the half-bakemono child. Oshina had not offered Tomoe the opportunity to see the child so far, and he never made a sound in the room of the shrine-house which was his and Oshina's sleeping quarter. An intrusion might not be welcome, and she might be blamed for curiosity, but she could not escape her promise to look upon the child and his situation.

She stood in the shrine's entrance a long time, making no sound. She heard Taro's long tail banging the floor, and Oshina saying something pleasant to him. There were none of the sounds of a child playing or moving about. If not for the clothing drying outside, one might suspect there was no child here at all.

"Oshina?" called Tomoe. Oshina immediately fell silent, although the dog's tail continued to thump lightly. "Oshina, please do not refuse me, for I would see your child. The tengu told me about him, so I will not be surprised; I do not come to revile you or your son."

There was no permission forthcoming, but there was no refusal either. Tomoe Gozen slipped off her sandals, pulled the longsword and sheath from her obi, and entered the shrine-house. She approached a sliding door along the partition, waited there a moment, then slid the door aside. Taro looked up from a comfortable position. Oshina had her back to the door, her body blocking the view of a child on a futon mattress. Tomoe moved sideways and saw the child lying there, and immediately she remembered where she had seen Oshina before. It was the homely face of the halfbreed bakemono which reminded her. The child's mouth was a crooked rent from center of jaw upward to the left ear; there was only one bakemono Tomoe knew about who ever had such a mouth, so the half-monster had to be his get.

"You are the Rooster Clan's daughter who was saved from a haunted swamp five or six years ago!" exclaimed Tomoe.

Oshina bowed. Her small voice said, "I had hoped you would not remember after so long. It was nice of you to help me at that time, and to help in the slaying of the monster who kidnapped me to that terrible place. You could not have known my shame had begun rather than ended; for I carried the monster's child. When he was born, I was cast out with him so that both of us would die. We wandered as beggars until finding this place. My son will be five years old in two days, but has no family to bring him presents."

Tomoe looked at the little boy's extraordinary ugliness. He lay upon his back staring into the shrine's rafters with dark eyes unblinking. He breathed lightly. One tiny fist opened and closed in a slow, pointless manner. "Why is he so still?" said Tomoe.

"He used to be playful," Oshina answered. "Now he never moves or speaks. He never cries out, and I must feed him by hand or he would starve. I have failed to be a good mother, or this would not have happened."

"It's very strange," said Tomoe, looking at the child's dark eyes. A shiver crept over her spine.

"I have named him Koshi, which means 'dead child,' because of his affliction. When we travelled, I called him something else, and he was a happy baby in spite of his ugliness. After he was older, he began to understand certain things too well. People were very cruel to us everywhere we went, and poor Koshi started to think he was the cause of our misfortune. One day he said to me, 'I am a monster-baby, mother; I am a monster-baby.' He had heard so many people say so when they threw stones at us and chased us from the villages. Shortly before I found this place for us to live, he became as you see him now. It is the result of our hard times that my son's spirit has fled to Hell, although his body remains healthy in the living world. I take care of him with the hope that his spirit will forgive my weaknesses and decide to return to Koshi's body."

The mother was too strong to shed a single tear. When her story was done, she bowed to her son, head to floor, and begged, "Forgive me, Koshi, if I have failed to love you well enough to make this life worthwhile."

Despite Oshina's lack of tears, or perhaps because of her fierce strength and sorrow, Tomoe was greatly affected. She looked at Koshi's terrible visage and saw in him a thing which exists in every child. What that thing was, Tomoe

Gozen could not express in easy words. It was a kind of innocence or lack of sinful feeling, a goodness universal among the young of every species and which awakens maternal instinct in every feeling heart: The goat who suckles the kitten, the wolf who suckles a bear's cub . . . one may be ugly to another, one may be the other's foe when grown, but every mother knows that every child requires concern, and she will overlook certain things.

Tomoe Gozen was overwhelmed with sadness to see the motionless child and his caring, lonely mother. The sorrow was too much to bear, so that the samurai found herself backing out of the tiny room in order to escape the feeling. Before she turned away, she said, "Forgive my intrusion," then ran away lest she be seen with tears in her eyes. If Oshina thought Tomoe ran from the child's appearance rather than from the mutual plight of mother and son, it could not be helped; Tomoe could not face Oshina's pain at that moment, and it would be unseemly for a samurai to weep; and so she had to flee.

For a while, Tomoe sat on the flat, mossy bridge watching the water rush underneath. She would like to be chivalrous in some way, but there was nothing she could do to mend the situation of Oshina and Koshi. Old Uncle Tengu was foolish to believe a single samurai could be a kami or protector to demon children. *She* could not help the brat. Yet it was a difficult thing to ignore the expectations of other people, even the expectations of a tengu, and even if the expectations were unreasonable.

Tomoe began to think it had been a mistake to save Oshina from that swamp those years before. It might have been kinder in the long run to have left her there. "It's not my trouble," said Tomoe, but could not shake away an illogical feeling of responsibility. She stood up abruptly and drew her sword full length, exclaiming, "I will be merciful and kill them both!" Her eyes looked fierce as she turned her gaze upon the main building of Lost Shrine. But she sheathed the weapon and sat down with the same abruptness, then rubbed moisture from the tip of her nose with the back of her hand. She said, "This is too much," and, "People must be stronger. It is weak of me to think of them." She folded her arms, unfolded them, then folded them again, and finally kicked one foot out from under herself to force a section of moss off the bridge and into the rushing water. She might have sat there in agitation until sunset, but for the sound of far-away chanting.

It was some sutra. It seemed to be coming from high on the mountainside. Many strong voices of bonzes and priests made the chanting audible for miles around, however faint. It was the yamabushi praying for Kiji-san to rest another day, to forgive the sins of mortals and not spill her molten, menstrual blood upon the world.

The sound of them reminded Tomoe that she had more important missions to attend. She removed a cloth-wrapped parcel from her obi. The package was longer than a shortsword and somewhat thicker, easily carried in the same way as a sword. She untied the cloth, unwrapped the contents, and revealed two objects. One was the shaku from the head of bonze Shindo's staff, which she had promised to return to the yamahoshi of Kuji-san. The other was the wooden, rune-carved sheath of a naginata. These two things represented the necessity of her visit to the two sects of martial priests on their respective mounts. She must be certain they would not compete with one another but would join arms for the march on Kyoto as soon as the leaves were falling in the valleys; and she must attend her private missions in the crater of Kiji-san, and through the fearful gate on Kuji-san.

Tomoe Gozen got to her feet again, looked at the shrine once more, and decided to put the mother and son out of her mind. A strong samurai does not waver from a course. Then, hardening her heart, she turned toward the sound of the chanting, certain she could reach the yamabushi temple well before Amaterasu had gone behind the western hills.

The easy, winding path to the yamabushi monastery would have taken a day and a half of pleasant walking; but there was a less leisurely way, one which was practically a vertical ascent. The bonzes rarely used it except in cases of emergency, so it was not always a clear route. It was marked by bushes which in spring-time would have flowers, but now were prepared for autumn. The weirdly twisted, root-bared and stunted shrubbery had been planted by bonzes of earlier generations, and looked very old. The gnarled roots and limbs were arranged as useful hand-holds (a climber must be careful lest the cliff-garden be injured). The rocks in the face of the ascent had been chiseled and altered to provide additional holds for fingers and toes, but never so obtrusively as to look like steps rather than a natural mountain wall. Tomoe's sandals were slung across her shoulder as she made the trek with bare hands and feet. She did not even wear her tabi-socks, for the rough ground would tear them too quickly.

Although the route was not difficult, it was progressively colder as the day grew older and she went higher. Along the climb, she found occasional statues of gods, and she offered each some quick, mild prayer. They were Buddhist gods and did not much enthuse her, but, as she was in their territory, she gave them each small honors. One of them was Ida-ten, a special god among warrior-monks, who stood for pious life and martial ability. Tomoe lingered before him in order to offer a more heartfelt prayer of respect than she had to the others. While she rested, she slapped the soles of her feet together and rubbed her palms vigorously, to work away the chill. Then she went on from the ledge, following certain sounds.

She heard the deep chanting of bonzes beseeching Kiji-san. The sound was far up the mountainside and echoed to Tomoe in such a way that she was not convinced of the direction. There was also the sound of rushing water which hindered her ability to understand the exact wording of the sutra. A counter-chant was going, too, sounding like a dozen or so young girls. This startled Tomoe, for she didn't think there were any girls trained by the yamabushi.

She came to the top of the mountain wall to a forested plateau. Now she could hear the chanting a bit more clearly. She also heard an unseen waterfall, hidden from her view, as were they who chanted, by the towering forest. The roar of the falls matched the bass notes of the yamabushi. The sweeter chanting of girls was like rain weeping through the cedars.

Her fingers and toes were numb. She sat upon a fallen log at the pathside and put her tabi and sandals on, then pulled her arms inside her haori to press cold fingers into the folds beneath her breasts.

The woodsy, level path led to a drum-bridge arching across a river. Beyond this was a stairway made of shale. Each step was a different shape and size, but all were flat; the ascent was easy. At the top, she saw the upper portion of the waterfall rising above tall evergreens. The river came out of those trees, eager for the valleys below. Tomoe did not know how close she might be to the monastery, but at least she was close to some of the men who lived there. She now heard the prayers distinctly, coming from the direction of the waterfall.

Guided by the voices, she found a trail, not so steep as the rarely-used route that she began from, but not so easy as the stairway either. Soon she came to another plateau of trees and ferns. Along the path she saw the abandoned shack of a woodcutter and, later, two statues of Buddhist deities, larger and fiercer than the ones she had come upon before. She bowed to them but did not linger. A creek—the crashing river's smallest conceivable tributary—crossed the trail Tomoe was using. She hopped casually over the narrow strip of clear, rushing water.

Eventually she came to the edge of a clearing and saw the place where the high, narrow waterfall connected with the lower river. A wooden platform had been built overlooking the pool at the base of the waterfall. A group of bonzes and a single priest were there, engaged in earnest praying. The priest was standing; the bonzes were on their knees around him. All rolled beads between their palms, eyes intent upon the glowing peak of the mountain. The yamabushi, unlike the yamahoshi, did not demand that novices shave their heads; so the bonzes as well as the priests had long beards and wild manes of hair. The hair of the priest was longest, and shot with white, and his robes were much heavier. The bonzes were clad in colorful patchwork garments intended for special rituals, and were armed with swords and spears. The priest's spear was longest, barbed, and decorated with strips of colored paper.

They looked magnificent, imposing, and pious. But it struck Tomoe Gozen as slightly humorous that they prayed against the eruption of Kiji-san, never aware of the true source of the crater's continuous glow. The Buddhists respected the celestial abode of the kirin, which was a holy monster, so that they would never approach or molest it as long as it respected their sanctuary as well. Therefore they had never gone up to look inside the mountain, to see what Tomoe Gozen intended to fetch.

As she watched the yamabushi in their serious endeavor, she began to think it a bad idea to let them know her intentions. If they knew she meant to visit the forbidden crater, they might hold her back, certain Kiji-san's wrath would be the result of her trying to injure the kirin. And certainly they would not want to accept the news that they had prayed these many generations to a volcano not really active; for Tomoe knew Buddhists to be stubborn in their beliefs.

There was the other chant, highly pitched, coming from elsewhere, but Tomoe could not at first locate its point of origin. The sutra they performed was not the same as the bonzes and the priest, but it was in harmony with it. Her keen ear located the source, and she was surprised. They were not girls but pretty boys, dressed in white, made to stand on a ledge beneath the frigid waters of the falls. The cold deluge struck the heads of these temple pages, flattened their youthful locks, rolled down their shoulders, and caused their white garments to cling to nubile, shapely bodies. They stood in an orderly group, undaunted, praying fervently that their suffering would appease the mountain for another night.

Tomoe did not interfere with the rites, but found a place to sit, trying to be warm and thinking how much more terrible the cold must be for the stalwart boys. They would become stout monks, and someday priests . . . if they did not die first.

When the ritual was done, the soaking pages came out from under the falls, revealing no discomfort, and joined their elders on the platform overlooking the pool. Together they faced the glowing mountain peak, and bowed. Then the entire procession retired along the path which would bring them near the place where Tomoe was sitting. She had willfully kept from their sight this whole while, planning to join them after their services were complete, and go with them to their monastery. However, a sudden plan came into her mind, which caused her to scuttle into the woods and keep low, letting the group of pages, bonzes, and priest pass without having detected her.

Her husband Yoshinake was still in doubt that the yamabushi and yamahoshi would leave their retreat to fight side-by-side in the Imperial City. The yamabushi, in addition to despising their rival sect, also took seriously their responsibilities in praying Mount Kiji into nightly silence. It occurred to Tomoe that if Kiji-san were to cease its threatening glow, the yamabushi would take this as a good omen, that the mountain intended to be calm especially so Her worshippers could aid the Knight of Kiso.

"It is not nice to mislead them like that," Tomoe said to herself, coming back to the path and looking in the direction they had gone. But some of the cleverness of her husband had rubbed off; she could not resist the plan. She would fetch the Golden Naginata *before* visiting the monastery, and it would be doubly easy to acquire their final agreement, when they perceived Kiji-san was quiet in honor of Tomoe's request.

It meant no comfortable quarters tonight, and it would not be possible to climb the cliffs to the crater by darkness. On the last stretch of path leading to the base of the waterfall, she had seen a woodcutter's shack, abandoned and broken in. She hurried back to this place and was pleased to find a cracked hibachi left there, in which she struck a fire and prepared herself for the night.

About the Hour of the Ox she was awakened by an icy rain and leaks coming in, so she built the fire up again. The rain sounded like a child's crying, reminding her for some reason of Koshi, although Koshi never cried. The rain increased, becoming the sound of a thousand children crying, and

Tomoe was given to thoughts of the Dry River in Emma's Hell, where the ghosts of children lived, and played, and were tortured.

The shadows were so cold and black that the fire wouldn't penetrate the corners of the dwelling. Tomoe began to imagine the place haunted. She had always been taught that by talking politely to ghosts, they would be less inclined to cause harm. She sat on her knees by the glowing hibachi and said, "If you are the spirit of Okio, take heart that I will visit you in a couple more days, and you can make your feelings known to me. If you are the spirit of someone else, please tell my friend Ushii Yakushiji that I am bringing him a gift, and will not try to make him leave eternal life in Hell if it is his wish to stay there." She bowed her head to one dark corner and then another. She said, "I am grateful for the courtesy of your house." The rain pelted the roof as she offered other platitudes. Time passed and she was still leery of going to sleep. A wind hissed through the cracks of the structure, and the dwelling shook throughout. The main central beam cried out in a voice which made Tomoe fall suddenly silent, speaking to the ghosts no more.

The sound had been familiar and yet it couldn't have been. The creaking wood reminded her of her mother's painful moans at her moment of dying. The hiss of wind through the walls was like her father when he was angry. In a moment, Tomoe found herself calling out,

"Father? Mother?"

Struck by sudden sadness, Tomoe dropped to her hands and bowed head upon the packed-earth floor. In the distance, she heard a temple bell ringing ominously behind the sound of rain, scaring the ghosts of the mountainside away. Tomoe looked up quickly and cried out, "Forgive the weakness of my filial piety! I have made amends to you and wed the Knight of Kiso as you wished, and have been a good wife to him. Rest happily father! Rest happily mother!"

She awoke with sun shining through the cracks of the poor house. She was not certain any of this had happened.

Above the final line of evergreens there was only snow and

rock. The peak of Kiji-san seemed close enough to touch, but this was an illusion of the clear air. She climbed the whole of the morning, Amaterasu high above her head by the time she came within arm's reach of the top. The route had not been as steep as she feared, but she was weary from the cold and the thinness of the air. Kiji-san and her twin, visible to the right, were not the largest mounts of the Karuga range. From her lofty view, Tomoe saw the range bend away in two directions, and she saw dozens of peaks higher than the easy one she had challenged. Yet the Twins were the most perfectly formed and conical of them all. Tomoe Gozen knew that she had come to a special and holy place.

Through the hours of her climb, a sweet, whispering, feminine voice had talked directly into Tomoe's mind, but the words were senseless and baffling. Now she rested, listening closely with her mind, certain that whatever communicated in this way would clarify itself if the listener would only open her mind completely. It was difficult for Tomoe to do this, for she was not certain such a voice should be trusted, and her leeriness was blocking the mind-sound.

As she squatted beneath the ledge of the crater, Tomoe Gozen unsheathed her sword, which was the sword of Madoka Kawayama, and breathed her foggy breath on the shining steel of it. Then she raised the blade above the ledge and used it as a mirror. Even fogged, the brightness of the Golden Naginata's reflection was hard on Tomoe's eyes. The naginata sat in a socket in the very center of the crater, with a constant flow of energy radiating from the upthrust blade. Tomoe lowered her sword, sheathed it, and waited for the spots in front of her vision to fade. For a while, she did not move, but listened more intensely to the voice inside her head. At last the message was clear: *Do not come to my domain*. It was the kirin, the holy monster, warning her away, as it must have done to yamabushi in the past, negating their curiosity.

"I must come," said Tomoe, her back to the outer rim of the crater.

Not to my domain.

"Yes, to yours."

Wendy Adrian Shultz

Not to mine.

"I cannot be stopped."

The kirin will stop you.

"We will see."

She removed the parcel from her obi, the parcel which was the length of a shortsword and twice as thick. She unwrapped it, removed the shaku first and replaced it in her obi, near the knot in back to keep it out of the way. The sheath was more important on this part of her mission. She placed it through her obi, but in front where she could snatch it to encase the magic weapon. The cloth which had wrapped the two objects throughout her journey was of the most immediate importance: it would serve as blindfold.

Tomoe hesitated about tying the cloth around her eyes.

"Kirin," she said, speaking softly but certain the holy monster would hear. "Let me see you once before I'm blind."

Blind. Blind.

"Let me see you."

Don't come to my domain.

"That part is settled. I would see you so I know what I must fight."

She withdrew the sword again, held it up so that she could see into the bright crater, but at an angle which would not reflect the Golden Naginata's terrible light. The shining clouds overhead were descending into the crater, falling in a swirl of mist, coalescing into the form of the monster. The kirin slowly became solid, its fierce white eyes looking directly at Tomoe's upheld sword, and into Tomoe's eyes.

The kirin's neck was longer than its whole body, and the body was that of a splendid, powerful deer, larger than a horse. Its split hooves opened and closed like iron vises. From its forehead three spikes protruded, the central one bending backward. Its muzzle was full of huge, round teeth. The exceedingly long neck was fully maned; and some otherworldly wind, which Tomoe could not personally feel, caused the mane magically to dance and sparkle. The fur of the beast was mottled red on orange, startling in its fiery brightness.

"The kirin is beautiful," said Tomoe, and the gentle but adamant voice replied,

Kirin is fierce.

The monster began to dissipate. Tomoe held her sword aloft, watching the kirin until the last possible moment, and was sad when it was gone. When it had vanished into colorful mists, Tomoe sheathed her sword, and tied the scarf around her eyes.

She climbed into the crater.

No further, warned the soft voice. *Go back.*

"I am resolved!" Tomoe shouted, running blindly over the flat ground of the crater's interior. She had memorized the position of every rock along the way and so was able to dodge obstacles although unable to see them through the cloth. She made it halfway to the upright weapon when a swirling mist threw her to one side. She was not sure how far she had been tossed from her intended route.

So it must be, the kirin's voice said sadly, and Tomoe envisioned in her mind's eye how the creature coalesced again. She sensed it becoming more tangible, knew that in a moment it would be solid and attack. She turned her blindfolded face until, even through the cloth, she could see the bright light of the Golden Naginata like a half-moon behind gauzy clouds. Immediately, she was on her feet and running toward it. She no longer knew where the obstacles were and so caught her foot in a depression; she went sprawling into a foolish posture. The kirin roared tigerishly and stomped the ground with its iron-hard hooves. Tomoe rolled away from the place where the hooves stomped, and carved upward with her sword, striking the neck to small avail. Common steel could not cut any part of the kirin.

Tomoe ignored the feminine laughter which answered her feeble attack. That laughter might have unnerved another. She lunged toward the handle beneath the light, pulled upward so that the Golden Naginata was in her hands. She now stood with the long-handled weapon above her head, its balde pointing toward the kirin. Its snaky neck moved right and left trying to find an entrance to bite Tomoe; but the samurai's senses were at their keenest, and the blade of the naginata was able to follow the kirin's motions.

I cannot be killed, the voice of the kirin whispered in Tomoe's mind.

"But you can be injured," Tomoe countered, and leapt toward the sound of the kirin's breath. It snaked its neck backward, the blade passing between its jaws. It made again the sound of quiet laughter, which Tomoe heard both inside her head and in the ordinary way, with her ears. She leapt at the sound of laughter, and the kirin was forced to give ground. Tomoe pressed the attack, but the kirin had tricked her into doing this. It grabbed the upper part of the naginata's handle below the blade and tore it from Tomoe's grasp! Again, the laughter. Tomoe was surprised, but more angered than upset, and she surprised the kirin in turn. She leapt blindly for its head, and it could not bite her without letting go of the naginata. She clung to the monster's gorgeous mane which was softer than silk and hundreds of times stronger. She was lifted up and up and shaken madly, but would not let go of her grip.

One hand knotted in the mane, Tomoe grasped with her other hand until she caught hold of the bottom part of the naginata's handle. She hung on while the kirin threw its neck around and tried to make her let go of mane, or naginata, or both. She did let go of the mane, only to hang from the naginata with both hands. The huge molars of the kirin were occupied on the handle so that Tomoe could be close to the mouth and not fear being bitten.

A split hoof of iron tried to kick at her, but the creature was not good at kicking toward its own face. Tomoe rolled over the handle of the naginata as though it were a mounted exercise bar, and with her sandaled foot, gave the kirin a blow to one huge eye. It roared a response, no longer laughing, opening its jaw in complaint. Tomoe landed on her feet, the Golden Naginata ready.

She wheeled around, sweeping with the weapon, but the kirin reared and an iron hoof kicked the side of the blade. Tomoe listened for every coil of neck, every movement of hoof. She knew the kirin was turning about, planning to kick with both rear legs. Logically she should leap backward, but she was not sure what the ground was like, did not know what she might trip over; and her mind was quick enough to suppose the kirin *expected* her to leap backward and fall. Instead, she leapt *forward,* the iron-hoofed legs missing her underneath, and she landed high on the back of the kirin.

You would ride? the feminine voice asked in disbelief.

The naginata was so long that, astride, it was difficult to cut the monster with the blade at handle's length. The kirin bucked like a wild, long-legged horse, twisted its neck to try to bite its rider. Tomoe pressed the butt of the naginata against the kirin's horns, pushed the head back. Then she let herself fall off in such a way that the kirin would think it had been an accident. As it reared to stomp her where she lay upon her back, the Golden Naginata swept quickly upward, catching the kirin in the breast.

Chill blood covered the blade. The kirin cried out in anguish—more for the loss of the treasured weapon than for the pain of any wound—and then returned to mist. Tomoe whipped off her blindfold but not soon enough to see the gorgeous kirin again. She saw only dawn-colored mists. She knew the holy monster would not reappear for a while, not until its wounds were healed.

You have won, said the kirin, and the voice had become sad and sensual, seeming far away. Tomoe heard no more.

She gazed upon the blade of the Golden Naginata, which glowed even through the filter of the kirin's rosy blood. The temper pattern was shaped like lightning, and this lightning-temper shined with a greater radiance than the rest of the blade. Tomoe said to the weapon, as though it were a sentient being, "I will call you *Inazuma-hime*, and we will be friends for a while." Inazuma-hime meant "Princess Lightning," and it seemed an appropriate title. Tomoe turned her face to the cloud-streaked heaven and called out a last time to the kirin, "Do not pine so much for Inazuma! I will return her when your wound has healed and your blood has worn from her metal! Then you may guard your treasure once again!"

Placing the miraculous weapon in the carved, unlacquered

sheath, the light of Inazuma-hime was completely doused; and though the day was not near ending, Tomoe sensed a darkness about the crater which was psychic, a sort of melancholy caused by the light of the Golden Naginata being doused and taken away. Although moved to pity, Tomoe Gozen hardened herself to the temporary theft, and descended toward the yamabushi monastery for her planned meeting.

On the third day after leaving Lost Shrine, Tomoe returned to see Oshina and Koshi. She was greeted on the bridge by the white dog. "How are our friends, Taro?" she asked, and scruffed the dog's big head. The rooster was loose, picking and scratching in a weedy patch of ground. The place seemed cheerier than before, especially in contrast to the severe monastery she had stayed in the previous night.

"Oshina!" Tomoe called. "I have come with a birthday gift for Koshi!"

Oshina appeared in the dark doorway of the shrine-house, wiping hands on the towel which hung from the front of her obi. She bowed and greeted Tomoe and, while as usual the young mother did not smile, Tomoe thought the woman was glad to see her. "I worried for you," said Oshina. "But I have made rice cakes so that we can celebrate your final visit." There was sadness in the promise of the celebration, for it was evident from the beginning that once Tomoe had visited the second monastery in addition to the first, taking Taro with her, neither the samurai nor the friendly dog were liable to come to Lost Shrine anymore. All the same, a small party with good rice cakes sounded like just the thing for Tomoe, who said,

"And to celebrate Koshi's birthday!"

Oshina nodded, and the faintest glimmer of a smile broke her melancholy expression. Tomoe entered the house, leaving the naginata named Inazuma-hime in the outer chamber, and leaving her longsword and sandals there as well. Lanterns lit the main room, and coals burned in a large ceramic pot, making the poor shrine-house modestly comfortable and homey. Koshi was propped up on a wicker back-basket so that he could see the affair, if he could see anything. His dark eyes still did not blink; his expression did not change; he did not turn his head when there was any motion. His little claw-like hands grasped the blanket which was wrapped around him. Oshina went into a dark, adjoining room to get the rice cakes. While she was out, Tomoe sat on her knees beside Koshi and whispered to him,

"You must be brave like your mother. You must return your spirit to your flesh. Life is very hard, I know; but half your blood is that of the Rooster Clan, so you can be as strong as a samurai if you try a little harder." She was going to say more even though Koshi seemed not to hear; but Oshina shuffled into the room with a large tray of rice cakes and pickles made from fernbrake. She sat the tray on the floor in front of Tomoe and Koshi. There was tea for everyone as well.

Tomoe ate with her fingers. "It's good," she said. Oshina broke her cake to feed part of it to Koshi. When food entered his mouth, he began to chew and swallow in a mechanical way. Where his deformed mouth turned down, he tended to dribble as he ate, but Oshina kept his face clean with a towel.

After eating two cakes and accepting Oshina's desire to refill the samurai's teacup, Tomoe remembered, "The gift!" She reached into her baggy sleeve-pocket and came out with a colorful paper ball. "It is not, strictly speaking, a gift from me, but from a wandering temple-clown who was staying in the yamabushi temple while I visited there. He was despondent because the yamabushi are not a sect to warm up to a clown, and no one but me was interested in his juggling. To cheer him up, I told him I would like to buy one of his juggling-balls for a young friend's birthday. He would take no payment, but gave the ball to me freely, saying he made new ones now and then in any case. So this small gift is from the temple-clown more than me."

Oshina took the light, round object in both of her hands, and held it before Koshi's face. "Do you see?" she said to the motionless boy. "The paper has crane-designs on it, Koshi! It means long life and courage!" Oshina smiled most widely now, though tears were in her eyes, and Tomoe Gozen was moved by the mother's happiness.

Then Oshina began to shed her tears for the first time, whether from gladness or sorrow Tomoe was uncertain. The young mother bowed to Tomoe rigorously as she said, "Thank you! Thank you very much!" which was embarrassing to Tomoe in the circumstance. She held Oshina by her shoulders to keep her from bowing anymore. Oshina wiped her eyes and then, turning to the pot of warm coals, dropped Koshi's paper ball within. Almost immediately, it caught fire, and Tomoe looked confused about the destruction of the gift. Oshina said,

"Now the spirit of the ball will find Koshi's spirit in the Dry River of the Hollow Land, where the souls of dead children live." Finally, facing Tomoe in a formal position, hands upon her knees, the composed and again-melancholy mother expressed her gratitude in a few unemotional words. Tomoe rubbed her nose uncomfortably, then drank the rest of her tea, wishing it were saké. "It is nothing," she insisted. "It is less than every child deserves."

The next morning she set out for the yamahoshi retreat on Mount Kuji. The eager dog ran ahead, up the mountain trail, chasing some bird or rodent Tomoe could not see. "Beware of foxes, Taro!" she scolded, laughing at him. They rose above the deciduous woods of the second mountain's base, to the tremendous evergreen forests higher up.

As she went, using the long handle of the Golden Naginata as a staff, Tomoe tried not to remember the contained, unebbing sorrow of Koshi's mother, or the sad state of the boy himself. She reminded herself instead of the good fortune she had had, meeting with yamabushi two days earlier. The *Zasu* or chief abbot had agreed to send the priests in his command, along with as many bonzes as could be rallied from outlying temples, to a village near Kyoto on the date required, where Tomoe Gozen would meet them and serve as their general. In addition, a particularly strong group of warrior-monks from a temple in the hills above Kyoto would be sent in advance, to give religious authority to Yoshinake's initial take-over. The Zasu further guaranteed that every animosity toward the rival yamahoshi would be set aside for the duration of their mutual service to Kiso Yoshinake. The head of the monastery had noticed that Kiji-san no longer glowed threateningly and, as Tomoe had predicted, this was taken as an omen in Yoshinake's behalf. Today, Tomoe hoped for equal luck dealing with the stubborn yamahoshi.

There was no quick emergency-route up Kuji-san, but neither was the regular path as winding and indirect as that which led to the other mountain's monastery. Tomoe went with long strides and found evidence of monks' activity well before nightfall. Before a grave-marking pole, several sticks of incense had been set in a pot, and none were yet burned more than halfway down.

The evergreens were extraordinarily thick and overhanging, so everything had a dark, ghostly appearance even in the day. Here and there among the trees, there were small dwellings whose doors were shut; but through wooden bars Tomoe could see that they housed individual Bodhisattvas or similar deities and relics. From within these dwellings she heard the murmurings of prayers, but did not see the bonzes. She proceeded along shadowy paths and up mossy stairways, wary of every dark place, as though expecting a mountain oni to leap out at any time.

It should not be dusk yet, but it was. The monastery was apparently situated in such a place that, during this season, the sun passed behind Kuji-san early in the day. Taro stayed close to Tomoe, as though he, too, worried about the forest's eeriness, and would be near to protect his mistress without delay.

Further up the way, acolytes with lanterns twinkling between the trees were going in a slow procession. They had silk cloths over their heads and were humming wordlessly as they went.

"Samurai!"

Taro yelped and Tomoe looked back abruptly. She saw a bonze standing lower on the stairway, a coronet upon his shaven head, his rosary dangling from one hand, a pole-axe in his other. He was not in a threatening posture, but Tomoe was leery of him, for she was unused to the idea of someone stealthy enough to come up behind her unheard.

"Did I startle you?" he asked. "I apologize."

He had a pleasant, handsome visage, and was young. Tomoe's mistrust eased away. She said, "I am Tomoe Gozen of Heida, come for the final decision about my husband's petition."

"My Buddhist name is Hagi-o," said the bonze, bowing. "I know little of the temple's politics, so cannot personally reply to you. Unfortunately, our Zasu has died in the night, and there are only a few novices such as myself guarding the premises, while those in authority are deep in mourning, meditation, and prayer. I do not know if anyone can speak with you tonight."

"I hope some meeting can be arranged," she insisted. "There are other matters as well, each needing timely consideration."

The young bonze led Tomoe to the monastery and through its gates. The place was situated on a bluff which made it almost impervious to attack, and was so hemmed in by trees that it was nearly impossible to see from any distance. Beyond the gate were a number of paths. She followed through areas not much less wild than the forest itself, then by several small vegetable gardens in which no one had tilled that day. She was taken past the chapel which stood hunched against the rear wall of the huge, enclosed grounds, coming to a long, low building with almost no lanterns lit within. Taro was made to sit outside. The bonze lit one lantern for the room Tomoe was brought to. He said, "You may stay here for the night. Perhaps tomorrow someone will be able to see you."

The bonze started to leave, but Tomoe made a disgruntled noise. She said, "There must be someone I can impose upon at once. Forgive my insisting, but how could I sleep tonight? The Zasu I came to meet has died; I do not even know who has taken his place. The Knight of Kiso has made certain arrangements previously. How does this untimely parting from the world influence past negotiations?"

"I know nothing of these matters," the bonze said, looking upset that she would put him in such a position. "We do not ourselves know who next will master the temple."

"Another matter, then," said Tomoe more calmly, taking the shaku from her obi. The bonze recognized it as soon as she removed the cloth. He exclaimed,

"That belonged to Shindo!" His expression at first looked puzzled. Then realization etched sorrow on his brow. "Has Shindo died also?"

"He asked me to bring this shaku to his fight-instructor, to apologize in Shindo's name for not returning as he had promised."

Young Hagi-o looked close to tears; and he made his handsome face quite ugly in his effort to hold back from crying. Tomoe could well imagine that there were not more than two such sensitive men in a place as severe as this, so that Hagi-o and Shindo would therefore have been close friends.

"It's been a sad day," said Hagi-o. "Please wait here for a little while and I will see who is available."

Tomoe was left alone in the quiet, dimly lit interior. The paper windows were as thin as the filament of an egg, through which she was able to trace the rising of the moon. A long time passed and, to calm her impatience, Tomoe watched the shadows on the rice-paper doors. The moon was a brilliant painter, making a naked branch into a silhouette against the paper. Tomoe sat on her knees, looking up; she looked at the seeming-painting. A breeze passed through the temple yards, and so the moon's brush-strokes were caused to shake.

Some insect, in the warmth and light of a garden's lantern, did not know it was time to sleep, and so was singing.

For all its austerity, it was a beautiful place, Tomoe realized; even if it were haunted, she would think the same.

The door behind her slid open. Hagi-o had returned so quietly that once again Tomoe had not heard him coming. "Shindo's instructor, Makine Hẹi, who I have told about the shaku, would like to receive it from you himself, as was Shindo's desire."

She followed Hagi-o past the main chapel, on the further side of which was a large building containing the dojo where bonzes were given martial training. It was dark within, and their shuffling footsteps echoed in the instruction hall.

At the far end of the gymnasium was a raised platform on which a huge, heavy-bodied priest sat facing a reliquary. His wild mane covered broad shoulders and hung far down his back. He was praying to the funeral tablet inside the reliquary while incense trailed from the bowl in front of it. The bonze waited until the priest had offered a sutra for every bead of his rosary, and then said,

"Instructor. I have brought her as you said."

Tomoe approached the platform and sat on her knees before it. The bonze backed out of the dojo and shuffled to his post of guarding the grounds this night. Outside, Taro whined a little. "Sohei," said Tomoe, addressing him by the respectful title for soldier-clergy. "Officially I am here about this monastery's allegiance to the Knight of Kiso. Unofficially I am here about the Gate to Hell, through which I petition entrance for a cause. Most personally, I am here about bonze Shindo, who performed the wedding ceremony for Yoshinake and myself."

The priest stood, still facing the reliquary, and bowed to the funeral tablet therein. Then he turned around to see Tomoe Gozen, but stood so much in shadow that Tomoe could not see his features. For an uncomfortable length of time, he stood there, a mountainous mountain-priest, his dark robes and rosary and shortsword and personal bulk making him a frightful, ghostly shape. Then he stepped down from the platform and approached the samurai, coming not too close before he got down on his knees as she. Now his face was visible, long-bearded and thick-browed and gloomy to extreme. Tomoe looked startled. Even with his hair long and face fully bearded, she recognized him. She exclaimed, "Goro!" for it was her lost friend Goro Maki.

"That is not my name anymore," his resonant, measured voice explained. "I am Makine Hei, chief instructor of the temple, and after special services tomorrow, head priest as well."

"Delightful news!" exclaimed Tomoe, but caught herself, for it was a sorrowful occasion as well, the previous Zasu having died. But she and Goro were old friends. She could be honest with him, and said softly, "There were doubts that the yamahoshi would ride with the rival yamabushi into battle. Now I see there is no more need for concern."

Makine Hei did not reply, nor alter his severe expression.

Tomoe regained her natural composure, for she had bad news to offer. She held out the shaku and said, "This was the head of a staff belonging to a bonze whom you instructed . . ."

"I know it," said Makine Hei, more quickly than he usually spoke. "It was forged in this temple and no two are the same. How have you come by so personal a treasure?"

"It was Shindo's last request," said Tomoe, halting before adding, "He was my friend, but it became necessary that he die. He agreed to it, but wanted to send his apology to you, for he had promised to return when . . . when . . ." Goro—or Makine Hei—made it difficult to continue. He scowled with so dark an expression that Tomoe almost regretted placing her longsword and Inazuma-hime in the outer room. She must imagine things, though, for this was her old friend.

"Shindo was a pious man, and innocent of bad feeling," said Makine Hei. "Who would require him to die?"

Tomoe could barely hide her shame. "My own Lord Kiso asked that I behead him, because of things he knew and which must be kept secret."

A rumbling sound rose from Makine Hei's chest as Tomoe placed the shaku on the floor and slid it halfway to him. Makine Hei reached forth and pulled the object to himself, then lifted it, then looked at it on all sides, its rings rattling faintly. The corners of his mouth were turned down, his brow knit tightly. He spoke to the shaku, saying, "*Ahu*," which meant stupid fellow, "I told you your soft heart would make you die."

Makine Hei stood in a flourish of long sleeves and robe, so quickly that Tomoe nearly winced from the threat of that motion, although not showing this feeling. But the huge priest merely turned toward the platform and went again to the reliquary and sat the shaku in front of it. Then, upon his knees, he picked up a tiny mallet and struck the bronze incense bowl so that it gave a high, pure, sustained note. Then he called angrily, "Shindo! How dare you seek forgiveness from me in this way! Did you not know that I am a man without a single heir? Did you not know I planned to adopt you as my son? How can I forgive you now!"

He stood in another angry flourish and went to the edge of the stage, looking down at Tomoe where she sat stolid but uncomfortable.

"You say you brought the shaku as a favor," said Makine Hei, "but I think you did it as a boast! How clever you must think yourself, strong as you are, stronger than Makine Hei's prize pupil!"

"You are too harsh!" Tomoe was injured by such words.

"It is impossible that the yamahoshi would aid the Knight of Kiso now! Do you not know that I have already been your own worst enemy? I am less *Sohei* than *Shugenza*!"

Now Tomoe's veneer of calmness was undone. She reared as far as she could without falling backward from her knees, for Shugenza meant "man or men of magic" and so Makine Hei claimed to be more sorcerer than fighting priest. She said,

"Bonze Shindo told me that the yamahoshi do not use evil magic, but seek to destroy it, or hold it inside Hell!"

"I am the exception!" the big man on the shadowy stage exclaimed.

It made awful sense to Tomoe, who felt stupid not to have seen what Goro Maki's nature had become. The yamahoshi committed their lives to understanding enough of supernatural evil that they could do it battle; but a truly bitter man could use this knowledge differently, to *become* part of the things others sought to defeat.

"It was you, then," said Tomoe Gozen, "who sent Tsuki Izutsu against me, against her very will!"

"It was I," Makine Hei admitted. "Many years ago you killed a warlord who was my master. It was my desire to avenge him by killing you before joining him through *junshi*. But my master's daughter loved you too well and refused me first the privilege of revenge, and then the privilege of going to Lord Shigeno by 'following-after suicide.' Don't mistake my feelings! I am not a bitter man and do not act for selfish reasons! I am pleased to live a retired life, and have learned that those warriors who seek great notice are weak-minded and deserve to be chastised. You gained fame after a battle that caused me ruin, although it was I and not you who behaved in accordance with the Way. You have merited punishment for a long time! I am the Fist of Buddha who will crush the evil pride from Tomoe Gozen!"

Saying this, Makine Hei leapt upon the floor of the dojo to strike Tomoe with the fist which clenched the rosary. Tomoe somersaulted backward and came up to a crouch, her shortsword drawn and slashing upward. The priest's rosary was clipped. Beads scattered and rolled noisily across the floor.

Makine Hei stood unmoving, a few beads left in his outstretched fist. Tomoe was equally still, a statue of a warrior crouched with shortsword held upward in one hand.

"Shugenza!" she addressed. "You cannot whisper magic charms against me inside the temple grounds, and you cannot punish me while I am armed and strong. Give up your resolution now!"

The other motionless figure answered, "My punishment is more subtle than fighting you at once. When I sent the oni devil into hell to fetch back the spirit of your friend Tsuki Izutsu, the soul of the oni was irrevocably bound to that of the nun; neither can survive without the other after their experience. Through the oni, I can control the nun, who has gained magic powers because of the additional possession of the Naruka she met while dead. She is the first instrument of my torture, for you must either kill your friend, or let her kill you; and you are punished in either event. The second instrument of my torture is a woman warrior like yourself, upon whom I have visited the unloosening desire to meet you in battle. Killing her will be the same as seppuku, for she thinks and acts as you did at that age. I have other punishments in mind, too! When your misery is its most profound, and you are the most forlorn, only then will I forgive your excessive pride, and I will come to you to fight, to free you from worldly agony, to show you my occult *kiaijutsu,* the art of killing with the voice!''

They glared at one another in the dark room for long moments of silence. Tomoe Gozen thought of many things to say, but could not make herself say any of them. She did not think Makine Hei understood his own motivations, and fooled himself if he believed he held no bitterness. Perhaps his retirement had caused him to go mad, for it was true he could have been a famous samurai; if so, then indeed Tomoe Gozen must confess some degree of guilt regarding his ruin. More likely, he had pursued the yamahoshi tenets without a clear mind and, in confronting evil to destroy it, had been destroyed instead. In whatever case, he was a terrifying foe to have.

Makine Hei lowered his fist and Tomoe Gozen relaxed her poised shortsword. The priest said, ''You seek the Gate of Hell? As the abbot has died, I am now the guardian! I will show you gladly, for it will be interesting to see if you can return without the help of the yamahoshi. Or will you change your mind about this excursion, knowing there is none to help you come out from the Hollow Land again?''

''I am resolved,'' said Tomoe Gozen. She sheathed her shortsword. ''I will have my weapons and a Shinto dog. What use the yamahoshi?''

''Bravely said,'' Makine Hei replied sarcastically. ''I am honored to point the way.''

In the outer room, she took up her longsword and placed it in her obi next to the short one. She took the Golden Naginata in her left hand, and stepped out into the night, following Makine Hei through the dark grounds. Taro growled at the big priest, with a voice as deep and disapproving as Makine Hei's. ''Be still, Taro,'' said Tomoe. ''Stay close to me.'' Taro lowered his head, looking properly chastened. Directly, they came to a low-walled garden of large stones arranged on small bits of gravel, and no plants at all. A group of young novices were called and ordered to push one big stone from its position, which requirement made them all look fretful and afraid, but they obeyed. The critically balanced boulder was heaved against by the young men until it leaned away from the black pit it covered. Taro sniffed near the hole, and Tomoe gazed calmly. Makine Hei took a lantern from one of the boys and held it out so that Tomoe could see there was a moist stairway leading down. He said,

"You will go first through the Land of Roots of the Hollow Land, where there is a dry river bed. A difficult trail will lead eventually to the Land of Gloom. The river is not dry in all places. If you drink from it, you will die at once. Should you find a way to escape, I will be surprised; if you do not, then I will put aside my animosity and judge you sufficiently castigated, and pray for your soul thereafter."

"You are generous," said Tomoe Gozen, descending the slippery stairwell. Taro was at her side, his tail tucked between his legs and his ears pressed flat. She turned around at the bottom of the steps and looked up from the pit, seeing the severe priest flanked by youngsters with worried faces. Then Makine Hei reached across the opening with both hands and, with his own great strength, pulled the boulder back with a thump which sounded all too final.

Darkness reigned with absolute tyranny.

There was no sound but that of a panting dog and the breathing of a samurai. The darkness was so total that Tomoe Gozen feared to take a single step, certain that she was falling into some bottomless hole. Slowly, she ran her hand up the shaft of the Golden Naginata and removed the carved scabbard from the blade. Now a ruddy, golden light revealed her habitat, including, truly enough, the black well into which she might have stepped. Of the stairway she had just descended, there was no evidence; of the boulder-covered hole, she could see no mark above. All around her were roots which obscured her view entirely. These roots hung down from the crust of the world and some were big as trees while others fine as hairs. They were like horrid, grasping appendages. There was a path which wound amidst these roots; and it was easy enough to follow by the light of Inazuma-hime.

As she went down the path in search of the dry riverbed,

she began to notice moving stars of light among the roots. These were the eyes of lizards reflecting the light of Inazuma-hime. Lizards such as these Tomoe Gozen had never seen on the face of Naipon, nor suspected lived below. They were miniscule and winged, flitting among the roots, grabbing hold of them here and there, watching her and Taro with round, malevolent eyes.

"You are too small to hurt us!" Tomoe shouted, and Taro barked at them as well. The lizards scattered away like a frightened flock of birds.

A footfall sounded behind, causing Tomoe Gozen to wheel about, but she saw nothing in the Golden Naginata's light. "Ushii?" she whispered, but no reply was forthcoming. Taro whined uncomfortably, wagged his tail with slow uncertainty, and looked at Tomoe.

The path grew narrower so that, in time, it was necessary to carve a better route. When Inazuma-hime cut a root, it would fall onto the ground and writhe like a dying serpent, then fade away to mist as though it had been illusion. After what seemed a very long time, Tomoe could make out no path whatsoever, and had to cut her way through every step. "I think we're lost already," she said to Taro. "Or we would have found the riverbed by now." Taro gave a short bark of reply, looking intensely in a direction Tomoe had not been leading them. His ears stood straight and rigid, and Tomoe knew that a dog's hearing was better than her own. Feeling somewhat relieved by the demon-dispelling swish of Taro's happy tail, she began to cut a path for herself and him, in the direction he had indicated.

Before much longer, she heard what Taro had noticed first. It was the sound of children singing. The song was a simple one, performed by a large number of tiny voices which became more and more distinct as the dog and the samurai came nearer. The words went, "Bless our mothers, bless our fathers, bless our brothers and sisters; keep them happy in the living world, where we no longer stay." Although the words were a bit sad, the sweet tune was pleasant, and hardly what Tomoe had expected to hear in the Land of Roots.

The next moment, she had broken out of the root-woods

Wendy Adrian Shultz

and stood abruptly on the bank of a waterless river. Here, there was a dreary, vague, weird light which hung in the air like vapor. But Tomoe kept her naginata bared anyway, against danger if not against black night.

Playing among the pebbles of the dry river were the singing children. Their numbers seemed to go in both directions for infinity. It was sad to see these shades of children, whose bodies were ill-clad or naked, and transparent to Tomoe's vision. They had no fireplaces to keep them warm, no toys to make them happy, no house to live inside, and no parents to give them love. The banks of the dry river were the only walls they had, the only things to define their wretched home.

The riverbed was covered with smooth pebbles and rocks, which made it impossible to walk in zori or geta. So the children went about their business with sore and naked feet. Their business consisted of more than their sweet singing. The smooth rocks served as surrogate toys, and they built little drum-towers with these, in honor of their lost parents. They also built little cribs for the youngest children. The largest children and the strongest cared for those who were too young to walk or who came into Hell crippled for some reason.

Despite the sadness of their spare and useless existence, they were remarkably cheerful children. As Tomoe stood on the bank watching them, she realized their brave, stout hearts found strength and satisfaction by singing their prayers of good fortune for their families. "Spare mother, father, brother, sister the misfortune of such an existence as ours!" sang the children, sincere in their desire to suffer for a filial cause, to keep others of their clans from having to retire to some part of the Hollow Land when they died.

They were proud of their work, too, for the rock-pile pagodas were precious to see. It was difficult to make the pagodas stand, because the rocks were round and would not stack easily. So the children struggled for success. Tomoe shook her head, unable to accept the Buddhist way of life and death, unable to understand why, if Buddhas were so merciful, children had to come to Hell, even when their lives in Naipon were too brief for them to have sinned.

Tomoe had yet to see the worst of these poor spirits' torment. Far down the dry river there was a commotion and what looked to be a smoky cloud. In that direction, children were crying and screaming. Tomoe watched in horror as the cloud came up the river. Soon she could see that it was a dusty storm of three-eyed devils not much larger than the children, but much stronger. They beat the children with whips and flails, knocking over the pagodas they strove so hard to build. "This is too much!" said Tomoe. The small bit of usefulness and pride the children were able to create among themselves in this bleak place were scattered and spoiled by the laughing, hideous devils. The innocent were smitten. Those who could run went in every direction to no avail, sometimes trying to carry the infants who could not walk. Those infants left behind in stone-built cradles had their beds kicked apart, and their tiny bodies rolled and dashed upon the rocky ground.

Tomoe Gozen could not hold back. She leapt into the riverbed with her Golden Naginata twirling. The smoky devils could not be cut into pieces, for they were intangible beings; yet the shining metal of Tomoe's supernatural weapon sent them squealing out of the riverbed to hide among the roots. Taro tore among the devils, too, and while his long white teeth could not hold them, they feared his jaws just the same, for he was a Shinto dog and they were Buddhist monsters. They could feel the pain of the dog's dislike.

When the devils were gone, Tomoe shouted, "Do not torment these children for a long time! Or I will come back and fight you!" The children began to dust themselves off, collect their friends, and take their places in order to rebuild their ruined pagodas, as they had done a thousand times before. They began to sing for the safety of their families, and things returned to their previous order. A child's translucent hand passed over Taro's fur, but not a hair was moved by that ghostly stroke, and the child, feeling nothing on his hand, went away looking sober.

There was only one child who had seemed unaffected by the horror, who neither took part in the building of pagodas, nor was sent fleeing by the smoky three-eyed devils. This child was particularly beautiful and richly clad. He sat on a high, smooth boulder near the further bank of the waterless river. In the beautiful boy's hand was a paper ball on which a crane-design was printed, so Tomoe recognized him as Koshi, although his spirit was so unlike his mortal flesh.

Koshi raised his child-perfect face to Tomoe, his round face with dark, slanting eyes, and smiled at her so charmingly that her heart was won. He said, "Mother sent this ball to me, saying it was from a strong samurai. Is that you? I have waited here to guide you, because you do not know your way around the Hollow Land and will get lost many times and have many problems without some help."

Saying this, Koshi leapt into the air and floated gently to Taro's back. Taro did not mind, for the transparent child was weightless.

"There's a trail beside the riverbed," said Koshi, pointing to a stack of rocks which made a stair. "We will go that route, in search of Okio's gaki spirit."

Taro went up the steps first, Koshi riding on his back. As Tomoe followed, she asked, "How do you know about Okio?"

"It's a famous tale in Hell!" said Koshi, sounding impressed with it himself. "His family used to live nearby, in a hut hidden among the roots. But Okio heard you were coming, and so took his family to the lowest part of the Hollow Land, to make it hard for you to reach him. The devil Naruka is down there, and has promised Okio not to let you get near enough to see him."

"Do you know of Ushii Yakushiji, too?"

"The flesh of him travels all around in Hell!" exclaimed Koshi. "But I am not sure he has a spirit. I haven't seen him in a while, so you don't have to worry." But Tomoe worried anyway. She had felt a stealthy follower from the first, and sensed who it might be.

Koshi, Taro, and Tomoe went down and down the path. Koshi indicated certain tricky bends, keeping Tomoe from being led a wrong direction. After a long time, there were no more children in the riverbed, and in fact the bed had become swampy and overgrown with pale ginkgo trees. The fan-shaped leaves of the trees swayed and made a wind, but it was not the wind which caused the leaves to sway. "We won't go in there," said Koshi. "There are too many snakes, bigger than you have probably seen."

Tomoe thought over this advice and replied, "I would like not to see them now." She followed Taro and his rider. The swamp gave out after another stretch of time, becoming a creek of crystal water. The creek became wider as they progressed, until it was a genuine river running down from the Land of Roots toward the Land of Gloom. The river bottom was pink and smooth, which made Tomoe wonder, but she said nothing, and only followed.

"The path ends soon," said Koshi, "and the river runs between two high cliffs. You must not look up the cliffs, or tiny devils will leap through the pupils of your eyes and eat your brains. You may not think it very likely, but please consider my advice useful."

"I will believe you," said Tomoe.

"We must walk along the shallows of the river. If you do not slip into the middle, you needn't worry about drowning or being poisoned."

Where the path ended, they climbed into the shallows and began the long trek between faces of two cliffs. The cliffs may have risen into eternity; Tomoe never looked up to find out. "Step most carefully," warned Koshi, who still rode on Taro's back as Taro swam alongside Tomoe. "We are walking on *Jishin-uwo* the Earthquake Fish, and if we wake him up, he will thrash around and cause catastrophe on Naipon above."

Tomoe knew about Jishin-uwo, the unbelievably huge catfish who slept beneath the islands of Naipon. It was worrisome to walk upon him, knowing that one misstep would not merely cause Tomoe to slip into the water to drown or be poisoned, but also annoy Jishin-uwo in such a way that thousands of lives might be lost in the living world when the Earthquake Fish thrashed and the ground above the Hollow Lands cracked and heaved. It was a nervous trip indeed, and all the same, Tomoe began to think it would not be as hard as she had imagined, since she had Koshi as her guide and had so far met no untoward resistance.

As they came to the place where the cliffs ended, Koshi said, "There is only one major obstacle between the Land of Roots and the Land of Gloom, and we must pass it carefully." The water became too turbulent to walk through, so Koshi led them out of the river and along a new path above the banks. The river broke into a fork, the further fork a raging rapids, the nearer one very still. They followed the quiet one until the sound of the other was left behind. Tomoe was surprised to see the water was tinted red. It was a specific shade which any woman of a given age, let alone a woman of war, could recognize at once.

The tinge became darker and darker until the river spilled into a big lake which was the deepest crimson.

"A lake of blood!" exclaimed Tomoe.

"It is the blood of warriors," said Koshi, "seeped down from the places where they died. I should have warned you not to make a loud exclamation like that, for now we have to worry."

The smooth surface of the blood-lake began to bubble near the middle. The bubbles began to move toward the shore. As they came nearer, Tomoe realized they were not bubbles at all, but *kabuto*, or metal war-hats, covered with the lake's thick fluid. The lake became more shallow nearer the shores, so that now she could see the heads of a dozen warriors coming out. Their faces were hidden behind monstrous metal masks, which like the helmets were stained with blood. Then she saw their bloody shoulders and arms, and their stained chests, and their legs. They were knee-deep in the lake of blood, slogging nearer, armed with swords and spears and bows and arrows—and everything about them was bright red.

Tomoe held Inazuma-hime ready, and tried to put herself in front of Taro and Koshi to protect them. But Koshi urged his mount forward as he said, "I can handle them!" When the blood-warriors came out onto the dry ground, leaving red tracks where they trod, Koshi rode Taro straight toward the fierce and frightful monsters. For a weapon, he had only his paper ball, which he held above his head. When he was near enough, he threw the ball amidst those who had risen from the lake.

In their horrific lives beneath the bloody waves, these unnatural warriors never saw anything as pretty as a ball, and so they fell upon one another fighting for possession of the rare thing. Koshi rode Taro back to where Tomoe stood, and Tomoe said, "You have given up your favorite thing."

"It was necessary," said Koshi, revealing no sadness. "You will have to save your strength for later."

They skirted the whole of the bloody lake and went along the red-tinged river on its other side, coming back to the fork once more, and following the clear-though-poisonous rapids to a place where the river became a waterfall larger than Tomoe had ever seen. She looked down into the Land of Gloom, which was a grey featureless plain mottled with moving shadows. It was so far down, and the wall so steep, Tomoe almost despaired of finding a path into that deeper country.

"Look!" said Koshi. "The Vault of Paradise!"

She looked skyward to where the beautiful, transparent child pointed, to the crust of the living world, the ceiling of the Land of Gloom which those of Hell called, incongruously, the Vault of Heaven. Across it in rainbow streaks were many precious metals, and like the Celestial River in Naipon's sky, there sparkled a stream of rare gems. It was as gorgeous a sky as Tomoe could ever have imagined! That all the gold and jade of humankind's desire was found beneath the ground should have been evidence enough that such things originated in Hell, yet Tomoe was startled to realize this, and to understand why these precious stones and metals corrupted the minds of men and women.

"And there!" cried Koshi, swinging his hand elsewhere. There was a cloud beneath the sky-roof and in that cloud were the ever-changing shapes of warriors battling eternally. Koshi named them: "Asuro! They fight for the spoils encrusted above their heads, never understanding that their highest goal is still too low to free them from the Hollow Land. I am told they are mindless killers up there! They are the souls of samurai too greedy and cruel ever to be born again! We are lucky they can never come down from their lofty position."

A path which Tomoe might never have found on her own was indicated by Koshi, who urged Taro off the cliff and onto the narrow route which zigzagged downward, alongside the magnificent waterfall. Once they had climbed over the rim, sound was suddenly muffled, and even the crashing falls made little noise. Tomoe had to speak, to be sure she had a voice! "The Land of Gloom looks less interesting than the Land of Roots," she said, relieved to hear herself. "I see nothing but flat ground and moving shades of grey. But there are no trees or objects to cast those shadows, so it is a curious if ordinary sort of land I see."

"I rarely go into the Land of Gloom myself," said Koshi, "but not because it is so dull. There is more to it than sanity can bear to notice; you should be grateful that the shadows are the only part you see."

A few bits of gravel fell from above, rolling past Tomoe's feet and on down toward Taro and Koshi. She looked back up the path to see what creature might have loosened those few rocks, but saw nothing.

As the bold trio went down the long, steep grade, Tomoe was visited by a sense of *déjà vu*. Suddenly certain she had walked this path before, she exclaimed in a loud voice, "I know this road!"

Koshi did not seem surprised that she would say this. He explained, "It is common for human souls to visit here, when the bodies are tired or sleeping, or when one is near to death, or in some kind of trance. You may have come here in your worst nightmares. Generally, if a spirit comes from a body which sleeps and is not dead, then when the spirit stumbles and falls from the heights, it returns quickly to its flesh, and the living body awakens in terror, never quite striking the ground below."

"I have often awakened with that feeling," Tomoe remembered.

"But you have come here in your body as well as your spirit on this occasion," said Koshi. "If you fall, there is no saving you, no waking."

They went carefully, Taro as sure-footed as Tomoe. Tomoe said, "But if *you* fell, Koshi, that would cause you to awaken at Lost Shrine, where your mother waits."

"You would push me?" asked Koshi, looking back over his shoulder at Tomoe with his eyes big and worried.

"It is not for me to make that choice for you," said Tomoe. "You are a beautiful child in this land your soul has found. If you go home to your flesh, you will be the half-monster once again, with only your mother and a few with gifted vision to know how beautiful you are inside. I can understand that the Hollow Land is no more hellish to you than life in Naipon. But you are the child of a samurai family, and no matter how a samurai may suffer, he must never cry out in agony, he must never give up. Think of your mother who loves you! Think of your lives to come, which may be better for you if only you can live this one through with strength and compassion, and with no thought for yourself."

They continued down the cliffside, Tomoe grasping the wall with one hand to keep her balance. Koshi admitted, "I am guilty of many things, not the least of which is a weakness of filial piety. I sometimes sit on a high rock in the Dry River and listen to the songs the other children sing, and those songs are for their families, not for the salvation of the suffering children themselves. When I see how brave they are, I know that I am the most terrible child of all, that it is true I am half a monster."

"I don't think you are such a monster," Tomoe soothed. "But I think you must consider very carefully your mother's devotion."

Koshi sighed and said, "I cannot leap from the cliffside now, for you would be left without a guide, and this trail might fool you yet if I am gone. Perhaps I will always find a good excuse like that! I am sorry for my mother and love her very much. But it is hard to believe she would be happier if I were with her, for I have caused her much pain by being born. I am sorry for myself as well, and would rather be the most beautiful child in a hellish place than the most hellish child in beautiful Naipon."

They were silent awhile, and careful of every step. At last they came to the bottom of the waterfall, which crashed mutely, and vanished into the thirsty ground. There was no river or anything that Tomoe could see out upon the flat plane. Koshi said, "I do not need to accompany you further. There are no obstacles now, except those which you cannot avoid, and no special landmark to prove your arrival, although arrive you must. The land out there is infinite, but at the same time it is very small; you cannot be lost. Time and distances are distorted, for which reason it is best not to stay long. You will find your way back I am certain, if the Naruka does not kill you as it boasted it would do. I will be waiting here, to lead you back the way we came."

"It may not be necessary to wait," said Tomoe. "I am sure I can find the way now that you have shown me once; and if I forget a turn, Taro will not. I am also not certain if I can return by the same path, to be perfectly frank, for a yamahoshi priest who gave me access to the Hollow Land has promised not to help me out again. In whatever case, your duty has been fulfilled, like the stout boy you are. Now your only concern should be about your mother. I should not lecture you, but a tengu-devil's tribe appointed me protector of demon children, and as you are half-bakemono, I am compelled to say these things. But the decision is yours in the end, like the decision to give up your paper ball. I once heard a Buddhist nun call the soul *tama-shii,* or 'ball wind.' Perhaps the paper ball was symbolic of another thing you must give up: your spirit's vanity. You will be called a monster in Naipon, it is true, but there will be those who love you just the same."

Koshi climbed off Taro's back, and Taro hurried away from the cliff wall to stand by Tomoe Gozen. Koshi said, "I will give every consideration to what you have said."

When they parted, Tomoe was not certain whether or not she had succeeded in the part of her task assigned by Old Uncle Tengu.

The shadows on the ground swirled like the shadows of waves and eddies, but whatever cast them remained on some level beyond Tomoe's vision. That they were ghosts and demons and ghostly things, she was sure. That they watched her passing, more certain still. But they did not make themselves visible, perhaps because the living were as ghosts to the dead and she was frightening to them; perhaps because they would not gladly challenge her Golden Naginata. But some of them must be bolder than the others, for she heard muted laughter and vague threats . . . nothing quite clear enough to understand completely. They were following alongside her and Taro, trailing behind, and dancing in front of her like clowns, jeering and pointing and having a grand party at her expense. At least, these are the sorts of antics she suspected. None of it could be seen. Nothing sprang forth to cause her harm.

The shadows rose and writhed like snaky mists, so it was never possible to see far ahead. When she looked upward, the colorful roof over the sky was hidden by fuzzy greyness. When she looked back the way she came, she could not see the cliffs; but she could find her way back when she needed to do so, for her feet left indentations in the gritty land, and she could follow these . . . if no one erased them.

The loudest sounds were the padding of her and Taro's footfalls. Now and then, she thought she heard the "crunch-crunch" of some additional pair of feet, but could not catch sight of anyone. The ghostly, invisible surroundings did not place any mar upon the ground, so Tomoe realized that if she were being followed by something more tangible than a ghost, it would leave a track similar to those of herself and the Shinto dog.

Suddenly she turned about and strode through the greyness, her Golden Naginata held forward like a lamp as well as for protection against any possible foe; and this quick tactic startled her pursuer, who was bent over busily smudging out his track and hers.

"Ushii!" she challenged, sounding angry. "A dirty trick to erase my trail!"

He jumped up and back, reaching for his sword but not drawing it. His hair hung loose about his face. He snarled. He was dirty and his clothes were tattered. He shouted back,

"I am proud to run errands for Emma, King of Hell! He suggests I keep an eye on you, for he does not like having living flesh marking up the ground. I erase my trail and yours to keep him happy!"

Tomoe said, "Those who dislike samurai are fond of calling all of us dogs. But my companion Taro is less slavish than you! If I see this King you serve, I will spit at his feet, for I have seen his treatment of innocent children, and I am unimpressed with Buddhist justice. Even a dog would not serve him!"

"You cannot know the Way of Emma!" shouted Ushii, angered to hear his master slandered. "Mortals cannot understand the Gods!"

"But you can understand?" asked Tomoe. She was sarcastic. "You can understand because, living here, you are immortal!"

Ushii became petulant. "I know my master is wise and benevolent."

"*Bakè*!" She moved toward him threateningly, but he withdrew. She said, "All you know is pain and madness! But I remember our old friendship and therefore have brought you a present. In exchange, you must shadow me no longer, but go your own way and pursue your own fate!"

"What can you offer me?" said Ushii disinterestedly. "I have a house in the higher country, among the roots. In it are many things. Everything I need."

"You need a healthier spirit!" said Tomoe. "A sword is a samurai's soul, and yours is rusted from neglect. Therefore I will give you this one. My own soul is temporarily invested in the naginata instead, and the soul of the sword I've brought with me belongs to someone other than myself."

She pulled the longsword and sheath from her obi and held these to Ushii Yakushiji.

"It looks nice," said Ushii, whining worse than Taro had ever done, easing forward to see it as a dog might sniff a bone. "Maybe I will accept your present."

"Good. You will be glad to know whose sword it was, and whose spirit resides within it."

"Tell me who," whined Ushii, acting now like a dog

whose head was patted, who had made friends with someone it had barked at before.

"It holds the spirit of your friend and lover Madoka Kawayama, who you slayed on a battlefield before casting your living flesh into Hell!"

Ushii held the sword and sheath, but began to shake the way a nervous dog would. He looked as though he might throw it down, but he was greedy to keep it, too, like a dog not trusting strangers yet eager for a bone. "Madoka?" said Ushii, cocking his head. He held the scabbard in one hand and drew the steel forth to inspect it and, seeing it, fell upon his knees and gazed the harder. "My face does not reflect in the polished steel," said Ushii wonderingly. "But I am not a ghost, and I should have a reflection."

"The sword reflects the soul," said Tomoe, still sounding angry.

"There *is* someone reflected here," said Ushii. "But it is not me. Is it you, Madoka? Do you forgive me for killing you? I have never forgiven myself. I have tormented myself in Hell to make restitution. Why have you never come to visit me before now? Did you love me not so well after all?"

"Ushii," said Tomoe, gentle to him for the first time. "You must get your master to let you go free, so that you can return to the face of the land a proper mortal, and throw yourself upon Madoka's sword. You have no soul left of your own, but his is strong enough to carry you into the next life. Then you can start again."

Ushii did not acknowledge Tomoe, but he must have heard. He asked the sword, "Have you waited for this occasion, Madoka? Have you come to take my life as I took yours? Are you strong enough to bear this soulless man into a better life? I have been immortal for only a few years. Perhaps I am not so addicted to it that I cannot throw eternal life away."

He stood abruptly, still not acknowledging Tomoe, but looking healthier than when Tomoe first found him. His shoulders were no longer hunched, and his eyes were more clear. He still gazed only at the sword as he spoke. "I will help you take revenge against me, Madoka! Then we can be joined in the next life as a single man!"

So saying, Ushii Yakushiji turned and fled into the greyness of the Land of Gloom, leaving a track which might later lead Tomoe to the cliff wall.

Taro had not been around while this was happening. Tomoe looked at the paw-marks on the gritty ground, and followed after the Shinto dog. She heard him barking, though the sound was muffled by the shadows.

"Taro!" called Tomoe, going quickly. The track led her to him soon enough. He stood with long teeth bared, and hackles raised upon his back, glowering into the shadows at something Tomoe could not see. But there was something there, for whatever it was had a voice, and it said in soft, unctuous tones,

"Call the *komanio* off of me." Komanio meant "hideous dog," and despite the fact that Taro was a handsome dog, he would not seem so to a creature of Emma's Hell. Tomoe stroked Taro's back until the hackles lowered, but she did not tell him to cease his careful watch.

"Who are you hiding there? Make yourself visible to me!"

The shadows wavered into a faint form, something like a tree. From behind the tree there stepped a woman dressed in red.

"Tsuki!" exclaimed Tomoe. "Where are your scars? Are you all right?"

She came forward with a pleasant smile, her walking staff held casually. "I have been cured of all deformity," said Tsuki. "We can be friends again."

Taro started to leap at the Buddhist nun, but Tomoe still held him by the hairs at the back of his neck. So busy was she restraining Taro that she did not act swiftly enough when the staff of Tsuki Izutsu swept out and struck the hand which held the Golden Naginata. Tomoe shouted and shook her smarting fingers, letting the weapon fall. Now she saw that Tsuki Izutsu was not cured of her scars at all. In fact, the scars that had previously been on only one side of her face were now on both sides, and Tomoe Gozen had never seen a more hideous woman. Tsuki snarled like a beast, and Taro snarled back.

The weird nun's staff struck Tomoe in the stomach, knocking her backward, further from where the Golden Naginata lay. Taro was free of Tomoe's restraint, and he leapt at the nun's throat, harried her, forced her back before she could deal Tomoe a third blow. Tomoe rolled to her feet, shortsword to hand, and as Taro was knocked away by the monster-Tsuki, Tomoe took his place, and sliced through the weird nun's neck.

Although Tomoe felt the resistance of flesh and bone, by the time her sword passed through the other side of the neck, it was already healed, so the head did not topple off. Tsuki's face twisted into an even more horrible scowl, and she laughed with notes so bass that Tomoe knew it was not the nun's spirit she was fighting, but the Naruka.

The Naruka showed its true shape, which was like a warrior carved in wax and partly melted, so distorted that it hardly looked human. What had looked to be a nun's staff before had become a *konsaibo*, a hardwood and iron cudgel long as a staff. Tomoe ducked a sweeping blow to her head, but Taro was less lucky, smitten in the ribs so hard that he rolled away, yiping. Tomoe hurried to keep the Naruka from striking the dazed dog again, deflecting the konsaibo's next blow with the flat of her shortsword. As Taro began to rise from his side, Tomoe rolled with another blow of the konsaibo so that it did not contact hard enough to smart; and as she rolled, she let loose of her shortsword and snatched the Golden Naginata from where it lay upon the flat ground. She came back to her feet in a ready posture.

"'Inazuma-hime will cut you better!'" she said, and swung her weapon through the Naruka's midsection, severing the monster in two. Strange to say, the monster did not die, for nothing born of Hell is truly living in the first place. Its legs ran one direction; its torso ran another on its hands. The legs and butt rushed Taro, stamping madly. The arms carried the torso toward Tomoe, and though the half-Naruka could no longer swing an iron rod, the sharp teeth snapped fiercely.

Taro grabbed the buttocks of his half of the demon, holding it in snarling jaws, while Tomoe cut the head from the other part's shoulders. Still the parts would not die or give up, so Tomoe used her naginata like a shovel and made a small hole in the ground and dropped the head in there, covering it over with grit. The other pieces could no longer see what they were supposed to do and could not fight effectively. As Tomoe stomped the ground flat where she had buried the head, the torso ran off into the shadows, and the two legs ran another way, and it is possible that neither part of the body ever again met up with its other half.

Tomoe reclaimed her shortsword and placed it in her sheath. Taro shook his body as though he were wet all over. Both of them were bruised by the encounter, but neither one complained. As they backed away from the site of the conflict, Tomoe staggered and Taro yelped, for the floor of a house had appeared beneath their feet so suddenly they almost lost their balance. The floor was covered with fine tatami mats from one side to the other.

A moment later there was a wall. On the wall hung a tall, narrow painting depicting the Fox Goddess, watching a billowing fire. In front of the wall there appeared a lacquered table on which sat a big vase. Another wall appeared, with rice-paper doors; and then there were the other walls as well, with entries to other rooms. Tomoe blinked her eyes in disbelief, and in that blink, there appeared futon bedding rolled out upon the floor. A dead old man and dead old woman were partially wrapped in this bedding, speared while making love.

Tomoe looked into another room and saw the old couple's grandchildren had been slain most brutally. She looked into the next room, expecting to see Okio and his dead wife as well, but somehow she had been fooled into returning to the first room, where the old couple sat up in a polite position and their futon was rolled up and put out of sight. Tomoe looked quickly into the other room once more, but the children were not there. Suddenly, they too sat politely, one to either side of their grandmother and grandfather.

Sitting higher, on a raised part of the floor near the tall, narrow painting, was the swordsmith and his wife, dressed like royalty, their eyebrows shaved off and painted high up on their foreheads so that they looked startled, their teeth dyed black, their hair arranged perfectly. Okio wore his bent swordsmith's hat, but otherwise might have been the Mikado himself, flanked by the august family, so regal did they appear. Seeing that they looked perfect as dolls set out on Girls' Festival Day, Tomoe remarked, "You have not done so badly here," feeling strange to be talking to a family of ghosts. They did not reply, as dolls would not. Now she suddenly noticed that none of them were as pristine in appearance as she had first imagined. For they all had big wounds on their bodies, and their nice clothes were drenched in crimson. "How unfortunate!" she exclaimed stupidly, but still none of them acknowledged her.

Taro watched from beside Tomoe, turning his head one way and then another, as though he, too, were confounded.

Tomoe discovered she was standing on a wet tatami, and the wetness was the fault of blood. Disgusted with her clumsiness, she lifted up one foot, but now the blood was gone. Okio's family had vanished also, while she was looking at her feet. There was only Okio left, and he was noticing Tomoe for the first time. He said, "You have defeated the Naruka who was to keep you from finding me. Why do you pursue me even to the Land of Gloom? I have no more control on you, now that you have retired my sword, and I am daily harried by the sutras of the priests with whom you left the sword I've haunted. Why not leave me be, since you are already free of my influence?"

"I am sorry if I annoy you," said Tomoe, who sat herself upon her knees in a formal posture. Taro lay upon his belly. Both of them looked most beseeching. She said, "My husband Kiso Yoshinake has become an unreasonable man because of you. He even threatens the Mikado. I saw no way but to come and beg you to set him free, to forgive his rash behavior in things past. There is no reason for you to be so cruel and to haunt his sword relentlessly."

"Yoshinake rushes headlong to his fate with open eyes," said the hungry ghost of Okio. "He does this cunningly and with willingness."

"You refuse my request?" asked Tomoe, looking sad.

"What can I refuse? I *might* be willing to forgive you for your part in the slaying of my chosen avengers, for you must obey a master and are not responsible. But there is no reason to say I forgive even you, because you have retired my sword in any case and, being beyond my reach, it no longer matters. Yoshinake can retire his sword of Okio as easily as you have done. My forgiveness is unnecessary."

"He refuses to put the sword aside," said Tomoe. "*You* won't let him give it up. If it were otherwise, I would not risk so much coming into the Hollow Land."

Okio reflected on this a few moments, then said, "I am impressed with your sincerity. But I, too, am resolved. I will think steadily about forgiving you. But, if Yoshinake wants like forgiveness, he must say it to his sword. He must make his feelings known to me. I think that I am being reasonable."

"It would be reasonable," said Tomoe, "if you had not already made him so stubborn."

"You blame his stubbornness on me? So. What else can I tell you? That your trip was wasted? As token of my concern, I will give advice regarding escape from the Hollow Land, but I can promise nothing regarding Yoshinake's fate. Have you any plan for leaving Emma's Hell? I do not think the yamahoshi have any intention of helping you."

"I have not given it much thought," said Tomoe. "When Makine Hei said he would not let me out again, I still could not waver. Going into Hell was the same as going into Battle. A samurai never asks how she will come out again. Those whose sincerity is the greatest, who strive the most going *in*, they are the ones left standing when the battle is done. Because I think like this, I have not worried about how I will get out, but rely on the sincerity of myself and the Shinto dog."

"Perhaps a little worry would not hurt you," said Okio. "There is a Gate to Naipon just as there is a Gate to Hell, and it was that gate used by Ushii Yakushiji when running errands for Emma outside the Hollow Land. None but Emma can let you through. Not everyone can meet him. But I will be glad to write a letter of introduction if you desire."

"I have sworn that I will spit at his feet," said Tomoe. "I will not ask favors of one who tortures children."

"If it were your resolve to serve nothing which tortures children," said Okio, "then life itself you would refuse to serve. I don't know if there is any other way from here, except through homage to King Emma. But I may have some good advice for you anyway. On your way upward, you will find obstacles difficult to surmount. It is important that you win almost every battle, for if you lose, you will die in the Hollow Land and never see your husband in life. But there is one battle you must lose. Which it is, I cannot say. Only, I will tell you this: Tsuki Izutsu and the red oni were bound spiritually so that they would be strong enough to win their way out of the Hollow Land. They were strong indeed, and won every fight without exception. In fact, they were too eager, and did not see that sometimes it is important to be more supple. As a result, the Naruka was able to invade their combined spirit, and both were driven mad. You, too, will be made insane by the things you have witnessed in the Hollow Land, and by the things you have failed to see around you . . . unless you know the one time you must fail. Otherwise, you may find yourself in need of a champion, someone bold enough to descend into Hell and destroy *your* Naruka and your madness."

Tomoe Gozen bowed before Okio and said, "I am grateful for your advice." When she looked up, Okio was no longer there, but in his place was a mound of broken swords, their handles missing.

Then the walls, painting, table, vase, doors, tatami, and floor faded from around her and she and Taro were left sitting on the gritty ground. Taro rolled his eyes and licked Tomoe's hand. Tomoe said, "Well, Taro, did I succeed in any of my tasks? If we cannot escape this place, how will we know if Koshi returned to his mother, or Ushii regained his soul? Unless we are sincere enough to find the way out, it will not be possible to see if Tsuki Izutsu is truly free of the Naruka and, if so, if she had the strength to free herself from Makine Hei's influence and the red oni. As for Lord Kiso, I think Okio was inclined to pity, don't you? We must return to know for sure!"

Tomoe Gozen hurried along the ground, following the track left by Ushii Yakushiji, searching for the face of the cliff which could not be seen through the atmosphere of the Land of Gloom. Taro was ahead of her, barking, seeming to want her to hurry. He was a white specter barely within range of her vision, and she ran to keep him in sight. There was a ghostly wind erasing the footsteps ahead and behind, smoothing out the gritty ground. Taro barked more, and the sound of him echoed faintly as from far away. Although there was no overt danger to detect, this was the first time on her journey that Tomoe fretted about what might lurk unseen among the shadows. Only when she realized the source of the weird echoes did she relax somewhat: the dog's barking returned from the face of the very cliff they sought! They found their way to the zigzagging upward path. Still, Taro insisted they go quickly; but the climb was difficult even at a slow pace. She must cling to the wall at times, and be sure not to drop Inazuma-hime. It was a tiring occupation. "Are you part goat, Taro?" she asked, breathing heavily, accepting his encouragement as he led on.

The mists of the waterfall coiled like serpents and mingled with the shadows of the land below. These mists and shadows welled upward, clinging to the clothing and hair of Tomoe Gozen. The Land of Gloom did not like to let her go. But mist and shadow have no strength, and she continued upward, feeling only a little sapped of energy.

When she reached the top, she felt some easement of spiritual attack, and realized after-the-fact how dearly the Land of Gloom had tried to hold her back. "We won the first battle," she said to Taro. "And I hardly knew we fought."

She had thought it would be the simplest task to trace their way back through the Land of Roots. But the upper country was as changeable as the country far below. The river seemed to flow from the opposite angle it had gone before, and Tomoe was not certain if she should follow the river pretending it had not moved, or try instead to go at the angle it had flowed previously.

"You must lead us, Taro," she said, but even he hung his

head and whined an apology. Above, far over the Land of Gloom they had left behind, she saw the clouds of battling Asura, their forms unstable, cutting each other relentlessly, although none of their severed parts ever fell completely from the sky. A loose arm floated off horizontally, elongating itself as it went, then growing a new body. How long Tomoe watched them, she did not know. It was exactly like watching clouds, the way they parted, grew, combined. As she stood gazing, her mouth hung open. She was fascinated by the Asura! Her breathing became more difficult as she gasped through her open mouth, her eyes fixed upward, eager to join the fray. She began to think: *How gorgeous the jade and gold of the Vault of Heaven! How rich I shall be if I can only get up there and chip away some pieces!* Her right hand reached upward longingly, for the fight and for the plunder, and she saw that her upraised hand was transparent like a ghost's.

There had been some annoying sound which she ignored for a long while, but now she realized it was her companion barking and jumping against her, trying to get her attention. Slowly she tipped her face down until she could not see the beguiling Asura or the Vault of so-called Heaven, and her hand became solid once again. She could breathe normally again, and Taro became less frantic. She looked at the Shinto dog and said, "Did I almost become a ghost, Taro? Have I won another battle? Come! We must take a chance and follow the river as though it had not moved. If we are sincere in our quest, we will find the way. Sincerity alone matters!"

They went along the banks of the poisonous river, the pink back of Jishin-uwo shining beneath the rushing waters. They came to the river's fork and followed the red-tinged tributary to the lake of blood. "We must be on the right trail," said Tomoe, but Taro did not look convinced. They went as silently as possible, and as swiftly, around the lake's circumference, careful not to rouse the blood-warriors beneath the waves. Before they had gotten all the way around, Tomoe spied a colorful object smashed upon the ground, surrounded by pools of crimson. She reached to pick up the crushed ball, but her touch destroyed it. It vanished in a puff of vapor.

They followed the other bank of the tributary back to the main river. It felt to Tomoe as though they were going a direction contrary to the one they had taken before. Although the path was similar, it was never exactly the same.

There were roots hanging downward from the sky, but they did not quite reach the ground, did not threaten to cling like tentacles or bar the way. At least, they did not threaten her and Taro at first. There was a place along the river where the roots did reach all the way into the water, drinking of the poison, and blocking the path above the bank. Tomoe said, "I do not remember any place like this from before, Taro! Can you sniff the way yet?"

Taro slunk close to the ground, ashamed. "Useless animal!" said Tomoe, annoyed quite a bit. Her naginata began to cut a path, but the roots oozed dark blood which Tomoe knew must contain poison from the river, and she and Taro came back out of the rooted place in a hurry. "We can't get through there," she said. "We will have to go around."

They followed the edge of the rooted place, until stopped by a high wall built of gargantuan masonry. In the wall there was an iron gate thrice as high as Tomoe's head. Now Tomoe was more confused than ever. "We must get out of this place fast, but are not finding the way!" she complained. "Aren't we sincere enough, Taro? Which one of us is holding us back?"

She pressed the iron gate and, despite its tremendous size, it swung inward. From inside wafted a horrifying odor. When she looked in, she saw a garden of rocks and raked gravel as stark as the place which hid the Gate of Hell in the yamahoshi monastery, though larger by far. There was a spraying fountain, the water of which was yellow, and it was the source of the noxious odor.

In the middle of the garden of rocks sat a monk with a pilgrim's staff, his head shaved, and he was fatter than was healthy. She could see him only from behind.

"Bonze!" cried Tomoe from the gate, wrinkling her nose because of the odor. "Do you guard some gate that goes away from here?"

The monk stood, his back still to her. Slowly he turned

around. His face was that of a demon, the mouth too big and filled with sharp teeth, the eyes glowing red, the brow deeply etched with infamy. The monster said, "I am Emma, King of Hell, and I have brought you here to offer you a retainership. I need a living being to run errands for me on the land above. I have recently lost my previous employee, and that is why I need another."

"I will never serve someone cruel as you," she said with supreme belligerence. "But I will search under these rocks for the doorway used by your last retainer."

She put the butt of the Golden Naginata against the nearest rock and, though she hardly pushed, the rock tipped over. There were only centipedes underneath. The centipedes had human faces.

Tomoe strode across the raked gravel, ruining the nice design the rake had made, and knocked over another boulder.

"Most destructive," growled Emma, but he did not stop her.

Other rocks turned over until there was only one left to try, and this one would not budge.

"I have found it, Taro," she said. Then, looking at Emma, she asked, "Will you keep me from looking under this one?"

"As you please," said the King of Hell, studying his pilgrim's staff as though he had no interest.

The rock still would not budge. Tomoe put her shoulder to it, but strive as she might, it would not tip over. She gave up struggling and said,

"Perhaps it is necessary to fight the King of Hell!" She raised her naginata above her head, her stance a challenge.

"What do you want of me?" Emma asked, refusing the challenge.

"I want the rock removed so I can go through the Gate to Naipon!"

"Did you not once boast that you would spit at my feet if you met me?"

"Twice I said so!" she eagerly confessed.

"I am less wicked than you think, Tomoe Gozen. A king does not always choose his country. To prove my goodness, I will grant you one request and one request only. What will it be?"

"The rock!" she said.

"Good," he said, and the rock fell over by itself. There was nothing but the biggest centipede beneath, its little human face screaming for fear of its exposure. Emma said, "There never was a Gate to Naipon here. You have given me the only vengeance I require. Do not insult me anymore! Now, leave my sanctuary and find your own way home, if there is any."

"I will do as you say," Tomoe replied, moving with Taro toward the gate. "I will neither serve, nor be served by, a monster who makes children suffer."

Outside, there were no more obstacles. The roots had withdrawn higher into the sky. She and Taro passed beneath the roots and came to the river bank again. They followed the trail between the coursing water on the one side and the forest of roots on the other side, until they came to the cliffs whose heights they must not gaze upon. They waded through the channel between the high walls, going along the spine of Jishin-uwo. Tomoe thought of her meeting with Emma, and wondered, "Did I win that time, Taro? I do not know myself if I did! Okio said I must win all but one encounter. Was that the one to lose?"

They ventured on, Taro swimming at her side. She said,

"Koshi said that time would be warped for us in the Land of Gloom; so we do not know how much time is left before the fighting in the Imperial City. It is necessary to go fast, but this sluggish river makes us go so slowly. If I am impatient, I may fall into the poison water, or awaken scaly Jishin-uwo underneath my feet. It is harder without Koshi helping, Taro."

They came out of the channel between cliff walls and regained the bank, making better distance once again. The river became a trickle, then a swamp with ginkgo trees which grew thicker and thicker until they practically filled up the riverbed.

The dog trailed behind the samurai, still no help in sniffing out the way. "If we come to the dry part of the riverbed soon," said Tomoe, "we will know for sure that this is the right direction." But the swamp went on for longer than she expected. She could see no end to it. If these things weren't trouble enough, there was some creature moving noisily among the ginkgo trees in the swamp.

Once or twice she caught a glimpse of the beast's long snout and oversized pig's body. When she tried to look at it straight on, it would hide; but when she pretended not to be paying attention, it was quite bold. From the corner of her eye, she saw it foraging among the fan-leafed ginkgo, digging in the mud with its tusks. It seemed to be finding rocks which it picked up with its snout and shoved into its mouth, masticating them with big molars, creating the terrible grating sounds.

Whether it foraged along this way without regard for the samurai and dog, and only accidentally kept abreast of them, or whether it went the same pace as they did for some cunning reason, Tomoe could not guess. She thought she had seen a beast like it before, but could not quite remember. It was so odd and ugly and strong in its appearance, it was hard imagining how she could have seen such a thing and forgotten it. Yet some memory tugged upward from her subconsciousness until she had a headache and gave up further considerations on what the beast might be and where she might have seen it.

After travelling long, and still seeing no sign of the dry part of the river, and hearing nothing of the children's pretty songs, Tomoe became frustrated and sat down on the bank to ponder the whole mess. She said, "In this swampy riverbed of ginkgos there stalks a noisy, chewing monster; and to the other side of our path the root-forest has become impenetrable. There is no other way but that which we have found, Taro! I know that I sincerely wish to find the way out of here. But we must both want to succeed or it will not happen. Why are you not helping?"

Taro held his head low, wanting to be forgiven.

"Maybe I should not blame you," she said. "Maybe I am the one who is less sincere than I believe."

She sat thinking.

"It is possible that I am not eager to fight in Naipon this time," she considered aloud. "My husband has made unwise decisions, but I must obey him. Perhaps one hellish road is like another, and I have become discouraged." She looked at Taro again, sharply. "I wish you could talk to me! I need advice on these many things. I was always taught, 'Consult even your own knee,' but my knee has never answered, and neither does bad Taro!"

She stood abruptly and the dog shied away, whining a bit, but not too much.

"Find the way, Taro! Lead us!" She stomped the ground demandingly. Then she stopped acting like a child, scratched her head, and observed, "Hell is not a good place in which to improve oneself. Come on, Taro. I will lead us."

When she turned to walk on, there was someone in her way. It was another bonze, dressed like King Emma, but with a sweet face and a pleasant smile. "Who are you?" demanded Tomoe, more confused by every complication. "Have you come in here to help me? Are you a yamahoshi? Your chief instructor is a bad man! He trapped me in here and I can't get out!"

The pleasant bonze bowed graciously. He said, "I am Jizo, and I have come from back this way, where I was helping some unfortunate children."

"I know you then," said Tomoe, surprised. "Jizo-sama, the Buddhist Saint, protector of small children! Well, I should think you're needed here. There are thousands of children hurting!"

"That is a terrible truth, and I try to be of some help from time to time, but there is only so much anyone is capable of achieving in this place." Jizo-sama looked forlorn and weary, but pleasant even so. "I hear you passed the Dry River some while ago and that you helped the children at that time. We are alike, then! Are we not? I have even heard that some Tengu devils declared you patron of their children!"

"I think that was a mistake," said Tomoe, almost indignant.

"Don't think so hastily," said Jizo-sama. "Don't be

afraid of responsibility. It may not always be possible to help everyone. Helping someone now and then is often the best that we can do. Also, sometimes we will fail. But so long as we continue, it is good enough."

"I am a warrior," said Tomoe, feeling slightly belligerent toward this too-nice bonze. "I haven't time to be a nanny, especially not to the children of devils."

"Sometimes I feel that way as well," said Jizo-sama, sighing deeply. "Well, I am glad to have met a kindred spirit in this country! But if you will forgive me, I must go. There are children and mothers begging my attention at shrines up in Naipon."

The bonze turned and started to walk away. Tomoe ran after him, saying, "You know the way to get up? You must show me!"

The bonze turned around and his face was that of Emma. Tomoe let go of his shoulder and stepped back from him, looking angry. "You tricked me!" she said.

"We are alike as I told you," said Emma. "If you were Buddhist you would know that Jizo is my brighter aspect, and I am not a trickster. You are a killer who helps children. So am I!"

"You are a cheat who makes a bad place to put innocent children, then helps them now and then for your own conscience!" cried Tomoe, and she charged with her naginata. Emma raised his pilgrim's staff and knocked the weapon right out of Tomoe's grasp. He said angrily,

"That was a clumsy attack! Do you think there is so much magic in your weapon that you can forget your skill? Your Inazuma-hime is good for fighting supernatural monsters, even the King of Hell himself. But it does not make you a stronger, better warrior. It is really only an ordinary weapon if you use it against a common warrior; so I knocked it from your hands as a common warrior would do. Hell has made your fighting form contemptible! You had better get out before it is too late for you!"

Saying these things, Emma turned away once more, and strode up the path with big, firm steps. Tomoe could not chase after him, for she must recover the Golden Naginata, which had been flung into the swamp near a big hump of mud.

"A nuisance," said Tomoe, climbing off the bank into the muck. As soon as she reached the Golden Naginata, the monster which had been following came running out from the ginkgo trees. Taro did not bark or move from his comfortable place high up on the river bank. He cocked his head and watched as though nothing mattered to him. Tomoe saw this and was convinced at last that it was Taro's lack of sincerity, not her own, which had kept them trapped! She resolved to leave the dog behind, despite the help he had been before, but for the present she must fight the monster. Inazuma-hime came upward in her hands, and the monster stopped in its tracks to avoid getting its snout lopped off.

It was no higher than a horse at the shoulders, but was stouter by far, like a bristly old boar. It had a boar's blunt tusks and big yellow teeth, flat for crushing rocks. It raised its ugly snout and trumpeted, its mouth yawning wide and its thick pink tongue licking out hungrily.

"I am not rock!" said Tomoe. "Go eat something else!"

The snouted creature paid no attention. It darted back and forth with such speed that it kept Tomoe from getting back up on the top of the bank; but it was not quick enough to get around her naginata's guard. If Taro would help, it would be easy to defeat the creature, but he only lolled his tongue and panted, disinterested in Tomoe's problems. The rock-eater ran forward, and the samurai tried to cut the fiend with Inazuma-hime. But the naginata was deflected against the creature's tusks.

It yawned its mouth at her again, a mouth big enough to gobble down her head in one swallow. When it charged the next time, she struck at that open mouth, but it only bit hard on Inazuma-hime and would not let go. Those teeth were made for chewing up rocks, and even the Golden Naginata could not cut through molars hard as that; but at least the molars could not undue the supernatural temper, and the blade could not be crushed.

The monster pranced forward, its molars still clamped firmly on the blade, forcing Tomoe backward. There was the big lump of mud behind her. The butt of the naginata was soon pressed against this. Though the mound was soft, it somehow managed to hold together and stop the snouted rock-eater from pushing any further.

Her back was against the soft mound, which felt like cold flesh. She began to think it peculiar that the heft of the naginata could not be pushed into the mud no matter how hard the snouted monster tried. She took as much advantage of the situation as she could, holding the naginata's handle with only one hand, and drawing out her shortsword to stab the monster on its big nose. She stuck the shortsword deeply, and left it dangling from the top of the snout.

The creature trumpeted and lurched away, letting go of the naginata. Tomoe felt the hump of mud moving in an unlikely way, and as the snouted creature was shaking its head in pain, the samurai looked behind herself to see exactly what she had been leaning against. There was a crease or fold in the mound which began to part in two directions. The mound was a gigantic eye! As it opened, she saw that it was pink and angry. It was the eye of Jishin-uwo, the earthquake causing catfish who slept beneath the mud and water of Hell's river, its body and its fins reaching to every subterraneous corner of Naipon.

The rock-eater finally shook the shortsword out of its proboscis and came at Tomoe madder than before. She held her naginata upward and knew that this time she had the correct angle to successfully cleave the rock-eater between its eyes.

Taro decided at that moment to join the trouble, but he did not help Tomoe. He launched himself from the bank, flying not toward the beast but toward the samurai. His white teeth were bared and it was evident that he intended to clamp a hold of Inazuma-hime's handle to ruin Tomoe's balance and defense. She turned the blade quickly, and Taro fell upon the ground cut in half, his two parts thrashing although he was already dead. At the same moment, the big mouth of the rock-eater came at her face so quickly she could not get away. The big jaws snapped onto her entire head. She could not see

Wendy Adrian Shultz

a thing. She was certain her neck would be bitten through in a moment.

In that moment of certain death, Tomoe remembered where she had seen such a beast as this: in her most terrifying nightmares. It was the *Baku,* whose stomach was strong enough to eat the least digestible things, such as iron and bad dreams. The Baku was a welcome sight if the dream were bad enough, for he would take the dream away and rend it like a piece of meat.

The Baku spat Tomoe away as though she were tougher and worse tasting than gravel or nightmares. She fell into the mud next to the horrible eye of Jishin-uwo. But the Baku was not going to let her off completely. It scraped the ground with its front hooves and prepared to attack with its two tusks lowered, intending to impale her. For she had hurt its nose when the only thing it intended to do was its usual favor; and the Baku sought revenge. Tomoe was too dazed to raise the naginata or pick up the shortsword near her fingers. She could hardly move; her mind was confused by the Baku's breath.

She would have been killed but for the ghostly, white horse rising from Taro's halved body. It was a warhorse, and one that Tomoe recalled having ridden into battle many years before! The white horse reared its legs to keep the Baku from doing anything more to Tomoe.

Jishin-uwo was beginning to thrash beneath the ground. The root-forest shook madly. Tomoe grabbed the shortsword and thrust it in its sheath. She held tightly to Inazuma-hime while scrambling to the top of the bank. The ghost-horse which was Taro's spirit stayed behind to hold off the Baku. Dust and stones were shaking loose from the sky above. Bits of roots were falling everywhere. A crack appeared in the ceiling of the Land of Roots, and Tomoe found herself in the thickest part of the root-forest, climbing toward the light of Amaterasu, the Sun Upon Naipon.

As she went, her mind fought against forgetfulness. The Baku had bitten into her memories, and she was not convinced she wanted to lose them. She recalled her adventures in the Hollow Land in snatches, but the larger portion of what she had seen and done was drifting from her mind. She realized that the Baku had been the challenger Okio had warned her not to defeat. The Baku was the monster against whom Tsuki Izutsu had failed to lose! Strong Tsuki had escaped the Hollow Land remembering every detail of horror. To defeat the Baku was to recall each of the crippling nightmares of one's whole life, and what sanity could survive a thing such as that? Taro had known it from the beginning, but Tomoe had cleaved him in half, misunderstanding his intentions.

Her guilty feelings for killing Taro faded from memory. She climbed the tendrils from the Land of Roots until she reached the crack in the ground above. There, she clung to an earthen wall while it shook with Jishin-uwo's annoyance; but she could not be made to fall back into the Hollow Land.

She clung also to a thought, one which the Baku could not have: There would be a funeral tablet for brave Taro, and he would have the death-services of a samurai.

She struggled onto the shaking surface of Naipon, saw that she was in a mapled valley, the trees of high autumn all around her. The limbs of the trees vibrated as the ground heaved and buckled. There were gorgeous leaves upon those branches, many of them falling because they were so shaken; and their falling was like a weird, colorful snow upon Tomoe's body. She knew it was nearly time to lead the yamabushi unto Kyoto, to reinforce whatever claims Kiso Yoshinake had been making. She was uncertain exactly how much time had passed, days being measured differently underneath the world. Haste might be necessary. But for the moment, she could only lie gasping air, while the crack she'd scaled from Hell partially closed itself. Everything ceased to toss about. Jishin-uwo invariably thrashed a few lighter times, once he'd been awakened, but for now the catfish rested in its new position.

As she lay, looking up through the red and yellow snow of leaves, through the dark sky-cracks of branches, she beheld the cloudy, bright sky, and her brow knit into a puzzled expression. She was certain she had just this moment escaped from Hell. Some of it was clear in her mind, but most of it had faded. She would almost be willing to swear by her very honor that she had fought the Naruka and talked to Koshi's spirit and given Ushii a sword and pleaded with Okio to forgive Lord Kiso's rashness . . . but thinking more carefully, these things began to sound most improbable. The specifics of each event were jumbled in her memory. The harder she tried to draw these actions into focus, the more hazy and unlikely they became. The Baku, the horse-spirit of Taro, the meetings with the King of Hell, and other important events, were forgotten entirely. Without these missing pieces, the parts she *did* recall refused to adhere into a logical, consistent picture.

In time, she rose from her weary posture and went in search of a lake or spring. A purification rite was of absolute necessity, considering where she had been. If she could find salt, she would rub herself until parts of her were raw! Afterward, she would proceed with haste to her rendezvous with the yamabushi, and her rendezvous with fate.

The following day found Tomoe Gozen going toward the pre-arranged meeting-place by means of palanquin, her Golden Naginata strapped to the vehicle's outside. The men carrying the braces on their shoulders jogged to a steady cant, going swiftly as Tomoe had directed. She lifted the bamboo curtain of the palanquin to see people swarming the other way, coming from two roads which met on this third. They fled the war in the Imperial City and the ruin by earthquake of their own small villages. The quakes had mainly ended yesterday, but presently, Jishin-uwo decided to give one final thrash before settling down entirely. At first she did not feel it, due to the bouncing motion of the palanquin. But directly the bearers were so tossed about that they dropped the box which held Tomoe, jarring her suddenly.

The peasants scurrying along the roads were thrown off their feet. Tomoe's palanquin bearers went down on their faces not only because of the shaking ground, but because they feared Tomoe's anger at being dropped so abruptly. She ignored their pleas to be forgiven, tossed the bamboo curtain over the roof of the palanquin, and sat inside watching the countryside convulse. Her expression was one of utter detachment.

A crack appeared in the middle of a rice field. It began stretching toward the palanquin. The bearers, seeing it, rose from the ground and staggered swiftly away, abandoning their occupation. Tomoe sat calmly, watching the crack approach her. It stopped short of the road, never quite threatening to devour her or anyone else. When this last complaint of Jishin-uwo was finished, the people began to rise from the dirt and gravel, dusting themselves, their faces nearly as calm as Tomoe's. Even peasants were resigned to such occurrences in Naipon, though occasionally bewildered to think a country divinely created and divinely ruled could yet so easily convulse with abundant disaster.

Tomoe went the last small way on foot. She smelled smoke before she actually saw the village, and knew the quake had caused fires the day before, and some of these still smouldered. The people swarming along the roads could do no better than forget their ruined homes, leaving valuables at shrines as offerings, dressing statues in finery, offering millions of prayers, and fleeing to the mountains or off to another province. What they carried in big squares of cloth upon their backs was the extent of their salvaged past.

As she strode against the tide of this exodus, many hands were extended, peasants trying to convince her to give them some coin. She had nothing to offer, so ignored them. Another samurai might have acknowledged them with the sharp edge of steel. The peasants may have hoped for exactly such an end to strife; but Tomoe Gozen did not draw her shortsword nor unsheath the blade of her naginata.

The naginata was a worry. The kirin's blood would wear away in one more week's time. Then there would be no protection from the blinding light of the weapon's supernatural temper. She recalled that it had taken her a year to perform the errand for bonze Shindo, to return the head of his pilgrim's staff to the monastery. It might be equally difficult to return Inazuma-hime to her place in the crater of Mount Kiji, with Tomoe's other responsibilities so numerous and so pressing. When the holy monster kirin was healed of its injuries, it might come stalking for Tomoe Gozen, and create trouble. She must be prepared, whether with apologies or strength to fight the beast again.

When she arrived in the village, she saw that hundreds had been crushed by their falling homes. There were few attempting to dig the bodies out. There were already evil odors rising from the bodies, so disease would soon come to scourge the survivors. The quake had not been severe in Kyoto, one refugee from that direction remarked; but the war itself was awful and it was considered a bad idea to flee the villages in the direction of the capital.

People wandered about on aimless journeys through the rubble. One staggering, bloodied fellow crossed Tomoe's path, staring blindly though nothing was wrong with his eyes. He dropped down dead at her feet. She stepped over him. In the distance, a religious maniac howled a Shinto prayer. Buddhists jangled rattles, sitting amidst destruction. Tomoe spied a child attached to the breast of its dead mother, suckling pointlessly. Above them, a poem was scribed in blood upon a fragment of a wall. It was the mother's final consideration: "The city falls in pieces. How serene the clouds."

There was surprisingly little looting, but one sad-looking woman upturned splintered floorboards and bent tatami mats as though in search of something in particular, something precious; but she looked confused, as though her quest was an unknown one even to herself. Her tattered clothing were grey from dirt. It was clear she had been a beggar even before the quake delivered instant poverty to an entire town. Her face was smudged with soot. Her arms were blistered, indicating that she had barely escaped one of the fires of the day before. He eyes were deepset and dark beneath. Even in such a condition, Tomoe recognized who this was.

"Oshina!" she cried. "Oshina! Why are you here?"

The woman looked up stupidly, then shouted back at the samurai, "Give me money, samurai! Give me food!" She came hopping through the rubble toward Tomoe Gozen, her hand reaching out, beseeching.

"Oshina, don't you remember me? Why have you left

Lost Shrine? Did it fall in the earthquake also?''

''The shrine?'' She looked more stupid than before, but then seemed to remember. ''I left Lost Shrine several days ago. I don't know if the earthquake hurt it.''

''Where is your son? Why is he not strapped onto your back?''

Her deepset, dark eyes pondered this question, for she scarcely remembered anything at all. ''My son,'' she said carefully, then it flooded back into her consciousness. ''Koshi! Koshi!''

''Where is he now?''

''Koshi-koshi!''

Tomoe grabbed the hysterical mother by the shoulders and squeezed hard. ''Don't act so funny, Oshina! I am your friend Tomoe Gozen! Don't you know? Have you abandoned Koshi at Lost Shrine?''

Oshina settled down and nodded vaguely.

''How could you do it! Oshina!''

Oshina looked into Tomoe's eyes and the look was so eerie and intense that Tomoe let go and stepped back. Oshina said in a low, whispering voice, ''Koshi's spirit unexpectedly came back into his body. I wanted to rejoice. But the first thing he said, as soon as he sat up, was 'Iye-iye-iye,' I-don't-like-I-don't-like-I-don't-like. Then he fell back dead completely. I left, forgetting even to bury him.''

''Poor Oshina!'' exclaimed Tomoe, frowning in an exaggerated but honest manner. ''I tried to help but only made things worse! Old Uncle Tengu made an error thinking I could be useful. Oshina! Let me help you in some way! How can I make amends?''

''Money, samurai. Food.'' She put her hands out. ''Or . . .''

''What else would you have, Oshina? I will get it!''

The woman did not answer at first. Then she threw herself at Tomoe's feet, looking up and clinging to the samurai's jacket, screaming at her, ''Kill me, samurai! Kill me at once! Then I will find my son!''

Tomoe pulled Oshina's fingers loose from the hem of the jacket and stepped away. She looked upset, but replied, ''As you desire it, I will." She withdrew the shortsword and placed the point against Oshina's neck. She asked, "You are certain?" Oshina's madness seemed to vanish from her dark, sad eyes and in that moment her mind was clear. She held her lips firmly together, and nodded for Tomoe to continue. The shortsword punctured throat and vein.

Oshina's expression was one of gratitude.

At dusk, those peasants who had no place to flee, or were too despondent to try, gathered up gold- and silver-leafed parts of houses, using them as firewood against the cold. Tomoe had been side-tracked trying to help these wretched people, but they were so afraid of her that it was hard to be useful. There existed a rift between castes so wide that even the gravest emergency could not bridge it for a while. Eventually she was approached by a black-clad yamabushi who, though a priest, did not respond to the peoples' pleading for religious services. He bowed to Tomoe Gozen, led her beyond the village by a narrow path, to a huge clearing where tents were scattered and banners flapped. Three thousand yamabushi camped there. There were more, she was told, waiting in the hills around Kyoto, and some who had already joined the first assaults on the city and surrounding points.

"The Knight of Kiso sent this," said the priest who brought her to the camp. He indicated a large armor-box which had the comma-pattern of Tomoe's personal crest printed on the outside. Within, bamboo armor lacquered shiny black with red silk lacing was neatly arranged. A newly forged shortsword and longsword were encased separate from the armor, the hilt ornaments made of gold. There was also a fan marked with Yoshinake's crest. That fan symbolized the field marshal, and she would use it to direct and signal events on the battlefield. The priest said, "There is a horse as well. The white one over there."

"We march tonight," said Tomoe. "We will be in our positions outside Kyoto as Amaterasu rises."

PART THREE

The Audacious Treason

Beneath Amaterasu the Shining Goddess there are many worlds, say the oracles, this one which we see, and others; and these worlds are varied one from the next in remarkable ways, while in other things they are remarkable for their similarity. Naipon, a divine nation, rises from the jade seas of each of these worlds, though many other nations cannot be found one world to the next; and the Yamato people, a divine race, are mighty in each of these places, though many other peoples are noteworthy only upon occasion. The fact of the matter, according to the oracles, is this: The fabric of the universe, and the universes within and without, would completely come undone, sometimes imploding upon itself, elsewhere dissolving into mists, other places bursting outward into tiny fragments . . . except that the anchor of everything is Naipon, which alone, among things known and unknown, holds all else together by its reliable and significant existence.

And in this country which lies like scattered jewels drifting on the ocean, there is one place more holy even than the rest.

This place, of course, is the Imperial City, where dwells the living flesh of Naipon, the august descendant of Amaterasu Herself; whose name in this generation is Go-Temmu, who has been kept in unpardonable seclusion by a clan once favored to be his guard but who became, by slow stages, his turnkeys. Who is to blame for this? The oracles ponder and speculate. Surely the Buddhas had nothing to do with it; positively the thousands of myriads of Shinto deities took no part. Gods do not smite gods as men smite men, so the felons must be mortal. Go-Temmu was a living god, mistreated by undeserving servants; an insult to Him blights humanity in the eyes of other gods as well. Who perpetrated such sin? The oracles venture cautiously: It was true the

Shogun in that *other* capital had once exiled the Mikado, but that was long corrected; it need not be discussed. Furthermore, did the Shogun command the Imperial Guards? They were not of his clan and he did not necessarily favor them; indeed, he had often sought to chastise them in small ways, but they thought themselves too mighty to notice.

Surely we are beginning to resolve the riddle (the oracles expressions approximated those of Bodhisattvas at the moment of enlightenment) of who the culprit is! The only ones to fault are the turnkeys themselves! (Or the *guards,* the oracles amended, begging the listeners' pardon, and looking most respectful.)

The offending clan was named Ryowa, which means circle of dragons. In other worlds they had other names, but their faces were the same, and their loss of faces too. Let it be known, then, that the Shogun sent a fierce general named Kiso Yoshinake to punish the Ryowa! (It took no oracular ability to see this.) Let it further be known that the Rising Sun General had never known defeat and did not expect to know it!

So said the oracles. They grew bolder as war approached and heightened. "See that comet," they shouted, more belligerent than pious, though they lived in temples. "It heralds the Ryowa downfall!" They also cried out, "See that red streak in the sky, persisting from dawn to dusk! It is Ryowa blood, about to splash the ground!"

That many of the oracles were men in *torikabuto* or monks' hoods may have had something to do with their rude prognostications. Some were yamabushi. As became widely known, yamabushi strode the highways along with the invading samurai, and many sects sympathized.

Most of the army was on foot, but there were generals on horses; and a sizable cavalry was obviously expected, since the first infantries were eager to control certain fields which were useless but for grass.

There were twelve famous generals under Kiso Yoshinake, one of them his wife, and four of them *shi-tenno* which meant "four great men." And great they were, and beautiful. These four rode steeds of shining jet and, when going side by side, they were themselves a horde.

The city which awaited terror sat in a quiet valley surrounded by temples and gardens and gently winding highways and brooks; there were placid lakes and slender waterfalls; and this city was inhabited by courtly aristocrats who were gentle and powdered and scented and innocent of fearful things, protected as they were by those veritable turnkeys, their guards, who themselves learned courtly manners so as never to offend fragile dispositions. The roofs of the city were tiled and the tiles were gilt with precious metal which reflected the sunlight and rivalled the dawn.

The recent quakes had done the city small damage. A single temple was thrown down, that was all, and it was the Temple of the Goddess Kwannon—an omen, that, for She presided over mercy. Gilt tiles were shaken into the gardens and streets here and there, it was true, but golden leaves and ruddy ones and leaves of somber brown had fallen from the peach trees and plum, cherry trees and maple, hiding the quake-made rubble. Kyoto looked serene in this leaf-covered state; it looked as though it rested on a softly brocaded quilt.

The war was already in progress when six unarmed yamabushi brought an oversized palanquin to the headquarters of the Ryowa. The headquarters was a place better than the one the Mikado lived in. The yamabushi announced that the occupant of the large palanquin was their heavenly patron. Inside was a statue of the warrior-monks' god, Ida-ten. They sat the transport outside the gate of the Ryowa clan's palace, a nuisance to those who came and went. A devoutly religious clan, no Ryowa would dare touch the holy thing outside their gate, nor attack the unarmed monks who brought it. Presently the six monks made camp in eyesight of the gate, the palanquin, and Ida-ten; whether they guarded their relic or wished to see who came and went from the military palace, this is not what mattered. The monks made this declaration: "Ida-ten is angry that the Ryowa have failed to live spartan lives as befit true warriors! He will sit here by the gate until the chief-generals beg his pardon!" The Ryowa leaders were incensed beyond reply. They repaired to secret meetings to discuss the situation. They suspected, but were not sure, that this was only a ploy to weaken their hearts, that Ida-ten was only a piece of wood and his transport merely a big fancy box. It might not be a religious matter at all, they argued, and began to convince themselves. Furthermore, the monks were frankly rude. They ought to be cut into pieces, whether or not it made some god angry. "There are other gods!" said the Ryowa council in their palace. The council was mostly men whose prime had left them, but left them wealthy. "Ida-ten is no one we need fear!" they agreed finally, deciding the best course would be to arrest the monks and set the wooden god afire. However, while this meeting was going on, a sentry had kept an eye on the six yamabushi, and on the fearful palanquin in front of the gate. The Ryowa sentry saw a peculiar thing, which was this:

A noodle-vendor had come up the street carrying on his back everything he needed to vend noodles. He placed the box of gear upon the ground, blew a spark into hot coals, and began to heat fresh noodles to sell to the yamabushi and whoever was bold enough to happen by. "I will pay homage to your god!" said the smiling noodle-man, and he went traipsing to the palanquin, bowing and humbling himself and saying beautiful this and beautiful that. One of the yambushi, noodles hanging from his mouth, shouted a sudden warning, "Don't touch him, noodle-man!" It was too late. The curious peasant placed hand upon the door of the palanquin and, before a single yamabushi could stand up and hollar a second time, he fell down dead in the street. "Too bad!" the monks lamented, giving the unfortunate fellow an impromptu service. Then they hauled him and his noodle-vending box away. The Ryowa sentry took news of this event to his superiors. The chief-generals became petrified. They still refused obeisance to Ida-ten, but could not bring themselves to burn the palanquin after all; neither could they threaten the six monks. Later on, someone thought they saw the very same noodle-man spending a lot of money in a saké house; but perhaps it was the noodle-man's twin brother, drinking to forget his loss of kin (and forgetting it quite well, judging by his laughter).

Ida-ten inspired fear only in those whose hearts were already weakened with self-doubt. Night and day, battles raged about Kyoto, and while the troops of Kiso Yoshinake were seriously outnumbered, the hearts of his warriors were more stout, and there were good reasons for this: they were righteous men. The coming and going of Jishin-uwo's unrest was another element in Yoshinake's favor, as things turned out. Although the capital itself was not much damaged, a Ryowa troop in an outlying post was swallowed up entirely, and in another case badly shaken up. Since Buddhist monks were so large a part of Yoshinake's invasion, it was possible to credibly proclaim the quakes to be the merest sampling of a holy retribution about to be visited upon the offensive clan holding the emperor in thrall. The august (and conspiring) child of Amaterasu was himself delighted by the prospects for freedom, prospects enlarged by every victory for the Knight of Kiso; therefore Go-Temmu wrote his own imperial testimony of heavenly (and hellish) intervention in behalf of the throne.

About this time, Tomoe Gozen brought a reinforcement of three thousand additional monks, which caused still other monks to rally; and martial nuns and wanderers added a motley flavor to the units. Even peasants asked to join the conquering horde, having been over-taxed by the Ryowa, and eager to be part of such a holy mission. Still the Ryowa outnumbered their foe, for the countryside was populated by that noteworthy clan; and even so, it hardly mattered, for Yoshinake was not merely the superior tactician with excellent advisors, but also wise in psychological warfare. The harassed clan, despite claims of being the gods-favored and hereditary defenders of the imperial house, were in fact utterly dispirited by the statements of the priests and oracles and the Mikado's own clever testimony. Consciously or not, the Ryowa accepted that supernatural disapproval had been earned by their self-serving policies.

The defending clan, enamored of religion, aware of their own misdeeds in recent years, and believing in the aforementioned retribution they must suffer, fought not for victory, but for valorous death. This, they were allowed. The armies of the Knight of Kiso dove into the Ryowa's superior numbers whose only wish was to die honorably and atone. A hundred battles were fought in those few days. There were heroes in each one, on both sides, whose praises would be sung in their home villages and provinces for hundreds of years to follow.

At the Battle of Dazai, beneath the blazing sun of autumn, Nenoi Yukika, one of the shi-tenno or men most favored by Kiso Yoshinake, and most trusted, led footsoldiers and horsemen against the famous Ryowa general, Sanehire. Nenoi Yukika was a neatly bearded man of middle years who sat high upon his black horse. His armor was black, his helmet black, his visage dark and stern. His arrows were fletched with raven feathers. The heads of these arrows were shaped like big turnips which could annihilate a man's eye then burst out the back of a skull, brains splattering in the wake. This black warrior directed the battle from the top of the hill, showing his marshal's fan this way and that way like the fine conductor he was, sitting this whole time upon his horse, the black horse with an iron mask and horns. Then Nenoi Yukika saw General Sanehire himself entering the fray, anxious as he was to die with his brave men. But who could kill this general? Who was strong enough? How could the Ryowa hero of numerous campaigns possibly die well, when his swords were too swift to let him? Thus did the hooves of a black horse plunder the grass, leaving sod upturned behind, down and down the hillside and into the fight. General Sanehire saw General Nenoi Yukika coming, and was glad. "You are my man!" Sanehire shouted, and Nenoi Yukika answered, "You're mine!" Sanehire was clad in red silk over red-lacquered armor, and on his helmet were the antlers of a deer. The red general and the black general met on horseback. The red general's rust-colored horse met the black general's night-colored horse. The steeds fought each other even as the generals fought; and when Sanehire fell, it was red on red on red, and he looked up at night above him, though it was bright of day. His last word in life was: "Excellent!" Then Nenoi Yukika cut off the brave man's head and put it high upon a pole, saying, "Now you will be able to see how valiantly your men die! How well all of you atone!" Then the dark general began to weep because of this splendor.

A different day, at the Battle of Fuhara, there was another proven man, who had grey in his trimmed whiskers but was younger than he looked; and his name was Tade Shimataka. He was as pale as Nenoi Yukika was dark. His armor was lacquered white. His helmet was white, and it was decorated with white pine branches. Around his shoulders was an arrow-deflecting cape which was also white. His arrows were fletched with doves' feathers, and their points were like closed beaks. His horse was black, which made Tade Shimataka look whiter, a ghostly rider. Tade Shimataka was also one of the shi-tenno; and his most wonderful fight was against the Ryowa ally Narita Hamba. Hamba was short and bow-legged, but you could not tell so when he rode his white-satin horse. He was broad-shouldered and bull-necked and thick-armed and was said to be the foremost archer of Naipon, able to draw a bowstring which three good men would be unable to manage together. Narita Hamba was called "General Ape" by rude men who were envious, devoid of manners, or apt to deride anyone superior. To Tade Shimataka, here was the opponent of one's life. Though they were on opposite sides of the large battlefield at Fuhara, these two men saw one another quickly. Tade Shimataka drove heel to horse and started off across the carnage to where Narita Hamba sat astride his white horse, impassive. Shimataka's arrows sang like birds through the air, but Narita Hamba understood arrows like some men know hawks, and cannot be scratched by them. He danced his horse back and forth, avoiding every quill, so that Shimataka gave up on this and spurred his black horse faster. Slowly, the Ryowa ally drew an arrow of his own from over his shoulder. More slowly still he nocked it. The heads of these arrows were shaped like sickle moons or cross-sections of teacups. They were wide enough to wrap halfway around a neck and sharp enough to cut clear through. The first arrow was unleashed and, before it was halfway to its target, a second was close behind! It was unexpected, the second arrow, because Hamba had moved slowly at first. Lord Kiso's marshal did not veer his horse or slow the pace or duck his head, but swept his longsword through the air and closed his eyes for a moment so that the splinters of the deflected arrow would not blind him. He swept his sword the other way, deflecting the second arrow just as quickly. Although it might be true that

WAS

no finer bowman than General Hamba lived in the whole of the country, it was equally the case that Lord Kiso's vassals were without exception masters of *yadome-jitsu,* arrow-stopping art. Tade Shimataka happened to be more skillful than the others. Thus Lord Kiso's famed "General in White" upon a black horse met the black-armored white-horse Ryowa ally face to face at Fuhara, exchanging cordial greetings.

Tade Shimataka's white cape swirled about him like snow. He was himself like snow upon a black mountain. "Fight me on the ground!" said Hamba, and Kiso's man was willing, though aware no man had ever won a grappling exercise with ape-armed Narita Hamba. They battled back and forth with pikes until Tade Shimataka's pike was broken, and then it was sword against pike, until Hamba's pike was broken. Hamba did not draw his sword as would be expected. Instead, he seemed to hunch down shorter than he was, his bowed legs becoming more so, then he sprang underneath Shimataka's swinging sword to catch the arm and hold it in a vise-grip. So they grappled this way and that way and it looked as though a stout black monkey had somehow gotten hold of a piece of white cloud and was wrestling it to the ground and tying it up! Lord Kiso's man's arms were quickly strapped behind his back and his chances of winning became bleak. But in the wrestling, Hamba's arrows had been scattered from his quiver, and Shimataka rolled over one of the iron arrowheads, cutting his bindings, but not letting on that he was loose. When Narita Hamba fell to strapping the legs of the cloud-colored man, one of Hamba's own arrows was snatched from the ground and smashed against the back of his thick neck. With a second blow of the knife-edged curve of the moon-shaped arrowhead, Narita Hamba's head and helmet fell into Tade Shimataka's lap. Shimataka, gasping for breath, exclaimed, "A loss to our country!" Then, as Nenoi Yukika had done at the Battle of Dazai, Tade Shimataka, at Fuhara, began to weep. These two men belonging to Lord Kiso had known lives of war too long for them to fail to recognize the pathos of all things.

Imai Kanchira on the other hand was scarcely more than a boy and for him war was new. He was so pretty that if someone ever succeeded in cutting off his head and taking it as trophy, someone else would surely say it was the head of a girl. He was the third shi-tenno, and Tomoe Gozen's brother. The fourth shi-tenno was Higuchi Mitsu, who was not much older than Imai. The pity of things had not yet settled into their intellects, so they were filled only with the glory and wonder of their own tremendous actions, untouched by the sorrow of lost lives and of an ancient, mighty clan crushed by youthful supersession. Imai and Mitsu fought side by side and laughing, giving contradictory orders to their men by means of their marshals' fans, causing the Battle of Shinowa to look more like a riot than an ordinary assault. The Ryowa forces were the more confused by this. With fighting on every side, it was difficult for the dying of either army to be sure they fell down facing the enemy. To fall facing away from the enemy would be construed to mean they died in cowardly retreat; but this might not be the case in confusion such as this. Higuchi Mitsu, whose faith was predominantly Buddhist, suggested that whoever fell in battle do so facing North, for Buddha died with his head to the North. Imai Kanchira, whose faith was predominantly Shinto, suggested that whoever fell in battle do so facing West, for that was the direction of Death. They laughed at their disagreement and the legion of samurai and yamabushi under their direction laughed also. There was much jesting on the field until the enemy was infected and, though routed, grinned and chortled. This is why the Battle of Shinowa is sometimes called The Happy Fight. The Ryowa army thought it a matter of honor to die in better humor than their foe; so one group of wounded, dying men got together and arranged themselves in a flower-shape; the petals their bodies formed faced in all directions. "How lovely!" cried Higuchi Mitsu, seeing the rent enemy like a red chrysanthemum on the ground. Imati Kanchira added, "They die prettier than we! Since we cannot compete, we should give up and not die at all!" Thereafter, there were no more deaths among the yamabushi and samurai led by Imai Kanchira and Higuchi Mitsu. Among the enemy, none were spared, and none ran away either, for they were having a very good time being cheerful.

On past occasions there have been tendencies to idealize the manners of a fallen foe, since it makes the victor appear the more vigorous to defeat surprising greatness. For the sake of objectivity, in the present case, it will not go unsaid, there *were* cowards among the old clan. To be sure, many of them changed their names and titles to escape to far provinces and live with relatives of humble station, and were never heard from again. Others disguised themselves as servants so as not to be captured, later shaving their heads to join priesthoods of a more sedate variety than the yamabushi. Still others, sometimes in droves, petitioned Kiso Yoshinake for commissions, and he allowed them to change sides, although he never trusted them very much.

Priest Kakumei set out one morning to prove the weakness of the foe. He was tired of these tales of Ryowa defeats which were glorious for both sides. Kakumei was a wide-built man and sometimes when he was approached by four or five friends, they would tease him by pretending not to see him there, and say to one another, "We must go around this wall!" Or, "Who put this wall up here?" His hair and beard were shaggy even for a yamabushi; and it was somewhat curly for, it was said, his grandmother was an Ainu wild-woman converted to Buddhism. On this morning when he set out, he wore no armor, maintaining that the Ryowa swords were too dull to cut his priest's robe. Nor did he take any sword or fighting pole or axe or naginata, sure as he was that his rosary was enough to frighten off such timid warriors as he would find. In preparation, Priest Kakumei had combed his hair and beard outward on all sides, so that he looked like a black-maned lion. He combed his thick eyebrows upward so that he had an angry look without trying. He wore high wooden *geta* on his feet, to prove it was not necessary to have easy footing to defeat Ryowa clansmen. He fixed upon his visage a look that made his eyes seem round and sharp, and went out by himself to face the enemy. He shook his beads at the Ryowa unit, and did they run away? They certainly did! What pious fellow wouldn't? This was a Buddhist priest! His only weapons were his beads and his awful face! Strike him down, and what could come of it, but gods' vengeance? Priest Kakumei chased a bunch of them this direction; he chased a bunch of them that direction. Always he held his rosary in front of him, deriding them in a thunderous voice. "Stand still and fight with me, thou cravens!" But only one would do so. Priest Kakumei fell upon this one and strangled him with the rosary. He kicked another with his geta, and broke the fleeing man's back. Another died of fright when Kakumei raised his arms, his sleeves hanging down like the wings of a black moth. It went on like this until the only one left standing on the battlefield was Kakumei, with a few corpses scattered in undignified postures. Thenceforth, when Yoshinake's generals told tales of Ryowa valor, Priest Kakumei would shake his beads and grumble.

On other past occasions there have been opposite tendencies to degrade the foe, to make them seem forever afraid, as they were before Priest Kakumei, or to make them seem cruel felons. By doing this, a victor wishes not to worry about becoming ill-judged for the slaughter. History will call the dead, "Too weak to live!" or else say, "Their infamy required this vengeance!" Such things must never be suggested about the dragon-circle clan. They were mighty. But they exceeded their station, and no one must do that. With some exceptions, they went down boldly. The boldest would not even consider amnesty or exile. The clan elders living in and about Kyoto and the chief-generals of the military palace were especially apt to perform seppuku before they would suffer the indignity of capture or defeat. Some might have escaped but refused to do so. Had there been hope of rallying in the future, they might have tried to live. But there would never be such a chance. Therefore they embraced self-immolation as the only acceptable behavior. Men such as these, along with their throat-pierced wives and sons and daughters, merited and received the highest funeral honors.

Nor had Kiso Yoshinake and his famous wife been mere table-generals through all this. For, grand as were the exploits of the shi-tenno and other field marshals, and of the troops, this grandeur paled beside the significance of Lord Kiso's and Tomoe Gozen's conclusive surge into the capital itself. Tomoe's white charger carried her through leaf-matted streets, and the blood of Ryowa made the leaves more gorgeous still. She slew fourteen famous generals in three days of battle—about each one a story might be told; and she slew lesser foes too numerous to recount. Her husband was of identical courage, despite having to retire from the field periodically to hear from spies and council, to decide tactics, to reveal his mental prowess in matters of war, and largely to bore himself with responsibilities beyond the sword. Each time he heard that Tomoe had taken another general's life, Yoshinake spoke lavish praise, then set out to do the same, lest it seem his wife was mightier, as some said Madame Hojo was mightier than her husband who was Shogun. Did this suggest Kiso Yoshinake was envious of his wife's fame or her strength? We shall never know for sure. He took joy in the knowledge that he and Tomoe were equally matched. Perhaps he had forgotten a battle with straw-wrapped bokens which revealed Tomoe Gozen the more prepared to die and, therefore, the greater warrior. Lord Kiso was proud of his wife, let there be no doubt. He boasted of her courage and her beauty. If she had killed fifteen famous generals and he one less, his feelings might have been otherwise. Or he might still have been glad; who is to say? The adage goes, "That which might have been was not," while the reasonable truth is this: Kiso Yoshinake relied upon Tomoe Gozen even more than his superb shi-tenno; for one of her was equal to the four of them, and the four of them were equal to one thousand times their number.

And was Yoshinake beautiful in battle? Ah! Upon his helmet were the horns of an ox. His armor was blue-black, the cords of it bright cobalt. His arrow-deflecting mantle was likewise blue, wrapped about his shoulders and scintillating as does the center of a flame. His arrows stood up high behind his back, fletched with blue feathers from an eagle's underwing, the heads shaped like candles' flames. With bow, rattan-wrapped and lacquered the same blue-black as his armor, it was said his only equal was the Ryowa ally known as "General Ape," who now was dead, so there was no one living who could equal Yoshinake when archery was considered. He strove through the defended streets of Kyoto, breaking that defense, taking off the heads of soldiers, dashing this way and that way on his dappled grey horse, a horse called Grey Cloud Demon, whose iron mask glistened in blue hues, whose fur was like blue ash beneath the blue flame of Kiso Yoshinake. Nothing withstood the fire of the Rising Sun General and his shining Sword of Okio.

Now and then Tomoe was able to watch her husband. Her heart swelled with pride in him. For herself, she felt only that she must fulfill her husband's mission, duty sufficing though she was shockingly devoid of vanity. But seeing Kiso Yoshinake, she knew she had chosen the proper lord, or been chosen by him, and whatever was the final judgement of them all, she would have no regrets. He had grown a beard this past month, blue-black like his armor and bow, and it hid his boyish charm, his girlish prettiness, but Tomoe Gozen did not mind, for now her husband looked like Hachiman himself, supreme god of battle, patron to Kyoto, fierce as a wild beast . . . and who else had a lord who looked like that? Who else such a husband? Yes, Tomoe Gozen was proud of him, but could not often hold back to appreciate his grievous beauty; for she herself was busy, like Hachiman's mother Jingo, serene and beautiful and ever close behind her son, conquering as he.

The days of battle passed quickly. Throughout this time, the headquarters of the enemy was watched by the six yamabushi with their palanquin containing the wooden god. Ryowa field marshals came and went, bowing to Ida-ten as was polite, but trying not to notice the six men camped beneath their noses. When everything was hopeless, when everything was lost and the Ryowa no longer cared if Ida-ten became angry, only then did they go out to the half-dozen yamabushi and beat them to death with clubs. Only then did they stuff the corpses of the monks into the palanquin of Ida-ten, and had this tribute taken to the Place of Tents which was Lord Kiso's moving camp. There was a message with the palanquin which said, "Ida-ten is a devil not a god! We owe nothing to him! Hachiman is the wargod of the

Imperial City, and He will crush the monks and monkish oafs!" The yamabushi were more insulted than Kiso Yoshinake. He had been called worse things than monkish oaf these past few days, sometimes by men he would not deign to hear or notice, others who he would engage in battle with or without insult. In fact, the message amused him; for he had been once or twice mistaken for the wargod Hachiman during the long battles, which resemblance caused the Ryowa to pale. And he had come to believe he was possessed by Kyoto's patron god. Therefore it struck Lord Kiso as richly funny that the failing foe called upon Hachiman, *called upon their enemy,* for aid. It may be considered a good thing, too, that Kiso Yoshinake was feeling too self-important to believe himself insulted; for the day Lord Kiso recognizes insult is the day the world burns with the fire of his rage.

However, the yamabushi were outraged that the palanquin was mishandled and the wooden god stained red. They thought Lord Kiso ought to respond more hotly than he was inclined to do. Tomoe Gozen, who had led the bulk of the yamabushi these few days, felt a certain responsibility to them, and said to her husband, "I will handle this."

She selected eighteen men of the yamabushi, men she had been impressed with in the battles. On her white horse, its horned mask lacquered white; with her red-lacquered bow and her arrows fletched with crimson feathers and points the shape of willow leaves; in her black enameled bamboo armor with bright red cords; with a white flag mounted on her back and sticking up high; with her helmet sporting a crescent moon of gold; with the Golden Naginata named Princess Lightning in her hand and two swords at her side; Tomoe Gozen led the charge through the gates into the garden of the Ryowa chiefs' headquarters. The guards, one hundred against eighteen, surrounded the yamabushi who were on foot and the woman who was on horseback. She paraded the horse before them, her naginata wavering before their faces, and they did not attack. The yamabushi were variously armed with naginata or swords or iron staffs with rings on top. They stood ready. Tomoe Gozen shouted loud enough for the generals inside the palace to hear, "With arrows and blades Tomoe Gozen of Heida, wife of Lord Kiso Yoshinake the

Rising Sun General, has fought her way into the palace yard with eighteen men at her side! We come to avenge the ill-considered treatment of Ida-ten! The weapons we bring with us bear names as famous as our own, including Inazuma-hime! The men left dead outside the gate could not stand against us. Can these one hundred here do better? See how they hesitate!"

The hundred men, insulted, started forward, but the weapons of the yamabushi went upward to the call, and Tomoe Gozen's Golden Naginata swept in front of them, and they held back once more. She shouted, "We will take our time doing what we must! Generals inside, do you hear this? We will take our time!" Then the battle was engaged with a flurry of strokes and limbs flying. It could have been finished quickly, but it was polite to give the chief-generals every opportunity to complete the rituals of seppuku, to say good-bye to one another in their palace, to write their death-poems and make known their last requests.

At length the final guard was slain, by which time the besieged generals had completed their rituals. All but one died with their bellies slit. The one general still living stepped out onto a porch to survey defeat.

This clan elder did not at first appear to be as old as Tomoe would have expected. He came out of the military palace, gazed upon the corpse-strewn garden, saw that only yamabushi were left standing, plus a woman on a white charger. His eyes stopped not upon the woman, but upon her Golden Naginata held to rest. As for himself, he carried a long spear; it was clear he intended to die fighting, being of a particular school which taught this to be the only Way. He said, "I refuse to die by seppuku!" His hand reached up to the spear's tip to remove the lacquered sheath. The two-edged, arm-long blade glistened eerie blue. Tomoe studied first the weapon, then the man, trying to guess his true age. His hair was coal black, but his eyes and gnarled fingers looked old. It could be none other than Tsuneme Heizan, who since his seventieth year had dyed his hair with ink so that, in battle, none would think him feeble and hold back.

"Grandfather Heizan," said Tomoe Gozen. "These eighteen monks were hand-chosen by myself and, as you can see, they have helped me slay five times our number, without receiving a scratch. Nevertheless, I am sure none of these fine men are strong enough to kill you."

"Only yourself!" Tsuneme Heizan agreed. Then he said, "Before we begin, allow me to tell you a story; it will not take long. When I was a young man, there was a blind warrior who bore the same naginata now in your possession. I remember her well. In fact, I was her first husband's rival, and her second husband's foe. The Ryowa clan contributed to her eventual downfall, but we relied on intrigue, not physical strength. All these years I have feared she might return, while at the same time I have been sad that she did not. Can you believe it?" He laughed at himself. " 'Old Man Heizan' they have called me, despite that my hair is not a bit white, as you can see; 'Old Man Heizan fears an aged nun!' But really what I feared was the Golden Naginata, which many times has killed me in my dreams. To overcome this fear, fifty years ago I commissioned the sorcerer-smith Jimei to forge this spear you see before you now. It took forty-eight mooncycles for him to make it, attended the whole time by fox-devils and spirits of the fire. To test it, I attacked Jimei, and killed him despite his magic; so this is his final and most remarkable creation. I have not used it since, for it was forged for one thing only, to destroy the weapon you call Inazuma-hime. Mine is named 'Bolt Catcher' and will finish off your lightning!"

Tomoe slid casually from the saddle, gave her quiver, her bow, and her white flag to one of the monks, and took a proper stance with Inazuma-hime. "I welcome it!" said Tomoe Gozen.

Tsuneme Heizan leapt down from the porch into the garden, an agile man despite his years. It was true he was skillful! He had, these long years, practiced every day. His style was the perfection of the Shinto Gods. It was the enlightenment of Buddha. Tomoe was impressed. When the two-edged spear struck the one-edged naginata, blue sparks and yellow sparks flew upward like fireflies, and the yamabushi moved away from this electricity. The armored woman stepped backward as the spear passed before her throat. Tsuneme Heizan blocked her return attack, and sparks flew upward again.

"Bolt Catcher is strong!" said Tomoe. "But what of Grandfather Heizan?"

"He also is strong!" said Tsuneme Heizan.

"I think so, too," said Tomoe. "But maybe his lungs are not what once they were. Maybe he will grow weary."

Sparks scattered a third time. The sorcerous spear and the Golden Naginata were evenly matched. Furthermore, Grandfather Heizan was without question Naipon's foremost practitioner of *yari-jutsu*, spear-art. But Tomoe Gozen was calm throughout, whereas Heizan grew more and more insistent, as though knowing he had only a few minutes to win, or thereafter be too tired. It was not long before Inazuma-hime scraped along the handle of Bolt Catcher, and Tsuneme Heizan's fingers were clipped away and fell onto the ground, writhing like wrinkled maggots. The sorcery-forged yari fell onto the ground as well, splitting a rock where one edge of the blade struck and rang. The old warrior slipped to his knees.

"Please," Tsuneme Heizan requested, "my coup de grace." He held his chin so that Tomoe Gozen would be able to pierce his neck. She handed the Golden Naginata to the same monk who had taken her arrows, bow, and flag. She drew forth her longsword, prepared to deliver the coup de grace required. She hesitated, feeling sad. Sweat dripped from Heizan's forehead, mixed with the ink he wore upon his hair, giving him a striped look. "That nun still lives," she told him. "The nun you loved and feared. Next to her convent is a peaceful monastery. Let me cut your hair and not your throat! What harm a little peace in your last years?"

"It's too late for such a thing," said Heizan, who had this while remained upon his knees, holding his fingerless hands against his waist. Now Tomoe Gozen saw blood seeping out from under the old man's obi. She realized he had committed seppuku after all, but, finding he could still move about, stuffed the belly-wound with cotton, wrapped his obi tightly to stay the flow of blood, and had come out to die in battle *in addition* to honored seppuku.

"The coup de grace," he asked again. Instead of stabbing, Tomoe reared back with her sword and lopped off the old man's head. To a nearby monk she said, "Wipe the ink from his face and place him over there with those young men." Then she took up the weapon called Bolt Catcher, took her bow and arrow and flag and Golden Naginata, climbed upon the white charger, and hurried to the Place of Tents to inform her husband they could take the military palace as their own.

By sorrow, by valor, by fear and by wit did the old clan perish or, failing that, fled into the west with two-thirds of Yoshinake's troops in pursuit. This was in accordance with the Shogun's wishes, though he remained in faraway Kamakura; so how could he have guessed what Yoshinake's additional intentions might have been? As soon as the Mikado could be imposed upon to confer suitable titles and authorities upon the Knight of Kiso, he would consider himself sufficiently qualified to march on the military capital, a fortnight's journey on, and take control of the military office, the bakufu . . . *that* was his intent. "My cousin and Madame Hojo presently rule Naipon," said Yoshinake to his wife, in a rare mild moment. "In a while, it will be you and I."

Although he said this; although he no doubt meant it to be a mutual endeavor from start to end; minds and reasons change, and Tomoe Gozen was at the brink of being severed from secret matters and discussions. When this came about, it would be her fault entirely; for she had too often been the conscience, and not the buttress, of Kiso Yoshinake.

It was not that she intended to be contrary. She strove to find some element of gladness in the prospect of Lord Kiso's proposed dominion. Her honor, her duty, these hinged not on power gained personally, but on service to her lord. It was the same for any samurai. The fact that serving the Knight of Kiso could be construed as serving also her own material and political interests was not invigorating, but unsettling. Yet it had been the same with Madame Hojo, stateswoman without peer. She fought beside her husband until they achieved regency through the Mikado; thereafter she influenced and sometimes dictated official policy, became, virtually, one and the same with the Shogun. She was younger than him by far; and whenever he should die, it was never questioned but that she would cut her hair and rule as *Ama* or Nun Shogun, regent to her child.

Tomoe Gozen tried to believe this course would be as admirable for herself as it had been for Madame Hojo. But the situations differed in important details, so it was difficult to hold Madame Hojo as the correct model, therefore difficult to applaud the possibility that Tomoe Gozen might rule Naipon at a husband's side.

Struggle as she might to feel better, what Tomoe Gozen felt was a strange and penetrating melancholy regarding this planned treason. To escape crippling sorrow, she sheltered within herself one major truth: If she served Lord Kiso properly, she need not fear anything else being in discord with her warrior's code. To be in harmony with ones lord's intentions was as much harmony as any wife, or any vassal, should require.

Even thinking this, sometimes Tomoe's tongue became sharp when it should not. Sometimes it was sharp when warranted, but no one liked to hear it.

When a quietness of sorts settled on Kyoto—when the killing at least had gone west—a good deal of celebrating arose within the city, at first instigated by the citizens who were glad the fighting ended. But soon events took on a ribald flavor unexpected by those native to the city, for the yamabushi were given to extremes of austerity *and* excess, depending on the day.

The liberator, his wife, his shi-tenno, and other important vassals had moved into the military palace (from whence the imperial palace was in view, connected by a private road and string of gardens). During a meeting between warriors of rank and sundry messengers, it was mentioned that the yamabushi were being wicked. The city yearned for a return to its usual placidity . A quieter observance of the liberation might be preferred. These were the couched and second-hand suggestions passed along from aristocrats . . . aristocrats not yet certain whether or not to be delighted with the loss of their turnkeys.

Kyoto had never known such unrestrained revelry as appeared able and willing to continue unabated. Gentle, courtly people soon felt not liberated from, but abandoned by, the clan who had protected them from such knowledge as they quickly gained. Was this, or was this not, abusive language and behavior? Were these or were these not truly holy men who went helter-skelter through the city drinking saké, making noise, and pushing people over?

A few more carefully worded petitions made their way into the meeting place of the palatial headquarters. Kiso Yoshinake was not the most subtle of men, except in certain matters of poetry, and he might have responded better to a louder plea, such as, "Call off your filthy, uncouth priests!" To the quieter requests he answered, "The city is their reward!" Perhaps he misunderstood the importance of the matter. When complaints persisted, he said, "No more!"

Already he was asking to be cut off from the needs of those he purported to oversee. Already he became a tyrant, and his rule scant hours old.

It may be supposed that about this time Go-Temmu in his slightly smaller palace at the far end of a lane, insulated from affairs as he had always been, began to doubt the promises of freedom. Kiso Yoshinake had not as yet requested conference. In itself this was mannerly behavior; go-betweens and messengers were the usual and polite means of communication between the two palaces. Yet Lord Kiso broke so many other rules; why not this one? The Mikado may well have observed this to be evidence of his own continued seclusion from matters of state. Yet he had means!

His palace, overlooked by the other, had a small but steady stream of messengers and servants going back and forth between the two. Few were authorized to walk the connecting road and gardens, but who would hinder such dainty people as these? Who more than they belonged upon that lane and midst those trees?

Both palaces came alive with intrigue—Go-Temmu's intrigues. The ears of pages and dancing girls were pressed to walls, striving for news of samurai intentions. Whenever a warrior caught some maid or page or old groundkeeper or cook or stablehand in those spying endeavors, they would threaten to cut off noses and ears; but in actuality, Yoshinake felt unthreatened by the Mikado's attempts to be abreast of news, and gave no order to interfere with any of his people. Around the chambers where important matters were discussed, enough guards were placed; elsewhere, let His Augustness play as many games as he desired! It was mere courtesy to allow him this.

Finally Lord Kiso made time to compose a most gracious correspondence which was taken to the Mikado by the boy who was Go-Temmu's personal companion. The boy was surly and effeminate and Yoshinake did not like him; but he merited some respect since he was the major go-between of these first communications.

The letter Yoshinake composed revealed him a poet indeed; it was quite a pretty tract, lavishing praise on His Augustness but also on himself; and the brunt of its meaning could be taken one of two ways: the *request,* or the *demand,* for favors and titles some of which were mere prestige and others of political advantage to the Rising Sun General. Dare Go-Temmu trust this self-named Liberator? Were there other choices?

Lord Kiso's dull meetings progressed. Tomoe interjected conservative advice which rubbed her husband wrong, and sometimes the shi-tenno sided with her opinion. Yoshinake was on edge already, awaiting the Mikado's reply, and therefore was unreasonable about almost everything. Late that evening, the surly and too-pretty page returned with the Mikado's missive. Yoshinake dismissed most of those in attendance, save Tomoe and the shi-tenno.

He was in such an ecstatic state that he could not focus his eyes or hold the letter without it shaking too much. The Mikado's own calligraphy! For all Lord Kiso's successes, fame, military expertise, and greatness, he was at heart and by origin a country lord, a provincial, a rough man from the mountains. Never in his life did he expect to hold a letter addressed to him by the Mikado's hand! This may seem a contradiction from a man with audacious plans; but such a contradiction was Kiso Yoshinake, in this and many things.

Without being asked, Tomoe Gozen took the paper from her husband's hand and read it to herself. Then she folded it and put it inside Lord Kiso's sleeve, so that he might take it out and look at it and smell it and feel its every crease when he was alone to do so. To the shi-tenno and for her husband's immediate knowledge, she made this summary:

"Tomorrow afternoon there will be a celebration for us and our chosen guests in the Mikado's palace, at which time the required titles and commissions will be given."

Kiso Yoshinake tried to sit with utter composure, a man indifferent to such things. But he could not disguise his feelings. He kicked his feet out from under himself and gave a shout of glee. The shi-tenno—dark Nenoi, pale Tade, young Imai, funny Higuchi—these men laughed with their lord. Tomoe Gozen stood and went outside.

Shortly, meetings came to a close, and Yoshinake's shi-tenno strolled together through the gardens between the Imperial palace and the military one. This garden was much larger than the one inside the gates of the newly occupied headquarters. The place was like a fairy-forest, especially at dusk, when the whole of the world was most surreal, faded, still. As it was autumn, only a silktree blossomed; but the garden was no less lovely. There had been no battles here; therefore leaves of maple, peach, plum and cherry were still a soft, untrampled mattress. Naked branches were black cracks against the redness and yellow of sunset. There were dwarf pines, green-black in the failing light, and these smelled sweet in lieu of spring's flowers. Servants of the Mikado's palace were about, although few at this hour, lighting garden lanterns as they passed between the hedges and along the magic forest's highway (the lane between the palaces). They were so ethereal in their movements, these servants, that they added to the fairy-quality of the place.

The shi-tenno divided into two couples, and, strolling on, they appeared as pairs of lovers; and indeed it was common knowledge, without the least ill-thought, that dark-skinned dark-clad Nenoi Yukika and light-skinned light-clad Tade Shimataka were the worst enemies of women. It might have been supposed that youthful, playful Imai and Higuchi were more likely to be lovers; but they had not considered it. Imai Kanchira looked so like his sister that, on times, Lord Kiso petted him, and Imai liked his lord's attention, but innocent man that he was, he never was aroused. Higuchi Mitsu was an extraordinary lady's man, his voice as smooth as his face, always eager to make some girl laugh and cause infatuation. In fact this was his weakness; a samurai should be more careful than Higuchi sometimes was. All the same, when these lovely men sat themselves beneath a leafless tree, upon the mattress of the leaves, it must have looked to be a tryst to anyone who noticed. Happy smiles were on their faces and they whispered things which might have been sweet promises, or not. A maid of court happened by the lane, saw them, giggled, and hurried on. Higuchi and Imai saw her in turn, but could not guess what she thought funny.

"There is Amaterasu's obi unrolled across the sky!" said Imai Kanchira of a stripe on the horizon. "Truly she has made herself ready for her bed."

"That rosy stripe has been there the whole day," said Higuchi Mitsu. "In fact I've seen it in the sky, unchanged but for position, on each day since your sister brought the yamabushi."

"That long?" said Imai. "I have not until this moment had the chance to notice!" He sighed, as though disappointed in himself, then added, "I must strive to notice such beauty as that more often."

Darkness completed its formation as the two men sat and spoke. In the dark, they became more serious in their conversings, and Higuchi Mitsu said,

"Imai, my stalwart, tell me: Do you ever nurture doubts about the thing our lord has planned?"

"Never for a moment!" said Imai, for Lord Kiso was his god. "How can you ask me such a thing?"

Higuchi Mitsu said, "We are among his council. Therefore it is proper that we, along with Nenoi and Tade, think in ways which other vassals never should. In order to give good advice, we must have previously considered every action and its possible outcome. We must even judge the intentions of ourselves, and of our lord. Think for instance of the sorts of advice Tomoe gives in council! It is advice which Nenoi sometimes seconds, so she is not just being a disagreeable wife. She has coined the phrase 'great treason.' Even Lord Kiso uses it, as though it were an irony and not a terrible fault. You cannot deny our lord is quite a stubborn man."

"An admirable trait!" said Imai of stubbornness, looking a bit upset with Higuchi's ruminations.

"What we've done until this day," said Higuchi, "serves equally the Shogun and Mikado, not only our Lord Kiso. From this day hence, this changes. The Mikado becomes our tool as he had been that of the Ryowa. The tool becomes a weapon against Lord Kiso's lord."

"Lord Kiso's only lord is the Mikado. Why serve first a regent?"

"That's what I asked *you*," said Higuchi. "For myself, I cannot answer."

"If I knew you less well," said Imai Kanchira, "I should question your faith in our lord. You talk as though you think we have merely shuffled power; but truly we have improved matters here. Why do you doubt it? I will not accept that Lord Kiso is an unreasonable man. If it seems so at times, it is only because his reasoning is beyond you and me."

"Beyond your sister also?"

"Perhaps she calls him unreasonable because her heart is frozen!"

"You think that?" Higuchi Mitsu did not ask his friend to pursue this notion, but said, "It's no insult to say Lord Kiso is stubborn or unreasonable; resolve is always like that, itself a noble thing. Nor is it a contradiction of fealty for his shitenno to consider these things." Higuchi quoted an old aphorism: " 'They who serve a wicked master are the noblest retainers. Who serves a kind master are never tested.' Do you remember a story, Imai, about a retainer named Hodo Doshijei?"

"Yes I do," said Imai, and told this tale: "Hodo Doshijei was beaten by his lord and sent on useless errands here and there. For this, he received too little rice to feed his family. Then one day his master received a letter from a wealthy acquaintance. The letter said, 'Lord Toba, you have a retainer by the name of Hodo Doshijei whose courage I admire. As my own retainers are useless men, I would like to receive Hodo Doshijei as a gift.' Lord Toba sent for his retainer and said, 'Useless man though you are, yet has someone noticed you, and this someone I dare not resist. Go serve him from now on!' Hodo Doshijei hurried home to tell his family, 'I have been given the opportunity for us to live more highly, but who would serve Lord Toba if not me? No one likes him, so there is none to serve him well enough.' Therefore Hodo Doshijei composed this letter for the prominent man who was seeking a third or fourth retainer: 'Sir. I am honored by your desire to have me in your service. As I have many children and live in poverty, I consider this the chance of my life. Yet my present master, who cannot afford a proven man, would be unable to manage his affairs if I abandon him. Though I go hungry everyday of my life, and my wife and children suffer, still must I beg you reconsider my master's position.' Soon enough Lord Toba received this final missive from his acquaintance: 'You have the only true retainer in Naipon! I have been impressed by his sincerity. Can you forgive my bad manners in trying to take him from you?' Lord Toba sent for his retainer and, when Hodo Doshijei arrived, thrashed him soundly and sent him on some foolish errand."

Higuchi Mitsu slapped his knee and said, "That is exactly the story! When first it was told to me, before I had the fortune to serve Lord Kiso, I used to think about Hodo Doshijei and ask myself, 'Was he a stupid man or valiant?' "

"He was exactly like us!" said Imai, glad to have discovered this good way of viewing Yoshinake's occasional irrationality. "Doshijei was an admirable man!"

Standing nearby was a samurai who had approached unnoticed, by accident hearing the end of this conversation. When she set foot off the swept lane, she was heard by the sound of brittle leaves crinkling. She stepped out of darkness, into the light of a garden-lamp, and stood above the two men who had been chatting beneath the leafless peach. "You should not talk so loud," she said, "or people cannot help but overhear." Actually she had heard very little; but, since she, too, knew the tale of Hodo Doshijei, she understood completely the good impressions Imai and Higuchi had about themselves. She said, "When your families starve to death, *then* tell yourselves you are men like Hodo Doshijei! When Lord Kiso's errands are useless and he strikes you about the shoulders when you bow, say it then! Hodo Doshijei was a selfless man, whereas *each of us benefits by what we do.*"

Higuchi and Imai looked between their knees, sitting formally beneath her gaze, a gaze as dark as that of Nenoi Yukika in his worst of moods. Seeing she had struck them to the core, and they were filled with doubt about their virtues, Tomoe Gozen softened toward them and said, "Nevertheless you are extraordinary men of battle and have minds as well. You are fine council for Lord Kiso. Please continue to remind him of his other options. If in the end he does not waver, we will see this to its end."

She brushed past them. They turned upon their knees to see her go; and they bowed a firm agreement, although she did not see them do so.

This was precisely the kind of conscience Tomoe Gozen had become for Yoshinake, his shi-tenno, even the yamabushi. It might have been that she could have presented these things in better ways. Good advice should not make men feel stupid. Even young men like Higuchi and Imai did not like to be made to believe themselves foolish. Wise, reflective men like Nenoi Yukika and Tade Shimataka liked it less. As for Lord Kiso, he could not bear it the slightest, scowling at the sting of Tomoe's blunt opinions. It would have been better to word things in such a way that those corrected were led to believe they thought such things of their own accord. But Tomoe Gozen was convinced her influence was small (which never was the case) and saw no need to do more than register her disapproval from time to time. The result was that many of her ideas were shrugged aside by men who otherwise must feel smaller.

From that moment in the garden, Tomoe ceased attending important meetings, thinking her input little valued. She did so of her own accord, but there were none eager to insist she come. That is how it happened that she was thereafter excluded from things Lord Kiso truly would prefer to share.

As the yamabushi had been mostly under her command, Tomoe Gozen was not certain she could ignore their reported behavior. She strode the nighted avenues of Kyoto to judge for herself. Everywhere was dance and laughter where that morning had been terror. The night was lit by multitudes of paper lanterns of every color and by the strangely luminescent band of rosy mist in the sky. Samurai and warrior-monks tested one another playfully, only occasionally injuring by accident; and as accidents were considered part of the games, none had vengeful thoughts. Girls and women who had never seen or heard such deviltry as was going on were less aghast than might have been expected. Many were titillated beyond recount. Some gave up their mildness in favor of indulgence. A few were glad to offer their virginity to bonze or samurai; although it was later avowed that fewer of those ladies were as virginal as purported. Many colorful costumes were worn askew. A city noted for its taste and etiquette came apart at its seams; but one could be of the opinion that the pretty ways of the Imperial City could do with these kinds of improvements.

She was less appalled than she had thought she would be, though there was very little which appealed to her personal sense of celebration. Perhaps those aristocratic complainers who sent letters to Lord Kiso were stuffy old men and prudish old women. Certainly there was no dearth of *young* nobility playing in these streets. Some of them may have thought it a kind of tribute to their liberator, himself a man from an unruly province, trained through youth by the mountain priests before he raised his armies. Many words of praise were said for Yoshinake; a fragment of a sentence heard here, another over there, informed Tomoe of this. Perhaps things did not go so badly as Tomoe had been fearing! If the citizens were pleased, then she had been wrong to tell him to be more attentive of their needs; Lord Kiso knew the situation better than she!

It was very odd to see these youths of royal families acting as they did. It was possible their emotions had been pent up for so much of their lives, only to see death so near in these past days, that now from sheer relief and reawakening, they were eager to aid in the propagation of the yamabushi sutra, whatever it might be, so long as it had something to do with the way the strong priests cussed as they pleased and swaggered.

But could it be that Tomoe Gozen was blinded by her tolerance? She had learned about the attraction of men like Yoshinake, and like the yamabushi, beside whom she was pleased to fight. Did such feelings for them cause her to look upon their celebration superficially? It was always easiest to see those who dance and laugh and willingly indulge in this or that. But what about the darker corners of the night? Over there behind a tree sat a girl, her obi trailing away from her body, for some cruel man had unwound it. She was weeping. Tomoe Gozen started near to see if she could help, but the girl got up and ran away, dragging her untied obi through the darkness. And what was that bonze keeping in his robe if not a rare piece of lacquer ware? Who else had bags of things? A muffled shout made Tomoe stop and turn around, but she did not hear it again, never knew what it was that happened. Now that she began to look closer into the eyes of those citizens who mixed so well with drunken priests and soldiers . . . was there not a little madness in their eyes? Weren't these once-coddled folk of Kyoto looking back at Tomoe Gozen with something of desperation?

She passed a temple which the yamabushi had taken over and turned into a saké den. It was the temple of a peaceful god—exactly the sort warrior-monks could not respect. The sound of gambling and lewd songs pulled Tomoe Gozen back toward this place, for she wanted to rush inside and reproach the men she had fought beside. But what use a token gesture? She stood at the bottom of a stairway, gazing up at the closed door to the temple, and there was fury in her mind. Dare she contradict her husband's proclamations? The city is *not* yours!

Before she could decide, the temple door burst apart with hardly any warning. Priest Kakumei himself came out backward, landing on his back at the foot of the steps. "Damn!" said the big wall of a man, as Tomoe Gozen looked down on where he lay, wondering who or what could toss him out like that. She turned her face toward the broken door, saw inside the ravaged temple. An old man with shaven pate had been tied up to the rafters, dangling with the rope about his waist. His eyes were clenched tight, but he could not close his ears to the blasphemies in his temple. What an awful thing to do to him!

Kakumei got up from the ground and brushed himself off,

looked at Tomoe whom he had always liked, and said to her in a chagrined fashion, "There's a *shoki* in there!" Then she saw the monster peering out. It was a thing too ugly to be a man, but somehow man it was, or parody of one. His face was flushed the color of peony blossoms. His hair, too, was red, like fire. In a funny way, he looked like a yamabushi, wild and hairy and strong; but certainly that red hair set him apart. Priest Kakumei said, "Those old shoki devils are attracted to two things: defiled churches, and saké. I guess we conjured him ourselves!"

Tomoe Gozen went into the temple and let the old priest down from the rafters. The poor fellow would not open his eyes and, now that he was loose, he quickly put his hands to ears, trembling. The shoki swaggered around the room but the yamabushi pretended to hardly notice. Priest Kakumei was following Tomoe, hovering about her. He was almost as big as the shoki but not quite. He said, "We must ignore the thing. They tend to go away if not noticed. There is only one other way to get rid of one, and I would not like to try it."

A drunken bonze came up to the resident priest who Tomoe had set free. This bonze tried to force saké into the old man's clamped mouth. Tomoe glowered at the bonze. He shrugged and left off. Meanwhile the shoki was being a nuisance, shaking empty saké bottles and saying things like, "None in this! None in this one either! Hurry-hurry! Give me wine!"

What a stinking den of iniquity she had come across, not one yamabushi sober, nor the wenches they had brought . . . fancy whores, for plain ones never lasted long in Kyoto, where etiquette so mattered. Hastily indentured servants (usually they farmed) came in and out from the back room of the temple, trying not to see the red-faced red-haired shoki (the yambushi advised them of this). They brought freshly warmed saké to replace the bonzes' empty bottles; and so the saké-loving shoki noticed who they were. "Sister!" cried the shoki, then, "Sir," but the girl servant and man servant hurried back into the other room. Tomoe Gozen lifted a full saké bottle out of the hand of a bonze. He looked up at her but did not try to get it back.

"Shoki devil," said Tomoe. "Here is a full bottle!"

The big fellow was like a fawning horse eager for something sweet. He came over and took the bottle and drank it down. The yamabushi gave a collective groan, for who could get rid of a shoki once it thought it could have what it wanted? Priest Kakumei groaned loudest, pulled his hair, and said to Tomoe Gozen, "What did I tell you? Do you know what you've done?"

"I've made him settle down a bit," said Tomoe, feigning innocence about the matter. She knew exactly what she had done. It would make the yamabushi think twice before committing more devilish acts, attracting worse devils than themselves, and ones they could not handle. She looked Priest Kakumei in the eye (she craned her neck to do it) and this is what she said: "I have never seen a fiend like this red-haired shoki in my life; but I have heard the best way to get one to go back to his secret haunt is to challenge him to a drinking-match. Is there none among the yamabushi who can hold more than a shoki?"

The shoki had finished off the bottle and began leaping up and down, shaking the entire structure. "More saké! More! More!" A bonze crept forward on his knees and held a bottle up, for it was no good ignoring him now. "Thank you!" the shoki shouted. "Thank you thank you!" He began to guzzle. He looked around the room and said, "Nice house!" between swigs. "Where is the incense pot?" Shoki liked to wear temple incense pots for hats. It was a most sacriligious thing to do. Tomoe Gozen gazed about the room and said,

"If the yamabushi are too cowardly to fight the shoki fairly, it is possible to stack the odds against him!" She looked at the shoki and asked him, "Would you mind?"

"Not me. I don't mind." He wiggled his red eyebrows and drank again.

"Good. See?" She addressed the yamabushi again. "The shoki is a good sport about it. Boil saké in a big pot until it evaporates a lot. Use the condensed brew for his cup, and ordinary stuff in your own."

"Good idea!" said the shoki.

"I think so too," said Tomoe. "Hurry-hurry!" she said to the servants, mimicking the shoki.

As any shoki can drink a lot, it was necessary to send all over Kyoto to get enough. By so doing, it was soon known everywhere that more than fifty yamabushi were trying to outdrink a shoki devil in a temple. Naturally, a crowd collected outside. More yamabushi came to see if they could drink more than a shoki, disregarding his head start. A huge container of stinking brew bubbled over the fireplace. The shoki drank this stronger stuff without waiting for it to cool. Now and then a boastful bonze decided he would try the shoki's brew; but these fellows did not last long. The others thought it good enough to measure ordinary stuff against the shoki's stronger.

Through the night it continued. Tomoe Gozen napped off and on, awakening once to a sad noise. It was not the sloppy, slovenly horde of sots that awakened her, but the soft, pitiful moaning of the defiled temple's priest. The old fellow had pulled himself into a ball, eyes shut tight, hands to ears, and he whimpered. Tomoe stroked his shaven head until he settled down a bit, but now and then he made some more unhappy noises. She understood a few words as he muttered miserably, and gathered that he thought himself to have been murdered in the wars, his temple burnt to the ground, and now the spirit of himself and of the temple were residents of Hell.

Before dawn, every yamabushi except Priest Kakumei lay sprawled upon the floor, out on the porch, or in the yard. The audience had camped around the place, some of them asleep. It looked as though there had been another battle, and here was the aftermath.

Tomoe Gozen, awakened and alert, waited for the final verdict. Priest Kakumei sat on the opposite side of a table from the shoki. The shoki wore an incense pot on his head. First the priest belched. Then the shoki belched. Then the priest emptied a cup of regular saké; then the shoki emptied a cup of condensed saké (or had the poor tired servants gotten things mixed up?). The crowd was thinning until the only ones who stayed were those who had placed wagers on the outcome, and even they were bored. There was only so much amusement to be had from watching yamabushi get sick and fall down. The final yamabushi, and the pet, were not doing anything different from a few hours before. Belch-drink. Drink-belch.

Something new did happen when Priest Kakumei reared up into a wavering posture, almost knocking the table down. Standing, he cried fiercely, "I am now so filled with courage!" Belch. "I am now so filled with courage!" He looked down to where Tomoe Gozen was sitting and he asked, "Where was I?"

"Filled with courage," she replied.

"Yes! I am now so filled with courage that I will fight the red-faced shoki with my fists!" He swung at the shoki across the table and the beast went cross-eyed when thus smitten. The pot fell from his head with a clatter and a crash. He reared up angrily, his face even redder than before. He grabbed Priest Kakumei by the shoulders, lifted him over the table, and threw him out the broken door as he had done many hours earlier.

"This is too much!" said Priest Kakumei, lifting himself to hands and knees. Then he fell down again quite silent.

Tomoe Gozen stood up and said, "Have you another name than shoki?"

"Kono Kasa," said the shoki. "You may call me Kono."

"Well, Mister Kono, you are too strong for the yamabushi to exorcise. That being so, how would you like to join my army? You will be good for humbling these men when they are too sure of themselves, or wicked."

"Will there be saké?" asked the shoki.

"Not very much," said Tomoe.

"Can I camp out in a temple?" he asked.

"I think a tent."

"Then I decline!"

"Very well," she said, drawing forth her sword. "I will take your head."

"I will join your army," the shoki reconsidered. "I hear the war is over anyway."

After so whimsical an adventure, by which she gained a strong member for her troops, it might have been presumed

Tomoe Gozen's mood began to glisten. It did not. She returned to the military palace gloomy as the day before, as liable as ever to register some firm complaint, in a manner to injure sensitivities . . . this being so, she chose to remain silent, bearing in mind that, on occasion, when nothing gentle could be spoken, nothing should be said at all.

There was a slow bustling about the headquarters, while breakfasts were prepared and samurai rose and primped at leisure. Few but the Four Great Men had been up for very long, and they were tucked away with Lord Kiso, their meetings securely guarded. Tomoe Gozen pretended to have forgotten the council meetings. She bathed, groomed, put on fresh clothing. She dressed in plain black hakama and white kosode blouse, over which she wore a black haori waist coat subtly patterned with waves. She found a straw hat she liked, and it was lacquered black. She carried it about, indicating her intent to be heading off somewhere soon. Several other samurai noticed she was planning to leave, no doubt to the tent-camp to check on troops. Yet they must have wondered why she was not with her husband and the shi-tenno, for those meetings were important. When she tied on her hat and went into the garden and toward the gate, she took not only her two swords, cast through the straps of her hakama and her obi, but also she had Inazuma-hime. This made witnesses more curious still, for there was no need of the naginata today. Celebration, not battle, was in the offing.

Before she had passed completely through the garden, she was accosted by a tailor. Lord Kiso had ordered special garments be readied for the afternoon ceremony; and this meant a dozen pairs of women's hands would be sore and aching by noon, hastily completing the necessary alterations of fancy court vestments. Tomoe suffered the apologetic tailor until she had the measurements she needed and was gone. Tomoe did not particularly look forward to parading gaudily along the lane between the palaces, in suits hindering easy motion; although she was mildly amused by the prospect of her husband in *eboshi* high-hat, sleeves dangling to the ground, and powder on his face. It would hardly fit his swaggering image; yet, perhaps, nothing less was quite polite in the company of court.

Tomoe Gozen proceeded to the Place of Tents, the tents being tarp enclosures devoid of roofs. Although she had not attended the pre-dawn meetings in the headquarters, nor peered into the council chamber to see what present decisions were being made without her restraining hand, she was nonetheless soon cognizant of new policy.

As she went among the troops in the tent-camp, she saw that all were at odds among themselves. Kiso Yoshinake had ordered a kind of purging of the troops. Fencing peasants were to return at once to their farms, under penalty of death if they refused. Wanderers were to hasten to their districts, the threat of execution encouraging them to do so. The wives of generals could remain; old precedents existed for this. But those small groups of martial nuns or others who were unmarried must either fall back among the camp-followers and whores, or else get themselves to their convents and other places. There had been no recognition of the value of these auxiliaries up until the day before. Nor was there an explanation of this sudden policy. But Tomoe Gozen knew her husband was sprouting nasty pretensions, master of Imperial Kyoto that he was, and would no longer suffer the motley nature of his army. Even samurai and yamabushi were not to mix, but were restricted to their own company, for this would lend a more orderly appearance to things. Yamabushi and samurai had mixed only to a small degree in any case; but this small degree must cease, and this official segregation was not good, in Tomoe's opinion, for the maintenance of a united force.

As the "lesser" warriors who were neither martial clergy nor of samurai blood packed their gear to leave, they were pitiful to see. Tomoe Gozen had trouble being Yoshinake's second voice in this matter. Therefore she became more silent still, passing through the tent-camp, pretending hardly to notice the mild but real unrest.

At the edge of the camp she was overtaken by the shoki devil. He wore the long, black robe of a priest, which surprised Tomoe. A white smile broke his flushed complexion. "Good morning, General Kono," said Tomoe. They bowed to one another. She had allowed him the unofficial title of General, which everyone would honor for so long as the shoki refrained from drinking saké. It was a terrible concession for him, but worth it for the title. Tomoe asked, "Why are you so gleeful? Everyone in camp looks sad."

"Clever shoki that I am," said General Kono, "I have converted to Buddhism so that I cannot be purged from the army by Lord Kiso's decree. I am a yamabushi!" The red-haired Kono Kasa thumped his chest with a big fist.

"I am glad," said Tomoe. "Please help the troops clean up the city. There is yet much to be done since war has ended."

General Kono agreed wholeheartedly and scurried off to useful labor, strong fellow that he was. Tomoe went her way.

It was yet early morning when she found herself off the main highway, wandering lonely trails upon the hillside. Once, she passed along a clearing, and lingered to peer upon the Imperial City in the low valley. How peaceful it looked; how attractive in every configuration.

Illusion: a wondrous possession.

How easily lost.

Before long she came upon a stream and followed it to a lake. She sat upon a fallen log and gazed over crystal waters. Though burdened with emotion, none of it was visible in her even gaze.

Pines dominated the high forest, surrounding the lake closely, their tops bowed in obeisance or to see their own images. The seemingly omnipresent rosy streak in heaven —a piece of dawn persisting day and night—reflected on the silver lake, a bolt of sheerest silk unrolled across infinitesimal waves. It was an unusual shade, that streak, unlike anything quite earthly; yet Tomoe Gozen had seen the color once before, and had these many days tried to convince herself it was mere coincidence. She did not like to admit some connection between the rosy light above Kyoto and the mist she had seen over Mount Kiji, coalescing into a holy beast.

"Kirin," Tomoe whispered, and her voice carried across the lake weirdly. "Your blood will not protect against Inazuma-hime's glare beyond today. Will you come to claim the weapon then? If so, I will not pierce you anew. I will not attempt to keep your treasure for another spell. It has already been used for its purpose in the Lands of Roots and Gloom; I should have returned it to you before now. I am sorry."

She stood from the log and moved to the edge of the lake, peering not at the rosy streak in heaven, but the one upon the lake. She bowed her head courteously, made several more apologies, held the Golden Naginata in front of her, horizontally in both hands, and cried out: "Oh mighty kirin of Kiji-san! Take your treasure from me now!"

A wind played over the surface of the lake, making the reflected streak appear to move nearer. Then it went back. Tomoe shattered the serenity of the setting once more, shouting, "I have come to understand your love of Inazuma-hime! If I keep her one more day, to lose her will be as though I lose my own heart!"

She stood there a long while, unmoving, expecting the fierce kirin to coalesce upon the water, come toward her like a mist, take away the treasure which was the beast's true love. But the kirin did not appear. The rosy band across the sky did not alter. Tomoe Gozen lowered her arms after some while. She removed the carved wooden sheath of the weapon, doing so slowly, for she was not certain what hour would find Inazuma-hime repossessed of blinding light. It was still rose-gold, shining, but not damaging of eye, rather, it was pleasing, although "pleasing" did injustice to the feelings it invested in its viewer. The beauty of that lightning glaze and temper gifted Tomoe Gozen with a tranquility lost of suspense, a restful peace. Her heart was almost bursting with a sense of ease; and Tomoe Gozen converted this excessive amity into a burst of inspired battle-postures as had never before been tried. Inazuma-hime thrust imagined opponents on the right, then left, and then the fighter twirled about, slashing a full circle, ending in a downward sweep which *stopped*, suddenly, all of this between one breath and the next. The movements had been more poetic than aggressive and, for the narrowest slot of time, she felt *in touch* with some harmony of spiritual and material wholeness, sensing Inazuma-hime to be a link, a circuit, connecting Universe to human selfhood. Tomoe then spoke quietly to the weapon. She said:

"I never thought to care for any blade as much as my

retired Sword of Okio. My present sword is jealous! But it, not you, must still possess my soul; the soul of another rests in you: the soul of the kirin. Why will the monster not claim you? Must I keep you near myself until I suffer greatly to be parted from your presence? Is that my punishment for taking you away?" She sighed, but not unhappily, for Inazuma-hime eased her feelings. "Last night," she said, "I dreamed. I was asleep upon my knees, leaning on some sad old frightened priest in a debauched temple; and the dream was just a voice which said, 'Mount Kiji is a temple also, the altar of which has been robbed, defiled, even as this old man's temple is.' The voice was sweet and feminine and courteous to me, but also very stern. I awoke knowing the monster kirin was near, would not rest or be happy until its altar was restored. I am very sorry for your true master, Inazuma-hime! I am very disappointed in myself!"

Then she sheathed the Golden Naginata and began to walk back to the city. She was surprised to be returning with Inazuma-hime still in her possession, convinced as she had been that it would be taken from her hands. Desire made her happy it was still hers to hold. Guilt, and knowledge that it would soon become a dangerous light, made her uneasy that the kirin ignored the call.

Yoshinake's entourage waited by the back gate of the military palace, preparing themselves emotionally for the parade to the other palace, the one at the far end of the long lane. They were never so nervous in preparation for war! They stood in awkward-looking bundles, posturing absurdly, trying to be comfortable in their heavy, gaudy robes. They each wore an eboshi: tall, narrow black hats with ties that went under the chin. They wore excessively high clogs or *geta* which went "clatter-clatter" as they milled about. They wore stiff, colorful, excessively flared hakama over several layers of equally uncomfortable garments. Atop everything they wore big overcoats of elaborately brocaded silk, long enough to drag the ground.

The shi-tenno tried to retain their dignity, and did not do too badly, but were less impressed with themselves than when sporting armor. Lord Kiso himself strutted about as though he felt perfectly at home in such finery, unaware that he appeared more the buffoon than any. Tomoe Gozen looked as though she was suffering most bravely. Two dozen other men, some with their martial wives, were fidgeting and worrying that something was on crooked (they were right). Everyone was overheated, as the afternoon was unexpectedly humid.

"Don't we look handsome!" exclaimed Lord Kiso. He was serious. Higuchi Mitsu laughed, but went quickly silent, realizing no one else thought the remark funny. Tomoe Gozen, standing at her husband's side, bowed to him with a reasonable degree of grace, then answered: "We certainly do look dressed up."

Lord Kiso turned, stumbling on the hem of his costume. An ox-cart was coming down the lane to fetch the one most honored among the guests. The others were to walk behind the cart in a stately procession. Such was the plan. A servant from the Imperial palace had previously instructed them in the etiquette of the situation; but he had done so tersely and not remained to see if it went well. Nobody looked as though they quite remembered anything, each looking to someone else and hoping to follow their lead.

The ox lowed on seeing this group. It looked at them in a startled way, and they looked back. The ox-keeper was having trouble convincing the beast to turn around, for it seemed intent on staring at these dressed-up warriors. It had spent its life giving rides to similar persons and had never stared like this before. Honored Ryowa warriors were always learned in manners of court, and were quite unastounding in their costumes which were worn with ease and grace. But in the present case, even a dumb animal could see something was amiss; it was apparently planning to stand there until it figured out more precisely what the problem was.

The ox's groom was an older fellow. He smote the animal's rump until it decided to pay attention. It turned about, revealing the rear end of the cart which had fold-down steps. Servants unfolded the steps and helped Lord Kiso enter the cart. It bounced and, as he had again stepped on the hem of his costume, he tumbled onto the floor of the transport in a clumsy heap. Everyone pretended not to notice while Lord Kiso struggled to discover some means of sitting on his knees within the cart's confines. There was room for no one but himself. The rest began to line up behind the ox-cart. Tomoe Gozen was supposed to be the first in line, but something happened which caused her to be last. That thing was this:

One lick of the ox-keeper's whip and the ox took off running as though chased by boars. The ox-keeper looked stunned. He began running alongside the cart, trying to get the ox to slow down or stop. It was very swift, convinced, no doubt, that uncouth plebians pursued. Imai Kanchira shouted, "Our lord is in danger!" Off he went, along with the other shi-tenno, running behind the cart and crying out, "Oh! Oh! Stop there! Oh!" They kept stumbling in their clothing and on their too-high geta, trying valiantly to keep their eboshi hats straight, and were not much help stopping the cart.

When the other vassals, their wives, and few privileged servants saw the shi-tenno run off like that, they thought it best to keep up, to show their concern was equal to that of the Four Great Men; or, if not to prove their concern, then at least to keep the parade coming in a manner somewhat in the fashion explained to them earlier (though faster than explained). The shi-tenno were making a terrible racket, and the wooden geta on everybody's feet went clickety-clackety, and the wheels of the cart rumbled; with all this, who could stop an ox? If it knew about oni devils and badger-spirits and such things, no doubt it believed its pursuers were such as those: impostors, not true Ryowa. Who could say the ox was wrong?

As for Yoshinake, he simply could not keep his balance in the bouncing, speeding cart. He kept falling on his back and floundering. The excessively long sleeves of his robe wrapped around his face and he could see nothing. He was, furthermore, blaspheming in a superb way, so that the ox-keeper, unused to such sounds, clapped hands to ears and gave up trying to stop the ox. Lord Kiso shouted, "Kill that man! Kill that ox's groom!'' which quotation excludes many elaborations on how the killing should be done and under what unhealthy circumstances. The ox-keeper may have understood, about that time, that Lord Kiso meant revenge for this indignity, and so began to placate the thrashing occupant of the cart, saying, ''Hold onto the rails, Honorable Sir! Hold onto the rails!'' Lord Kiso caught the rails in his fists and thereby ceased to flap about like some wounded hawk. In fact he found his balance quite nicely and this caused him to smile. He shouted over the din of the swift parade, ''Is this the way to do it?'' He stuck his chin out proudly. The ox-keeper, long beyond his youth, could not keep up with the cart any longer; but he did manage to say, before dropping out, ''Yes, that is exactly the way!'' Then he left off running altogether, fanning himself with a scarf in one hand, patting his forehead with it, watching the whole entourage dash past noisily in clogs and crisply crinkling costumes.

Tomoe Gozen was last to arrive at the gate because she walked, much as had been instructed at the start.

Sweaty and stinking in their cumbersome clothes, the whole group gave over their longswords to servants at the door, and were given folded iron fans instead. They were permitted only their shortswords within the Imperial palace, and even these must not be drawn under any circumstance whatsoever. The iron fans were token replacements for the longswords, to be worn in the obi where the longsword ordinarily belonged. This custom was ages old and nobody questioned it; if they had been of a mind to question it, their fears would no doubt be alleviated to note that not even the castle residents responsible for protecting the premises carried longswords. The only exceptions ever made were, upon occasion, dancers, whose swords were mere decorations permanently adhering to their sheaths.

The iron fans were called *tessen* and were commonly cast in one piece so that they did not really open. Only one of these fans was not of the artificial sort: Kiso Yoshinake was given a special example, more carefully made with several parts, opening the way a wood and paper fan would do. He realized this difference immediately, and felt immeasurably honored, justifiably privileged. He opened the fan and followed after the servant, fanning himself expansively. It might have gone without saying that Yoshinake was in a fine mood. He was beaming! He looked this way and that way and was most impressed with everything he saw, though truth be told, there was not much to be seen in the hallways. But the atmosphere impressed him anyway; indeed, he was wholeheartedly overawed by the wonders he imagined were behind every door. This was the house of Amaterasu's godchild after all. Where gods or godlings lived, that was heaven. Kiso Yoshinake thought himself strolling through the corridors of paradise. The entourage behind him was perhaps less inclined to swoon, observing that their own headquarters, taken from the ousted Ryowa, was in fact the finer dwelling.

They were conducted to a huge chamber where serving girls waited with trays of covered food. These girls were sitting near the walls, behind pillows on which the honored guests were to sit. They looked nervous and afraid when the doors first slid open, for they had been told the warlord Yoshinake was ferocious. But seeing who tumbled in, these girls began to grin in an unbecoming fashion, and had trouble looking serious for a while.

Yet another servant (the palace crawled with them) showed the group their places. Directly, everyone was seated neatly along two walls, one side facing the other.

The center of the floor was bare, polished wood. The sides of the room were covered with tatami mats, and the pillows arranged on top of some of the tatami floor-coverings. Yoshinake and Tomoe sat nearest a raised area which was a stage. Imai Kanchira and Higuchi Mitsu were next closest. Across the way, against the further wall, dark Nenoi and pale Tade had positions of honor nearly as important as their lord and Tomoe Gozen, except the stage was not quite centered. On the stage itself there was a large screen, behind which the Mikado would later sit.

Yoshinake's bright mood dimmed with disappointment. He had thought the Mikado would be waiting to receive him. Perhaps he thought there would be a shining man upon an elaborate dais. Lord Kiso looked about the room, seeing for the first time that it was an ordinary enough place, at least there was nothing shimmering the way he had dreamed it as a child. The home of the Sun's descendant *ought* to shine, oughtn't it? Well. Yoshinake was a grown man and must have known in his heart that the Mikado's palace would be made of the same stuff as castles and temples. Still, the child in a man can live a long while; and it is sad, sometimes, to let a part of that child go. Yet there was relief as well as sadness in Yoshinake's manner, for at least he need not fret that he manipulated some god instead of a man.

Everyone sat rigid in their fancy clothing, in the most formal of postures, waiting. The maidens uncovered the trays, and the entourage poked at rice and pickles and radishes, everything prepared in pretty ways and arranged within the bowls in pleasing patterns. No one ate much. There was saké before long, and this the warriors were more eager to receive, nervous as they were.

Tomoe Gozen watched her husband carefully. He was out of his own, for sure. How magnificent he would have been, coming here in full regalia, armor a-clatter, face stern, manner curt but profoundly courteous. By his expression, he was no longer pleased, no longer blind to his awkward appearance, no longer awed by his surroundings. The food was food; the wine was wine; the tatami were tatami; the wooden beams were only made of wood. What else he should expect was hard to know, but surely he expected more than an ordinary feast and drink in an ordinary chamber . . . or to be left there waiting.

No one spoke, or at least not really. The maidens plied the men and wives with pointless questions, but the answers were quick. There was no atmosphere of gaiety. Rather, the atmosphere was as stifling as the court costumes. The Mikado would arrive, they were told, in good time, from some other part of the palace; but time was passing, rice became dry, nothing interesting happened.

Lord Kiso scowled terribly, craned his neck, tried to see behind the screen. Tomoe leaned toward him and whispered, "Be patient this while, husband. The Mikado no doubt fears your intentions are no better than were those of the Ryowa.

You must show him you mean only respect, and tolerate his slow arrival.'' Lord Kiso made an even more sour face, but nodded with understanding; still, he was hurt, as would be any spoiled boy expecting praise and getting silence. In a while, Tomoe added, ''Our men are edgy, too. See how they squirm? They accept saké too quickly. We must set them an example.''

Kiso Yoshinake knew by his wife's words that he must be calm at any cost. Further, he should extend his strong personality across the room to hold at bay the ready impertinence of his vassals. All were being tested by the Mikado's tardiness, and they must not fail. They must not believe his Augustness was in any manner at their beckoning.

The vassals and other invited guests were taut as strung bows and needed to be more relaxed.

Unexpectedly, Lord Kiso stood. He was eager to meet the challenge of putting his men, and himself, at ease. Every eye was on him. He held his iron fan outward to one side, opening it section by section. His posture was dramatic. When he spoke, it was not with military toughness, but with the lively tone of an entertainer. He said, ''As you know, Imai Kanchira, youngest of the shi-tenno, has been learning to play the *tsuzumi* drum and to recite tales of our conquests! It is proper that every samurai have some art beyond his sword.''

Tomoe saw her husband's intentions and said very quietly to a serving maid, ''Quick, fetch a drum from somewhere.'' Yoshinake was still speaking in his sweet, introductory manner:

''You may also know that I was at one time famed for my 'hermit dance.' It has been a while since I have had the chance to practice my boyhood skill. Perhaps those gathered here will help me to discover whether my 'hermit dance' is rusty or still bright.''

Imai Kanchira, red with embarrassment, but smiling with the joy of it as well, took the tsuzumi which the maid had fetched, and held it upon his shoulder, prepared to strike it with his right hand. Yoshinake faced Imai and bowed one time. Then the warlord moved to the center of the floor and

Wendy Adrian Shultz

took a stance as might an actor in a play, an illusion increased by the brocaded robe and glistening silk hakama. Crouched thus, he raised his fan straight upward and closed it with a *snap*.

Imai struck the drum: *pohmp*.

Only that once.

Imai chanted in his sweet boy's voice: "I am the Knight of Kiso, Rising Sun General, famous from Nikko to Nagasan for my arrow-deflecting art!" He struck the drum twice more: *pohmp-point*. Yoshinake turned a full circle as the line was chanted by his vassal, moving his fan out and across as to deflect arrows in slow motion. He no longer looked the least awkward in the colorful costume. It suited him well, just then. Imai sang the next line: "By dint of trenchant blows has his Augustness been freed from the nefarious circle of dragons!"

Lord Kiso made three powerful sweeps of one arm, turning his head slowly, his face fixed with an actor's fierce expression.

"In battle I met Toriyoka Gembei and sliced him through the neck!" *Pohmp, pohmp-point*.

Yoshinake ran forward to Nenoi Yukika, sweeping the closed fan toward the dark man's neck. Nenoi feigned the loss of his head, slumping forward.

"I grappled Kunugi-no-Nara and bit a hole in his throat!" *Point point pohmp*. Lord Kiso scurried to the opposite side of the room going at a stylized, bow-legged trot, baring his teeth at Higuchi Mitsu, who sat next to Imai. Higuchi was delighted to pretend his throat was bitten, and fell over on his side in hammy death.

Pohmp! Pohmp! "My well-known horse Grey Cloud Demon and righteous Sword of Okio fought on without my taking note!" *Pon-point*.

Yoshinake went back to the other side of the room where light-skinned Tade Shimataka awaited his turn to be killed.

"General Yohara refused to die when his arm was cut off!" *Point*.

Tade Shimataka let his arm go limp when Yoshinake's fan

pointed at it. Imai struck the tsuzumi a number of times, rapidly, stopped suddenly, shouted, "So I chopped off his other arm as well!" *PHOMP POHMP PHOMP POHMP*. Tade's other arm went limp.

This went on some while, until most of the vassals in the room, their wives, and ultimately the servants, were all tipped over, pretending to be dead, but sporting tremendous grins. The serving maids were starting to die just as someone interrupted.

It was the surly page who appeared on the raised stage. He stood in front of the Mikado's screen, gazing in a haughty fashion at the dancing warlord, his Tsuzumi-playing vassal, the assorted warriors and guests and the palace's own maids . . . . most of them stretched out in idiotic postures playing dead. Such a gaze of disapproval did that boy have! What right had he? Kiso Yoshinake froze in mid-step, turned his head to see the boy upon the stage. Those spread out on the floor sat up one by one, making themselves more dignified (or trying to), each seeming embarrassed to have been caught at such play. Imai Kanchira peered sidelong at Higuchi Mitsu and, as though to spite the silence that fell upon the room, smote the drum once more: a sharp sound: *Doh!*

The boy on the stage said, "The Mikado is present."

The hush was more startling then. Everyone began to bow. Kiso Yoshinake hurried toward the place of honor, settled to his knees, last to bow and first to look up, hoping to see the man behind the screen. He did not know what the Mikado looked like. As a child might wish a glimpse of some hero, Yoshinake maneuvered his head back and forth, hungry for a chance to see Naipon's living flesh.

The haughty page before the screen was heavily powdered and lightly perfumed. There were brow-smudges made high on his forehead. His court costume was of brilliant colors, suited to his young age. His tabi socks were red, like a girl's. This fancy lad held a scroll in one hand and, with the other, began to unroll it before his own eyes. The moment the boy began to read it, Lord Kiso realized it contained the very commissions he had requested.

"By right of services to His August Son of Amaterasu,

Go-Temmu the Living Flesh of Naipon awards Kiso Yoshinake, the Rising Sun General, the high title of Grand Councilor, in addition to which he shall henceforth be made Commissioner of Police."

Yoshinake visibly swelled. His face was tight with excitement. His right hand clenched the iron fan tightly. Tomoe Gozen, too, could barely suppress a smile, for she liked to see her husband thrilled as this. The boy on the stage read further:

"His Augustness also bestows upon the honored Knight of Kiso the position of Commander of Guards, in addition to which he shall henceforth be made Protector of Shrines, Temples, and Treasures of Art."

A long breath issued from between Lord Kiso's clenched teeth as he grimaced with a kind of ecstatic pain. Tomoe thought her husband might swoon for sure, tipping on his side and groaning. He managed not to do so. His eyes were wide and round as he listened to the page who was still not finished. The page unrolled the scroll a bit further and continued:

"Further is the Liberator of Kyoto to be made Bodyguard to the Sixty-Six Provinces, in addition to which he shall henceforth be appointed Barbarian-Suppressing Generalissimo."

This last title made him, effectively, the Mikado's regent: Shogun. Lord Kiso's dream was realized in that moment. He placed a hand upon the floor before himself, needing balance, staring at nothing, like a man wounded near to death. Then, of a sudden, he realized the page was done, the highest position a samurai could achieve had been achieved. Lord Kiso began to bow many times in rapid succession as a mere peasant might do, and saying in a loud strained voice, "Thank you! Thank you very much!" which was not at all the correct procedure, but disarming in its way, and appropriately humble.

The scroll was rolled tight, a band tied around it, and a servant took it from the Mikado's personal page and carried it to Kiso Yoshinake. His hand shook to accept it. His thoughts may have stroked the realization that he was now fully qualified to march on Kamakura and take the military capital as his personal seat of government . . . but more simply, his mind was filled with a less specific delight, an unnamable pleasure which knows no thought, no reason, but is like a shining light at the center of the self. He snapped out of his daze a moment, looked up at the haughty page, and made his promise:

"I shall be the Unifier of Naipon!"

The page did not look at him. Instead, he clapped his hands three times, and a line of dancing girls came into the room from a door beside the stage. They were dressed in archaic costumes, an older type of eboshi hat on each of their heads, robes trailing the floor, a straight variety of longsword attached decoratively to their obi and sticking out behind like tails under overcoats. Young female musicians appeared, too, with stringed instruments and bells; they sat on the floor in front of the stage. The twenty dancers arranged themselves in rows upon the hardwood portion of the floor, between the two rows of honored guests. The musicians began performing (Imai Kanchira surreptitiously played his tsuzumi with the young women) and the dancing commenced. The audience quickly settled into comfortable postures. Saké went freely among them, and only Tomoe Gozen did not partake. Everyone watched the spectacle of grace and elegance which the dancers represented. Everything grew merry.

The page was sulky. He stood before his master's screen, watching all of this, never smiling; but he could not dampen the mood of Yoshinake's success. Nenoi Yukika stood from his pillow, skirted the room to join Lord Kiso for a moment, and in his master's ear whispered, "I will make that rude boy my lover."

Tomoe barely heard this said; Imai was not paying attention. Yoshinake looked askance at the pouty, disapproving face of the Mikado's page and companion, then at the dark face of Nenoi, and said, "Please feel free." Nenoi returned to his side of the room, leaned to Tade Shimataka, and exchanged a joke and laughter. Both of them began to stare at the page upon the raised part of the room, no longer affronted by his unforgiveable hauteur.

Tomoe Gozen whispered to her brother, "Imai, please

refrain from drinking.'' He registered surprise at her insistence, but obeyed without question. She volunteered an explanation: ''Our Lord Kiso is more drunk on his achievement than on saké. If it were otherwise, he would notice that these dancing girls are not soft-looking like these other women of the court. I think they are stragglers. I think they are Ryowa clanswomen.''

At that very moment, the decorative swords proved not to be decorations at all. The women had maneuvered themselves before the chief vassals and Tomoe and Lord Kiso, their maneuvers seeming innocent parts to their dance, until steel licked out toward the faces of the guests. The musicians ceased their performance, sat quietly, and were clearly unsurprised by the event.

When the music and merrymaking became a stillness; when there were straight, old-fashioned swords pointed steadily at eyes and mouths and noses; when even the most honored and heavily titled Yoshinake must hold his head back lest his throat be pricked; there was a loud roaring sound, and it was Lord Kiso shouting,

''The meaning!''

The young woman before him raised her sword a little, until it was between his eyes. His own hand clutched only the iron fan in one hand, the scroll of titles in the other. He had no longsword to match hers, nor did any other of his company. He might draw his shortsword rapidly enough to win . . . but there was a matter of honor in obeying old traditions. It would cost face to draw the shortsword in the Imperial palace, despite the present treachery. Kiso Yoshinake worshipped the emperor despite the plotted use of him; and thereby, not even a country warlord like Yoshinake, unmannered though he could be, would break the cardinal rule. No matter what provocation, it remained unwarranted to use the sword.

The boy who had this while remained before the Mikado's screen shouted back at the warlord, ''State your true intentions, O Knight of Kiso!''

His reply was quick and honest.

''To rule Naipon!''

"It was expected!" said the boy. "Thirteen days ago, a giant favored in Kamakura, by the name of Uchida Ieoshi, was a guest of this palace, under Ryowa scrutiny most of his stay. Before he left he managed to inform us that the Knight of Kiso had been authorized to attack the Ryowa, that in fact there were, at that very moment, warrior-monks and samurai gathering in the hills around Kyoto. We were delighted by the prospects! However, the giant told us that he had personal reason to suspect your capacity for treason if the Ryowa were cast down. Uchida Ieoshi planned to hasten to Kamakura and beseech the true Shogun to prepare a chastisement. Today, we have received advance word from spies that Ieoshi and another of the Shogun's most trusted vassals, Wada Yoshimora, are mere hours from the city! Your treason cannot succeed!"

Yoshinake's boyish excitement drained completely. His grip upon the scroll was so tight that the narrow binding snapped, and the scroll unrolled across the floor, the paper blank. Such a look was on his face that Tomoe Gozen feared her husband's response more greatly than she did the swords pointed at everyone's neck, including her own.

Uchida Ieoshi, the very son of a jealous swordsmith, had long conspired against Lord Kiso and Tomoe Gozen in his desire to destroy the last two Swords of Okio. He had come upon some useful information, it could not be doubted. Tomoe had in that hour seen her husband raised to the height of success, then plunged into the depth of failure. How would he react? Not slowly. Not mutely. Not meekly. Of this, Tomoe Gozen was sure.

His fingers had been digging into one of the tatami mats, which suddenly he raised up, toppling the woman who threatened him with sword. Tomoe Gozen whipped the iron fan from her obi to smack her own doom aside. Imai Kanchira used his tsuzumi drum in a clever way, pushing it on the end of the sword which threatened him, standing as he took his iron fan to fight. The room erupted into violence; and each of Yoshinake's retinue used *tessen* in lieu of swords. Therefore none dishonored themselves drawing shortswords in the Imperial palace.

The Ryowa dancers were strong, but they were dancers after all, not practiced warriors like those attacked. In ten heartbeats, they lay defeated, their skulls caved in by the iron fans, or else their arms broken by the swift defense. As good measure, the musicians were slain, too; perhaps there was spite in that. Only one among Lord Kiso's group had been slow and therefore slain.

Yoshinake was not placated, of course. He dashed onto the stage and thrashed the pretty boy who cowered and tried to run, but crumpled with skull cracked. Lord Kiso pushed aside the Mikado's screen, bellowing in rage. There was no one behind the screen. No one had been there the whole time.

The ceremony and titling had been a sham designed to make him waste the day while men marched the last miles from Kamakura. Kiso Yoshinake knew that he had been insulted more gravely than any man had ever been, that he had played the fool better than it had been played before. The anger of him was terrible to see. He stood upon the stage and called out to his vassals:

"Already Kyoto may be surrounded by the first troops. They await signal to attack, no doubt, or for the bulk of our enemy's forces to arrive. Clearly, we are unable to take the Shogun by surprise in his own city. Nevertheless, we will destroy his armies! We were outnumbered three to one by the Ryowa, yet we barely suffered. Now, many of our troops pursue the Ryowa westward, and the Shogun will have sent forces six times what we have at present. Therefore you must use cleverness to win! Any trick will do! We will not be overwhelmed!"

The room cleared in a moment, all but Lord Kiso, Imai Kanchira, and Tomoe Gozen, discounting the corpses of the women. Lord Kiso stood yet upon the stage, an actor of the final scene, gazing at the floor between his feet, musing bitterly. In a moment, he cast off the gaudy overcoat, untied the silk hakama and let it drop to the floor, and stood in the somewhat plainer kimono underneath. He crossed the stage, approached a lantern, peered down into the fire of it. The flame, surprisingly, was blue.

"Husband."

Lord Kiso did not reply, did not move. He gazed down into the flame.

"Lord Kiso!" shouted Imai, his face sad. Still there was no answer.

"Husband," Tomoe repeated, knowing that he heard. "I have left a gift for you beside your armor in the military palace. It is a spear forged by the sorcerer Jimei fifty years ago. It shines blue to match your armor and your helmet. It is a good weapon for you."

He looked up at her sharply. "I have the Sword of Okio!"

"That sword has been your ruin. The Shogun's vassal Uchida Ieoshi has replaced your position in the bakufu. He would not have ferreted out information against us but for that sword."

"I will have no other!"

"I ask only that you inspect the spear before casting it aside. I confess to you that when I was away those few weeks, I visited Okio's spirit, and believe he may have forgiven us; but I cannot be sure. If we had not treated his champions unfairly, no doubt his swords would have helped you and me in our mission to rule Naipon. The Shogun, after all, permitted the giant to hunt down the swords and break them, and to slay Okio's family because he refused to leave this capital for the other. What more fitting vengeance than to replace the offending Shogun with Kiso Yoshinake, Okio's strongest champion? But the strength has bled from the sword. If Okio no longer hinders us, he at least is no help."

This matter was settled long ago, and Yoshinake would not change now. He refused to reply to his wife again. Instead, he bent to pick up the lantern. He tipped it sideways in his grasp, so that its paper walls caught fire. He descended the stage, moved toward a paper window, used the lantern to set the window, and hence the wall, on fire.

"Lord!" cried Imai Kanchira, running forth in surprise.

"The Mikado's home will burn!" roared Lord Kiso, moving from the heat of the wall. The flames went upward toward the beams. The wooden structure would be easily destroyed. Lord Kiso moved toward the exit, his face that of a madman, flames growing behind him. He said, "His Augustness will be flushed from his hiding place. To escape the blazes, he must use the stone stairway down; the other exits are made of wood and so will be aflame. I will wait for him at the bottom of the stair."

"You would keep him hostage?" said Tomoe, aghast, barring her husband from the exit. Yoshinake looked at her sternly, insisted,

"No! I will save him from the unfortunate blaze!"

Imai Kanchira stepped backward, out of the room, a look of horror upon his face. His disillusion was sudden and complete. Tomoe Gozen bowed to her husband and replied,

"Please be a good bodyguard for his Augustness." Then she turned and fled the burning palace, pulling her brother with her.

Tomoe Gozen and one thousand yamabushi were responsible for the defense of the northern highway. They marched along this route, a few of them on horses. There is a point along this highway which rises up sharply. It is known as "City Viewing Spot." Here, Tomoe Gozen in black armor and moon-crowned helmet reined her white charger about to gaze upon Kyoto. The yamabushi turned also, although they would never have yielded to the temptation without their general's example.

Already it was night. A moon hung low upon the city. The streets were filled with frantic people, mere ants from this far view. The Imperial palace was an inferno. The ants uselessly cast buckets of water at the base of the burning structure. Sparks ignited surrounding woods, hence to the small dwellings scattered among the trees. The moon's silver and the fire's gold shone across the whole of the city, making Kyoto grander than its norm. Such beauty could destruction be! In that moment of her life, Tomoe Gozen was moved to rare tears, and the yamabushi to fervent prayer. They fell upon their knees at City Viewing Spot and chanted a sutra for each bead of their rosaries; and Tomoe recognized the chant as the same used for stilling Kiji-san, the mountain which the yamabushi believed would erupt without their attention. Did they think the city would stop burning if their prayers were good enough?

Tomoe's sorrow was twofold. In her mind's eye, she saw her husband standing with his back to flame, his eyes the same bright fire. Her passionate gaze met his and they were silent for a moment, devoid of challenge or condemnation. How odd that she should think in that moment of their having failed to sleep together even once since her return with the yamabushi! There had been no opportunity. Their respective duties kept them here and there and never in the same place for a night. She wondered if his thoughts matched hers in that moment, remembering the night prior to her trip to the Karuga Mountains. That night, his obi fell away like a flaccid snake; his kimono unfolded like a screen. She had smelled of camphor, he of camelia oil, and the odors mixed as their bodies clung. Now, at City Viewing Spot, she fancied she could smell that combination; and the nostalgia of it filled her with longing. It was not exactly a sexual longing, despite the thing she remembered; it was less definite than physical desire. She longed for something they had never truly captured. There had almost been something between them on that night which seemed so long ago, something more than duty, honor, battle. Today, Kyoto burned, and Tomoe's heart was ashes. The thing that she and Yoshinake nearly found together would never be pursued. Win or lose the current fight, the intensity of their lives would never again be focused on that frailest part of human interaction, that inconsequent emotion, love. They had let the moment pass; it could never be regained. She had been a cynic before; she had thought such a thing as love could not exist in such a world as hers. Now she thought it did exist, but for her and Yoshinake, it had been put aside too long. Forever after there must be only duty and fate between them. It should be enough. Yet, whatever the reason, and despite the fact that she would never let it be known why, Tomoe Gozen was very sad.

The yamabushi finished their prayers; the march went on, beyond view of the flaming capital. A scout, or spy, met them along the way, informed them that but one mile on, a troop of six thousand shogunate warriors had raised a camp off the highway, planning a dawn attack. "They wait for other troops to find their positions on all sides of Kyoto,'' said the spy. ''They are well-hidden because of a hill between them and the road; but the hill could be your advantage, rushing down on them.'' Tomoe gave orders to the scout: slip into the camp, set fire to tents at the proper moment, create diversions and confusion among the enemy.

There were scouts of the enemy along the way also. The yamabushi proceeded slowly, sniffing the air, listening for a place that was, perhaps, *too* quiet. Not one enemy spy must pass their knowing! Seven were ferreted and slain. An eighth was captured alive, but killed himself before speaking.

Tomoe informed her men that they would be outnumbered six to one; and Priest Kakumei replied, ''Well met! It will make the fight more even!'' But Tomoe Gozen would not be impressed by such blind valor. She told them Lord Kiso's order was to be clever. She said,

''You have seen my Inazuma-hime in action many times. Unfortunately, I cannot use her in tonight's battle, for reasons you will know soon enough. But there is yet a value to the Golden Naginata, if you will heed closely my advice. Our horses must be blindfolded and left this side of the hill we are about to approach. When a whistling-arrow is launched, you will charge down into the enemy camp with all ferocity. *Under no circumstances look behind yourselves even for the quickest glance!* There will be a light upon the hill which the enemy must face. It will render them blind. Even so, they will fight well; but if each of you slays six, we will win. If curiosity causes you to disobey and look back, it will be your last sight, live or die. I hope you understand.''

She sat astride her charger, looking upon her army, and her sorrow did not escape them, though they could not know its varied sources. She asked, ''Where is General Kono?'' The red-haired shoki hopped to the front of the ranks. He wore his recently acquired yamabushi robe, which was too short to cover his shins, and a bronze pot for helmet. He carried a spear and had a longsword in his obi. He was proud and warlike in appearance, but a bit too happy in demeanor. Tomoe told him, ''You are strong as ten, but frankly very clumsy. There is no armor big enough to wrap around you, and you will be vulnerable to enemy swords. Will you leave my army and go back to where shoki devils come from?"

"It is not so easy to get rid of me!" said the shoki.

"Big as you are," said Tomoe, "I think you are young, devils growing faster than men. If a child like you were slain in this, I would feel burdened."

"I am less a baby than you think!" It was no use trying to dissuade him.

"Then fight well!" said Tomoe.

"I will!" said the shoki, looking more serious now. Tomoe said, "It is time." This is how it went:

Tomoe Gozen, a shoki devil, and one thousand sohei crept silently to a hilltop and peered down upon a camp where not even a campfire was lit and no sound was made. Directly, at three points simultaneously, fires erupted in the camp, shouts rose up, and half-dressed samurai went running helter-skelter for a nearby stream and back. More fires sprang up, and the enemy became more confused in their efforts to stop the blazes, unable to find who started them, a shadow in their midst. Unseen atop the hill, Tomoe Gozen strode to the highest place and planted the butt of the Golden Naginata where it would stand on its own. Then, she took a bow and set a whistling arrow to it, announcing the attack to the enemy when the shaft sang forth. The yamabushi burst from the top of the hill, shouting Buddha's wrath, their weapons raised high. The samurai below scurried about more and more frenetically, trying to douse the fires and simultaneously don armor as fast as they might, snatching weapons, coming to the edge of the camp to meet the yamabushi.

When her men were near the foe, Tomoe Gozen reached up with eyes shut and removed the wooden sheath from Inazuma-hime and placed this sheath in the back of her obi where it would not be in her way. Then she stepped in front of the shining weapon, a black shadow against incredible light, and she drew forth her longsword to descend into the mass of battle.

The shogunate forces were unprepared for a night attack, and less prepared for the night to be made brighter than any day. They watched the avalanche of bonzes and priests, and then the light appeared, and the bulk of the samurai were instantly blind. The yamabushi carved crazily into the ranks of startled, blinded warriors. Of the six thousand, perhaps a sixth had caught on it time to protect their eyes, or had been busy fighting the fires in the camp; but even these dared not face toward yambushi with open eyes without suffering the fate of their fellows.

The yamabushi showed no mercy. Samurai sometimes cut their own numbers, since they could not see. The yamabushi were hindered to a lesser degree, for they dared not turn to protect their backs from samurai who slipped by; and samurai, already blind, could fight in any direction. Many of Tomoe's men died because of this; yet none doubted the yamabushi would win. If fights elsewhere went as well, under the leadership of Imai, Higuchi, Nenoi, Tade, and Lord Kiso himself . . . the cost might be tremendous, but Kamakura would remain their ultimate prize.

Tomoe Gozen had a personal mission and scarcely watched the slaughter. She recognized the family emblem on the burning tents and flags, and went searching through the camp for Uchida Ieoshi. She stood among the flaming tents, her back to the shining hill, and shouted, "Tomoe Gozen of Heida, wife and vassal to the Rising Sun General, challenges Uchida Ieoshi to meet me in armed combat!"

There was no reply. She heard only the din of battle behind herself, the roaring fires to each side. Irritated to be ignored, Tomoe shouted,

"The sword-thieving shogunate general is a coward as I thought!"

Then there was reply. Uchida Ieoshi stepped out from the side of the one unburning tent, the flames and the Golden Naginata playing light on him, making him seem a supernatural presence. He was two heads taller than Tomoe Gozen, the tallest man she had ever seen, and wide enough to match his height. His armor was glistening black; the length of his sword would dwarf another. Such a monster he appeared to be! But his eyes were black from having seen Inazuma-hime, and he seemed uncertain where his foe might stand. He said, "You dare to call me coward?" His voice was a thunder-drum. "It was you arranged to fight blind men. Very well, come and meet a sword of Uchida-clan make!"

He drew forth an astonishingly long blade and Tomoe Gozen stepped back from the rush of the blind man. She did not back away from fright, but because he had stung her with his accusation, and she could not deny it. But for Lord Kiso's order to be clever, she would never have used that trick.

"Uchida!" Tomoe shouted, thereby telling him where she had moved. He turned his sightless gaze on her, raised the overlong sword. "Uchida! I am binding my eyes so that our fight is even!"

She cast off her helmet, for the giant wore none, and inside it was a length of cloth folded into a square as padding. She unravelled it, tied it about her face, and said,

"Now, my foe, we may fight!"

Thus it was engaged.

Between the clash of yamabushi with samurai, and the ruffling of fires, it was impossible to judge the subtleties of movement. The ear was not enough defense. She could hear Ieoshi's feet digging on the ground, but could not be sure how he held his arms; she could hear a rapid motion of his sword, but a slow attack was nearly soundless; she could hear his breath but not his heartbeat. But her foe's handicap was the same; he could follow her no better.

With only a general idea of body placement and approach, they fought awkwardly. They would nearly stumble into a fire or almost fail to block the other's stroke. Each recovery was ungraceful. Though Tomoe was quickest, the giant's strength was phenomenal. When Tomoe blocked tremendous blows, she could not easily hold her place, and so staggered back and back.

Exceedingly long blades were often badly tempered; but this one would not break against hers. Perhaps only her retired Sword of Okio could have matched a sword forged by Uchida Ieoshi's clan. It was no use lamenting about that.

They moved away from one another, she cocking her head left and right to hear his every motion. His thunder-drum voice began to recite an old poem or prayer, and the sound of it was unnerving. "I have wandered from the dark world upon a darker path. Shine on me, Brother Moon! Shine on me, O bright celestial river! Show me the way to the True Eternal Dark, and let me bring my foe!"

He struck her sword so well that, to keep her sword in hand, it was necessary to fall with it, roll across a burning coal which made the lacquer of her armor stink. She regained her feet, stood silently, listening. He tried a subtler attack, aware that such was harder to detect. She countered with the same, so neither gained advantage. Tomoe answered his threatening prayer with a promise: "When I kill you, I will give your armor to a shoki devil who is big enough to wear it!" He did not take the insult literally, knowing nothing of General Kono, but he was insulted no less, and hardened himself still further to the test.

Both were reliant on their sense of hearing, but Tomoe slowly came to realize there was another sense to use: that which distinguishes heat from cold. When Uchida Ieoshi moved against a burning tent, he was like a huge black shadow cooling her flesh. She could detect the shape of him, down to the placement of his arms. As his extra long sword went up above his head, she turned her own sword straight toward the center of the shadow she perceived, and charged with such force that she rammed the point of her sword through his armor and into his heart. In the same space of time, his sword had merely reached its upward apex, and now he dropped it behind himself. Tomoe Gozen jerked her blade out, snatched the blindfold from her face, and saw the giant tumble like a cedar.

The din at the bottom of the hill had died away. Of the thousand yamabushi, three hundred were left standing. Of the samurai, not one.

At that moment, the voice of Kiji-san whispered in the ears and minds and hearts of the surviving yamabushi. That same voice was heard by Tomoe Gozen not as a mountain's soul, but as the femininely urgent voice of the holy kirin. And perhaps the kirin was the spirit of the distant mountain after all; perhaps it was true that in placating that spirit with daily sutras, the yamabushi kept the volcanic peak at peace. The voice within each of them said:

Now have I served you as you, for generations, have served me.

The rosy streak against the starry heaven began to pull itself together in a rounder shape, then to funnel down toward the top of the hill.

"Don't look up there!" warned Tomoe. "Like this!"

She cleaned the blood from her sword, breathed a white breath upon it, and held the steel in such a way that she could see Inazuma-hime's reflection. The yamabushi observed her method and did likewise, three hundred mirror-surfaced blades held aloft. So doing, the yamabushi collapsed upon their knees in religious ecstacy, for they saw their god coalesce beside the weapon, its furred but serpentine neck turning in such a way as to look once upon them all. Was there something of tutelar concern in the monster's huge, moist eyes?

As it took Inazuma-hime's handle in its jaws, the kirin once more became a rosy mist; the weapon became golden sparkle; then both of them were gone. In the aftermath, Priest Kakumei approached Tomoe Gozen, his generally fierce features softened and seemingly aglow, and he said,

"Kiji-san has watched over us this while. Now the spirit of the mountain has gone home, as must we."

Tomoe Gozen bowed to the priest and thanked him with utmost sincerity for the aid of the sohei.

"There is one thing more before we go," said Priest Kakumei; and he pointed toward the dimly glowing remains of a burnt tent. Beyond the cinders, outlined in the darkness, sat Kono the shoki devil. He had found a large gourd of saké and, apparently, spent the entire battle drinking. Tomoe was incensed.

"Kono Kasa!" she shouted, anger in her voice, denying him his unofficial but much beloved title. "Strong boy though you are, you were no help to us at all!"

She still held her sword to hand, and approached the devil with a meaningful expression. He crawled away, dragging the saké gourd with him. Priest Kakumei stopped her, saying,

"He is our responsibility, who conjured him by our bad manners in Kyoto. Since he has converted to our faith, we will take him to the monastery. Perhaps there we can yet teach him to fight!"

The shoki bowed before Tomoe's wrath, begging her pardon. Priest Kakumei helped the pitiful devil stand. Tomoe Gozen only turned her back, went to retrieve her discarded helmet. Then she returned to the side of Uchida Ieoshi and said to his corpse, "You can keep your armor after all. But I will take your head to my husband who you have harried for so long!" She bent down and placed her shortsword behind the dead giant's neck, and pulled upward, cutting flesh and bone. She cast a pin through the head's topknot and carried it away, leaving the yamabushi behind to deal with their dead.

On the highway at dawn, where Tomoe rode toward Kyoto, someone waited. This someone sat astride a chestnut horse, its iron mask the color of dried blood. The rider was likewise clad in ruddy colors, the armor being lacquered the shade of rust, and an umber arrow-deflecting cape hanging loose at one shoulder. The warrior wore an iron mask the same hue as that worn by the horse. The helmet fitted to this mask was unornamented, and designed to hang low at the back of the neck. A most practical helmet. The weapons of the warrior were these: *hoko* (a spear of foreign design, with a secondary point extending from one edge), an *ono* axe strapped to one thigh, and the long and shortswords mounted from the armor. Attached to the back of this impressive samurai was a high pole with flag, and on the flag was the family seal of Uchida Ieoshi.

The iron-masked face of the samurai tipped down enough to see the trophy Tomoe had tied by its hair to her saddle: the head of a giant. An angry breath issued from the mask, and the warrior spurred the chestnut steed into action. Tomoe drew her longsword and began the long gallop to close the distance between herself and Uchida Ieoshi's avenging masked vassal. At that moment, a heavy-set priest in black garb and wild mane of hair stepped out from the shadowed woods and onto the road. He stood between the charging pair, facing the masked vassal, and raised his *shakubo* or shaku-headed staff to make a religious or magical sign in the air. The rings of the shakubo rattled. The vassal lowered the hoko, veered into the trees, and kept going along some path without breaking speed.

"Sohei!" Tomoe shouted to the priest, reining her horse up short. "Why this interference?"

The huge, almost corpulent figure in black hemp robes turned about, and Tomoe saw that it was Makine Hei, self-proclaimed her worst enemy. She corrected the previous title of sohei to,

"Shugenza!"

Birds greeted the morning with pleasant songs, incongruous with the shadow of the sorcerer-priest so near. The severity of Makine Hei's expression was suddenly broken by a smile, but the smile did not look comfortable on that face.

"I only happened along this way," said Makine Hei, as though such a coincidence were the least likely, especially in his own case of sorcerous machinations. He continued in a cordial fashion: "You may be pleased to learn the yamahoshi cast me from their order for sealing you in Hell and for singly deciding the yamahoshi would not ride with Kiso Yoshinake. So I have not been made their abbot after all, but am only a wandering sohei doing penitence."

"Or a wandering shugenza," she amended. "Since you have avoided the high office of Zasu, it leaves you free to pursue me. Is that so?"

"You misjudge my intentions! Did I not just now save you from the masked vassal?"

"I would hardly think so," said Tomoe.

"You do not believe my sorcery caused your attacker to continue through the forest with no thought of turning back?"

"I have no idea about that. I only know you bring nothing beyond mischief for me. Such a man have you become."

"Perhaps so," Makine Hei admitted, and his strained smile was gone in an instant. "I have practiced my occult kiaijutsu since last we met. May I demonstrate?"

"As you wish."

Makine Hei turned his great bulk to face a certain tree, in

which numerous tiny birds of morning chittered, unaware of danger. Makine Hei's deep voice began to hum a note so low Tomoe Gozen could barely hear it, but she felt its modulation in her chest, and did not like the feel. The birds ceased their songs at once, and fell from the branches of the pine, flapping on the ground, dying in agony. When Makine Hei ceased the barely audible sound, only two of the stricken birds recovered, hopping drunkenly into the underbrush. Then the shugenza turned back to Tomoe Gozen, the depth of his hatred fully realized upon his visage. Tomoe Gozen made her charger walk backward, duly worried about his surprising power.

"I am not yet so good at it that I can kill you with my voice," said Makine Hei, but he said it with a grim nicety which did not ease her worries. "Soon I will have perfected it. Until then, it is better that you live and suffer more! I have brought news: Your husband has let his hostage go, a virtual confession that holding the Mikado captive was an unjustifiable offense, an admission of defeat. Wada Yoshimora has pursued him to Awazu, where the last battle is taking place at this moment; you will need to hurry or not get there before it's over. Lord Wada looks forward to meeting you, and is doubtlessly disappointed not to find you at Yoshinake's side this morning. Not only has Lord Wada set his heart on having your husband's head, he has also set his heart on you. He has three warrior wives already, and would make it four."

Tomoe would have cursed, but did not wish to interrupt her informant. He went on. "That masked vassal I turned aside from you is this moment heading to join a force which will cross the river Tai and join Wada Yoshimora at Awazu for the final thrust against Kiso Yoshinake. The end is upon him! Can you reach him in time? Can you turn the tide that has set itself against him? I would like to see you try!"

Tomoe Gozen's sword was yet to hand. She spurred her horse almost without thought, bearing down upon Makine Hei with her weapon raised, leaning from the saddle. But the shugenza stepped backward into the shadow of a tree, and was gone. Tomoe Gozen did not stop to lament her failure to destroy the sorcerous priest; rather, she forced the white charger to the limit of its endurance, speeding to Taigawa Bridge, hoping to stop the legion of the masked vassal from joining Wada Yoshimora on the further side.

At Taigawa Bridge it went like this: Tomoe Gozen built a fire in the middle of the bridge, then waited on the far side, hoping the wooden structure would burn through before the army against Kiso Yoshinake could put the fire out. The army led by the masked vassal was only minutes behind Tomoe. Soon a hundred horses and riders, along with several hundred samurai on foot, had gathered near the torrential river to survey Tomoe's handiwork. The vassal gave orders Tomoe could not hear, but their content was soon evident: Samurai scurried to the riverside with hats or anything which would hold water, then scampered back up the banks, running to the center of the bridge, trying to douse the flames. Without buckets and with only a few leaky straw hats and shallow metal helmets, there was not much effect, and the fire grew larger. The masked vassal made a second command, and ten horsemen galloped wildly through the flames, the horses screaming for the pain of it, but obedient to their riders. Tomoe, astride her white horse, met them. Only two could come at her at one time on the narrow bridge, and so she fell them two by two. The horses continued by without riders.

The masked vassal sent ten more, and twice as many additional men on foot. They came at Tomoe, their lacquered bamboo armor blazing, their horses' fur singed and tails alight, the men themselves badly festering. Tomoe held the bridge's end against them, her longsword flashing one side then the other of her prancing steed. Then an arrow took the horse and it went down, but Tomoe landed on her feet and fought without any loss of momentum. The masked vassal unleashed a second arrow, which Tomoe did not deflect; it stuck into her armor without penetrating as far as her body. A third arrow did the same, but Tomoe busied herself fighting those attacking her on horses and on foot. The end of the long bridge was soon clogged with corpses, atop which stood Tomoe Gozen, waiting for the next onslaught.

By then the bridge had burnt through enough that to send ten more horses would only cause it to collapse. The masked vassal made a sweeping gesture which sent the troops scattering east and west along the river's banks, searching for another place to cross. Those who had been uselessly trying to douse the blaze were directed to empty their last helmetfuls of water on the masked vassal and horse. Tomoe saw her drenched foe spur the horse onto the bridge, leap into the flames and come out steaming, just as the bridge began its plunge into the Tai.

Tomoe went backward, for the pile of corpses she had been standing on were sliding down the tilting length of the collapsing bridge. The masked vassal was determined, as was the horse. The sliding bodies were leapt; the incline was scaled by four sharp thundering hooves; and the fiery bridge was left tumbling behind.

As the masked vassal bore down on Tomoe Gozen, she threw herself onto the ground to avoid the edge of the hoko spear. She rolled to cut through both front legs of the rust-hued horse. It went down, the vassal tumbling over the horse's head, but rolling to a stance. Tomoe stood waiting with sword upraised.

"I am Tomoe Gozen, wife and vassal of Kiso Yoshinake," she announced, for such formalities were often performed between warriors of equal stature.

"I know," said the masked vassal, insulting Tomoe by not returning an introduction. But the vassal's hand moved toward the mask, unhooked it from the helmet's brim, and let the mask fall away. Beneath: the youthful, smiling face of Azo Hono-o. She said, "The head you bore away from battle, which has fallen with your horse into the Tai, was the head of my paramour. I must have revenge!"

"So it was you!" said Tomoe. "You who provided Uchida Ieoshi with the information he required to topple my Lord Kiso! Only you knew about the revenge-raid for the Imperial swordsmith Okio. Only you could have given the giant what he needed to sway the Shogun from favoring my husband!"

"So you must have vengeance also," said Azo Hono-o lightly. "There is no evading it now. You and I must fight."

Azo did not look the least unhappy about events. She had lost her hoko in tumbling from the horse, but presently she unstrapped the axe from her armor, and said,

"This will crack your helmet! You will die!"

Tomoe's sword blocked the downward blow of the axe before it struck her helmet; but she had not anticipated Azo Hono-o's fist striking her jaw. Tomoe was dizzied by the expert blow, yet blocked the second swing of the axe well enough, and countered with a swift cut toward the midrift of the other woman, failing the mark as the axe swept down to avert the sword.

"I am unmatched at *onojutsu*," said Azo Hono-o, holding the axe aloft in a boastful way. She backed away to see Tomoe shake her shaggy, dizzy head. "But I am better still with *this*." She drew her longsword and attacked with axe and blade. Tomoe blocked the sword, felt the axe smash upon her helmet and glance off.

"You make a lot of noise fighting," said Tomoe, trying to sound unimpressed by Azo's style; but with two blows to her head, Tomoe Gozen could not see very well. Azo Hono-o swung both weapons simultaneously: two overhead attacks which left her belly unprotected. Tomoe turned her longsword sideways and up to block both of Azo's weapons, at the same time raising a swift kick into the woman's stomach. Azo stumbled. Tomoe pursued, slashed toward Azo's shoulder. The blow was blocked with the axe's handle, but Tomoe's sword cut through that, and Azo went to her knees, dropping axe-handle and sword. She clutched her bloody left arm. Tomoe could have killed her then, but held back.

"I've won," said Tomoe quietly.

"It is only a scratch!" said Azo, but when she let go of her left arm to reach for her longsword, the left arm came loose from its armor and dropped onto the ground. Seeing the depth of her scratch, Azo Hono-o demanded,

"Kill me!"

"I won't," said Tomoe. "You are too much like me."

"Cruel to let me live!" Azo shouted, snatching up her sword and standing erect. Tomoe sidestepped a feeble assault and said to Azo,

"You must live. Grow strong. Try for me again." As Tomoe strode away toward Awazu, Azo Hono-o watched, pondering this last advice.

Tomoe Gozen went across a field where none but she was standing. It was a garden of twisted arms and raised knees blossoming red. Arrows and swords were the weeds of this garden.

Birds fed. Tomoe's longsword scattered the evil black crows. Now and then she succeeded in carving one or two of them out of the air as she passed by. The rest of these grim scavengers merely settled back to pecking at bloody wounds and tearing out eyes, as soon as Tomoe had gone by. She found a man still living, if barely, and he was of Yoshinake's army. She knelt to the man. He looked at her without much recognition, without the least strength, so drained of blood and pale was he.

"Where is Lord Kiso?" she asked softly, then, "Where are the shi-tenno?"

The man coughed, smiled (no, it was a grimace), and said, "Lost. All. Lost." Something caught in Tomoe's heart. For a second the world ceased to exist. Then she found herself and managed to ask,

"They were killed?"

The fellow rocked his head from side to side, a negative reply. He moved his crimson fist to one side of his stomach and made the ceremonial motion of belly-slitting. Tomoe grabbed that empty hand, as though the man had really tried to kill himself, and she would delay the act. Her eyes looked up, then down. There was panic in her. If Lord Kiso had repaired somewhere to perform seppuku, it would not do that she was not with him. She must commit junshi or "attending suicide" at his side.

She held the dying man's fist tight and there was no softness left in her voice when she demanded, "Where have they gone for the ceremony! I must be there! I must die with them!" The mortally wounded samurai understood this well. He pulled his hand loose from hers and pointed toward a stand of pines which guarded an area of leafless maples low on a hillside. Tomoe Gozen stood, but the dying samurai groaned in a pleading way. He had placed his hand to his belly again, his eyes holding those of Tomoe. She said,

"I understand."

She unsheathed the man's shortsword and helped him hold it in his weak, shaking hands. She helped him sit up. She knelt behind him, intending to help him guide the blade into his stomach. But sitting up drained him entirely, and the man died, a rush of blood at his mouth and nostrils. Belatedly, she gave him the aid he wanted, pulled his blade inward. Then she left him with hands frozen to the hilt of a shortsword buried in his flesh, lying on his side.

From the stand of pines, she could see Kiso Yoshinake sitting on his knees in the maples further down. No battles had been fought here. The ground was padded with crisp, brown, uncrumbled leaves . . . the autumn colors had mostly faded to browns and greys. On Yoshinake's left side sat pale Tade Shimataka and dark Nenoi Yukika. To his right: Higuchi Mitsu, whose humor did not show, and Imai Kanchira, whose youthfulness was undisguised by the first downy hint of beard. None of them wore armor. They were in white under-kimonos, the closest thing to ceremonial suicide garments they could expect on such short notice.

In their laps were lengths of white paper, on which they would write their death-poems. Each had his own brush, but would share an inkstone, wetted with their joined spittle.

They turned to see Tomoe Gozen loping down the hillside, waited for her in silence. She virtually plowed onto her knees amidst them, and she was ready to die with them, it was sure. The shi-tenno bowed to her as she sat there panting, but Kiso Yoshinake did not bow, scarcely looked at her as he said,

"Wada Yoshimora has withdrawn to allow us these few moments. I do not think it is necessary that you be here."

These were harsh words, though perhaps he thought mostly to spare her. Tomoe could not believe what he said; he would never have said it to the others with him. She could not reply. Her shock was evident, so her husband added more gently,

"Death is shared between men, life between a man and a woman. What would people say if the Knight of Kiso died with a woman?"

To Tomoe Gozen, these words were not kind, but outrageous. She said, "You can say this, after we have shared more than a year of death together?"

"It was a different matter then," her husband replied. The shi-tenno were silent. By their downcast appearance, Tomoe Gozen knew they would be glad to die with her. Kiso Yoshinake alone was unreasonable. Yet he alone could make the decision.

Never before had Tomoe Gozen been disobedient. Now, however, she began to strip off her armor, casting it away from the circle of these men, until she sat in only black hakama and white kosode blouse, her longsword behind herself, her shortsword on the ground before her knees. She said, "We must be swift!" She withdrew a piece of paper from her undergarment's sleeve. In other circumstances, such paper was used to clean blood from ones sword. In this case, it was for writing her death-poem. "I burned Taigawa Bridge, but enemy troops will find their way across the river soon. They will join Wada Yoshimora, find us, and take our heads. We have only a little time!"

"It won't do," said Yoshinake, unyielding. "Your duty is to live, to pray for us on each anniversary of our death. Who else would do so if not you?"

"Someone will do it!"

She was desperate, it was clear. But Yoshinake needed to say nothing more. Even if she died, she might be unable to follow him, if she had gone upon the journey through disobedience. Her duty was indeed to pray every year for their spirits. She lowered her face, defeated, ashamed, stricken because she could not die with them. Suddenly her brother staggered up from his knees and fell down again in front of her, shouting through tears, "Sister! I will die for both of us! I will be a brave Yamato hero!" His face was so twisted with fear and agony that it was doubtful he could be brave even for himself. Tomoe touched his face, and knew she dared not reveal her own hurt regarding her exclusion, for she would need to be strong for Imai and the others, witnessing their act with appropriate somberness. "Take good care of him," said Tomoe. "Be his best councilor."

Lord Kiso, too, saw that Imai Kanchira was afraid, and he

Wendy Adrian Shultz

said to him,

"Imai. You are young and beautiful and it is a shame for you to die. It is easy to admit it, for have we not sympathy for the flowers that die for sake of summer, the leaves that fall for sake of winter? Sympathy is not regret. Failure is as noble as success, or nobler, if we are single-minded in our approach, blithe about our individual and collective evanescence. The bravest are also the most transient: the dying toll of a temple bell; the day cherry blossoms tumble all as one, seeming winter's deathly snow despite the mildness of spring. Take heart in this, Imai! We will be admired for this moment! We have surmounted the hateful duties and presently may free ourselves from this inconsequent world. How fortunate we are!"

Imai Kanchira was encouraged by these words. He returned to his place beside Higuchi Mitsu. He was ready to die. To the shi-tenno, and peripherally to Tomoe Gozen, Yoshinake continued,

"What have we sought for ourselves but this? Did we think we were seeking the conquest of foes when what we sought to conquer was nature? Did we dream of the unification of clans, while actually wishing to push back whatever was not 'us?' It is trees we fear, and rivers, and the ground our blood will nourish. Unable to confront our grimmer, simpler destiny, we play as though such things as power and wealth—or, more nobly, duty and honor—are our true intentions. But we are not so selfish as that, and we are more afraid. There are no victors, and few consolations. We have sought a world which obeys our voices and our swords. In this we have failed. In this, men will always fail."

In the distance was a clatter of hooves, the cries of Wada Yoshimora's final assault. The enemy were further than they sounded, for they were numerous, raising a din. The shi-tenno calmly wrote their poems. The poem of Tade Shimataka went like this: "The world is an empty, fleeting place/ There is nothing left behind which is real." Nenoi Yukika, the dark man at fair Tade's side, wrote without emotion: "We are dawn's dewdrops blasted from existence/ We were never stone." Higuchi Mitsu had loved life too well to write anything so melancholy, and so his poem was simply, "It has been beautiful to see all that I have seen." Tomoe Gozen took the inkstone from man to man, so that each might blacken his brush. By her brother she lingered, and held his hands until he was calm enough to write:

"Age shall never weary me
or make me slow.
It is proper to go quickly."

They read their poems to one another, moist-eyed all, but finally unafraid. Lord Kiso, the true poet among them, read last what he had written. His voice was clear and strong. The words held both his vanity and his true power:

"Maples shed Fall colors
I become a picture
embroidered on the leafy brocade."

Then Nenoi Yukika raised his longsword to Tade Shimataka's chest, and Tade Shimataka raised his longsword to Nenoi Yukika's chest. Higuchi Mitsu and Imai Kanchira faced one another similarly, longswords held between the breasts of their closest friends. In a moment, they were finished. Each lay upon their sides, pierced to their hearts. Thus had they committed junshi to accompany Kiso Yoshinake on his final journey.

Yoshinake faced Tomoe Gozen, but they were far apart. He had no final words for her. His shortsword lay before his knees, and with this he should slit his belly; but he reached behind himself instead, took the Sword of Okio and unsheathed it. He wrapped his own poem around the blade so that he could hold the steel toward himself, and he exclaimed, "Okio! Be revenged on me!" Then he pierced his left side and slowly drew the sword through spleen, intestines, liver, kidneys, stomach; blood gushed onto his lap, but his face revealed no pain. He withdrew the sword, stuck it a second time beneath his diaphragm, and pushed the sword downward to complete the cross. He set the sword aside and waited. He waited until he was as pale as Tade Shimataka, then paler; until he was as weak as the man Tomoe had found on the battlefield. Though blanched, his expression did not alter. He did not fall backward. He did not fall forward. But he was dead.

Tomoe had watched without the least expression. Her brother, her friends, and her husband were before her, and she the only witness to their last moment. She had the inkstone. She had a brush. She had the paper which had been intended for her final words. Upon this paper she wrote a sort of lament for family and friends, thinking as she wrote that her desire to better herself with every passing day had never been achieved, that even in today's great act, she had not been allowed participation, and there was no greatness in her. If she were wrong, she did not realize it.

The sound of soldiers was louder now. She would have to flee East to relatives, perhaps to Shigeno Valley where she had served as a retainer before marriage. But she did not hurry. She finished her poem, and read it aloud to the men dead before her. Eventually, it would be printed on their grave markers, and it would be repeated by many a vassal serving lords who reached too far:

"Like a dream
is the life of a samurai
from which, awakened,
no memory remains."

EPILOG

Duel at Hisa Yasu Bridge

A hot, stifling, humid summer storm ended suddenly in the night. The overhanging cedars wept outside Shan On's cottage at the edge of Shigeno Valley Cemetery. It was not yet dawn. The nun clad herself in white robe and yellow hood. She rolled her bedding and put it inside a closet. It was by no means chilly even in the pre-dawn, but she built a small fire for cooking. Soon water was heated. As seaweed boiled in the covered pot, the nun listened to the sound of wind playing through the cedars and to the false rain stirred from the shaking branches. The only light in her house was that from the hibachi's orange coals.

In the corner of her tiny house was a place where once a dog had made its bed. The dog no longer lived with her, indeed, she knew by now, no longer lived at all. A tablet with the dog's death-name sat in that corner, surrounded with things the dog had liked and played with in its life. The name on the tablet was "Raski," more commonly a horse's name.

Because Shan On was old and lived alone, she did not often feel compelled to rise before the sun, particularly not during the long-enough days of summer. But her dreams had been troubling, and that is why she began her day somewhat earlier than usual.

When the seaweed had boiled a while, she added a few

diced vegetables. These she cooked very briefly, then removed the pot from its hanger above the coals, adding miniscule mushrooms before the bubbling stopped. To the cooling liquid she added a paste of fermented soybeans and salt, which dissolved instantly. This was to be her breakfast. She had made too much, and this was odd; for she never wasted food.

Shan On was not given to premonitions, but she felt at present a definite anxiety, as though something were reaching into her very being to make its needs known to her. Had this something to do with her unsettling dreams? She could not remember the nature of the dream which awakened her. Yet some echo of nightmare persisted, not in her mind, but among the weeping cedars.

Before she could eat a bowl of soup, she was distracted by a scraping on the stairway leading to her house: a nailed shuffling almost like a dog, but not a dog, for it sounded like two feet, not four. Shan On was accustomed to hauntings. She stood, leaving her bowl of hot soup sitting on the floor. She moved toward the door and, trusting to her varied gods, undid the latch and moved the door aside.

There was no beast or ghost standing on her steps in the windy morning gloom overlooking the graveyard. It was a woman. She was dressed in a red kimono. She was thin, as happens when one fasts too much. She wore a hood similar to that of Shan On, but it was a startling red, like the kimono, not somber yellow. The hood was of odd design as well, for it completely hid half the woman's face: only one eye and half her nose and mouth were left exposed. This half-face was very beautiful.

The red nun carried a sturdy walking staff which might double as a weapon.

"Have I met you before?" asked Shan On.

"I think you have, one way or another," said the enigmatic nun-in-red. She entered the dwelling without invitation and limped toward the hibachi, expecting to be fed.

"Yes, I recall," said Shan On, who went to a drawer from which she took an extra bowl and chopsticks. "You were a fortuneteller, is it so? Your face was masked from me then, more so than now, shadowed by a big straw hat. But I recognize you by your voice. You have become a nun the same as me? I hope you are more satisfied than you seemed before."

"Not the same as you," said the red nun. "But I am satisfied enough. When first we met, I called myself Naruka, after a hell-creature. Before that, I had been someone else."

"Who are you now?" Shan On asked uneasily. They both knelt in the ember-lit room and feasted. Shan On watched the red nun sip *miso* soup from the corner of her half-hidden mouth, and snatch bits of vegetables with the chopsticks.

"I am not certain I can answer 'who' I have become. Will it suffice to say I presently use the name I had before? Please call me Tsuki, as in 'moon,' Izutsu, as in 'curb of the well.' "

"Shan On," said the white nun, introducing herself. "It is a foreign name."

"Yes it is," said Tsuki Izutsu, as though Shan On could have been wrong about her own name. She sipped more of the soup, then said, "Your miso is nice, but you have made too much for you and me. Could I impose on you to place whatever is left outside the door?"

Shan On thought: *What a strange request.* She asked, "Have you a shy friend?"

"I think so," said Tsuki Izutsu, as though she were less certain of this than she had been of Shan On's name's origin. Shan On ladled a third bowl of soup and set it outside, then closed the door and rejoined the red nun. Shan On asked,

"What have you come to me about?"

"I will be frank about that," said Tsuki. "I have been searching for several months for a friend. Her name is Tomoe Gozen, whom you know. It has been rumored that she died at the Battle of Awazu; but one of the Shogun's generals, Wada Yoshimora, continues to search for her, so the rumor of her demise was unconvincing. I searched for her in Heida. She has not returned to her hometown, for it is watched by Yoshimora's spies; and to go there would endanger what is left of Tomoe's family, mainly her grandmother. I looked several other places, which even Yoshimora's spies would not think of, but Tomoe Gozen had not taken refuge anywhere I looked. I believed she would return to her previous master here in Shigeno Valley when possible, but at the castle they told me she was turned away, I suspect because Madame Shigeno's heart has become hard lest softness be used against her to topple her estates. I am not certain where next to look. Although I have the ability to 'see' matters which others cannot see, my friend hides even her thoughts, so I cannot detect where she might be. My searching brought me this far. Did she come to you after Madame Shigeno refused to reinstate her as a retainer?"

"I cannot be so frank," said Shan On, "but I will try to be honest. I am not sure that I could trust you with privileged information, supposing I had such knowledge to share. I admit I saw Tomoe Gozen several months ago. She was distraught and convinced she had no friends. Madame Shigeno has rebuilt the wealth of this valley in part by playing enemies against enemies—or, it might be, friends against friends—never taking sides. Although she can be cruel, she is well loved by the people of this prospering valley; therefore there were few to whom Tomoe Gozen might turn for sanctuary, if Madame Shigeno said, 'No.' I did as much as I was able, helping Tomoe to understand how it would offend Wada Yoshimora for Madame Shigeno to keep Tomoe Gozen as retainer. Yet Tomoe was not much soothed by my explanation, for there was an additional matter. Although Tomoe had asked, about two years ago, to be relieved indefinitely from duties in this valley, it is debatable whether or not she was free to wed without her master's permission, which permission was never requested. Madame Shigeno has never forgiven Tomoe Gozen's marriage. That is why the mistress of Shigeno Valley declared Tomoe an unfit retainer and refused her audience. So, even were it politically safe or wise to keep Tomoe Gozen, there was too little trust for this to come about. It was crippling for Tomoe Gozen to understand this."

"She has not sought employment elsewhere?"

"I cannot tell you."

"But you know?"

"I cannot say."

"You are most polite in your unreasonable replies," said Tsuki Izutsu, her tone mocking Shan On's gentleness.

"Be forgiving of my ill manners," said Shan On, setting her empty soup bowl aside and bowing apologetically. "I know by the way you carry your staff that you are a fighter. I have no illusions that you are weak, just because you limp; and fewer illusions that I could defeat you, for I know only a little self-defense. Therefore I do not wish to offend you; but there is not much I can tell."

"It is a matter of confidentiality," said Tsuki Izutsu.

"It might be," said Shan On.

"Listen to me please," said Tsuki Izutsu, setting her bowl aside as well, and placing both hands on the floor in a beseeching posture. "As I said, sometimes I know things which I have no obvious means of knowing; yet I am rarely mistaken. Tomoe Gozen needs me. I owe her many favors and cannot let her down."

"Perhaps you mean to kill her with your staff," said Shan On. "I do not have your way of 'knowing.' I fear the powers you seem to possess. You project your will and your emotions. I can exert myself against your will, but your emotions cause me to feel sadness and confusion. How could I trust you with a friend's life?"

"I owe her much," said Tsuki Izutsu. "Once I was possessed by three devils: an oni, a naruka, and a sorcerer more wicked than the first two. Because of Tomoe Gozen, I am free of most of these monsters. I must suffer only the oni devil now. I am resigned that he is part of me, and I am part of him. Please be certain that neither myself, nor my 'shy friend,' mean harm to Tomoe Gozen. If you are doubtful, I will gladly allow myself to be bound in ropes, if only I may see her."

Outside, some creature slurped noisily at the miso on the step. Shan On ignored the sound, and said, "I am moved by what you tell me. Yet, if it were true, as you believe, that I know what became of Tomoe Gozen, wouldn't I also know her present needs? How can you be sure she requires your presence, if I do not know it myself?"

"I am convinced of her present unhappiness," said Tsuki.

"If it were so," said the white nun, "can you easily

change it? I think not."

"Consider these things," said Tsuki Izutsu: "Tomoe Gozen believes her path is one of failure. She tried to help her husband in a task which could not be achieved. She tried to regain a past retainership, but was called faithless and turned away. What other things plague her with a sense of unworthiness? How much can *I* trust *you* to know? That she once set out to seek vengeance for a gaki spirit, but performed the deed so badly that the spirit still would not rest? That a tribe of Tengu devils proclaimed her protector of devil children, but her efforts in behalf of a bakemono child were of tragic outcome? That her one 'success' as far as she can see was to convince a psychotic samurai to return to this cemetery and throw himself upon the sword of his own best friend? There is more than this, too! Subconsciously she knows that it was her own awkwardness that awoke the Earthquake Catfish, killing thousands. And she hurt you as well, killing your white dog out of sheer ignorance."

"None of these things justify Tomoe Gozen's self-doubt!" said Shan On, sounding angry for the first time; and as Shan On's anger was rare, perhaps it was because she believed Tomoe Gozen *should* feel guilt for some of these things.

"Yet she does have doubts," Tsuki stated firmly. "She needs to know she has not failed at everything. *I* am her one success."

Tsuki Izutsu stood abruptly, hovering over the white nun, staff to hand. She said,

"Take me to her at once!"

"I refuse," said Shan On, not cowering. "Attack me if you must. By your actions, I know how I should trust you. I would die rather than betray her."

Tsuki Izutsu raised her staff above her head and said sharply, "Judge me as you wish!"

Near a large creek running through rice fields on the outskirts of a village in Shigeno Valley, there was a nondescript hut consisting of two rooms. It had wooden walls, two high windows covered by rice-paper, a thatched roof, and an entrance with a curtain of woven grass. Around the hut, tall grasses swayed in the afternoon's hot, humid breeze. Shigeno Castle was not visible from this place, nor was any other important landmark or sight, which was the reason for the hut being built where it was. Called *sangoya*, it was a place of "women's impurity" as far as men were concerned, and a retreat as far as women were concerned. It was by no means a secret place, for it could be found easily, were anyone interested. Yet it was never discussed around men. The sangoya was shared by peasant women while menstruating or giving birth.

The larger, front room had a small, high window. The interior was usually dark. There were two hibachi for cooking purposes and, in cooler weather, warmth. Presently the room was stuffy; no fire was wanted; the transient residents had been eating mostly pickles, occasionally augmented with hastily made bowls of noodles. If evening were cool enough, they would make rice with red beans, the red beans symbolizing menstrual blood and believed to have magical properties. Although summer made the sangoya uncomfortable, and the single door was not large enough to allow reasonable circulation of air, the women nonetheless enjoyed themselves. Menstruation taboos provided each of them with short vacations from the drudgery of farm life. Clearly they did not view their "impurity" with much loathing, since it meant a time of rest, of gossip, of cultivating friendships with other women and helping each other, away from the auspices of men, which had its own pleasant ramifications.

The back room was smaller and also had one window near the ceiling. A birth-rope hung from a beam. On this, a laboring woman could hold herself up as a child was being born. It was occasionally a gruesome scene of blood and shouting and clinging to the rope while an old midwife assured some frightened, sweating mother-to-be that, no, you will not die. Sometimes the mother did die, of course, but it was really quite rare, the midwives being skillful *onnano-miko* wise in the ways of women's health. Usually childbirth was not a gruesome sight in the least, no more troubling than when a dog or cat gives birth. Easy birth or difficult, every mother was expected to spend twenty days in that back room, resting, recovering, getting to know her child, receiving guests, accepting gifts of food, and strictly observing this purification period. "Hut Visiting Custom" was called *koyamimai;* the custom was performed mainly by village grandmothers, in addition to whomever was menstruating on a given day. Grandmothers from each peasant family made *fu* or gluten bread for the new mothers, and thereby were not excluded from the sangoya because they no longer bore children or menstruated. By the end of twenty days, every grandmother would have visited at least once.

There was presently only one mother in the back room. She had six days to go, then she would be declared purified, and could leave with her child. There were complications in this particular case, for the mother's breasts had thus far refused to lactate. Wet nurses came several times a day. Everyone waited for the mother to give milk, although by now it was suspected she would remain dry.

In the front room there were, at present, four menstruating women, including a girl who had come for the first time, who was receiving special attention as a result. They talked about the non-lactating mother, not minding that she could overhear. They worried about her and her son. They worried also about her sad state of mind. Of equal importance to the conversations was the fact that the new mother was not a peasant. They did not know who she was exactly. They suspected she was of the *kugé* or royal class, outcast for some reason during last year's wars in and around Kyoto. They were wrong to think her kugé, for she was *buké* or military calss; but without weapons, no one could be expected to realize this.

She was Tomoe Gozen, who Shan On had sheltered for many months, until time to come to the sangoya.

Someone might have guessed the woman's actual identity, except that no one who asked about Tomoe Gozen had suspected she carried Kiso Yoshinake's child; so the connection was difficult to make. The women speculated that the mother was some princess instead of a warrior, and invented romantic nonsense to appease their own curiosities. They could not discuss the woman outside the confines of the sangoya, for occurrences inside these walls were customarily discussed nowhere else (if the mystique of the sangoya were ever broken, and menstrual taboos no longer observed, it would mean only that women were given no vacations whatsoever). Every woman in the village was aware of the fact that *someone* of probable importance reposed in their sangoya, but no man of the village had a single clue. Peasant women kept little from their husbands, fathers, brothers . . . but the sangoya was a special exception. Therefore ancient customs provided much security for Tomoe Gozen.

Tomoe's bed was made of two kinds of straw and a grass mat atop this. Once a week, the bedding was burned by the riverside and new bedding prepared for her. This was part of the post-childbirth purification. Although she did not feel the need to remain on her back the full twenty days, custom was demanding in this regard, so when she had visitors, she remained prone.

At the moment, a wet nurse fed the boy who had not yet been named. The wet nurse was a well-meaning woman who encouraged Tomoe with such words as, "Do not worry, you will be able to feed him soon," without the least realization that Tomoe did not care whether or not she lactated. The peasant was not sensitive enough to see maternalism was not strong in this one woman, preferring to believe the new mother's melancholy was the fault of her milklessness.

A grandmother from the village came to the back room of the hut, offering pleasant banalities and toothless smiles. She had brought more of the bland fu which Tomoe ate with small gratitude. In the other room, young women chattered like squirrels. Outside, the creek babbled, too. Tomoe could find little to say to either the wet nurse or the grandmother, so they kept each other company instead of her, and Tomoe was glad enough to be ignored.

To be sure, Tomoe had mixed feelings about her offspring. Months earlier, when she first admitted she carried Yoshinake's child, she was pleased to think some part of her husband would survive him. As for Tomoe's own family line, there were cousins enough to sustain it. But Yoshinake's clan was being systematically rooted out and exterminated by the Shogun's spies. This one progeny alone went undetected.

It did not mean she relished the prospect of motherhood.

There were moments when she was alone with the child, forced to cradle him lest he cry, when she knew years of *this* would be appalling. Blessedly, he slept almost constantly during his first weeks of life. The sangoya was warm as the womb, and the boy might be unaware that he was out into the world.

Her feelings caused her to feel badly about herself. She was not callous toward the child, but could not help her aloofness from him. Whatever instinctual attachment mothers must have for their own babies was missing from Tomoe Gozen. She doubted this was a natural response, but it was *her* natural response. She simply did not want the child.

She was eased to know there were practical reasons to unburden herself of the infant. He must be protected from the enemies of Tomoe Gozen. If by any chance the spies of Wada Yoshimora learned that Tomoe had hidden in a peasant sangoya, they would suspect the existence of a child, who could not be left to live, to grow, to become the avenger for Kiso Yoshinake. For the child's sake, Tomoe must disassociate herself from him. She would not become Yoshimora's prize under any circumstance; the perverse general collected warrior wives much the way other lords collect rare swords. She must have her freedom to fight or flee as she thought best, without involving an infant in the danger.

Wada Yoshimora had twice been to the Castle, disbelieving Madame Shigeno could have refused to reinstate Tomoe as vassal. Each time, his men had gone along the road in view of the sangoya, never thinking to search a peasant parturition hut for the well-known woman warrior. Tomoe might place herself beyond Yoshimora's grasp forever, were she willing to cut her hair and retire from worldly matters, to be a nun. But she had her pride after all; she had often been glad of her fame; such notice was the wish of many samurai, and it was hard to give it up. Additionally, she had never been devoted to the Buddha, so it would not make her comfortable to be a Buddhist nun; and a Shinto *miko* was a following not easily pursued unless trained from childhood.

The wet nurse left, leaving the child in his own straw matting. He was fed, contented, and asleep. The old peasant grandmother followed after the wet nurse, keeping up their conversation, forgetting to say goodbye to unresponsive Tomoe Gozen. Alone but for the sound of women chattering in the other room, Tomoe rose from her bed and stretched her muscles. She had never gone so long without practicing her various weapon arts. She wished Shan On would come and release her from this place, disregarding the twenty day purification time valued by the peasants.

She stood above the sleeping child. He had been ugly the first week, red and wrinkled. Now he was as beautiful as any child could be, yet Tomoe Gozen still could not appreciate him. She said, "What shall I name you?" She had no idea. "How ironic that you should be my one success, the thing I least intended to do." She raised her visage to the high window and saw the momentary shadow of a hawk upon the rice-paper. It made her wish, again, that she were free of motherhood's implied vassalage, free to roam as a hawk across the mountains. Perhaps Madame Shigeno was right to mistrust Tomoe Gozen, who had come to resent servitude. She whispered to herself, "I am after all a ronin in my heart. Neither lord nor child can hold me anymore. I have grown too much, or grown too small. Whichever way, I cannot be mastered. Yet what is a samurai who cannot serve? She is nothing. She does not belong."

There was unexpected excitement in the other room. The menstruating women were chattering about some visitor.

This is why Shan On began to trust Tsuki Izutsu:

At dawn, the red nun stood above the white nun, the threatening posture momentarily convincing Shan On that her visitor meant harm. But Tsuki Izutsu meant to be judged by everything she was, and everything she had ever been, and by her power opened up her mind to an unprepared Shan On. They were not memories *per se* that Shan On saw; she did not come out of Tsuki's mind having witnessed death and ascent from Emma's Hell, for instance; nor had she experienced Tsuki's mind as a series of dissertations on the nature of herself. Rather, what she touched was the essence of the red nun, stumbling over scars which held together the old Tsuki and the new Tsuki, the old with gentle humor and the new with constant pain both physical and emotional. The leg, how it hurt. The love of all things living, how it ached and washed pale. The fear of shadows, how it welled then ebbed away. The part of her that wished only to destroy, how shallow *that* part was, how insincere. In a moment, Shan On was free of Tsuki's bared self; surely to have been smitten by the red nun's staff would have been less painful. Shan On gasped air as though she had run a dozen miles. She looked up from where she sat upon her knees, up into the one visible eye of Tsuki Izutsu, the eye shining in the dimly lit room.

"How could I have known?" Shan On whispered, uncertain what it was she knew.

Tsuki Izutsu did not pity herself, and Shan On would not pity her either. The nun in white robe and yellow hood felt, instead, a fierce admiration for the spirit that bore so much and yet was unbroken.

At the same time Shan On knew that she was dealing with a woman capable of natural, raw sorcery. Could she have fabricated and projected this admiration and the emotional peaks and valleys, convinced by means of hypnotism that Shan On had seen the furthest edges of Tsuki's heart and mind? It was a thing to be considered. Shan On had been raised by a *miko,* a Shinto priestess, and it had been the shame of Shan On that there had been no natural sorcery in her, nothing to be trained and honed. Were it the red nun the priestess had raised and tutored, what a great prophetess and healer Tsuki would have been!

"As you are wise enough not to pity me," said the red nun in a surprisingly gentle voice, "be kind to yourself as well, and spare no envy."

It was true she had experienced a moment's envy, for what would Shan On have given to have pleased her aged guardian before the old miko died. As it were, the priestess on her deathbed told her, "You are not intended to be a Shinto priestess, for your mother is a Buddhist nun, who sends that other pantheon to watch over you with care." How sad a day it was! To lose one mother and regain another. Shan On's faith ran too deep for her to abandon the Shinto gods, but she took a yellow hood in honor of her blood-mother, and honored simultaneously the Buddhas and Bodhisattvas. What Shan On lacked in supernatural ability she made up for by her wonderful capacity for faith in gods of all sorts. It rendered her an admirable exorcist, though she could not conjure, and she had become a foremost advocate of *shinto-ryobu,* the Two Ways of the Gods.

"As you have seen my spirit," said Tsuki Izutsu, shattering the silence once more, "so have I entered the door of your most quiet existence. Please believe that we do understand one another perfectly."

Shan On was much older than her ageless face implied, and wise in her ways, if conservative. And she was trusting. If it were her own life at stake, she would not hesitate; but it was the fate of Tomoe Gozen she was asked to give in trust. There was still the possibility of sorcery at work, breaking down her will: the same sorcery Tsuki Izutsu sent ahead of herself, to be sure Shan On made soup enough for three. The same sorcery which created that momentary, overwhelming link of minds (and had the red nun done this consciously?). Shan On considered all these things before she said,

"I will not give absolute credence to the strength, or the weakness, you have revealed about yourself; although if what I saw was true, surely there is no greater being in this world than you. Yet I will trust you, not for what your sorcery unveiled, but for what I see with my own eyes. By your actions and your words I know that you are wounded, and I have seen this also about Tomoe Gozen. You have tried to make me understand that Tomoe needs your presence, but what I see instead is that you need hers. Perhaps, indeed, you are each the poultice the other one requires."

Tomoe's last six days in the sangoya were spent with Tsuki Izutsu ever near. The daylight hours remained a nuisance of heat and interruptions from village grandmothers and menstruating women, all of them well-intending busybodies, and of a class Tomoe Gozen frankly could not relate to for long periods of time. The evenings were more pleasant, filled by endless conversations between herself and Tsuki, sharing one another's feelings until long into the nights.

"I am glad that I was of use to you," Tomoe said, and truly it provided her a sense of tremendous relief to know her trip into the Lands of Roots and Gloom had been of some avail. In the warm evenings, Tsuki sat half-clad, unashamed of the scarred half of her face and body where Tomoe was concerned. Tomoe added, "But the oni devil lurks among the grasses outside the sangoya, and you rarely show the whole of your face to others. Perhaps I was of less use than a better life required."

Tsuki sat in the dim moonlight filtering through the rice-paper window. She coddled Tomoe's child, for Tomoe did not wish to do so. Her lame leg could not be folded beneath herself, so her position was informal, one leg sticking out and the other held close to herself. Tiny baby hands reached up and stroked the ruined part of Tsuki's face; her own hand, the one with crooked fingers, touched the child's face in turn.

"We must each of us bear our scars and devils," said Tsuki. "It is not so hard for me."

Often, in those few days with Tsuki, Tomoe was set to considering her own scars and devils, evaluating her sense of failure, confronting her personal and varied guilts and easing them away, planning what she would do with her future, arranging in her mind the pieces of her life. She weighed her widowhood with Tsuki's lifelong chastity; it was discussed until they had no more to say. Tomoe's reluctant motherhood was compared to Tsuki's quick maternalism. Each considered their past acts, sometimes inconsequential, sometimes ferocious, often of doubtful intent or outcome. In some of these things it was decided that Tomoe was the stronger, and in other things they agreed Tsuki was the most able to cope. Their weaknesses and faults, strengths and positive attributes, tended to balance one another: where Tomoe was uncertain, Tsuki felt secure; where Tsuki was confused, Tomoe saw an answer. Each woman soothed the other. Toward the end of that week together, they realized they were more alike than not, different as their lives might be.

"Have you thought to cut your hair?" Tsuki asked in the middle of one night, suggesting that Tomoe be a nun. "You said you feared to be like Okumi, the nun who told you of the Golden Naginata; but not all sects require seclusion, as I myself am evidence. You could be *komuso*, a wandering mendicant. Then it would cause Wada Yoshimora a loss of face to pursue you, for what pious man could lust for Buddha's woman? Also, it would cause people to say, 'How strong she is, to give up her family and retire from worldly things.' Whereas, if you continue to pursue the fame of a samurai, people will say, 'How wicked to abandon her sweet child like that.' ''

''I have thought these very things,'' confessed Tomoe. ''It is a dilemma for me. Were I to cut my hair as many widows do, surely it would be an affront to any Buddha whenever I might pray, for it would be the Thousands of Myriads I addressed instead of Him. Also, though I would be judged better to have abandoned this child for a holier life, than if I abandoned him for continued fame as a warrior, still in my own heart I would have to cope with what I had really done—that is, failed to love him. Few will know of my child in any event, so there is only me to judge myself. All that I have known is bushido, and I think I will continue to pursue the Way, and try never to regret the things I have lost or left behind.''

''Forgive my trying to choose your path,'' said Tsuki, lowering her face. ''Only you can know what is best for you.''

On the last day in the sangoya, there was a ''Going Out'' celebration with several grandmothers, three menstruating peasants, the red nun, and the sangoya's midwife: Shan On. Tomoe was embarrassed by it, and felt dishonest clad in peasant cottons, holding her child as a loving mother might. She forced herself to smile and tried to show that, yes, she felt gratitude to these women, although throughout the twenty days she had been mostly rude or despondent.

It was early afternoon when she, Shan On, Tsuki, and the unnamed child left the last ashes of burnt bedding by the river and walked toward Shan On's house by Shigeno Valley Cemetery. Tomoe handed the child to Tsuki, and did not look at him during the short trek. To the side of the road, the oni devil hid, followed, curious and jealous of the way Tsuki cooed to the baby.

The women and child arrived at the house by the cemetery. There, Shan On made bitter tea, which fitted the occasion, and there was trust and relaxation while they sat together. After a while, Tomoe traded the peasant cottons from the sangoya for her hakama trousers and haori waistcoat, which Shan On had kept. She bowed to her swords and apologized to them for more than twenty days of neglect. There was, among the things Shan On had kept for Tomoe, the carved wooden sheath of the Golden Naginata.

"Shan On," said Tomoe, "you may already know that this sheath was long kept by your mother. It has been passed along to me, but my path will be difficult, and I can guard no possessions beyond my swords. I do not think I would be remiss to let you keep the sheath safe for me, or for the next hero of Naipon who needs it for some cause."

The white nun received the sheath with pleasure, and ran slender fingers over the carved surface, sensing it was a holy and magic thing.

"Have you decided about the child," asked Shan On, who had not been privy to six days of conversations between Tomoe and Tsuki Izutsu.

"He has been discussed," said Tomoe, looking quickly to the bundle in Tsuki's arms. "There are wet nurses in the Castle. They attend the babes of vassals' wives. Tsuki will take my child to Madame Shigeno, who is not the sort to marry, and so requires an heir by adoption. Only she need know the boy's parentage."

"You can do this?" asked Shan On.

"You know I can," said Tomoe.

"Do you know that Wada Yoshimora has put guards and spies along the roads out of this valley? His informants knew that you visited the Castle many months ago, and, though you were turned away, none saw you leave the valley."

"Tsuki mentioned it to me," said Tomoe.

"How will you escape?"

"You have returned to me my swords," said Tomoe.

"There is another way," said Shan On, not liking the promise of more violence. "I will go into the castle-town where samurai live, and cause a rumor to be spread through the gay district. The rumor will be that you are hiding in some storage house behind an inn. The nearest men serving Wada Yoshimora are those who guard Hisa Yasu bridge, over the north forest river. They will be first to respond to the rumor and search the storage houses. At dusk, you will be able to slip over the bridge and away from Shigeno Valley without interference."

"If you would be so daring," said Tomoe, "I will accept your plan."

"I will go at once," said Shan On. "The summer days are long; I have several hours to plant false information here and there. Please do not be anxious, but wait until the sun is low."

"Do not worry about me after this," aaid Tomoe Gozen. "And do not let yourself be detected as my friend."

Tsuki stood in the open doorway, watching the white nun walk the path through the cemetery, off toward the castle-town surrounding Shigeno Castle. Tsuki held Tomoe's child in the crook of one arm, and her walking staff was held in her other hand.

"You must go also," said Tomoe. Tsuki stepped out of the cottage without looking back, but asked softly,

"Will we meet each other soon?"

Tomoe did not answer. Tsuki Izutsu limped down the stairway from Shan On's house to the graveyard. It was important for the two nuns not be seen together, but Tsuki must use the same route through the cemetery, toward Shigeno Castle. There, by whatever means necessary, she would gain admittance to the castle, and audience with Madame Shigeno. Already, her desire went ahead of her, influencing the thoughts of guards who might otherwise stand in her way, sending Madame Shigeno herself a priming message of curiosity about a nun-in-red and something she would bring. This ability to "pave the way" was but one of Tsuki's half-realized magicks.

At the foot of the steps, at the edge of the cemetery, Tsuki Izutsu turned around and looked up at the doorway to Shan On's house. But Tomoe Gozen was not standing there, did not watch Tsuki go, did not say goodbye to the nameless child. It was best this way.

In the solitude of the cedar-shaded house of Shan On, Tomoe groomed herself in preparation for the road. She brushed her long hair, retied it at the nape of her neck, and completed other cleansing rituals. She had done these things earlier in the day for the Going Out ceremony at the sangoya; but it was necessary to observe the etiquette of grooming before any important venture. As she performed these personal chores, she meditated on a variety of subjects, and viewed herself as from an objective plane. Some of her thoughts were of the child. Only three besides herself would know about him; but this was best for his survival, not some dread secret of her own, kept lest she suffer the judgements Tsuki had described.

Outside, it was so warm that no bird wanted to sing. There was no wind, so no branches were stirring. The silence comforted Tomoe.

Inside her haori jacket, near her belly, was a small bundle of provisions for the road, which Shan On had prepared in advance. Among the various small items was a funeral tablet upon which was printed in tiny letters the death-names of the shi-tenno, including her own brother, and above these four names were slightly larger characters: Kiso Yoshinake's title, Rising Sun General. Tomoe removed this object from her jacket and placed it on the floor in front of her. It was smaller than most such tablets, for it was intended especially for travel. She spoke to this tablet a long while, as though her husband and the Four Great Men were truly with her. She told them about the things which had transpired of late, and of her immediate plans.

Thus, in meditation, prayer, and private ceremony, the afternoon passed more quickly than she had thought possible, and dusk approached its verge. Tomoe Gozen closed up Shan On's house and started through the cemetery, lingering a moment by the monument raised to Madoka Kawayama and Ushii Yakushiji, the monument with the rustic god on top. Ushii's remains now resided in this grave as long intended, beside his life-long friend Madoka. Tomoe did not speak to them, but she bowed slowly and held her bow several extra moments. Then she lifted her face to the sky, no tear evident, and started off toward the north forest.

As she went along the highway—boldly, as though she were not a hunted woman—it did not seem that she was beginning something new, but drawing out an end. She wondered if there could be anything unexpected in her life

Shultz

from here on. Although she had made her decision to adhere to the Warrior Way, what additional fame could she achieve by this means? She had risen higher, and fallen further, than any woman or man of Heida, and the folk of her hometown, and all Naipon, could never sing her praises louder than today. Fame was a hollower reward than she had long imagined; the greatest pride was yet too small a thing to see or touch. Now, to continue in the only thing she had ever known did not enrich her mood, but made her feel as though she were a gaki spirit, a hungry ghost wandering the Eternal Isles unreconciled. Truly, she had been ready to die at Awazu at her husband's side; it was as though she were already dead. Though her sorrow and guilt had been mostly healed by the time spent with Tsuki, and she felt no regrets, neither did she feel as intense about life as she had felt in other times. She did not believe she could ever regain that sense of energetic action.

The road rose steeply out of the valley, leading through thick forests. The warm breeze raised dust to annoy her. Sunset's colors faded into grey. She did not know what waited outside Shigeno Valley, what was worth achieving. It wore upon her to consider the samurai Way might be, just possibly, a thing of vanity, not holiness. How could she dare nurture such a thought? Surely it was only herself that was vain.

She heard the roar of the river before she saw the waters. Then she saw the high, wooden bridge. Shan On's plan had worked, for none of Wada Yoshimora's men waited for her there. But there was someone else: the black-robed yamahoshi outcast Makine Hei, standing in the center of the bridge, a straw hat like an inverted bowl upon his head. He was fully armed with sword and iron-reinforced pilgrim's staff, and blocked her chosen route with his huge bulk. Tomoe did not break her stride until she reached the beginning of the bridge, and there she stopped. Upon her visage, there was no emotion. His face was hidden beneath the brim of his large hat. Tomoe asked,

"How could you have known that I would come?" There was less query than resignation in her tone.

The sorcerer-priest untied his hat and tossed if off the bridge; it spun, descending to the rapids far below. Makine Hei's deep, resonant, unmodulated voice replied: "I had lost you for a while, but have watched you closely these last six days."

Now Tomoe did register surprise. In fact, she seemed upset. She knew that Makine Hei could not have been lurking near the sangoya, so what he told her meant one thing:

"You can still see through the eyes of my friend Tsuki Izutsu."

Makine Hei turned his head from side to side, and Tomoe was visibly relieved by his negative reply. "The oni," he explained. "I can see through *his* eyes. Would you like for me to tell you what he is seeing now?"

"No," said Tomoe, wishing no news of Tsuki's venture to the Castle. She said evenly, "What you tell me means you know about my child, and your magic still is close enough to Tsuki that you might cause her harm if she is unwary. For these two reasons, I should kill you if I can. But I remember you as Goro Maki, as dear to me as my own brother who has died. I cannot believe you are only Makine Hei, a wicked shugenza, evil man of sorcery. That is why I ask you, let us put aside our grudges here at Hisa Yasu Bridge. Hisa Yasu means 'everlasting peace,' and it is proper for us to each forgive the other at a bridge so named."

Makine Hei's terrible visage seemed almost to soften, but only for a moment. Tomoe put foot to bridge and began to approach the shugenza. He said,

"You are a fool to attempt placating me this way. You have not suffered the indignity of a clerical life, but have wallowed in recognition for your deeds. I will never change my mind."

Still, she approached. The man of sorcery did not draw his sword, nor raise his *shakubo*, the fighting stick with ringed shaku at its tip. Tomoe recognized the shaku as the one once belonging to bonze Shindo, the monk she had beheaded at Kiso Yoshinake's command, and who Makine Hei had loved as a son.

She stopped in front of him, close enough to be smitten by

the shakubo if Makine Hei wished to try. Shindo, though unjustly slain, still would not approve his shaku being used to strike Tomoe.

"Goro," Tomoe whispered, hoping to awaken his old self. In reply, Makine Hei began to hum a note so low Tomoe barely heard it; but she felt it sure enough. She staggered back, clutching between her breasts, for her heart felt as though it had been snatched in a tightening fist. She fell at once upon her knees, groaning, unable to catch a breath. She looked up into the face of Makine Hei, her foe, and could find no trace of Goro Maki, her friend. She tried to speak to him anew, but could force no word from her convulsing lungs. The deep sound made in Makine Hei's throat and diaphragm intensified, and she could hear it better, and feel it more painfully. His kiaijutsu was perfected; clearly he could kill her with his voice. She wondered if it were necessary to do it slowly due to some limitation, or if he drew it out only because his cruelty exceeded vengeance. Surely he lengthened it out of cruelty, for she was nearly helpless, and he might at least have drawn sword to end it mercifully, but did not. She would like to think better of him than this, to believe it took his entire concentration to achieve this much, and that was why he could not use the sword to end her torture.

She tried to stand, then tried again. The sound was a weight upon her shoulders. She managed to find her feet, staggered toward the railing of the bridge. Makine Hei turned his mountainous self in order to continue directing the killing sound her way. He seemed to need no breath.

Soon she was blinded, or at least could see no more than vague shadow. Her fingers pained her, like a rheumatic old woman. Yet she clenched one hand around the hilt of her longsword and lurched toward the sound Makine Hei was making, drawing her sword in a rapid, even arc. The sound ended suddenly and she staggered halfway to the end of the bridge before she found her vision. Makine Hei was behind her; she turned in time to stop him striking with the shakubo. Only then did she see that she had clipped his beard in her rush, and more, cut into the throat itself to still the awful sound, to free herself from the blinding agony. Yet he pursued her with the pilgrim's staff. Blood flowed down the front of the shugenza's robe; Makine Hei was a crimson fountain. Yet he was still breathing, through the neck's gash and not through mouth or nose. Blood would fill his lungs eventually, so he would not breathe for long; but in the meantime, his throat burbled a sickening froth, and he refused to abandon the fight.

A blow to her head was averted by her sword, and when he struck again, her sword came down and cut the shaku loose from the staff. It was the only amends she could make to Shindo, who would not want to be involved in this.

Makine Hei drew steel. He attacked, attacked again, and Tomoe Gozen was hard-put to block the tremendous, well-aimed cuts. His red throat smiled at her. His blood spattered across the bridge called Everlasting Peace. How long could he fight her when so badly injured? She had seen low ranking footsoldiers of mediocre training fight on and on despite mortal wounds. By contrast, Makine Hei was a highly skilled samurai capable of conserving strength, a priest with meditative skills which slowed the body's functions, and a sorcerer into the bargain. She could not guess how long the grisly battle might endure. She was caught between a desire to deal him a merciful last blow, a reluctance to strike again the man who was once her friend, and the immediate fact that her mixed emotions became quite without pertinence when it was tough enough to keep herself alive.

At length he began to slow his fierce pace, for death could not be held back forever. She thought she saw an opening, but he had tricked her. Nearly cut by his trick, she leapt backward to the bridge's rail and barely kept herself from toppling over the side. Makine Hei's sword went up, ready to slash down, but she rolled along the rail and the sword cut through wood and not Tomoe. He pulled the sword loose, turned on her again, but she performed a dance of evasion while blood gushed from his opened throat, until there was so little blood left in him that the flood became a trickle.

The big man plunged to his knees and the whole bridge quaked. He glowered at her with hatred unabating, but he looked pitiful also, for he had failed in spite of cruel sincerity. He tried to stand, much as Tomoe had done when held down by the sound of his voice; but he tumbled backward to lie upon his back on Hisa Yasu Bridge. Tomoe approached him, not certain he was harmless. She realized her face was wet and suspected she had been cut without realizing; but the moisture was not crimson. She wiped away sweat and tears and knelt beside the expiring man who was warrior, priest, sorcerer, enemy, and long ago a friend.

She pried Makine Hei's fingers loose from the sword. Although he had changed the hilt of the sword so that she would not recognize it, she had known the instant weapons crossed that it was her own Sword of Okio which Makine Hei had stolen from its retirement in a temple. No doubt he believed the haunted blade still hated her, and would help him in his vengeance; but Okio had forgiven her after all, and she might wield this sword again.

She shook blood from the sword she had been using, sheathed it, and placed it on Makine Hei's chest, drawn a knuckle's length as was done for the dead. But Makine Hei lived yet a little while, his malevolent eyes still watching her. She sheathed the Sword of Okio and placed it through her obi, next to the shortsword, guardian of her soul.

"I have killed a friend," she said, disregarding his hateful glower. "I am not made sad by the Way, but it is possible that it has made me weary. Although I dare not and cannot question the tenets of bushido, I have come to doubt the means of my adherence to those tenets. If honor and success means always the death of friends, then there is something I have failed to comprehend. If I am to find some method of overcoming my vanity, to pursue the Way more sincerely, to better myself each day, and champion those I love instead of watching them die, then from this moment on my road must change noticeably. You were bitter to have retired, Goro. Would you feel avenged if it were me as well as you?"

Having spoken to him this way, Tomoe Gozen drew forth her Sword of Okio and held it behind her head. She cut the long, black, gorgeous ponytail hanging down her back. What remained of her shorn hair fell forward to frame her face. She placed the bound length of hair upon the chest of Makine Hei, beside the sword she had traded him. Her last words to him were, "Perhaps here, on Hisa Yasu Bridge, we have both found peace after all."

Silent thereafter, she kept him company until the dusk became the evening, until Makine Hei was dead; and only then did she continue across the bridge and through the forest. Waters roared behind her. A breeze murmured above. The trees rustled among themselves, passing on the news of what they had seen. A cricket sang: symbol of good fortune. A crow responded with a hoarse contradiction. Tomoe Gozen vanished into the early night.

dondo haré

NOTES ON PRONUNCIATION–

The lyric quality of Naiponese, like our own world's Japanese, is easily mastered phonetically. Vowels are limited to five distinct sounds: A E I O U are AH EH EE OH OO. There are no silent vowels. As with Italian, ending vowels are sounded. Therefore, Tomoe Gozen's name is pronounced, with hard O's, TO-MO-EH. Kiso Yoshinake's name is KEE-SOH YO-SHE-NAH-KEH.

As a rule, syllables are stressed equally. An exception is the combination "ai" which has the separate syllables "ah" and "ee" run together to form a hard "I." "Naipon" can be correctly pronounced NAH-EE-PON, or with the vowel-Y, NY-PON. The combination "ei" can be separated into "eh" and "ee" or run together as a hard "A," so that the yamabushi priest's name, Kakumei, can be either KAH-KOO-MEH-EE, or more quickly, KAH-KOO-MAY, depending partly on dialect. (Because dialects vary throughout the 66 provinces, almost any "close" pronunciation will be correct somewhere!)

Other examples from the story include Azo Hono-o, AH-ZOH HO-NO-OH; Tomoe's brother Imai Kanchira, EE-MY KAHN-CHEE-RAH; and the giant Uchida Ieoshi, OO-CHEE-DAH EE-EH-OH-SHE. Minimal practice will reveal the utter simplicity of the pronunciations.

ABOUT THE AUTHOR; ABOUT THE ARTIST

I, Jessica Amanda Salmonson, haunt used bookstores for interesting non-fiction books, which are ever-so-helpful in the art of the fictioneer. I have recently discovered a book of medieval inns of France, another on the Yankee peddlar, an old book about fiendish women who murdered and robbed and had a good time, an even older one about women's derring-do at sea, a 30s tretise on homosexuality among the Dorians, a 50s Marxist pamphlet about the history of "Negroes" in "modern" cinema, a turn-of-the-Century history of "Siam" by someone who seems to have made everyting up, and a mid-19th Century collection of Swiss Folktales including a story about the Virgin Mary as a knight who seduces maidens. Somehow modern fantasy and science fiction rarely approach the richness and imagination of these; so I've learned not to be influenced by my colleagues' fiction, in as much as I want mine to be interesting.

She, Wendy Adrian Shultz, and the above-mentioned "I," share popcorn beneath the shine of subtitled movies, crepes and espresso while watching the ferries cross Puget Sound, funny clothes made of natural fiber, street music, and vegetarian sushi. She used to be an art teacher but is presently trying to make a living from the art exclusively, an uphill struggle against a system which prefers to grind its talented few into dust but ultimately wears its own arms to nubs trying.

Together we share an awe for the beauty and transience of life which even the world's multitudes of villains cannot destroy.